by Clare Lydon

custard
books

First Edition April 2023
Published by Custard Books
Copyright 2023 Clare Lydon
ISBN: 978-1-912019-04-5

Cover Design: Kevin Pruitt
Editor: Cheyenne Blue
Typesetting: Adrian McLaughlin

Find out more at: www.clarelydon.co.uk
Follow me on Twitter: @clarelydon
Follow me on Instagram: @clarefic

Also by Clare Lydon

Other Novels
A Taste Of Love
Before You Say I Do
Change Of Heart
Christmas In Mistletoe
It Started With A Kiss
Nothing To Lose: A Lesbian Romance
Once Upon A Princess
One Golden Summer
The Christmas Catch
The Long Weekend
Twice In A Lifetime
You're My Kind

London Romance Series
London Calling (Book One)
This London Love (Book Two)
A Girl Called London (Book Three)
The London Of Us (Book Four)
London, Actually (Book Five)
Made In London (Book Six)
Hot London Nights (Book Seven)
Big London Dreams (Book Eight)

All I Want Series
Two novels and four novellas chart the course
of one relationship over two years.

Boxsets
Available for both the London Romance series and
the All I Want series for ultimate value. Check out
my website for more: www.clarelydon.co.uk

Acknowledgements

I first considered writing a women's football romance in 2015. However, back then, the game wasn't nearly as advanced, and crucially, I wasn't as invested. However, slowly but surely, that started to shift.

The Women's Super League got more money and coverage, and I went to a few games and watched on TV. The Women's FA Cup Finals drew big crowds at Wembley, and I was there to cheer the teams on. I went to international friendlies and Champions League games. I started following my beloved Spurs, along with my local team, Charlton. This was the game I loved, but played by women. As a football-mad kid who was barred from playing after the age of 11, I was amazed and enthralled. I wanted more, and in the summer of 2022, I got it.

July 31st. Wembley Stadium. I was part of the sell-out crowd that witnessed the Lionesses' glorious European triumph, the day where everything changed. Women's football, in the shadows for so long, finally stepped into the spotlight. These women were elite athletes, playing their game on their terms. I was captivated. Suddenly, I knew it was time to start writing about women playing football and ultimately, falling in love. The perfect match.

And so, to this book. *Hotshot.* My ode to women's football and the beautiful game. Within these pages, I hope I've captured the essence of what it takes to be a pro. I hope I've shown how much I love football. How much I admire the women who defy expectations and play: from the early 1900s to the present day. Being a female sports star is still bucking the norm of what it is to be a woman. Well done to everyone who runs after every ball and goes in for every tackle, at whatever level. Your actions are slowly changing the world.

Where to start with my thanks? First, to my early readers, Angela, Sophie and Kathy who gave me the initial thumbs up. Then to my stellar ARC team, who had to work extra hard to pick up all the Britishisms I initially had Sloane thinking and uttering. Writing US characters as a Brit is so hard, and evidently, I like to make life hard for myself. Silly Clare. Special tip of my cap to Henriette, who caught more than most!

Cheers to my talented trio of professionals who make sure my books look and read as best they can. Kevin for the gorgeous footy cover; Cheyenne for her crackin' editing; and Adrian for his expert typesetting. I love having you all on my side and couldn't do this without you. Thanks also to all the bloggers and readers who've shown such enthusiasm for this book in the run-up to launch. I hope you love it!

Bundles of gratitude and huge love to my wife, Yvonne, for coming to all the games with me. Especially all the Spurs ones, where we kept losing and I kept pouting. You followed women's football way before me, so you were a key inspiration in writing this, too. Even if your first love is Arsenal. (Although, whisper it, Arsenal's club level is pretty nice to watch a game in. Epic loos! Shame about the Arsenal-branded lager.)

Thanks also to Sam, my first footy kickabout partner. What might have happened if we hadn't been banned from playing, age 11? Thanks to Emma for humouring me in our uni footy team. I scored a great goal once, but it was offside. I was the last to know, sprinting away, arms aloft. Sad times. And to my family, especially my late dad, for instilling my love of football, and for taking me to my first-ever Spurs match in 1988. We beat Blackburn in the League Cup. Gazza played. Glory days.

Finally, to the Lionesses. The summer of 2022 was so special, I still get goosebumps when I think of it. My wife and I were at the 8-0 thumping of Norway in Brighton. We were also there at the thrilling Wembley final to see you beat Germany 2-1 on home soil. I've been a football fan all my life, attending hundreds of games. That European final was honestly the best footballing experience of my entire life. And holy fuck, we won! Here's to many more inspirational days of women's football. Many more days of inspiring the world with your bravery.

I hope this book entertains and inspires in equal measure.

This one is from the heart.

Thanks for reading.

If you fancy getting in touch, you can do so using one of the methods below. I'm most active on Instagram.

Twitter: @ClareLydon
Facebook: www.facebook.com/clare.lydon
Instagram: @clarefic
Find out more at: www.clarelydon.co.uk
Contact: mail@clarelydon.co.uk

Author's Note

This book is told from the perspective of the two main characters: one American, one English. I made the decision to use UK English spellings throughout, to save confusion for you, but also for me. I've tried to make sure Sloane thinks and speaks as an American, but I'm sure some things have slipped through the net. If she refers to petrol instead of gas, to jumpers rather than sweaters, that's on me. I hope at least she takes the elevator (not lift), sits on a couch (not sofa), and takes to the field (not the pitch). Even though we speak the same language, it's only when you come to write a book, you realise how difficult it actually is. Be gentle with me.

For Emma, who could have been a contender.

Chapter One

A brisk wind ruffled Sloane Patterson's short, blonde hair as she stepped out of the Boeing 777 and onto the wobbly metal staircase. She glanced at the melancholy sky, punctuated with dark clouds. Crucially, it wasn't raining. Everyone had told her that was all it did in England, especially here in the north. The first tick in her New Life column. Even if this was the UK's idea of summer.

She climbed aboard the VIP bus (essentially just a bus with VIP printed on a card stuck to the window), then tried to pin down the emotions zipping around her body. Excitement. Trepidation. What-the-fuck-have-I-done-ness.

But she was here now. No turning back. Hot nerves lit up her system. She clutched a pole as the bus swung into motion. Falling over within minutes of arriving wouldn't be a good look. Especially not on her bad ankle.

What had her LA therapist, Jackson, told her? "If you think of it as a bad ankle, it will become that. Think of it as a strong ankle. Repeat the mantra every morning. Make it your strongest ankle possible. Your best asset."

Sloane glanced down. *You're my very best ankle.* Then she rolled her eyes.

Jackson wouldn't be pleased.

"Are you sure you want to do this? Do they even know about women's soccer over there?" her mom had asked, as if she was a world soccer expert. Or even an expert on Sloane. She was neither.

When Sloane replied that the UK was the home of soccer, her mom had tempered her argument.

"Men's soccer came from there. They're a bit backwards when it comes to women's soccer, aren't they?"

Sloane had assured her the Women's Super League was established, and here to stay.

Her mom wasn't convinced. "I'm just saying, it's a big commitment. You can't just hop in a car and come home if you're feeling blue."

Sloane knew that. But when was the last time she'd gotten in the car to go visit her family? She'd been blue plenty over the past year, but her parents were never her first port of call. They were her parents, not her friends. Often, not even very friendly parents.

Plus, Sloane was sure about this. She needed to get away. A fresh perspective. A new culture to acclimatise into. A new club to give her something to strive for. A place different enough, but somewhere where they spoke the same language. She'd had offers from Spain and Germany, but England had won out.

The past two seasons in LA, she'd been in cruise control. Coming to Salchester Rovers was something completely new and challenging. That it would take her mind off the mess that was her love life was an added bonus. She'd spent the first hour of the flight wondering what Jess was doing. If she was thinking about her. Until she'd had harsh words with herself and put on *Wonder Woman*. Two hours of Gal Gadot was enough to distract even the hardest of hearts. Then she'd drunk three glasses of champagne and fallen asleep. Sloane wasn't a big drinker. Her mind told her that now, still trying to start up like an old, dusty computer.

The bus lurched to a stop outside the main building, and Sloane walked through the door and down a shiny white corridor. She was completely alone. There had been others in first class on her flight, but they'd been shepherded elsewhere.

A new country. Where she knew nobody. It was just her and her thoughts.

She took a deep breath.

She could do this. She'd scored the winner for the US in the World Cup final. But that had been easy, just muscle memory and repetition. Conversely, she'd never uprooted her life before. Hell, she'd hardly ever flown on her own before. She was normally surrounded by teammates and staff, safe in the cocoon of her club. Off the field, Sloane had gotten used to not thinking for herself. Things were about to change. Ever since she'd told her agent yes, she'd thought about nothing else.

The click-clack of heels on the shiny floor interrupted her thoughts. She was more used to hearing the click-clack of studs on the concrete that surrounded soccer fields. A woman in jeans and a mint-green sweatshirt walked towards her. She beamed a welcome.

Sloane straightened up. She glanced down to check she hadn't spilt anything down her sweatshirt, and ran a hand through her hair.

"Sloane, it's great to meet you."

She knew her name. The woman extended her hand and Sloane took it. Her excitement crackled up Sloane's arm.

"My name's Sara and I work for the Lancashire Airport VIP service." She had a voice that could knock the froth off coffee three tables away.

Sloane rocked on her heels and resisted the urge to rub her ears.

Sara paused, glanced at the floor, then back up. "Honestly, it's a thrill to meet you, and I'm super excited you signed for Rovers. It's just what the team needs this season, especially as we're fighting for the league, cups, and a Champions League spot." Sara shook her head, slipping her professional face back on. "But I don't mean to overwhelm you with expectations. I know you just had a long flight, and you're probably tired."

Sloane smiled. She met fans like Sara wherever she went, but she was always grateful for them. "A little thirsty for sure," she said. "But it's always lovely to meet someone who follows the game. I'm going to do my best to help the club on all fronts."

"Great, great," Sara replied, nodding like one of those Chinese lucky cats. "Let's get you through security. I've got someone sorting your bags, and then a club delegation is waiting in the car park. Plus, of course, there are a few fans waiting en route."

Warmth flooded Sloane. Fans had turned up. It happened wherever they went in the States, but she had no idea if it would happen here. Her mood brightened instantly.

"Sounds perfect, thanks Sara."

Sara beamed at Sloane saying her name.

Sloane knew all the tricks. Impressing women was the same whether you were charming a potential date, schmoozing a journalist or pleasing a fan. Turn your attention fully onto them, remember their name and repeat it back. It was a sure-fire way to make that woman feel like the centre of your world. It had always worked great for Sloane. Right up until it didn't. But she wasn't going to think about her.

Sloane produced her blue American passport and handed it to the man at border control. She was almost due a new one. Her photo was from nearly nine years ago, when anyone aged 28 was ancient. Yet here she was, 28 and not on death's door just yet. If you'd told 19-year-old Sloane what was going to happen in her life and career over the next decade, she'd have been pretty pleased.

"Welcome to the UK, Ms Patterson," the customs officer said, with a smile that emphasised the dimple in his cheek. "I hope you settle into your new job." He paused and leaned forward. "But not too well, because in my house, we're fans of Salchester United." He gave her a wink.

Sloane let out a hoot of laughter, and her shoulders loosened. She hadn't realised how tense they were until that moment. She peered at the man's name badge. Simon.

"Thanks Simon, I needed that laugh. But I'm sorry to be the bearer of bad news. Our Rovers are going to give you a soccer lesson this season, and I plan to be right at the centre of the action." She returned Simon's wink, and could still hear him laughing as Sara pushed open a set of double doors into the shiny VIP arrivals lounge.

Sloane blinked as camera flashes popped and the volume exploded. She grinned. If her mom could see her now.

Maybe coming to the UK was the right move, after all.

Chapter Two

Ella stood and stared at Salchester Rovers' elite training facility in front of her. The impressive new building had sprung up in the last five years, providing state-of-the-art training pitches, gyms, accommodation, and recovery for the men's and women's teams, as well as the youth set-up. Now, it was her workplace. She balled her hand into a fist. Deep breaths. In through her nose, out through her mouth.

This was it. Two degrees and nearly a decade working with her own clients, she'd finally landed her dream job. Scratch that, she wasn't arriving here to play football just as she'd wished when she was a little girl. However, when that dream hadn't come true, the next item on Ella's list was to work at Salchester Rovers in some capacity. Here she was, ready to start work as the women's team's very own performance and lifestyle coach. The first of her kind in the Women's Super League.

How proud her mum would have been. How stoked her family and friends were. She'd even allowed herself a moment to be proud of herself.

She took another deep breath and grabbed her new, posh black bag from the back seat of her metallic-green Mini. First day was all about looking the part. Fake it 'til you make it. It had been a while since Ella's previous first day. Just after her mum died. She'd faked that day just fine. If she could do that, she could do anything.

An impressive-looking black car with tinted windows pulled up a few feet away.

Ella bent to see who was inside, but she hadn't added x-ray vision to her list of achievements yet. She straightened. Did she need her navy blazer from the back seat? The July sunshine was fairly hot, but this was Salchester. It could change in a moment. She hesitated, then grabbed it. She might be overdressed, but it was better to look professional on her first day. She could suss the rest out as she went.

"You think you'll be able to handle the job, Ms Carmichael?" the People manager had asked in her interview. "These are Women's Super League stars. Players who get recognised when they walk down the street. Some of them are famous faces worldwide. The game's expanded in ways you'd never have thought possible ten years ago. Now, the women, just like the men, are superstars. How do you think you'll do working alongside them?"

Ella was aware things had changed since she'd last laced up her football boots. However, the question hadn't fazed her. She was used to dealing with professional athletes. She was a skilled and experienced elite performance coach, who'd helped sports people from all walks of life. She'd handle every person in the same way she'd treat any client – with care, respect, and with a professional attitude.

She'd also told the interviewer she'd expect the same in return. "We're all on the same side, with the ultimate aim of getting fit, healthy players – in body and mind – onto the pitch to do the best they can for Salchester Rovers."

That, of course, was the professional answer. The one she'd practised in the mirror prior to her interview. But right now, the reality of her new job started to sink in. She was working at the heart of her childhood team. Butterflies flapped in her chest, and she smoothed them down. The team she'd come to see with her family as a kid, the team she still supported to this day. Only now, she had a front row seat to every game. A behind-the-scenes pass to every day.

She'd been hired first and foremost to look after the women's team. To make sure their mindset and lifestyle were as fit and finely tuned as their bodies. She wasn't a psychologist, the club already employed them. Salchester had hired her to work part-time in a brand-new role to help the team level up. To do for them what she'd done for other athletes. To make them the best.

Because this year, Salchester Rovers were set to fight not only for the league with their arch-rivals, Salchester United, but also for the FA Cup and a second consecutive top-four finish. They'd spent big in the transfer market. They'd brought in Ella and a raft of other staff. Salchester Rovers were taking their women's team just as seriously as their men's.

A car door slammed behind her. When she turned, a hooded figure got out of the shiny, black car, slinging a holdall over their left shoulder. The holdall looked expensive. Ella was useless when it came to labels, but her cousin Marina had given her a crash course when she'd learned about her new job. "If you want to get on with the players, especially the big ones, you're going to have to get to know their lives. That means being up on fashion." Her eyebrows had almost joined together when she spoke, she was that serious. This person's bag was brown with gold. Louis Vuitton? Ella was 90 per cent sure.

Ella shrugged on her blazer, hitched her bag up her shoulder, and locked her car with a beep. She walked along the pavement and was just about to steer around the hooded figure, when whoever it was pushed their hood down and stepped back. Right onto Ella's shiny black brogues.

Pain shot up her leg and she let out a yelp.

"Shit! I'm sorry!"

An American accent.

Ella blinked, then focused. Then took a huge intake of breath.

Holy shit.

The woman holding the designer bag, who'd just stepped on her foot was none other than the best striker in the women's game right now. Salchester Rovers' new signing, Sloane Patterson. Queer pin-up. Very out. And very fucking good at football. In signing her, Salchester Rovers had broken the world record transfer fee for a woman. Sloane was a media staple, a darling of the tabloids with her English midfield dynamo fiancée Jess Calder, and a very big deal. Her job was to take the club to the next level. It was part of Ella's new role to make sure she was in the right head space to do just that. Hence, she wasn't going to shout at her for standing on her foot.

Instead, Ella shook her head. "No problem," she replied, making light of it. "I'm just glad I didn't step on your foot. That would have been worse."

Sloane let out a hoot of laughter. "Depends if you'd broken a metatarsal. Then the inquests would have started, right?"

"I do not plan on breaking your foot now or anytime." Ella cleared her throat. She was having a normal chat and a laugh with the world's best striker. This was her life now. No big deal.

However, it was one thing dealing with a world-famous basketball player, or a gold medal-winning hurdler or diver. Ella knew what it took to get to the top of any sport, and anybody who made it had her total admiration. But she'd never been starstruck before.

Until now.

Ella had seen Sloane play a few times, and she lived up to the hype. Talented, ultra-competitive, and always first to the ball, no matter what. Her results spoke for themselves. She showed up in the big games and scored big goals. Now, she stood in front of Ella, her face fitted with an American-pie smile.

"Is this your first day?" Play it cool. Ella had told her boss dealing with players would be no trouble. But that was when she'd had time to mentally prepare, with questions to ask them, research to fall back on. She hadn't delved into any of the players' backgrounds in depth yet. They weren't due back at the training ground until next week, and she didn't want to rock up to any meetings with pre-conceived ideas. The only thing she knew about Sloane? Fabulous legs, toned arms, lethal with both feet, gorgeous fiancée.

Sloane shook her head, the famous crease in her brow. "Yes and no. I mean, yes, this is the first time I've come to the training ground. The club car dropped me off. Very nice service. I'm here to say hi to the manager. I think she wants to make sure I've arrived and have no plans to run away before the rest of the players turn up next week."

"And do you?"

Another gentle laugh. Sloane was nothing like she was on the pitch. There, she was a force of nature. In real life, she appeared laid back. The ideal combination.

"I don't know yet." She held out a hand. "I'm Sloane Patterson. But I have a feeling you knew that."

Now it was Ella's turn to smile. She couldn't quite laugh. Not when Sloane was waiting for her to shake her hand. She gulped, but managed to propel her hand forward and grasp Sloane's. It was warm and soft in Ella's embrace. She did her best to ignore that. She really had to get over her childish crush.

But holy fucking hell, she was touching Sloane Patterson!

"Ella Carmichael. Nice to meet you, Sloane." She leaned forward. "I did know that. It's my first day, too. I'm the new club performance and lifestyle coach, so I think we'll be seeing a lot of each other."

"Thank goodness you do actually work here. But the blazer tipped me off." She swept her gaze over Ella. "You look very professional."

Ella did a mock bow. "Why, thank you."

What the actual fuck, Ella?

Sloane unzipped her black hoodie and tilted her head towards the building. Her golden hair glinted in the morning sun. "Shall we walk in together?"

She couldn't quite believe this was happening, but Ella went with it. She fought the urge to get her phone out and Insta-story this moment to the world.

She fell into step beside Sloane. As well as her posh bag, she also wore Nike trainers Ella had never seen before. They were probably made specifically for her. Ella followed Sloane on social media when she remembered to look. She was always in the latest fashions, with the latest trainers to match. Or sneakers, as she would say.

"Have you worked with other soccer teams? I'm impressed they've got you on the books. Performance and lifestyle coaches are not the norm."

"Salchester Rovers are the first team to have one, I'm told. We're breaking new ground. I usually work on a freelance basis. I have my own practice too, working across a few different sports. But the club have brought me on-board three days a week to work with the teams, with the option of more if required. I'm also going to be part of the women's team on matchdays. I'm really looking forward to the challenge." She wasn't lying. "I'm also very excited, as I'm a lifelong supporter."

"I better be on my game then, right?" Sloane grinned. "My brother was the same when I played for Houston. Loves that team for no apparent reason, as we're from Detroit. But every time I had a bad game? He'd call me and give me shit." She raised her gaze to Ella.

Ella was struck by just how blue Sloane's eyes were. She'd noticed them before on TV. But in real life? They held you in place and wouldn't let you go. Ella bet they'd been the reason for many broken hearts over the years.

"I'm sure you're going to do great and give your all for the team. I've seen you play. You've got mad skills."

They reached the front door of the training ground, and Sloane stepped forward. "Ready with your first-day smile? Want to practice it on me first? Here's mine." Sloane made an exaggerated face.

Ella snorted. She couldn't help it. She was charmed.

"Definitely go with that. Lucy Harris won't fail to fall for it."
Lucy was the Women's team manager.

"Thought so." She nudged Ella with her elbow. "I'm
nervous. You nervous? People think I don't get nervous, but I
feel okay telling you. You're a psychologist, right? It would be
bad not to be nervous."

"I'm not strictly a psychologist, just a humble performance
and lifestyle coach." Ella smiled. "But I agree, it would be
bad. Everyone gets nervous and wants to make a good first
impression."

"Especially when you come with the reputation like mine.
Never shy away from a tackle. Outspoken bad girl." She put a
hand to her chest. "But that's on the field. Underneath it all, I'm
a big softie. You believe that, right?"

"I never listen to gossip. I take everyone at face value. I
know what people say about a number of players, but I reserve
judgement until I meet them and know the facts."

Sloane raised a single styled eyebrow. Full, as was the
fashion these days.

"Smart woman. I like you."

Ella stored that comment away to tell her cousin when
she spoke to her. Marina was going to absolutely freak.

Sloane pressed the intercom, then opened the main
door when the receptionist buzzed them in. When the glass
door clicked shut, two figures rose from the blue sofas in
reception. They both approached Sloane, and gave Ella a
quizzical once over.

"Sloane," one of the men began. He gripped Sloane's hand,
and she dropped her posh holdall on the shiny, polished floor.
"How are you? We're absolutely thrilled you could make it in.

Good to get you acclimatised before everyone else shows up. The personal touch for our new star player."

He still pumped Sloane's hand, the muscles in his forearm flexing as he did. He wore a tight black polo shirt, black jeans and a surprising lemon belt.

"Just happy to be part of the team, Paulo, thanks for the welcome," Sloane replied. She threw a smile Ella's way. Like they were in this together.

Ella smiled back. Should she stay here, or go to reception? Probably the latter, but she'd waited here too long now for the transition to be easy.

"Sorry, is this a friend of yours?" asked Lemon Belt, aka Paulo Martinez, Salchester's chairman. His Spanish accent danced across his English words.

"This is Ella Carmichael, your new elite performance and lifestyle coach," Sloane told him. "She's starting today, too."

Paulo gave Ella a warm smile and a quick handshake. "Welcome, Ella. I'm sure Beth can sort you out if you go over there." He wafted his hand in the direction of reception, but his focus remained solely on Sloane, the star.

Ella took the hint. "Have a great first day, Sloane. I'll see you around."

"I'll make sure of it," Sloane replied.

Ella allowed herself a small grin, then made her way to the reception desk.

Sloane Patterson was not who she expected at all.

Chapter Three

"How's the new flat?" Lucy Harris put both hands behind the back of her head and focused solely on her new charge. She wore a Salchester-blue training top with the initials LH on the front. Every time Sloane saw Lucy on the sidelines on TV, she was dressed in her tracksuit, as if she was ready to come on and change the game. At 40, she was one of the league's youngest managers, having only hung up her boots six years ago.

"It's good. Nice view of the city. I appreciate getting the penthouse." She'd spent the first couple of nights breathing in her new city while staring out at the nightscape laid out before her. She'd needed a sweater, though. She'd been here a month now, and it was only getting worse. Even in August. In LA, August nights were still no jacket required.

"You earned it. Keep scoring goals for us this season and you can stay there." Lucy tapped her pencil on her desk and gave Sloane a wide grin. "That was a joke, by the way."

"I wasn't worried. Goals are my currency."

Lucy gave her an appreciative nod, then sat forward. "And are you coping with the weather?"

"It's a skill I'm yet to grasp, but I'm sure it'll come in time."

Her manager gave a proper laugh to that. "You're the first

major US player to come to this league, and I think a lot of them are put off by the weather. But they shouldn't be. It's actually better to play in once you get used to it."

"I'll take your word for it." Sloane had already ordered an electric blanket.

Lucy was a legend of the women's game. Someone who'd won it all at club level, and was now one of the most respected managers in the league. She'd taken over Salchester when they put their women's team together only five years ago. Little by little, the team had got stronger and were now ready to challenge for the league. Sloane was well aware that Lucy wouldn't stand for anything less than full commitment to the cause. She was ready to do just that.

"You know some of the girls, but I wanted to ask – would you like someone to show you around the city? I can arrange one of the staff to do it if you like?"

Sloane shook her head. "I'm good. I know Layla, I'm sure she'll show me the sights. Plus, I've already been photographed, which surprised me. I haven't just won the Euros, I'm not a Lioness."

Lucy sat back in her black leather chair. "Yes, but you're engaged to one."

A chill sluiced through Sloane's body. Was she? According to the rest of the world, yes.

"Plus, last time I looked, you were still a World Cup winner, still closing in on the record for the highest number of international goals scored by an American woman."

Sloane waved a hand. "I don't take much notice of records. I'm just surprised people know who I am. I haven't even played a match yet."

"You made the back pages. You're a star, Sloane."

"I was hoping to fly a little more under the radar here."

Lucy narrowed her eyes, then shrugged. "If it helps, you might be a star out there," she pointed out of her office window, "but in here," she circled with her finger, "in this training ground and on the pitch, you're just a part of the team."

"The way I like it, even if we call it a field. But field or pitch, I agree." Sloane replied.

"Good. My plan this season? To mould the team around you. I know you dropped deep to get the ball more with your last team, and that's a great facet to your game. But I want you to be the figurehead for us. We've got a great young striker in Nat Tyler. She's very excited to learn from you. Take her under your wing. Share your experience. She's already a fantastic talent and she's a born goal scorer. But pairing her with you is the dream ticket." Lucy snagged Sloane with her intense gaze. "Plus, we have a blistering midfield with Millie Welsh and team captain, Layla Hansen, who you know. But most of all, I want you to be happy here. I told you on the phone, I want to know my players on and off the pitch."

Sloane remembered this conversation with her old coach in Cali. Back then, *she* was the young, hot striker, being paired with the older, more mature teammate. Also on the team was Jess Calder, a promising midfielder. When they met, sparks flew, and their passion on and off the field had translated into goals galore. Sloane was well aware that your life off the field always infiltrated your life on it. However, she'd made a pact with herself coming over here. To be happy and content, and to focus on herself and her game. Nothing else. Especially not Jess.

As part of that game plan, Sloane cracked the best smile

she could muster. "I'm here for a new experience, and part of that is playing to the best of my ability in a new country and a new league. I'm excited to be here, and I'm hoping my life off the field will be so dull, I have to make all my excitement on it. I'm 100 per cent committed."

The manager tilted her head, then gave Sloane a firm nod. "I know you're committed. I've seen you in action." She paused, pinning Sloane in place once more with her gaze. "I also know that relocating brings its own challenges, even for a seasoned pro like you. My door is always open for matters on and off the pitch. Plus, we've employed a performance and lifestyle coach, so use her, too."

Sloane bit down a smile. Ella. She pictured her laughing face in her mind, her mass of brown hair. She'd liked her immediately. Thought she could be a friend. Was she allowed to make friends with the performance coach? She might not have a choice. Having friends off the field was just as important as having friends on it. They'd met once in the opening few days of her time here, and then, nothing. When Sloane had asked, she'd been told that Ella had a scheduled work break to coach existing clients elsewhere. She was in demand. That was a good sign.

"I will. I'm just excited to get started." Sloane was a winner. Lucy was a winner. This was set to be a fantastic partnership.

Lucy tapped her pencil once more. "One more thing. I'm introducing a personal stories session before every game. Where players and staff share something we don't know about their journey. Obstacles you've overcome. Or something you're still dealing with. I'm going to go first. Would you be happy to do the second share?"

Sloane nodded. "One hundred per cent."

"Great. One last thing. How's the ankle?"

Sloane ignited her brightest smile. "Feeling good. Great, even. Ready for the new season and everything it brings."

Chapter Four

"Come in, come in." Ella rose from her seat and ushered Sloane into the front row of the cinema room. However, this wasn't used to view the latest blockbusters. Rather, this was where the players came to view their performances and those of other teams. Where they analysed what they'd done, and what they could do better. Also, where they had one-on-one wellbeing sessions with Ella.

It was a far cry from Ella's playing career, where the facilities had been non-existent, and the manager had screamed at them when they did things wrong. The world had changed since then, as had techniques for dealing with players. Nobody responded well to sharp criticism handed out like a slap in the face. Lucy demanded high standards, and she made sure the players were met with an arm around the shoulder, and a gentle shove in the right direction when needed.

Meanwhile, Ella's job was to accentuate the positives, figure out ways to move forward, and wrap any shortcomings in a sandwich of can-do. Her task was to go deeper, and see where players could improve off the field, which then transferred to the pitch.

Even players like Sloane Patterson.

Who looked annoyingly stylish, even in a standard club tracksuit.

"Good to see you again. I've been looking out for you since our first day, but you've been elusive." Sloane flashed her charming grin, tossed her banana skin into the bin to her left with a slam-dunk shot, then stretched out her long legs as she settled into her red-velvet seat. "Just finishing my lunch." She took a swig of her coffee, winced, and set it down. "This stuff is lethal. Tastes like hot, melted tyres."

Ella sat two seats along from Sloane. "I agree. It's why I bring my own into work." She tapped the side of her nose. "Top tip."

"Noted."

"Good to see you again, too," Ella continued. "I had a couple of clients at the European aquatic championship and I'd already agreed to go with the team. Hence this is my second first day."

Sloane raised an eyebrow and finished chewing before she spoke. "How did they do? I imagine, with your help, they swept the board."

There was that charm again. But this time, Ella was prepared. The first time they'd met, she'd been starstruck, a fan. This time, she was in control, and she had the questions.

"They did well. But we're not here to talk about them. We're here to talk about you. You've been here three weeks now. How are you settling in?"

Sloane nodded. "Good. Great. I'm getting stronger and sharper physically, and the team is great."

"Lucy tells me you're training well. That's not a surprise. You're one of the world's best football players."

"Soccer, but we'll agree to differ."

"The best striker in the business. With an attitude, too. A hotshot, literally."

Sloane's eyes creased for a moment. "A hotshot? I hope in the nicest possible way?"

Ella contorted her face in an effort to keep it still. She hadn't meant that to come out of her mouth. "Of course. I've only heard good things about you. You're more than fine on the pitch. But what about away from training? Have you been out with some of the girls?"

Another nod.

Ella wanted to dive deeper, but it was unlikely to happen in the first session. Clients were always buttoned up physically and emotionally when they first chatted.

As if confirming that, Sloane sat up and crossed her arms over her chest before she spoke.

Text book.

"It's all good. We've been out after training to Shot Of The Day, the coffee shop Michelle runs with her wife."

Ella was yet to go, but she knew it was a popular destination. Michelle Howard was a stalwart of the team, coming to the end of her career. She and her wife had opened their coffee shop last year, very close to the training ground. With alcohol generally off the menu, most players' drug of choice was caffeine. Ella needed to find her own coffee shop to frequent now she was working here regularly. She could go there, but it was a player hangout.

"And in the evenings? I've just moved into my own flat here and I don't know anyone in the local area. I know it can get lonely." She was born here, but her family moved two hours east to the coast when she was nine. Salchester was still their closest big city, the hub of the north, just over two hours on a train from London.

Sloane hugged her body a little tighter, and creased her brow. "I'm used to that. I like my own company. I've got Netflix, I speak to my brother, and Jess." Her mouth twitched.

Ah, yes. The fiancée Sloane had left in the US. It wasn't unusual in their line of work, but Ella wanted to know why.

"How's Jess doing?"

"She's good. Busy with her team. We're both focusing on our own careers at the moment. A soccer player's window is short, so this move made sense for me right now."

Ella pressed her tongue into the side of her cheek as she gave Sloane a reassuring nod.

A flash of vulnerability worked its way across Sloane's face, but she covered it up by clearing her throat. She dropped Ella's gaze.

"But she'll be in the country for international camp in October? Lucy told me you're staying put and not going back for yours."

Sloane flinched.

It was almost unnoticeable.

But Ella noticed.

"If she gets picked. But that's in Surrey, not here."

"You won't see her?"

"No plans as yet. The schedule's very tight."

That answer told her all she needed to know. Sloane and Jess were on the rocks, and that could impact Sloane's footballing output this season.

"You're settling into the city, though, that's great to hear.

First game coming up when we head to Germany on our pre-season tour. What do you think will be your biggest challenges?"

Sloane took a deep breath, then gave Ella a defiant stare. "Bedding into an established team is going to be key, but I've done it before, so I'm ready for it." She dropped her head, sat forward, then turned to Ella. "You don't have to psychoanalyse me. I'm quite an open book on the field. I've read a lot of performance books, and I used to have a coach for it. I know what to do. There will be challenges, but I'm ready to meet them head-on. I thrive on challenge. I like to take risks. I've had success and failure and know they're both important. I live for the pressure. Bring on the first game."

Now it was Ella's turn to raise an eyebrow. Sloane was talking in clichés. "If you make me redundant, I'm thrilled." She was lying. Her skin prickled under Sloane's stare. "I get that you've done this work before, and you've read all the books. But if you're that well versed, you know there's never a time when you have it all figured out. This is a constant journey of learning and relearning. Of making yourself vulnerable and brilliant again and again. You can do it on your own, or you can do it with me as your cheerleader." She paused. "I don't know about you, but I've always been a fan of cheerleaders. Someone on your side, willing to spin and tumble just for you? That sounds like the ultimate to me."

Maybe it was time to throw in a personal titbit to pull Sloane back from the defensive edge? She didn't normally do it so quickly, but Sloane was a different case.

"My mum was my cheerleader. She never looked great in the short skirt, and her pom-poms were a little worn, but having her in my corner gave me wings. That little bit extra every time

I came up against a challenge. That's what the management team here are for. Lucy, the trainers, physios, nutritionists, psychologists. Me as an added extra on the side. We're here to fight your background battles and make sure your path is clear, so that when you're on the pitch, all you have to think of is you and the game."

Ella waited to see if her psychological trick had worked.

Sloane exhaled and her shoulders relaxed. If body language was anything to go by, it had.

"You said your mum was your cheerleader? She's not anymore?"

Ella gulped. She'd opened the door. She had to step through. She gave a slight shake of her head. "She died eight years ago. I know what it is to go through the world without your key cheerleader by your side. You can do it, but it's harder. That's why when I'm offered any others, I take them. Life's tough enough."

"I'm sorry to hear that." Sloane bit her lip. "And I wasn't being dismissive. I need cheerleaders just as much as the next person." She stared at Ella.

"Good to hear because I'm paid to be here, so I'd do it whether you like it or not."

At last, a genuine smile.

Ella returned it. "Shall we try that question again. What do you think will be your biggest challenges?"

Sloane considered the question before answering. "Gelling with an already settled side. Getting to know my teammates off the field as well as on. Learning the patterns of play. Getting the transitions right. Staying up the field as the manager wants. But that'll come in time." She paused. "This week, my biggest challenge is smiling into the camera looking like I mean it at my Nike photoshoot. I always get a bit self-conscious at those things. I could never be a model. It's harder than it looks."

Sloane lowered her gaze to the floor, then looked back at Ella. Sloane lied: she could totally be a model. But also, her guard was down. She was finally admitting a weakness.

"And they can't eat anything but dust. You wouldn't catch me wanting their lives," Ella replied.

"I'd much rather be scoring goals."

"Me, too." Ella winced. This never happened when she was talking to divers and hurdlers, did it?

But Sloane hadn't missed it. "You, too? Did you play?"

Ella bit her lip. "A long time ago. But this isn't about me. This chat is all about you."

"What if I want to know about you? Isn't this relationship both ways?" Sloane snagged Ella's gaze and held it.

Ella's insides rocked unsteadily under its heat. She'd love to share her story with Sloane. But this was not the time or place. She took a deep breath and shook her head. "Maybe one day when you've told me a bit more about yourself. This is a two-way conversation, but I need something to work with."

Sloane didn't drop her gaze. "Maybe in session two we'll both uncover a little more. You can tell me about your soccer career. I can tell you a bit more about how I have been lonely some evenings." She sucked on her top lip and held up a hand. "But that's not a problem. It's part of the job. It's one I'm used to."

Ella knew that was true. She almost offered to meet her for a coffee. But that would be unprofessional. Ella was here to do a job for the team, just like Sloane.

She'd get her to talk eventually.

Chapter Five

Her thigh muscles ached, and she knew her butt would be sore tomorrow. But it was the good type of sore. The one she'd take every day. Where she knew she'd worked her body, and that her muscles were getting stronger every day. Sloane still remembered the season she'd had on the sidelines with an ankle injury that never quite healed. Two weeks had turned into four months of growing frustration, as she watched her teammates lift the title without her help. She still got a medal, but she hadn't earned it. This season, she wanted to earn everything she got and take this team to the next level. That included her famed penalties, which she'd just finished practising.

"Thanks, Becca, you're a star!"

Salchester's goalkeeper gave Sloane a high five, then hurried off the field ahead of her, her ginger ponytail swaying behind her. "Can't stop, gotta get to my mum's for her birthday!"

Sloane shooed her off the field with her hands. "Get going, then." Becca disappeared into the changing rooms.

"Good shooting today, Hotshot."

Sloane smiled at Layla as she fell into step beside her. Layla had stayed out with her while she practised penalties, as Sloane did every session. Layla's Norwegian accent was still there in the background if you listened hard enough. However, years spent outside her home country, both in the US and now the UK, meant that her accent had a mix of everything. Part Texan, part Lancashire, part Oslo.

She and Layla had played together at college, had come up against each other in the US league, and had found themselves on opposing teams in international tournaments for their country, too. Layla was a creative midfield general, her speciality unlocking defences by playing killer balls to forwards. Sloane loved those types of players. Unselfish, playing for the team. Plus, they always made someone like her look good. Strikers were always inherently selfish. It was in their DNA.

"Forty-seven out of fifty penalties. Not bad. But I think you were the hotshot in training today." Sloane nudged Layla with her elbow as they walked.

Layla batted away her compliment with a wave of her hand.

"How you settling in, Patts? I hear you got an apartment pretty central. When I arrived, they put me in the usual block they reserve for new players. But clearly, you're a special case."

Sloane held up her hands. "I had nothing to do with it. I think my agent might have done, though."

"Closer to the action," Layla replied. "Not that you're after any action." She shook her head in disbelief. "I'm married, and you're engaged. Who would have thought it when we were tearing up the league and kissing any girl who'd have us back in the day?"

"Who indeed?"

Their boots click-clacked on the concrete as they stepped off the grass and through the glass doors to the locker room.

Sloane heard the facilities were good at Salchester, but they were better than anywhere she'd been before. Training on a velvet carpet of green grass trimmed to perfection. To her right, a wall of glass that housed a state-of-the-art gym. Beyond that, huge treatment and meeting rooms, where she knew she'd find Ella. This was a step up from where she'd been. Men and women training at the same facilities, viewed on equal footing.

"Interesting story from Lucy today. You're up next when we get to Germany. You know what you're going to say?"

Sloane shook her head. "Not yet, but I'll mull it over."

Lucy had started training today by telling them about her career, and how she dreamed of playing in bigger stadiums when she was young. However, back then, the women's game wasn't in the right place, and teams played on terrible pitches with no facilities. "At one point, because my parents didn't accept me as a lesbian, and football paid nothing, I slept in my car for a few months," she told them.

There had been gasps all round, including from Sloane. But luckily, her story had a happy ending, and she was now managing in those bigger stadiums she'd dreamed of playing in. "The FA is still run by men. The right to play was withdrawn once, so always remember those who fought to get it back. You're standing on the shoulders of giants. Enjoy it, live your best life, but never take it for granted."

Sloane hadn't given much thought to what she was going to say before their first game in Germany, but she wanted it to be something personal, to show she fully trusted them, just as Lucy had done. Maybe she could share the story of her parents? She'd never done that before, mainly because it was *hugely* personal and vulnerable. It fitted the bill perfectly.

"How's Jess?"

Sloane's skin prickled. What had Layla heard? The women's game might have gone global and picked up a slew of new fans, but it was still a small world. When relationships began or split, it was pretty common knowledge once the grapevine had done its work. However, seeing as Sloane didn't actually know what was happening with her relationship, she'd be surprised if Layla did.

"Good." Short answers. That was what she'd decided she'd give if people asked. She knew they would, of course. She and Jess were a power couple on and off the field. They scored goals, as well as sponsorships and big-money deals. They were two of the highest earners in the global game. But they were still just two women, navigating their long-distance relationship. Sloane knew there had been many column inches written about their lives since she'd agreed to this UK move. YouTubers had gone to town. Twitter had gone into meltdown. Jess staying put in the US hadn't helped the rumours. However, they hadn't said a word to any of their friends or colleagues. As far as anyone was concerned, Sloane and Jess were still very much together, and still committed to their relationship.

"She coming over for international camp in October? If she does, it'd be great to catch up."

If Jess was picked, she'd be on UK soil. Sloane had pushed that issue to the back of her mind. "I'll let you know. I'm speaking to her later. We have to see how our schedules are going to pan out. You know how it is when you're in different countries and playing in different leagues."

They arrived at their pegs and Layla took off her top,

revealing a well-toned six pack. She got up every morning and did 200 sit-ups. Sloane knew this because Layla never tired of telling her.

"You know what happened when Courtney and I tried living in different countries. It quickly went south. My advice? Stay in contact, get comfortable with phone and video sex, and don't go too long without talking. Otherwise, things might spiral where you don't want them to go." She stroked her firm stomach. "Now, are we going for coffee after this at Shot Of The Day? Michelle told me this morning that Suzy made fresh chocolate Guinness cake last night."

Sloane glanced Layla's way. "So long as you drive me to the city first so I can pick up a coffee machine. Then, coffee after that sounds perfect."

* * *

A gaggle of excited teenage girls were in the coffee shop when they arrived, as was often the case. Because the cafe was owned by a Salchester legend and her wife, fans often hung around hoping to spot a player. Sloane posed for photos and signed autographs before taking a seat. She took a first sip. Damn, it was good. The Guinness cake was sold out, but this was worth the trip. This flat white reminded her of cups she'd drunk in the Cali sunshine with Jess. Perhaps she'd have to come to Shot Of The Day more often.

Sloane's mind flashed to Ella. Had she tasted this yet? She'd love the stuff in LA, too. She'd fit in there. Ella's upbeat, incisive energy was very Californian, unlike her accent, which Sloane sometimes found hard to understand. Maybe the energy came from her determination to be the best and make everyone else the best around her, too. It's what everyone did on the West Coast. They studied, they ate right, they tried to upgrade their lives.

The team at Salchester was good, but she wasn't sure they had that extra *something*. Yet. She could help to bring it. So could Ella. Sloane was sure Ella had given her all on the field. What level had she played to? And why had she stopped? Sloane was intrigued. Ella was the person she'd most like to get to know. The squad was great and there were some good characters, but she'd met their types before at her previous clubs. The studious ones. The tactical ones. The physical ones. The rookies.

In contrast, she'd never met an Ella before.

After 45 minutes, she bid her goodbyes, before taking herself and her new coffee machine home.

Sloane walked in her front door, set down the machine and threw her keys on the island. This place still felt like a cold, empty shell. She needed to warm it up. Outside, drizzle stained the floor-to-ceiling windows. That was a new word she'd learned since she got here, too. Drizzle. Sloane was pretty sure it didn't exist in LA.

She kicked off her sneakers, then flopped down on the grey couch, ripping off her socks and wriggling her toes. Today's session had been a good one, her penalties on point. They needed to be. It was her job this season, and like she always said, the best time to start preparing was now.

She pulled her phone from her pocket and went to her Instagram. She scrolled down, right through to last year. She stopped when she got to the photo of her down on one knee, proposing to Jess on a Hawaiian beach. It was meant to be the ultimate romantic proposal, captured by a photographer at sunset. Only, the heavens had opened and it poured down. For Sloane, that had made it more real, more special. Jess, however, had been less than thrilled at getting soaked. What the camera didn't show you was that her bad mood lasted the whole evening.

Sloane rested her head on the couch arm and shut her eyes. She'd told Ella she was lonely eventually, but she hadn't said why. She missed LA. She missed her friends and her brother. But she didn't miss Jess. That said a lot.

Her phone lit up in her hands.

Video call coming in from Jess.

Fuck.

Sloane dropped her phone like it was on fire. Had she manifested this call with her thoughts? She tried to control her breathing, ran a hand through her hair. She didn't have time to check what she looked like. Did it matter? Jess had slept with someone else, so did she even care?

Sloane cleared her throat and swiped up. Every muscle she had locked up.

Jess appeared on screen, her face pixelated, before coming into focus. She looked tired.

"Hey." She tried a smile, but it didn't quite reach across her face. "I thought I'd call seeing as I'm twiddling my thumbs on the sofa." She paused. "How are things up north?"

Sloane blinked. She was up north. In Lancashire. When she first landed, she wanted to call it the Midwest, but apparently that wasn't a thing in the UK. "Things are good. Your country's idea of summer is a little whack, but so far, I can't complain."

"Nice apartment?"

"Flat to you," Sloane said with a smile. "The penthouse. It's lit. I'm having parties every night, of course."

"I bet. I saw some pics of you online out with Layla having coffee at Shot Of The Day."

"That was quick. It only happened about two hours ago."

"Fans are speculating whether you're an item." Jess gave her a pointed stare.

Sloane rolled her eyes. "People have got too much time on their hands." She paused. "Anyway, as far as the world's concerned, we're still engaged, aren't we?"

"Just the world?" Jess had the good grace to cast her gaze downwards at least.

"You tell me, Jess. You're the one who slept with someone else and then wouldn't talk to me before I left."

Jess winced. She never was very good with the truth.

The silence stretched. Then it stood, and stretched again.

"How's training going? Are you killing your penalties?"

Soccer. Whenever Jess was nervous, she always brought the conversation back to soccer. It was her love language.

"Don't change the subject. Are we ever going to talk about this?"

Jess sighed. "I wanted to come and see you before you left, but you know our schedules never matched."

She'd never been good at nailing down her priorities.

"I don't want to do this on the phone, you know that," Jess continued.

"We don't have much choice. This is about us. Our future. You told me Brit was a short-lived mistake." She still didn't truly believe her. But Jess was Sloane's fiancée and she loved her. Or at least, she had until very recently. It wasn't so easy

34

to throw in the towel. "We agreed we'd think about what we wanted over the summer. The summer's nearly over."

"Not in LA."

Sloane stared into the camera. She wasn't playing here. They needed to resolve this for both their sakes.

"Brit and I are over. It was a stupid tour fling that got out of hand. I told you that."

"You're still teammates."

"And that's all we are." She sighed. "I want you, Sloane, but you moved across an ocean, so where does that leave us? You know it's always been you. Ever since we met." Her eyes shimmered as she gulped.

"Telling me it's always been me and then cheating on me? That's not love, Jess. That's some form of weird bullshit. Something I'm not sure I need in my life anymore."

"Are you still wearing your ring?"

Sloane looked to her finger. She was. She wasn't sure why. Maybe because once she stopped, it really was over. She didn't want to fail at this. Sloane didn't fail. Not at soccer, not at life, not at love. She could already hear her mom telling her she told her so. That gay relationships don't last.

She nodded.

"Keep it on, please. We're not done. I'll call you next week. I love you."

Tears pricked the back of Sloane's eyes. A part of her would always love Jess, too. But she was 90 per cent certain that wasn't enough anymore.

Chapter Six

"I cannot believe you've waited nearly a month to give me any gossip about the delectable Sloane Patterson. Has she told you what's going on with her and Jess? I am going to freak if they've split. They are the couple that could. The ones I love the most. A perfect mix of US-UK heat, mixed with skill and cuteness and all manner of fuckability." Marina caught her breath on the other end of the line. Then she was right back on it. "I follow them both on Insta. Jess has a lot of Britney Navas and Wanda Rutherford on her page. If she and Sloane have split up, you think they're a throuple?"

"I can't give you anything as good as you're already making up." Ella pulled into her parking space, killed the engine and pressed her head against the headrest. It had been a long day, and she'd had a team meeting before she left with Lucy, the physios, and other training staff. Sloane was carrying a slight knock on her ankle so she'd sat out full training today, just as a precaution. But Ella wasn't going to share that with her blabbermouth cousin. Marina wouldn't be able to resist spreading the news all over social media, even though she'd promise not to. Ella already knew she had to limit what she said to anyone about the team. She couldn't have things getting out that could influence the set-up of opponents.

Marina wouldn't consider that. She'd just be thrilled with the gossip.

"All I can say is she's a pretty normal person. We've chatted about her settling into the city, and I've seen her at training. She lives in the penthouse of my block, but we haven't bumped into each other yet. She's down to earth, so if you want me to tell you she demands her kit is washed with jasmine-scented detergent and only drinks her water at room temperature, you're going to be disappointed."

Marina let out an audible sigh. "You're absolutely the worst person to be doing this job. Make something up for me at least. Remember, I'm coming to see you in a few weeks, and I expect a tour of your workplace. Maybe even an introduction to your favourite player."

Ella spluttered, unclicked her seatbelt, then hopped out of her car, keeping the phone glued to one ear. "Never in a million years, but good try."

"You have to hand it to me," her cousin replied. "Seriously, though. How's month one been? Are you settling in? Mum told me you spoke, and your divers did well."

Aunt Ursula had called earlier in the week. "They did, the whole staff are really pleased, which is great. But that wasn't the main focus of our chat."

Marina groaned. "Let me guess. That was about you finding a woman. If it sounds familiar, it's because she had the same conversation with me last night. She wants grandchildren. If they come from you, that's good enough even though it's not technically correct."

Ella smiled at that. "She didn't drop the grandchildren bomb. She was softening me up, because she wants me to come home for Christmas, which I'm not sure I'll be able to do."

"I bet she was pleased about that."

"Thrilled." Ella paused. "But back to dating. If you come over, you'll have to show me how to use the app you set me up on."

"You're a grown woman, surely even you can swipe right?"

"Evidently not, seeing as it's been on my phone for two months."

"You're too bloody busy, that's your trouble."

Ella grabbed her bag and her groceries from the back seat, locked the car with a beep, then approached her building. She felt in her jacket pocket for her house keys, but her fingers touched nothing. She frowned. She checked the opposite pocket. Same deal.

"I gotta go, Marina. I'm at my front door looking for my keys, and I can't juggle you at the same time."

"Any excuse. Call me if you fancy lunch this weekend, okay?"

"I will. Love you." Ella rang off, went to pocket her phone, but in the process dropped the handle of one of her shopping bags. Her two-litre carton of milk fell out, as did a multipack of Wispas, eggs, and tampons. Of course it was those items.

Ella sighed, put her bags on the floor, then got down on her haunches to pick up her shopping. In the car park, an engine stopped, then a few moments later, a familiar pair of club trainers appeared next to her. She looked up to see Sloane.

In seconds, she too was down on her haunches, helping to pick up Ella's shopping. Ella managed to grab the tampons and the milk, but a blush worked its way onto her cheeks as Sloane stood, holding her chocolate bars, along with the slightly cracked and soggy eggs.

"I think you might have to perform emergency scrambled surgery on these eggs if you want to salvage them."

"I think you might be right."

Sloane bent and picked up one of Ella's shopping bags. "I wondered if we might bump into each other soon. Let me give you a hand up to your apartment so you don't have any more mishaps."

Ella thought about saying no, but the likelihood of more mishaps was rife. She nodded. "Thanks, that would be great." And Sloane had wondered about bumping into her? Her mind spun on its axis.

They got into the lift, the forced proximity giving Ella goosebumps all over. She smiled uneasily at Sloane as the doors shut and her gaze skittered around the space. Was this them trying to be friends outside of work? The lift doors closed as she tried to work it out in her head, then mentally slapped herself. It was just a colleague doing her a good deed. She needed to be more chill about things.

But she'd followed Sloane on her socials since the start of her career. Liked numerous posts. Watched her game and her life grow. Now she was in a lift with her.

It was still weird.

Ella reached over to tap her floor button.

Sloane reached over to do the same thing.

Their fingers collided, and Ella jumped.

Beside her, Sloane blushed.

How did she know the floor she lived on? Ella pressed floor five, and the lift moved. She avoided looking at Sloane again.

The tip of her finger glowed hot.

When they reached her floor, Ella threw herself out of the lift as if she were on fire.

Which she sort of was.

* * *

"Probably not as fancy as your penthouse." Ella cleared her throat and pulled her shoulders back, determined to take control of this situation.

Sloane followed Ella over to the kitchen and put her gooey eggs on the counter. "More homey, though." She pointed at the far wall. "You have a picture up. That's more than I've been able to manage in my few weeks here."

"I managed to retrieve some bits and bobs from my storage unit." Ella smiled. "It's nice to have stuff around you. It makes you feel settled." She paused. "If you want to go to Ikea and do a picture run, I'd be happy to take you."

Having dumped the eggs on the kitchen counter, Sloane ran her hand under the tap and dried her hand on the tea towel, before neatly folding it and placing it back on the cooker handle. "I might take you up on that."

Ella nodded, trying not to panic about the thought of choosing picture frames and tealights with Sloane. Marina would go bananas. She had to remember that Sloane was just a normal person. Freakishly gorgeous and talented, but normal, too. She probably loved Ikea meatballs and mash the same as anyone. Even global sports superstars had to eat. Although Wispas might not be high in her diet.

As if reading her mind, Sloane picked them up from the counter. "Are these any good? I love trying new snacks in all the countries I visit." She held up a hand. "Not that I'm visiting here, but you know what I mean."

"You should definitely try them," Ella replied. "Wispas are my weakness. But if you ask nicely, I might give you a bite."

Did that sound like flirting? It wasn't meant to be. Stop it, Carmichael. "Do you want anything? A coffee, maybe?" Well styled out.

A shake of her head. "Bit late, but water would be lovely."

Ella indicated her sofa. "Take a seat, I'll bring it over."

"I can get it, just point me towards your glass cupboard."

"Above the sink." Ella grabbed the fridge items and stowed them. She'd tackle the eggs once Sloane had gone. She didn't need to see her scramble eggs.

When Ella looked up, Sloane stared at the magnetic-framed photo on her fridge.

Ella clutched the bag of pasta she held a little tighter. This was straying into Sloane finding out more about her before the other way around. Not the way it was meant to work.

"Is this you?"

The photo was of Ella, aged four. She had massive Lego hair, and was dressed in full Salchester Rovers kit, one leg up on a football, both arms flexed in a show of strength. It always made people laugh, including Ella.

"Yep, that's me, future football star, aged four."

"Was your mum behind the camera?"

Ella nodded. "Always. Encouraging me to be what I wanted to be." She pointed to the photo underneath, where her mum was eternally 40. Always smiling and cheering her on. "That's her."

Sloane leaned in. "You have her eyes. And her big hair."

"I know." Everyone told Ella that.

"What about your dad, is he still alive?"

Ella shook her head. "Never in the picture."

Sloane nodded, then studied the photo of her mum again. "I like her silver necklace, too."

"It was a favourite of mine as well. The pendant had a compass engraved on it. Mum was a big believer in destiny, in following your life course. That represented it. I had her necklace, but I lost it when I sold her house and we cleared everything. No idea how. It upsets me to this day." She still harboured a vague hope it might turn up one day.

Sloane turned her head, her gaze intense and full of sympathy. Ella normally shunned those looks. But with Sloane, she didn't want to.

"That has to hurt. But you still have the memory of it, and the photo. Memories are the most important thing." Sloane paused. "I had a ring I lost in my move, too. I still miss it." She gave Ella a sad smile. "You must miss your mum."

"Every day. Apparently, it gets easier. I'm not sure that's true." Ella squeezed her eyes to ward off threatening tears, then put the pasta away. She grabbed the salmon and yoghurt and put those in the fridge. She didn't want to talk about this now. Luckily, Sloane moved the conversation on. Ella was grateful.

"Family is one of the reasons I came to the UK. One of a few. I want to find out more about my roots. My great-grandparents met and fell in love here. He played for a local non-league team, Kilminster United, about ten miles from here. I want to find out more because my parents know nothing, and they're not that interested. But I think it's important to know where you come from. It makes you who you are."

Ella nodded. "I wouldn't be who I am without my mum's support and love. I'm sure the same can be said for you. Whatever worked for your grandparents was probably passed down through the generations."

Sloane held her gaze, then walked over to the lounge area, water in hand. Then she turned to Ella. "Actually, I was hoping to get along to watch my great-grandfather's old team this weekend for a special game they're having. A pre-season fundraiser." She paused. "If you're free, would you like to come with me?" Her face spelt hesitation. "I'd rather not go alone, and it would help to have a driver as I'm still not comfortable on the wrong side of the road. I'll pay for gas, and I can buy you coffee and cake. Or a half-time pie because I'm told that's a thing at English stadiums." Vulnerability streaked across Sloane's face.

Ella wanted to reach out a hand and tell her it was all going to be okay. Instead, she said, "A chicken balti pie?"

Sloane's body relaxed. "If that's a thing, then yes."

"It's a thing. A disgusting thing that your nutritionist would probably advise against, but it's a thing." Ella tilted her head. "You don't want to go with Layla? You're friends with her."

Sloane put her water on the coffee table and shook her head. "She wants to spend as much time with her wife and son before the season gets underway. Whereas we're both new here, and there's nothing in the rulebook that says we can't be buddies."

Ella shook her head. "Very much not. Plus, I'm free and in need of mates. Kilminster, you said?"

Sloane's smile lit up her face. "Thank you. The game starts at 3pm, so shall I pick you up around 1.30pm?"

Something fluttered in Ella's chest. She ignored it.

"I'll look forward to it."

Chapter Seven

"Is this what you were expecting?"

Sloane scratched the back of her neck and gave a small shrug. "I don't know, but it's what I grew up with. I like their kit, too: old-school, with no sponsors. Very retro. Just the smell of the grass, the choppy white lines. You're so close you can see the grazes on the players' knees. I love going to flash stadiums and watching massive games, but I also love this type of soccer, too." She stared at the couple of hundred or so spectators gathered for the fundraiser. "I promised you a pie, too, but there's not even a pie stand."

Ella pulled a Wispa from her bag. "Shameful lack of pies, I agree. But I can offer you this to share if you'd like?"

A grin twisted onto Sloane's face. "Sharing your Wispas, I know what they mean to you. I would love that, thank you." The wind whipped up and Ella's thick hair enveloped her face. She fought it off. It would drive Sloane mad, but it suited Ella.

It hadn't escaped Sloane's notice how easy it was to be around Ella. At least, when she was away from the training ground. There, Ella was part of the staff: sent to evaluate as well as help. That's why Sloane hadn't given much away in their first meeting. She shielded her feelings in exactly the same way she liked to shield the ball. She hadn't known Ella during their first session, but she knew her a little better now. Now, here they were, sharing a Saturday. They'd driven here, sharing nuggets from their lives. Spending time with Ella outside of work was like opening her diary.

Maybe Sloane needed to chat to someone about Jess. She couldn't call her family. Her brother was still away with the navy. Her parents were disinterested. Plus, all her other friends were involved in soccer. They knew Jess. They might talk to Jess. Even her good buddy, Alex, was Jess's midfield partner in North Carolina. All her usual avenues were cut off. Ella would be the obvious candidate.

The ball flying high in the air close by snapped her from her thoughts. A defender for the away side and a midfield player from the home team went up for the ball and their heads smacked in the air with a sickening thud as the ball clattered into the advertising boards nearby and rebounded onto the field.

Sloane winced and clutched the iron railing that came up to her waist in the ramshackle ground. She'd been on the end of a few of those incidents herself, and at best they gave you a deafening headache, at worst, concussion. She hoped it wasn't the latter.

When the whistle blew for full-time 15 minutes later, Sloane clapped and cheered the team's 2-1 win. Meanwhile, one of the head-clash players rubbed his head as he walked from the field.

"You okay if we head to the clubhouse to see if I can find out more about my family? I called earlier in the week, and they said it would be open."

Ella gave her a firm nod. "Of course. We've seen the game, but that's only half the job, isn't it? You're here to sleuth."

Sloane smiled. Sleuth. She liked Ella's turn of phrase. Super British.

They walked across the soft, slick grass – it had rained overnight – then stepped up onto the covered wooden porch and yanked open the white clubhouse door.

Sloane blinked. This was no grand clubhouse like one of those plush buildings with soft couches and lux bars in gated Florida communities. This clubhouse had a scuffed grey floor, white collapsible tables with red plastic chairs, and at the end, a small, almost apologetic bar. However, it was filled with fans, buoyed by their win, pints in hand. It might be a sad space, but the people inside were anything but.

"Shall I get drinks, or do you want to speak to someone?"

Sloane hadn't arranged anything specifically. She pointed over towards the soccer photos on the far wall. "Let's have a look at those first."

When they landed in front of them, Sloane was drawn to the older black-and-white ones. If he'd lived, her granddad would have been 81. Her great-grandparents were both born in 1920, and he'd played here in the late 1930s. Did they even have photos back then? She was pretty sure they'd have one or two.

A hand on her arm made her look up at Ella. "What was your great-granddad's name again?"

"Robert Patterson."

"In that case, bingo!" Ella stabbed a framed photo right in front of her. "This is a photo of him about to score in a league

47

game in 1938. Just before the war broke out." She shook her head. "I feel a bit emotional, and it's not even my family." She ushered Sloane closer.

Sloane peered in, and sure enough, Ella was right. There was her great-granddad, with a crew cut, ball at his feet. A prickle of pride gushed through Sloane and happy tears threatened, but she swallowed them down. She'd hoped to find evidence of him, but she never thought it'd be this easy.

Beside the photos was a notice asking for club sponsorship. Maybe that's why their shirts were sponsor-free: they couldn't find a company willing to do so. It explained why the clubhouse was so tired if they were short on money.

A chair scraping along the ground behind her made her turn. In it, sat head-clash man. Sloane stepped sideways and gave him a grimace.

"How are you feeling? It was quite the clash back there."

The man, a boxer's cut above his right eye, heavily coated with Vaseline, gave her a weary half-smile. "I've had worse, but I might not be drinking ten pints tonight. I don't need more of a headache than I've already got." He touched his right temple, as if checking it was still there, then pointed at the photo. "I saw you looking at that when I sat down. That's my great-uncle in that photo."

Sloane's heart almost stopped in her chest. She pointed again. "This guy?"

The man gave her a smile. "That guy."

"Well, hot damn." She gathered her breath and her thoughts. "That man is my great-granddad, so I guess that makes us related in some weird way."

The man tipped his head to the right. "It does? But you're

American." He paused, as if assessing her words. "Hang on. You're related to Robert?"

She pointed to her chest with her index finger. "My great-granddad."

"Fuck."

Sloane leaned in and held out a hand. "I'm Sloane."

He shook her hand slowly. "Ryan." He winced again. "Sorry, this is not my finest hour."

"Great goal, though."

He grinned. "Thanks."

The team manager approached, carrying a pint of water. He put it on the table in front of Ryan. "Get that down you, lad. Stay hydrated at all times. No beer for you tonight." He eyed Sloane, then held out his hand. "Matt Cook, team manager."

"Nice to meet you, Matt." She shook his hand. His shirt collar was half in, half out of his black sweater. Sloane imagined that was Matt's signature style. "Sloane Patterson, new fan."

Matt paused mid-shake on hearing her name. "Sloane Patterson? As in, US soccer sensation, Sloane Patterson?" His eyes widened.

Oh shit. She hadn't expected to be recognised here. Sloane gulped, then nodded. "I wouldn't say sensation, but yes, I play."

"You play?" Matt's voice went up an octave. "You've signed for Rovers and you're a big deal." He laughed. "What are you doing here?"

Ryan stepped in and explained, and Matt put his hands on his hips. "I never expected that. So, you're after history? There's loads. You need to speak to Barry over there," Matt pointed. "He's the official club historian. There's nothing he'd like more than to fill you in."

"Bore you to death," Ryan interjected.

"Yes, but when he has a purpose, he's less… prone to wandering. Okay, maybe not, but what Barry doesn't know, you don't need to know. Speak to Barry." Matt glanced at Ryan. "Your mum's not coming today?"

Sloane's heart sped up. "Your mum would be my what? Some distant cousin?"

Ryan screwed up his face. "I don't know, but she'd love to meet you. Especially if you're a famous footballer. Are you famous?" He paused. "My girlfriend would love to meet you, too. Big fan of the women's game."

Matt nodded. "She just signed for Rovers in the largest transfer ever in women's football. She's playing at the official stadium in her first home match of the season."

Ryan blinked up at her. "Blimey. Nice to meet you then, famous distant cousin."

Matt produced his phone. "You mind if we snap a photo for social media? It might mean we get some new fans if they think you're coming. You will be back when the new season starts?"

"When the schedule allows." She leaned in so Matt could snap a selfie. He looked very pleased as he keyed in a caption. "Sloane Patterson. Kilminster United fan. How about that." He paused. "If Robert was your great-granddad, there's a story about your grandparents you should hear. Especially given who you are." He shook his head. "But it's not for me to tell. I think Cathy would love to do the honours on that one."

"Cathy?"

"My mum," Ryan said.

"You need to be a bit more excited that you're related to Sloane," Matt told Ryan. "She's won the World Cup."

"My mum is going to freak. The first game she's missed in ages and this happens." Ryan rubbed his shoulder. "We'll come and see you in your first game. Family solidarity."

That warmed Sloane all the way through. She'd never had that before. Her brother had always been away. She could count on her hands the games her parents had attended in her lifetime. If she was married to a man, maybe things would be different. Or maybe she'd been looking in the wrong place for family all along.

"But what's this I need to know?"

Ryan shook his head. "I only vaguely know. Speak to my mum. She'll fill you in." He paused. "Are you my distant cousin, too?" he asked Ella.

She'd stood back while Sloane chatted, but now Sloane ushered her back into the group. "This is Ella, a Salchester colleague. She kindly drove me here today." They all shook hands.

"I'm not an American cousin. I'm Lancashire born and bred." She gave the group a proud smile.

Matt flashed his phone, where the snap of them was already getting traction. "This is getting more attention than anything else I've ever posted before. The power of celebrity."

"Can I get your number so my mum can get in touch?" Ryan asked.

Unease spread through Sloane. She didn't give out her number easily, even to potential family. She'd been burned this way before.

"Is it okay if I take your number, or your mum's? I don't give out my number, I hope you understand."

Matt slapped Ryan's shoulder. "Have some respect. That's like asking David Beckham for his number, you idiot."

Ryan blushed, and gave Sloane his mum's number. "I'll tell her to expect your call."

"Tell her to count on it. Particularly now I know there's a secret I need to know."

* * *

"That went better than I expected." Sloane clicked her seatbelt into place as Ella reversed out of the club car park. Ryan stood at the door waving. She waved back. "You think he took offence I wouldn't give him my number?"

Ella shook her head. "He's waving at you from the door, so I think you're good. If he did, he'll realise soon enough why. You're public property."

"Sometimes I hate that."

Ella glanced over. "But I'm sure there's plenty to make up for it, isn't there? It comes with the territory. You get very good at something, and people are drawn to you. They want to know how you got there and how you do it. It's basically what my job is, too. Working out what makes you tick and helping you figure out how to harness your power fully."

"You don't have my number, either." Sloane grinned over at Ella as she pulled out onto the main road.

"I wouldn't give it to me. I'll just send you annoying emojis at inappropriate times."

"Eggplants?"

"Too obvious. I go down the dancing ladies and cats route."

Sloane smiled. She was glad she'd bumped into Ella on their very first day. It had created a strange camaraderie between them which she wasn't sure would have been there otherwise.

"Thanks for coming to watch today, too. Jess never really

liked coming to watch local games with me. Especially men's games. She was very women only, and she liked a certain type of stadium, even if it was empty. For someone who loves soccer so much, I never understood. We used to argue about it."

Ella drummed her fingers on the steering wheel as she pulled up at a red signal. "Used to?"

Sloane felt her cheeks flush. She wanted to talk to someone, and Ella was right here. "I don't think you'll be surprised to know that things aren't all great with us."

"I got a feeling, seeing as you're living with an ocean between you. But I didn't want to assume, because plenty of people do it."

"We're not officially broken up because we're engaged. If that hadn't happened, it would have been easier to walk away." Sloane paused. Should she share the whole story? She was already shin-deep. "Obviously, this is off the record?"

Ella nodded, keeping her eyes on the road. "Obviously."

Sloane exhaled. "She cheated on me when we lived apart in the US. Three months after I proposed. I only found out a couple of months back, and I was ready to throw in the towel, but she wants to try again. But she cheated with a teammate. She says it was short-lived, but they're still on the same team and in the same city. What I know is that she was sleeping with her *and* sleeping with me. That's hard to come back from." Understatement of the year.

"I can see that." Ella licked her lips. "And I'm really sorry, too. I remember seeing your proposal, it was all over my socials. It was very romantic."

Sloane snorted. "It was for me, but it clearly didn't mean that much to her. We had a conversation this week, but she doesn't want to talk big things over the phone. I tried to see her before I left, but she could never see me. Or didn't want to." Her skin itched just thinking about it. "I'm not sure where we're at. Or maybe I am. But we're still officially engaged, so I'm in limbo. I'd like a clean break, but it's not so easy when you've loved a person as long as I've loved her." Sloane's throat went dry. This was far more than she'd shared in ages with anyone. And she hardly knew Ella.

She clamped her mouth shut. Perhaps she'd said too much already.

"Sounds like it's a lot of what Jess wants, and not much of what you want." Ella's knuckles flexed as she gripped the wheel. "Speaking as your friend, and not your performance and lifestyle coach. Although this shit can really affect your performance." Ella clicked her tongue. "But sorry, I probably shouldn't be wading in."

But maybe she should. It was nice to hear someone else's opinion. Someone with a fresh perspective. Perhaps Ella was right, too. Jess was the one who'd messed up. Now she was the one hanging on. Sloane had got angry, then Jess had talked her around. Perhaps she should get angry again.

"How about you? Are you in a relationship?"

Ella laughed. "With myself, yes. With anybody else, no."

"At least you're happy." Sloane wriggled in her seat as the truth of that statement hit her. She wasn't happy. Hadn't been for some time. She needed to take control with Jess. Do what she wanted to do with her life, just like Ella.

"I am happy, but my family aren't. My aunt and uncle would like me to meet someone, but I think it'll happen when it does. I don't want to push it." Ella glanced left and gripped the wheel tight again. "When it's right, I'll know. My family think I'm not romantic, but I am." Her cheeks blushed fuscia pink. "Which is why I liked your proposal. I'm sorry it went sour."

Sour. Sloane sat with the word for a minute. It was a good way to describe her year of being engaged. "It's nice that your aunt's invested, though." Even though Ella's mum was dead, she still had close family. More than Sloane.

"It is, although our ideas for my life clash sometimes. She thinks you can't be happy on your own. But I have been. That's not to say I wouldn't like to meet someone, but it's got to be someone right for me. I'm not going to settle for someone just because the clock is ticking to get married or have kids, or because society thinks I should."

Sloane balled her fists. Ella was speaking her language.

"If I think about Jess, there were a few red flags which have surfaced since we parted. The sleeping with someone else was a huge one, but there were others I ignored, too." Not considering moving with Sloane when she got the offer she couldn't refuse in LA for one, even though the team were interested in signing her as well. Also, her love of one too many beers, and her habit of texting in the middle of the night while tipsy or drunk.

"Sometimes it takes distance to see these things. We're all learning as we go. I'm sure you had good times, too."

Sloane nodded. "We did." Although they were getting less easy to remember. "When was your last relationship?" Was that too personal? She'd shared about her life, so Sloane hoped it was okay to go there.

Ella hesitated before she spoke. "Four years ago. We were together a year. Reba was a city financier, and our lives just weren't on track. Money was an issue, as was her addiction to her work. Something had to give in the end, and it was us." She shrugged. "Since then, there's been nobody. Hence my aunt getting worried. My mum was a single parent, and I'm an only child. She also never had much luck with relationships, and my aunt worries it's rubbed off on me. That I expect the worst. She doesn't want me to turn into a loner. I think that's family code for weirdo."

Sloane laughed. "Give me your aunt's number, and I'll call and tell her you're anything but a weirdo. I'd say you're a great listener, and perhaps the first new friend I've made since I arrived in the UK, which I appreciate. Plus, you've met my family now, too. More than Jess ever did."

"I'm honoured," Ella replied. "For what it's worth, you should sort things out with Jess, one way or the other. Life is always better when you're living it authentically. Doing what you truly want. You're already doing that career-wise. You just need to get your love life in order." She shook her head. "And this morning I did not wake up thinking I'd be giving Sloane Patterson relationship advice."

She put a hand to her chest. "You should ignore me. I'm the woman who's never held down a relationship longer than a couple of years, so what do I know? Peak performance in elite sports, that's my area of expertise. Relationships? They're a mystery."

"I think you might be wiser than you give yourself credit for."

Their apartment block came into view. Beside it, the dipping summer sun shot hot flames into the river water. It looked like a piece of modern art.

"That's pretty," Sloane said. "I miss the Californian sunsets over the ocean, but that river view has a charm all of its own."

Ella slowed the car, then turned right.

Automatically, Sloane flinched, fearing for her life. She still wasn't used to being on the wrong side of the damn road. "I'm glad you're driving. I swear, I would have turned straight into oncoming traffic."

"It's just practice."

Ella leaned her elbow on the door. She looked effortlessly cool. Like she was in a road trip movie, about to drop a pearl of life-changing wisdom.

Sloane admonished herself.

She'd never thought that with Jess, either.

"I've driven on the right in mainland Europe and you always have your share of heart-stopping moments, but then you get used to it." Ella steered the car off the road and parked in her allotted spot. Then she killed the engine and gave Sloane a shy smile. "If you want, I could take you out to give you some practice in wide spaces where you're unlikely to crash into anything. Then we could progress to roads."

"That would be amazing." She had to get over her block of driving here. She wanted her independence. "Are you sure you can handle it?"

"I'm a very patient person, it comes with my job. Plus, you can drive, it won't take long. A couple of sessions to cure your nerves."

Sloane turned in her seat. When Ella did the same, she caught a waft of her floral perfume. It was the perfect fit for this English rose. She felt a pulsing sensation low in her stomach. Sloane blinked hard at her own thoughts. She wasn't sure where they were being generated, but it wasn't from her normal brain.

She cleared her throat. "You've got yourself a deal. Thank you." She paused. "For what it's worth, I agree with your aunt. You should get out there and meet someone if you want to."

Interesting declaration.

Ella rolled her eyes. "Don't you start. My cousin set me up on the Honey Pot dating app, but I'm not all that keen."

"Not when we're about to go away on a pre-season tour. But when we get back, you should date. I'm going to follow up on this," Sloane gave a wag of her finger. "You can, so you should. I'm off women right now for obvious reasons. But imagine if I went on Honey Pot, all the attention I'd get." Sloane shivered. "It's why I tend to date people I meet on the field. They're known quantities. You never know if people are genuine when you're famous. Even just a little like me."

"I think you might be more famous than you think. You're even known at Kilminster United."

Sloane laughed. "A fluke. Ryan had no idea. Shall we make a pact? I'll give my relationship some serious thought if you commit to at least looking at Honey Pot."

"Even the name makes me squirm." Ella paused. "But my family would be pleased."

"One date might get them off your back."

"There is that."

"Do we have a deal? For the record, you're getting the easy end of the bargain."

Ella grabbed her bag from the back seat, then held out her hand.

Sloane took it, then tried to contain the jolt that surged

through her body on contact. Her gaze jumped to Ella. Had she felt it, too? The air in the car grew very warm, and her heart began to sprint.

"We have a deal." Ella's voice was steady, but her cheeks had turned scarlet.

Chapter Eight

Ella had never been to Germany before, but she liked what she'd seen so far. The team were staying in a central Frankfurt hotel with a fantastic sauna, spa, and steam room suite on the top floor that Ella earmarked to make use of later. One plus point of being staff was she also had a room to herself, unlike the players who had to share. Even hotshots like Sloane. Ella smiled at that thought. She was far from the hotshot the media made out. She was a normal person, navigating her way through life like the rest of them.

The other part she'd enjoyed? The private plane they'd flown on. She was living the dream. She'd sent her cousin a selfie from the plane, with the team behind her.

I hope you got a couple of those cute bottles of bubbly on your private plane! Marina texted.

Ella grinned and typed, *We're an elite sports team. We're not on a trip to Ibiza.*

You've changed. Marina added, followed by a line of eyeroll emojis.

Ella stepped off the coach onto the sparkling clean pavement outside the hotel. Lucy was right behind her, wheeling her branded club suitcase.

The team checked in at the swanky reception, their blue

tracksuits and Nike trainers looking out of place in the opulent lobby. The space was filled with gleaming white pillars, along with gargantuan pots of deep pink and purple flowers. Crystal chandeliers hung from the ceiling, while expensive, layered scents infused the air with calm.

Ella recalled flying to play a team in France during her playing days. They'd paid their own fares, travelled with their knees against their chests, carried their own bags, and stayed four to a room in a budget hotel. The jump to this was staggering.

To her left, a bell boy wearing a pillar box hat was getting a selfie with Sloane followed by an autograph. Ella stood back, marvelling again at her friend's fame. She and Sloane might be crossing paths for a brief moment in their lives, but Sloane's fame was deep-rooted and never likely to leave her. Ella would never be able to understand that.

"Team meeting in an hour in conference room A. Get settled, then be there for 5pm. Sloane's going to share a story from her career then, too." When Lucy spoke, the whole team stopped and listened, as if she were the most feared teacher in school. If she had her whistle, Ella imagined everyone in the lobby would have stopped mid-task to pay attention, like the well-schooled Von Trapps. Everyone including the desk staff and bell boys.

Ella waited for the team to disperse, with only a brief glance in Sloane's direction. She was sharing with Layla, while Ella's room was next to Lucy's. They got the lift up together.

"I was watching on the plane, seeing who sat next to who, who spoke to who." Lucy spoke directly to Ella, and didn't once glance at her own reflection in the floor-to-ceiling lift mirrors. Quite the self-control. "The youngsters seem to be settling well."

Ella smiled. "They are, but some of them are so green, it makes me laugh. I'm sure I was never that useless in real life when I was 19." The music in the lift wafted around them like a soothing balm. This hotel took relaxation seriously.

"Take Nat. Such a sweet striker of the ball, fabulous football brain. Such a prospect, she's frightening. But on Tuesday when I had a session with her, I asked her if she was missing anything from home. Her answer? Her mum's spiced scrambled eggs on toast. I told her she could do that herself, she's got a flat with a kitchen. But she said she wouldn't know where to start. She can score a goal in front of thousands of fans, make the right decisions in a split second. But ask her to do something for herself and she's stumped."

Lucy ran a hand through her short, dark hair and grinned. "Tell me about it. I had to show Brie how to lace her own boot the other day. She said she could do it criss-cross but not straight across. I showed her it's not that hard."

"But life skills apart, I think the young ones are doing fine, and the newbies are settling in, too."

Lucy thrust her right hand into the pocket of her navy suit and appraised Ella. "I saw you chatting with Sloane in the lounge at the airport, too. I know we all think she's fine, but she's a newbie, too. Even if she is older and won everything there is to win."

"Not a Women's Super League title, an FA Cup, or a Champions League."

"That's to come." Lucy wagged her index finger as she spoke. "But seriously, she's okay? I asked her, and I think I believe her."

Ella pressed her tongue into the roof of her mouth and willed her cheeks not to flush red. "She's fine. She lives in my block, so we've got to know each other a little outside work. She's enjoying the UK so far. Plus, she bought a new coffee machine the other day, so I think she's planning on staying."

The lift reached their floor, and they both stepped onto the bouncy carpet and walked to their rooms.

"Those players run on coffee. Wait until they hit 40 and can't sleep a wink after drinking it." Lucy smiled as she walked. "I'm really pleased she's chatting to you, though. Beyond your work remit, it's good for her to have a friend she can count on who's not another player. I was always friends with staff when I played, and I valued those relationships so much." She paused. "I know our paths didn't really cross that much back in the day, but are you still in touch with any of your old teammates?"

Ella shook her head. It was something she regretted, but when she made the decision to walk away from football, she cut all ties. "Not really. Which is why it's nice getting to know these players, seeing how things have changed. Including the rookies, and even superstars like Sloane. I'm looking forward to her session today."

Lucy nodded. "You think they're a good idea?"

"I think they're more than that. They get everyone to trust each other more. They're a stroke of genius."

Chapter Nine

The hotel conference room was like every other Sloane had ever experienced in her life. Flip chart. A horseshoe of chairs and desks. Shaded out windows. Coffee, tea, biscuits. She was sure many business deals had been hammered out over these desks. But today, Sloane stood at the top of the horseshoe, right hand in her club tracksuit pocket, her bottom lip clutched under her two front teeth. She was trying to stay calm, but she'd never shared her full story before. She'd decided today was time.

"Okay, everyone." Lucy clapped her hands. "Let's have a bit of silence for Sloane's story. She's bravely stepped up to share the first tale from a player. Next up will be Dan our head physio, and after that, I'll choose another player. Listen, learn, respect the speaker's bravery, because it takes courage to speak your truth. Phones away, please, ears open. And remember, whatever is shared in these sessions doesn't go any further. Circle of trust." She smiled. "Or rather, horseshoe."

Everyone laughed, and the mood relaxed.

Sloane gave her a nod, then cleared her throat.

"Thanks Lucy, and thanks also for your powerful story last time out, which I've thought about a lot since. Now, I figured it was time to share mine." She pulled her shoulders back and put a palm to her chest. Her heartbeat surged beneath her fingertips. This was new territory.

"You know me as Sloane Patterson. You've probably got fixed views on who I am, based on how I play, how competitive I am, my playing record, and what I've won. But what you don't know is the struggle it took to even get to play soccer. Because my parents didn't want me to."

She looked around the group, seeing the surprise register on everybody's face. She'd only ever told this story to close friends. A couple of her old teammates in LA. Jess. Not even Layla knew the full extent. But if Lucy wanted them to be vulnerable, to open up to each other and make them trust each other, this is what she had to do. But the one person she avoided eye contact with was Ella. That might make her stumble.

"I grew up in Detroit in a good neighbourhood. Me, my parents, my brother. To the outside, it probably looked like we were a tight-knit family. We were always well turned out for school, we were well fed, we had a nice house, and we always attended church. Religiously, you might say."

A few smiles at that.

"But my parents took religion to the extreme. They believed boys and girls should behave in certain ways. Having a daughter that wanted to play soccer was not part of their plan. Instead, they tried to force me into playing violin, and into dancing. But the only dancing I wanted to do was on the field. My whole childhood was a long battle to get my parents to take me to soccer. They refused, but a very kind neighbour stepped in. He was taking his daughter, and he took me, too. Without him, I wouldn't be standing here today."

Sloane paused, then took a steadying breath before she continued.

"As I got older, I could take buses myself and get rides with teammates. Very briefly, when I started to get noticed, my parents rallied. But it didn't last. They couldn't contemplate me having a career as a soccer player. My mom told me it brought shame on the family." She paused. "A young girl kicking a ball on a field. That brought her shame."

Sloane shook her head again. She still recalled the razor-sharp slice of that comment. To this day, she didn't understand it.

"I've tried to change my mom's mind on this so many times, but I've learned to let it go. You can probably guess she was less than enthused when I came out to her, too. A lesbian soccer player for a daughter. Not what they ordered. But here I am. Living my dreams. Playing the game I love with people who love it just as much as me.

"Soccer gave me the family I needed when my own let me down. It gave me a home and a purpose, and it allowed me to lean into the absolute best version of me I could muster. I will always be grateful to the sport, but also to all of you. Because soccer is a team sport, and I am a team player. What I'm saying is, if you really want something, if it's in your heart, you'll always find a way. Even if it's painful at first, things get easier."

The scars might have healed over, but they were always there.

"My story is not out there in the public eye. I've always been able to celebrate my victories with teammates, coaches, girlfriends, and occasionally my brother. Nobody notices that my parents aren't there. Their choice, their loss. They still never come to my games, never acknowledge the two most important parts of my life: my career and my identity. You only get one life, and my own experience has taught me to live it on your own terms and nobody else's."

Stunned silence descended on the room. You could honestly hear a pin drop.

"That's it. That's my story. I hope it helps you understand me a little more." Sloane sucked on the inside of her cheek, then broke into a hesitant smile.

The applause that followed was deafening.

Sloane cast her eyes to the floor, embarrassed by the attention. When she looked up, her gaze collided with Ella's. She made a fist and pressed it to her chest.

Sloane's heart bloomed red.

* * *

After a full day of training in super-sunny conditions, the following afternoon the team had a game against Eintracht Frankfurt, who'd finished third in the top German league last season. When they ran out onto the field, Sloane swallowed her nerves just like always, then tilted her head back as the adrenaline and excitement flooded her system.

A couple of thousand fans, most of them decked out in Frankfurt's black shirts, made some noise in the concrete stands that flanked one side and one end of the field. This was Salchester's first major test with new players in the starting line-up, including the new strike partnership between herself and Nat. She was determined it would start well.

Ella had organised a cooking session with them both

earlier this week to build their relationship on and off the field. They'd made pancakes from scratch, with lemon and sugar, as well as the savoury type with mushrooms, spinach and cheese. Both were delicious, but it had confirmed to Sloane she should definitely turn down any offers to do MasterChef. She'd sweated enough over combining flour, milk and eggs.

Nat was quiet at first, but then she'd opened up a little. Pancakes were not a staple for her, not like in the US. Her mum was Pakistani, so Nat had showed them how to make chapatis instead. She confessed it was the one thing her mum made her learn before she left home. They went just as well with the savoury topping.

Sloane knew there was more bubbling under the surface though, as did Ella. When Sloane had shared her personal story with the team, Nat had come up to her afterwards and given her a hug. No words, just a hug. Perhaps it had resonated, Sloane didn't know. After all, there were bigoted parents in every country, not just America. She'd heard a couple of the girls talking to Nat about the movie *Bend It Like Beckham*, equating it to her. She was sure that got tiresome. There weren't enough Asian women involved in UK soccer. Nat could be a trailblazer. Sloane hoped she had the support behind her.

Whether it was their bonding session with Ella, Sloane's personal story, or the fact they were well drilled on the training ground, once the whistle went, things clicked. Sloane's touch was like silk, every pass paying off, every twist like poetry. She hummed with satisfaction every time she touched the ball. It was one of those days when the ball simply stuck to her feet, when her shots hit the mark. She lived for this.

After a cagey opening and with 20 minutes gone, Rovers'

no-nonsense midfielder Welshy scurried down the middle, leaving a trail of stunned defenders in her wake. Sloane followed her, but Welshy delayed a little too long before releasing the ball, and the final defender blocked her pass.

However, the ball pinged out to Sloane, who took it down first time on her instep. She swept her gaze to see what was on. To her right, wingback Cally signalled for the ball, but she had a defender with her. Up ahead, Layla made a dash left, then right, taking two defenders with her. It was a clever run, and it opened up space – which Nat ran into.

Quick ball, decisive action. That was how you won games, and how you won life. With the brick wall of a German midfielder tracking her, Sloane dinked right, got the extra yard of space, then chipped a ball over the top for Nat to run on to.

They were on the same wavelength.

Nat took the ball down in the penalty area as smoothly as she'd rolled her chapati, sized up the angle in a micro-second, then rolled it smartly past the keeper with the outside of her right boot. She turned, arms aloft, mouth aghast. She'd just scored her first senior goal for Rovers, and she looked as if she could barely believe it.

Sloane ran to celebrate with her.

"You're a fucking legend!" she shouted, smothering her in a hug. The rest of the team did the same, and Nat emerged with a massive grin. Sloane knew it would last for days.

"You're the fucking legend," Nat told her, with a grin.

They high-fived on their way back to the centre circle. Job well started. Not yet done.

They took their slender lead into the second half, as the sun cranked up its dial. Almost from the kick-off, Nat thundered down the left wing as if jet-propelled, before cutting it back for Sloane on the edge of the area. She took the ball in her stride and saw the keeper set for a far-post shot. Sloane shaped her body to shoot that way, before hitting the ball towards the inside post. The shot hit the back of the net before the keeper even moved. Sloane raised her eyes to the sky, and grinned the sweetest grin. 2-0 to Rovers.

She wasn't done, though. Ten minutes later, Layla surged into the area and was brought down by their centre back. Frankfurt was reduced to ten players, and Sloane stepped up to take the penalty. She was supremely confident. Sometimes, she just knew. Plus, she practised this shit every day for occasions just like these. When the ref blew her whistle, Sloane sized up the keeper and sent her the wrong way. The net rippled, and Sloane had her brace. She ran left, did her trademark jump and fist bump, then turned to take the acclaim of her teammates. Days like these? She would happily live them over and over again.

When the final whistle went, Salchester had triumphed 3-1. The teams embraced, then Sloane took time to sign autographs and pose for photos with a cluster of fans near the dugout. When she walked towards Ella and threw her a satisfied grin, Ella held out her arms, and Sloane accepted the hug. When they pulled back, there was something in Ella's eyes Sloane couldn't quite pin down. Respect perhaps? Appreciation of her talent? Maybe something else?

"Good work today, Hotshot." Ella's gaze lowered to Sloane's grazed thighs and her bleeding knee. She'd collided with a defender towards the end of the game, but that was the life of a soccer player.

Sloane followed her focus. "My knee's stinging, but the win makes it better. Although I'm looking forward to a hot shower."

Ella blinked, then gave a quick nod. "Of course." She flicked her head right. "Get in the changing room, soak up the adulation. Tomorrow, we work some more."

"More pancakes?"

Ella gave her a wicked grin. "You should be so lucky."

Chapter Ten

The high spirits were still there later when they went for a Korean meal. The location had been picked to challenge the team's tastebuds, but also because it had a private room that offered karaoke. Ella wasn't sure what it was with sports teams and karaoke, but they always seemed to love it. Personally, she thought it was a fate worse than death, and that was just listening. She'd always ducked the microphone at any karaoke she'd ever been to, and she fully intended to do the same here, even though she was technically a newbie. However, surely being staff gave her a free pass? Her intention was to sink into the background and hope everyone forgot her. Plus, she was sat next to Lucy, and nobody was going to hassle her.

Lucy stood and clapped her hands. The 40 people around the long table fell silent. "Okay team! Great performance today, good to get some minutes on the pitch and in the legs. We'll have a proper debrief tomorrow before our next game the day after and talk about what we need to work on. But for now, enjoy this Korean feast. Try all the various meats and the vegetables, even the kimchi. I guarantee you, it's nicer than Nando's."

Ella stifled a laugh. She liked Nando's as much as the next person, but the reverence it was afforded by some of the younger players made her smile.

"And the microphone is coming around the table, so make your song selection. First up, the newbies have to give us a song." Lucy pointed across the table and three seats down at Sloane. "You're up first, Patterson. You shared your story, now it's time to share your hidden talents."

Sloane's mouth dropped open and she put a hand to her chest. "Why me?" Sloane held up a fork in protest.

"Because you're old enough and ugly enough to take it." Lucy gave her a wink.

"Whatever you say, boss." Sloane stood and pointed down the table. "I nominate Nat after me. Pick a song, Tyler."

"Already done!" she replied with the confidence of youth.

In the end, Nat went first as Sloane had to take a phone call just as the microphone appeared. She walked back in as Nat was launching into her version of 'Sweet Caroline'. Nat wasn't the tallest player at 5ft 5, but you'd never guess that from her performance. She held the notes, got everyone involved, and when she galloped into the final chorus, she stood on her chair and led the whole group. Even Ella joined in. Nat finished with a flourish and jumped down to great applause. Then she ferried the mic down the table and leaned over to pass it to Sloane.

"Follow that, partner."

Somehow, Ella knew Sloane would accept the challenge with gusto. You didn't get to be such a top striker without being competitive, after all. Sloane walked over to the machine, keyed in her song, then came back to her seat as the opening notes chimed through the speakers. 'Can't Take My Eyes Off You'. A karaoke classic and a massive crowd-pleaser. Ella should have known.

Plus, the way Sloane handled the mic and didn't even look

at the screen told Ella this wasn't the first time she'd done this. Whoops from the crowd as she got into her stride, whirling her way to the showy chorus, then walking down Ella's side of the table. Ella swivelled her head to follow Sloane's progress. She couldn't do anything else. She was transfixed.

Sloane shimmied past Ella, her close presence lifting the hairs on the back of her neck.

Sloane smelt of bergamot and success. When she reached the chorus, the whole table joined in as Ella knew they would, singing at the top of their voices. Beside her, Lucy had a grin on her face. By the second verse, Sloane was on the opposite side of the table, back where she'd started. She arrived at her seat, three down from Ella, but didn't sit. Instead, she, too, got up on her chair and sang the final verse as if she were a pop star and not a star striker. There were a lot of similarities. Showstopper, crowd-pleaser, dream-maker.

When Sloane reached the final chorus, she sang it to Viv two seats down, then flicked her gaze to Welshy, sat next to Ella. Then finally, to Ella.

When their gazes connected, a firework went off in Ella's chest; one with enough force to make her suck in a gasp. She swallowed it down and tried not to flinch as she stared at Sloane. What the hell was that? She'd spent enough time in Sloane's company of late. They were friends, nothing more.

But Ella didn't remember the last friend who made her tremble in the way Sloane just had. Who made her breath come in rasps. Who made her forget everyone else in the room and focus on her alone. The lights dimmed. The volume went low. Until all Ella could see was Sloane, and all she could hear was her elevated heartbeat.

She glanced left to Lucy, who was grinning and clapping towards Sloane. To her right, Welshy was doing the same. Nobody else had noticed.

However, when she dared to look back at Sloane, her gaze hadn't shifted. She stared at Ella with an intensity that made Ella's muscles clench. When she could wrench herself away, Ella dropped the connection, and so did Sloane. Only then did the volume turn back up and the lights return to their former level. Ella stayed still, not daring to move or look anywhere else but at her nearly empty plate. She took a sip of her fizzy water, and hoped they'd leave soon.

She wasn't sure what had just happened, but the sooner they were back at the hotel, the sooner she could go to sleep and pretend it hadn't. It was just a blip. She didn't like Sloane in *that* way. And even if she did, nothing could happen. They worked together, and Sloane still had a Lioness fiancée.

Whatever had made her chest explode needed to pipe down.

* * *

Her mouth still hummed from the taste of red chillies, garlic, and ginger as she entered the hotel lobby, struck again by the lush floral arrangements. A hand on her shoulder made her glance right.

Sloane.

Her stomach dropped. Sloane's skin was exquisite. Silky, almost otherworldly. She really had to get a grip.

"Your hair looks nice today." Sloane narrowed her eyes. "Different, somehow."

"I had it cut. It reduces the volume by half. It'll be back to normal in a couple of weeks."

"Right." Sloane looked at her feet, then back to Ella. "I also noticed you got out of singing a song at dinner, which wasn't strictly fair. I was looking forward to hearing you sing." She tilted her head to one side as she spoke, then swirled a finger around Ella's face.

Ella followed Sloane's fingertip precisely.

"I can't quite work out if you'd go Taylor or Florence. Or maybe something old school, like Kate Bush or Abba."

"I can't hold a note, so I decided to let the group off my awful singing. If you've ever heard me, you'll realise it's a good thing."

A large group with dozens of cases entered the lobby. Sloane and Ella shifted left to let them past.

"Nice try, but you owe us a song. Maybe on the plane home." Her face lit up with a lopsided smile.

Had Sloane's smile always been so magnetic?

"I hope you're going to share your story when it's your turn, and not duck out of that, too."

"Everyone's got to share, so I'll take my turn happily." Ella paused. "Talking of which, that was really powerful stuff from you yesterday. It was a really vulnerable story to share. I liked seeing that side to you. I hope I see it more in our sessions, too."

Sloane licked her lips and shrugged like it was no big deal. Ella knew it was.

"I can be vulnerable. I'm American, remember? Plus, with my background, I've been in therapy for years. It's what we do best. Navel-gazing."

"Don't make light of it." It was a defence mechanism Ella was well acquainted with. She'd used it for years after her mum died.

"I wasn't." Sloane stopped, then sucked on her top lip before she continued. "You want to grab coffee in the bar before we go to bed? I might share more for you to ponder."

Sloane talking to her about going to bed wasn't helping. Ella had to get out of here. Back to the solitude of her room. Away from Sloane.

She shook her head. "I'm knackered after today, so I'll skip it." She tilted her head towards the lift. "See you tomorrow."

Sloane gave her a slow nod, went to say something else, then shook her head. "See you then."

When Ella got to the lift, she turned. "Sloane?"

When Sloane's gaze met Ella's, her expression was expectant. "Yes?"

"It's Taylor. Every time. Who else?"

Ella got back to her room, closed the door, and let out a breath. She pressed her back to the wood.

Yes, she'd always admired Sloane from afar before she met her. For her skills, her passion, and her toned muscles. But getting to know her proved to Ella that Sloane was all those things and so much more. Sometimes when you met stars you admired, it was a let-down. Not so with Sloane Patterson. She was vulnerable, open, funny, sexy. And damn, the woman could sing, too.

Ella took off her clothes, gratefully unclipped her bra, then brushed her teeth and fell into bed. It was at times like these she wished her mum was here to call. Her aunt was a great stand in, but it wasn't the same. She and her mum used to chat about everything, but she'd have to cope with this herself. She recalled developing an attraction towards her therapist once, which was highly inappropriate, but she'd talked herself out of it. Also, she'd eventually changed therapists to make her life easier. She wasn't about to leave this job, so she had to work around it, using all the psychological tricks she knew.

Her thoughts were just that.

Thoughts.

She could ignore them.

Chapter Eleven

When Sloane woke, her pillow was damp from her dribble. If her adoring fans could see her now. She wiped her mouth with her forearm, then rolled to the other side of her pillow. Beside her, Layla's bed was unmade, but her roommate was nowhere to be seen.

Sloane's phone lay on top of her mattress where she'd left it last night after scrolling through photos of yesterday's game that the club had posted on their socials. She was pleased with her performance, with the link-up with Nat, and also that Ella was on the sideline to watch. Yes, Sloane wanted to impress her new teammates and her manager, but that was work-related. Now she'd gotten to know Ella, she wanted to impress for other reasons that she couldn't quite pin down. Friendship? Possibly. Nothing more.

Sloane was still engaged in all but name, and very much not on the market, even if she was almost single. The thought made her stomach hurt. She couldn't face dating again. Perhaps that's why she was holding on, too. It was like Ella had said, once you reached a certain age, putting yourself out there again was tedious, as well as scary as hell.

She rubbed some sleep from her eyes and reached for her phone. When she clicked it awake, the message notification winked at her from the top of the screen. When she saw who they were from, Sloane's stomach twisted a little more. Three messages from Jess. What the fuck?

Looks like you were having fun last night. I know what it means when you sing that song to someone in public. Who the hell is she? You're not screwing the manager, are you? Because that's below the line, even for you.

No sign off, no kiss.

Alarm slithered through Sloane like a rattlesnake. She rolled onto her back and held her phone in the air, stabbing Instagram to see if that held answers to Jess's cryptic message. She was tagged in three stories. She stabbed again, but lost control of her phone. It fell and hit her on the nose.

"Ow!" That happened at least twice a week. She was surprised she hadn't broken her nose. It smarted as she picked up her phone, but she ignored the pain.

There was an agreement in the team they wouldn't post anything incriminating on any social channels. She braced as she clicked on the first story. It was of Nat's song, Sloane singing the chorus, arms aloft. Nothing there.

But it was the next one that made her sit up. It was her singing the final chorus of her song, stood on a chair.

Sloane inhaled deeply. "Fucking hell."

She hit the chorus and winced. She wasn't a terrible singer, but she was no Adele, either.

However, it wasn't the singing she was focused on. Whoever took this video was stood behind Ella and Lucy. During the final part of the chorus, Sloane's gaze was focused solely in that direction.

Sloane gulped. Most people wouldn't pick anything up from this. Jess wasn't most people. She'd seen something. It was only now Sloane looked at herself, she could see it, too.

She took a lungful of air and put the phone in her lap. Her stomach nosedived.

She liked spending time with Ella, but she didn't have energy or headspace for anything more. Ella felt the same. They were both job-focused. Nothing had happened. So why did she feel so guilty? Why was her mind already scrambling over mental rocks for something to tell Jess? She had nothing to refute. Yet it didn't feel like that at all. As she watched the story through one more time, then again, then again, something that tasted very much like guilt crawled into her mouth.

She didn't like cheaters.

She didn't like being cheated on.

She hadn't cheated.

She needed to remember that.

What if other players saw what Jess did? What if Lucy thought she liked her?

Sloane covered her eyes with her hand.

Even worse still: what if Ella was right at this second watching this story and realising the look in Sloane's eyes. What if she'd seen it last night? Was that why she said no to coffee and hurried off?

She chewed on the inside of her cheek. She'd done nothing wrong. She'd just sung a song. She dashed off a reply.

Of course I'm not screwing the fucking coach. I'm still engaged, and I have standards.

It was a low blow, but Jess had asked for it. She had some fucking nerve accusing her of things. Sloane had done nothing wrong. Jess had no right to be watching what she was doing. She should be focusing on herself. But Sloane knew what soccer players' lives were like. There was an awful lot of free time, an age to watch social media again and again, and wind yourself up. Jess had clearly been doing that.

Sloane clicked on Jess's Instagram and saw reels of her training for North Carolina. There was also a reel Sloane hadn't seen from a week ago, with Jess out playing golf with Britney. The woman she'd had the affair with.

Sloane ground her teeth together and tried to compose herself. Jess was such a bare-faced hypocrite. The way she looked at Britney as she swung her club? Like she wanted to eat her? Sloane could sing to Ella for days and it would never match that. Mainly because Jess was watching someone she'd slept with. The difference was night and day. Sloane clicked over to Britney's Insta, something she hadn't done for a few weeks, and saw reels of her and Jess embracing post-goal.

Something snapped inside. Sloane was a rational person, but this was over, wasn't it? Jess calling her out for singing a song, when she was probably still sleeping with Britney? Sloane's breath sped up. She was so done. She called up the message box again. The gruesome script of their breakup had kept her awake many nights, replaying its lowlights, and her skin still crawled in the aftermath. This past summer had all been about what Jess wanted. Nothing about Sloane. Just as Ella had said.

That was about to change.

You come into my messages acting like you're the victim? Fuck you, Jess. I saw you playing golf with Britney. Celebrating on the field. It's clear as day you're not backing off like you claimed. I know what we said the other day, but why don't we just grow up and see what's in front of us? Make this break permanent and call off our engagement. Nothing's going on with me, but you're paranoid it is. Shouldn't it be the other way around?

Jess is typing…

Sloane checked her watch. It was the middle of the night where Jess was. What the hell was she doing up?

Jess is typing…

Jess is typing…

Then nothing.

Sloane pressed her head against the headboard and breathed out. Wow. Four years and thousands of promises all boiled down to this moment of nothing. She waited two more minutes, then sent a message because Jess was clearly too scared to call it.

Take this as my exit. Our engagement is officially off. Feel free to fuck whoever you like.

She pressed send, sighed the heaviest sigh of her life, then jumped out of bed. A swarm of bees took up residence in her head, but she tried to ignore them. She got dressed into her tracksuit pants and training top on autopilot, arriving at their private room for the breakfast buffet.

There were only five others already there, including the assistant coach Jonas, teammates Cally, Nat, and the missing Layla, plus one of the physios. She couldn't recall his name. Ken? Kai? Definitely began with a K. Sloane waved at them, then walked to the buffet and helped herself to scrambled eggs, baked beans, and toast. She'd got a taste for baked beans since being in the UK. She slopped the beans on her plate and some splashed up on her training top.

"Shit." She put down her plate, but it was only when she went to clean the stain, she noticed her hand was shaking. She bit her lip and took a breath. Had she done the right thing? She'd just ended her relationship, blown up her engagement. Or perhaps Jess had done that months ago?

She picked up her plate and put it down on a nearby table. Then she walked to the coffee machine, pressed some buttons, got a mug of black liquid, added milk even though she wanted cream. She liked Europe, but their lack of cream in coffee was an issue. As she walked back to her food, she tripped on nothing and spilt half her coffee on the floor in front of her.

She stopped. It was a good job they didn't have a game today. She'd be useless.

"Sloane?"

She glanced up. Nat. Looking very unsure. Her gaze diving around, anywhere but Sloane.

"I wondered if you had five minutes to have a quick chat? Somewhere private?"

Sloane held out her top, still coffee stained, and shook her head.

"Can it wait until later? I'm sorry, I'm a bit distracted this morning. It's just not a good time."

Nat stared at her for a second, then gave her a brisk nod. "Of course, no problem." She hurried off and out of the dining room.

Sloane frowned, as concern sat in her stomach. She should have made the time. But today was not a good day.

A hand on her back stilled her. She turned carefully so she didn't lose the rest of the coffee over whoever was behind her.

When she saw Ella's concerned gaze, she wanted to put down the coffee and fall into her arms.

What the hell? They didn't even know each other that well. But right now, Sloane could do with a friend. But she couldn't collapse in the breakfast room. That was way too public.

"Everything okay? You just tripped over…" Ella glanced at the floor. "Nothing?" She studied Sloane's face. "Plus, you look a little flushed."

Sloane took in Ella's perfectly oval mouth, as if she was seeing it for the first time. Her impossibly smooth skin. She leaned in to inhale the scent of her floral perfume.

That was not normal behaviour.

She straightened up, then shook her head. "Just in a rush to get to my massage with the physio and thought I'd throw coffee and beans everywhere."

Ella wore tailored royal-blue pants and a sky-blue shirt. Her pink belt provided a pop of colour, and highlighted her slim waist and defined hips.

Sloane couldn't stop staring. "You look nice today. Very professional."

She smiled, and her face lit up. "Doing a talk later to the

staff, so thought I'd make the effort." Ella paused. "You sure you're okay? You seem out of sorts."

"I'm fine." Sloane skulled what was left of her coffee, glanced at her abandoned plate, then back to Ella. "In fact, I've gotta dash. I'll grab a croissant, just don't tell Lucy I had no protein, okay?"

Ella mimed zipping up her lips and throwing away the key.

* * *

"How's your ankle holding up? Feeling okay?"

Sloane winced as Dan the physio put pressure exactly where she didn't want it. But that's what physios did. It was their job. She nodded, trying to keep her face neutral. It wasn't easy.

"It's still a bit sore, but I do my maintenance exercises and it's manageable. I can still play soccer, that's the main thing."

"Football now you're in the UK," he joked.

Sloane forced a smile. "It'll always be soccer to me."

Her ankle hadn't been the same since the only big injury of her career two years ago, and she had to take particular care of it. She told everyone it wasn't an issue. But it was. That was even after all the physio and performance work she'd done. Maybe Ella could help her overcome any niggling injury doubts.

But she wasn't sure seeing Ella right now was the best thing for her health, mental or physical.

That thought made her frown.

"Why the sad face?" Dan looked like a guy Sloane's brother used to play basketball with. She hadn't liked him, but Dan showed none of his traits, thankfully.

Sloane shook her head and smiled. She wasn't about to confess her inner woes to her physio. That wasn't his job, even though she was sure he'd heard his fair share. Today's session was about her body and nothing else.

"I was just thinking about my breakfast this morning, and how I spilled it down my top."

He laughed. "You're good with your feet, you can't be good with your hands all the time, too. That would just be greedy." He worked his way up her leg and massaged her thigh.

Sloane closed her eyes and tried to shut down the thoughts buzzing around her head. But her mind was like a flickering movie, serving up images of Jess, her and Jess in happier times, Jess and Britney, and finally, Ella.

Ella had made it onto this movie of her life?

"Great match yesterday. You and Nat seem to have built up a good rapport already, which bodes well for the season."

Soccer chat. Thank goodness for soccer chat. "It does," she replied. "She's got skills, and I think we could really do some damage to other teams this season."

Dan nodded. "Your penalty, though." He shook his head in admiration. "You're not afraid to be brave and vulnerable, which is what penalty-takers need to be. Same with your amazing personal sharing session this week, too. But that penalty was the key point in the game. They were coming back into it. You miss that penalty, the momentum swings. At 2-1, anything can happen. But you scored it, it's 3-1, it's a different vibe."

Sloane nodded. "There's a reason I practice as much as I do."

"I know," Dan replied. "There's a reason we work your muscles every day so you can do just that." He grinned at her. "Teamwork makes the dream work, right?"

If only everything was as simple as soccer. She and Jess used to be a team. No longer. Now, she was flying solo.

It was a strange feeling.

* * *

Ella glanced at her phone: 30 minutes until team talk. Today they were getting a personal story from assistant coach, Jonas. Everyone was learning so much about each other through these, and Ella couldn't wait for the next one. She sipped her coffee in the hotel lobby and checked her emails on her phone. She had a couple of new business enquiries to answer, and a message from Aunt Ursula, asking about her trip. Maybe she'd reply now.

She called up WhatsApp and clicked in the reply box, but a presence nearby made her look up. Nat stood beside her, biting her lip.

"Nat, hi! You okay?"

She nodded, looked at the floor, then eventually back to Ella.

"Good." She toed the carpet with her left trainer. She was already dressed for training, white socks pulled up beyond her ankles. She'd add shinpads, longer socks and boots just before she left for the field. "I was just wondering if you had a minute."

Ella nodded, then laid her phone on the small wooden table in front of her. "Of course." Her messages could wait. She gestured to the space on the sofa next to her.

Nat sat down.

"I was talking to Sloane the other day, and she mentioned you used to play football professionally."

Ella had to concentrate, as Nat's scouse accent was strong. She was from Bootle.

"I did." She wasn't sure where this was going. "An injury cut my career very short."

"Sorry to hear that."

Nat glanced over at reception, where a man was checking in with the most luggage Ella had ever seen one person attempt to manoeuvre.

"It's just... good to know you get the pressures we're under."

"I do." She still had no idea what Nat wanted, but she'd let this play out. Nat clearly wanted to talk.

"I tried to talk to Sloane a bit ago, but she had coffee all down her and seemed distracted. Then I thought of you."

"Right."

"It's just... what Sloane said in her team talk. It's sort of where I am now." Nat took a deep breath. Then the words tumbled out of her, as if she'd been storing them up. Which she probably had.

"My parents are supportive of me playing football, to a point. They don't understand, they're not football fans – being Pakistani, Mum far prefers cricket – but they want me to be happy. However, I came out just before Rovers signed me, and they're not happy about that. I thought Mum would be tough because being gay isn't exactly okay in Asian culture, but Dad's taken it badly, too."

She exhaled another long breath, then looked up. "I don't know why I'm telling you this, but Sloane's story made me feel like someone might understand. All the other girls here, if they're gay, their families are supportive. Sometimes it can feel like…" She shrugged, then wiped her palms up and down her face.

Ella's heart went out to Nat. Parents could be so cruel, especially when they were talking about someone as young as Nat. Ella's mum had always been supportive, but Sloane had lived that life. She was living proof that things got better, even if you had to make it happen for yourself. It was something you never got over, but you learned to live with.

However, the pain of parental rejection was still raw for Nat. Ella so wanted to make it better instantly. She'd do the best she could.

"My mum always accepted my sexuality and my career choices, so I won't pretend I've experienced what you or Sloane have. But I've met plenty of sports stars who've had family issues; with sexuality, and dealing with parental expectation. It's tough, I won't lie. Especially at the start. But your parents might just be in shock. They may come around. Most do, so remember that. As Sloane would admit, she drew the short straw." She gave Nat a tight smile. "But you have to remember this is your life, and your dream. You're already doing better than most. You've scored your first goal, and sung your first song. You're living the dream."

Nat gave her a genuine smile. "I am. But that's what makes it hurt a little more. Because why can't they see that? Why can't they be happy for me? They think football turned me gay, but I was always gay." She shook her head. "I want them to come to games, to see me play. I want to make them proud." When she glanced up, her eyes were shiny.

Ella reached out, took her hand and squeezed. "I'm sure they want to. Give them time. Meanwhile, play the best you can because making yourself, your teammates, and the fans proud is what you're playing for the most. You can't control other people's reactions to anything you do or anything you are. Concentrate on what you can control: being the best footballer and best queer role model possible."

Nat snorted at that. "I don't think I'm anyone's role model."

"You'd be surprised. You're not just out and proud, you're one of a handful of Asian players in the league. You're making a difference, even if it doesn't feel like it. Representation matters." Ella squeezed her fingers again, then let go. "Have you spoken to your parents since you arrived?"

"A couple of times, but they never call me. It's always the other way around. I'm worried I won't be able to go home when we get Christmas break." Her lips quivered as she spoke.

Ella sat forward and held her gaze. "It's hard to do, but it really is a waiting game. It's only September. December is a while away. I'm sure they'll welcome you home by then. Hang in there, and keep doing what you do best. I'm sure they're following your career, whether they admit it or not."

Chapter Twelve

They were seven weeks into the season, and the team was unbeaten, with five wins and two draws. They couldn't have asked for more. The new signings had settled in, Sloane especially was scoring for fun.

Ella waited for Sloane in her office – she was going to drive them home for the second time this week. The first time, she'd been slow, steady, and super-nervous, not how Ella had imagined. Today, Ella was going to get her to relax, take things easier.

Since the pre-season in Germany, Sloane had kept it mainly professional with Ella, focusing solely on her training and performance. They'd chatted a few times when Ella was in, but something shifted on their trip, and Sloane had kept her distance. There had been no coffees or knocks on her front door. Just the promise of a driving lesson, which was happening today.

Sloane wouldn't be drawn on her love life in their performance sessions. From the look of Jess's socials, she'd already moved on, but Sloane didn't want to talk about it. However, she had opened up about her mindset, and about her injury fears, which Ella knew were well founded. She'd had her own to deal with, and that hadn't ended well. She wouldn't wish her outcome on anyone, let alone the best striker in the world.

Her phone lit with a message from Sloane, saying she was waiting outside. Ella shut down her laptop, and waved at Lucy through their clear office wall. She beckoned her in. Ella packed her bag, then stuck her head through Lucy's office door. While Ella shared her space with three others, Lucy had hers all to herself.

"How did the sessions go today? You're not in the next two days, right?"

Ella shook her head. "Nope. Everything is good. I've been helping Nat with her decision-making confidence, Amy said my shepherd's pie recipe was a winner, and they're all ready for this weekend. Big game against the league leaders. Everyone's in the right head space. They just need your words of wisdom to guide them now."

Lucy nodded. "I was wondering if you'd like to share during the pre-match talk next weekend? This week's is big, but next week is against our arch rivals."

Ella blinked. "Me? The biggest match of the season so far?" She pointed to her chest then glanced over her shoulder, just to check Lucy hadn't been talking to anyone else.

There was only her.

"Yes. You've been there, done it. I've already told my story." Lucy led from the front, and she expected her team to follow. "You told me your story – now tell it to these kids. Tell them what it means to have it taken away. Tell them to go out and seize the day. Be vulnerable. Take a chance." She paused. "Or say whatever you want to say. You up for it?"

Was she? Ella had addressed conferences before, been on

a stage in front of hundreds of delegates and done it with ease. But smaller groups were always more pressure. People listened more. You could see the whites of their eyes. But she'd got into this job to make a difference. If this was what it took, then so be it.

"Count me in," Ella replied.

* * *

Ella still couldn't believe the club's fantastic facilities, nor that they were shared with the men. Everyone she'd met so far was friendly and open, which was terrific. She loved the atmosphere both teams fostered together, and wished more clubs took this on-board. When the men and the women worked together, sharing facilities and stories, it was better for everyone. Maybe she could suggest to Lucy both first teams had a regular social sharing session. Food for thought.

As Ella walked towards her car, she spotted Sloane leaning against one of the carefully planted trees in the car park. She was dressed in a club tracksuit and trainers with a woolly hat – "this is not California!" as she constantly told Ella – but she wore it better than anyone. Sloane was one of those people who could wear a bin bag and look great, whereas Ella had to work at it more. Maybe she could ask Marina for help when she came around to see her new flat. Her cousin was far better at style than her.

"Is that the world-famous striker Sloane Patterson leaning against a tree like she's doing a shoot for her own 'In The Style' range?" Ella blinked. Her playful tone was new.

Sloane gave her a slow smile as she straightened up, stuffing a wrapper into her pocket.

"Why haven't they asked me yet? I should be upset, right?" She walked around to the passenger side of the car. "They should get me doing a collection. I'd make it queer as hell, and ladies all over the world would love it."

"I agree," Ella replied. "I was just thinking I need to freshen up my wardrobe. You could inspire me." She came to stand beside Sloane. "I think you're on the wrong side, by the way." This had happened the first time Sloane drove, too.

She shut her eyes and shook her head. "It's not my fault if you insist on putting the driver's seat on the wrong side, is it?" She snatched the key fob from Ella's hand and opened the door. Once settled inside, Sloane adjusted the seat and mirrors, then stroked the steering wheel.

Ella tried not to pay too much attention.

"Have I told you I love your car, by the way? Small, but perfectly formed. Also, the colour is lit."

Ella beamed. "My car says thanks. I assume you drove something bigger in LA?"

"I did. A Subaru gifted to me. Bigger than a Mini."

"But not as cute."

Sloane gave her a look Ella couldn't quite decipher, then tapped the digital display on the dashboard. "I was going to apologise for being late, but you can work until whenever I guess. Whereas once my 50 penalties are in, I'm done."

"There are always performances to make better: you on the pitch, me inside minds and bodies. How many did you score today?" Ella snapped her seatbelt into place.

"Forty-two. Not bad, but not great either."

"You're very hard on yourself. Forty-two is pretty bloody great. Who was in goal?"

"Miira and her massive hands, so I guess it's not bad." Sloane sat back in her seat, palm to chest. "But if I get to the stage where perfectly acceptable is okay, please slap me. I've always been exceptional. Fifty is exceptional. Anything else is a fail."

Ella shook her head. Miira was the first team's back-up keeper, and she could pick up a baby with one hand, no bother. "You know perfection isn't possible, right? Especially against Miira."

"I know, but I refuse to believe it."

She'd missed this over the past few weeks. Their ease with each other. She needed a friend like Sloane in her life.

Sloane started the engine, then adjusted her position and sat tall. "Okay, enough talk, I need you to be on guard so I don't kill us driving home."

"Those words will make me take notice." However, as it was gone 4pm and the car park was nearly empty. Ella was confident they'd at least get out of there without serious injury. "Have you ever had a crash?"

"Never."

"Stop catastrophising, then. Remember what we said about living in the moment, not worrying about the past or the future?"

She grinned at Ella. "Yes, ma'am."

Those words sent a parade of tingles up Ella's spine. She ignored it and focused on the shiny watch on Sloane's wrist. "Is that new?" She pointed. "I don't think I've seen you sporting much bling before. It's pretty cool."

"From a new sponsor, it arrived at the weekend."

"It must be nice to have cool stuff just turn up on your doorstep." Ella couldn't imagine it. She was still thrilled with her club tracksuit, training top and jacket with her initials on. That made her an official member of staff more than anything else in the world.

"I guess I'm used to it."

"You should remember it doesn't happen to most people." It was also a reminder to Ella how different their lives were, despite their commonalities. Financially, they were worlds apart.

Sloane glanced her way, then nodded. "I do. I have to wear it a number of times in public to get my money from them. I'm trying to get used to it." She jiggled her wrist. "It's pretty heavy. Plus, who wears watches these days? Doesn't everyone just use their phone?"

Ella held up her wrist, showing off her not-so-flashy watch. "I do. But then, I'm an old-fashioned girl at heart."

"I like that about you." Sloane eased the car onto the main road, with no hiccups. "You're an English rose, from another era."

Ella didn't quite know what to say to that. Was it a compliment? Or was Sloane saying she was a stick-in-the-mud who wasn't up to date with the modern world? She might have a point. It didn't stop Ella's cheeks heating to inferno level.

She was just forming a response, when Sloane tried to turn into the wrong lane at their first junction.

"Hard left!" Ella shouted as her heart rate sped up to breakneck speed.

Sloane jumped, swore, then made a course correction. "Godammit!"

"Take it slow." Ella reached over and involuntarily put a hand on Sloane's knee.

They both jumped again. Heat swirled around the car as it wobbled, before Ella put a hand on the steering wheel.

"We're going to get home in one piece."

"If you say so." Sloane kept her eyes firmly on the road.

"Take a right at the next junction. That's the second lane, okay?"

Sloane nodded, and managed it.

She was fine when she was purely driving. It was only at junctions that she came unstuck. Once she'd taken the next junction correctly with no coaching, Ella's heartbeat slowed slightly.

"You should come over and see if there are any clothes you want from my pile." Sloane glanced at her briefly, then focused back on the road. She pulled up at a red light. "If you were serious about getting new clothes. I get sent them all the time and I'm not going to wear them all. We're fairly similar in size, give or take a few inches."

"That'd be great." Ella was still trying to put the fact she'd grabbed Sloane's knee out of her mind. "Have you heard from your cousin, by the way? Ryan's mum? I know you said you were hoping to get in touch with her a few weeks ago."

"We're planning on getting together soon. I haven't really had the head space or the time since the season started. I wanted to focus on that first, get off to a good start. I already have enough outside influences in my life, so I figured there was no rush. I've waited my whole life already. But she seemed cool on the phone." Sloane paused as she pulled away. "One of those outside influences is Jess, by the way. We broke up officially when we were in Germany." She took a deep breath. "You might have seen her with Brit on her socials. Looks like they're showing the world it's official now."

Ella hadn't expected a confession today. She flicked a

piece of lint from her trousers. "I'm sorry to hear that. Are you okay?"

Sloane nodded. "I called it. Should have done it months ago. I'm just surprised she sat on it for as long as she did." She exhaled a long breath. "But it's all for the best. In the aftermath, I've worked out that I'm completely over it. I just needed it to be official." She glanced at Ella. "I'm serious about the clothes, okay? Come around, see what you like."

"Okay." That was an expert change of subject, but Ella wasn't about to push for any more.

They drove the rest of the way home in silence, save for Ella uttering a few "first lane," and "follow the blue car" to back Sloane up. However, just as the first time, once Sloane was into the groove, she found her driving mode. She pulled up in Ella's space and sat back with a smile.

"That was 60 per cent less scary than the first time. In a few more weeks, maybe I can think about getting my own car."

"Big steps, make sure you're ready," Ella joked. The slight tension that had been in the air from Sloane's confession popped. Ella was glad. She didn't want there to be weirdness between them. She got out of the car and Sloane followed. She locked it, then gave the keys to Ella. Their fingers touched and Ella fought the frisson that ran through her whole body. However much she tried to deny it, it was there.

When Sloane fell into step beside her, Ella shivered slightly. Maybe it was colder this November than she'd thought. When she glanced at Sloane, she was wearing an expression Ella couldn't read.

"Now I've blurted out my shit love life – or rather, complete lack of – what about you? Have you swiped right yet?"

Ella shook her head. "My cousin's coming over tonight, and I know she's going to badger me." Ella checked her watch. Marina was due in half an hour.

"Badger you?" Sloane tilted her head. "What the hell does that mean? I hope no wildlife are going to be hurt in your apartment tonight."

Ella spat a snort of laughter. "No animal cruelty, I promise. I'm almost vegetarian, if you discount the chicken and fish I eat. Plus, the occasional steak."

"Vegetarian of the year." Sloane gave her a slow grin. "You want to come up for a quick coffee? Or to look at some clothes?"

Ella shook her head. "My cousin's due any minute for her tea and a glass of wine."

"Tea and wine? A bit overkill on the liquids."

"Tea means dinner up north."

Sloane made a face. "I am *never* going to get the hang of UK English, I swear."

"Stick around, and we'll have you talking proper in no time." Ella paused. "Plus, I also have some work to do for a client meeting early tomorrow, so tonight's not good."

Sloane smiled. "I always forget you have another job. That you're in demand." Her breath swirled around her in the cold evening air. "Not that I'm surprised, because you're amazing." The timbre of her voice went low.

Ella gulped. She wasn't sure what Sloane was or wasn't saying here, and she didn't have time to work it out. "I never take it for granted, and I give my all to everyone I work with. You're all special to me." Ella glanced at her watch, then back at Sloane. "I have to go."

Their gazes connected. Ella stared into Sloane's azure blue

eyes. There was so much behind them. So much going on. She was in serious danger of drowning.

"I'm sorry I've been elusive over the past few weeks. I've just had a lot to work out, with Jess and everything. But I've done it now. I've missed our chats, but it's just been a weird time."

Ella put a hand on Sloane's arm. She'd missed their connection, too. "You don't owe me an explanation."

"I disagree," Sloane replied. "I just want you to know, you're pretty special to me, too." But as soon as the words escaped her mouth, Sloane looked like she wanted to scoop them back in and swallow them whole.

A loud gong sounded in Ella's heart, but she shushed it internally and flailed around for words to reply with. Anything. Something. It was no use. She couldn't locate her next sentence. Eventually she managed: "I'm not in Thursday and Friday, so I'll see you for the game on Sunday, if not before?"

A wholly inappropriate response, then.

Sloane gave her an exaggerated nod. "Sunday, sure," she muttered.

Right at that moment, Marina's sky-blue Corsa sailed into the car park and screeched to a halt. Marina had never done anything quietly since the moment she was born.

"And that, with perfect timing, is my cousin."

Marina slammed her car door and waved Ella's way.

Ella waved back, panic flitting through her body. Had she said anything inappropriate about Sloane to Marina? She didn't think so. Mainly because there had been nothing big to say until just now. When who-the-hell-knows-what had just happened.

Feelings swirled around them in the evening air. Sloane Patterson had just told Ella she missed her. That she was special.

Ella wasn't sure what to do with that fact. She wanted to hold her breath, still the moment, allow this fizzing thrill to vibrate through her. But that wasn't an option with Marina coming down the path to where they stood, completely oblivious.

When she got to Ella, she scrunched her face and wriggled from foot to foot. "I am busting for the loo! Can you open your door so I can get to your flat before I pee myself?"

She was doll-tiny, with liquorice hair and a whirlwind personality that left anybody who came into contact with her in a spin. Mainly in a good way.

It was only when Marina fully focused on Ella, and then the person standing next to her, that she stopped talking.

"Holy shit!"

Ella closed her eyes and sighed. She'd wondered if Marina was going to embarrass her. She had her answer.

However, Sloane had clearly seen this before from the wry smile on her face. She extended a hand to Marina. "Sloane Patterson. You must be Ella's much-talked-about cousin, Marina."

She was a charmer. Ella had to hand it to her.

Marina opened and closed her mouth like a goldfish. "I am!" she said, clearly delighted to have been a topic of conversation. "But whatever she's told you, I'm at least 50 per cent better in person."

Sloane snorted. "I have no doubt, I've met your cousin." She shot Ella a quick wink which melted her on the spot, then shook Marina's hand.

When Sloane eventually managed to pull her hand away, Marina gazed at her own skin, then back up to Sloane. "Are you joining us for tea?"

Sloane immediately shook her head. "Ella just let me drive us home so I can get some practice in. Driving on the wrong side of the road is killing me. At least you play soccer the same way, so I'm thankful for that. Every time I get behind a wheel, I fear it might be my last."

Marina threw back her head as if that were the most hilarious thing in the world. "I'm sure you're not that bad."

"No, she did nearly kill us on the way home." Ella glanced at Sloane. Their gazes froze, and in that moment, Marina disappeared. All that was left was Ella, Sloane, her heartbeat, and the cold waft of their breath in the evening air.

Until Marina wriggled one more time. "You think we can go in before I pee myself?"

The three of them shuffled through the door and into the lift. Sloane pressed the buttons for her floor and Ella's.

The lift door closed, and Ella didn't know where to look. Certainly not at Sloane.

They stopped at Ella's floor. She gave her cousin her key, and Marina flung herself into the corridor.

"Number 24, loo's first on the right!" Ella shouted.

Marina gave her a thumbs-up.

When Ella turned, Sloane's left foot held the lift door open. She was slow to raise her gaze. "See you Sunday for the game, then?"

Ella nodded. Football. That was safe ground.

She had no idea what the rest was.

Chapter Thirteen

Sloane stood and came in for the pre-match locker-room huddle. Every game was the same: stand in a circle, arms around each other, followed by a motivational talk from Lucy. The manager was good at them, Sloane had to give her that. Sloane had worked with many coaches in her time, and Lucy Harris was up there with the best. As usual, Lucy stood in the middle of the team, waiting for a hush to descend. It never took long. She had the power.

"Do you feel that?" Lucy tilted her head upwards. "It's the hum of anticipation. We've got a sell-out crowd today, and we're at the home of our arch-rivals, Salchester United. If you need more motivation to get out there and show the fans what you can do on a football pitch, then you shouldn't be here. Anybody need more motivation than that to make our fans proud for their biggest game of the season?" Lucy cast her gaze around the group.

Sloane led by example, shaking her head with vigour.

"Good," Lucy said. "But if you do need more motivation, I've asked Ella to say a few words." Lucy glanced to her left. "Over to you."

Sloane's skin flared hot as her friend stepped into the centre of the team circle, and Lucy stepped back. Sloane couldn't think of anyone better to do this. Ella was a scholar of the game, and she was wise beyond her years. She was also calm. She made Sloane calm. She had the same effect on everyone she met.

"I want to tell you a story." Ella cast her gaze around the circle. As her rich, hazel eyes met Sloane's, she stopped for a millisecond, but then carried on.

Sloane took a breath. She appreciated that extra attention, no matter how small. Sloane's radar wanted Ella on it every chance she got.

"You know me as your performance coach. A mentor. But in my past life, I was a footballer, just like you. A good one, too. Creative midfield was my position, just like Welshy and Layla." She pointed at Rovers' numbers seven and eight, the engine room of the team. Millie Welsh gave her a grin in return.

"But when I was 19, I was playing a match and went in for a 50-50 tackle. Just as I had a thousand times before. Only on this day, my knee wobbled, something popped, and I went down writhing in pain. I knew it was bad, but I didn't know how bad. I'd torn my ACL." Ella took a moment to let her words sink in.

Sloane's breath stalled. How did she not know this? Maybe she hadn't been a very good friend so far, after all. She made a note to ask for more details.

"Back then, we had little to no support for the women's team. I had the NHS for treatment, but that was it. There were no specialists on hand, no club doctor to consult. The women's teams didn't have physios or facilities to rehab like you have today. I went in for the operation, but it didn't go well. In fact, I had to go back in a couple of months later. Then, I had to rehab solo." She waved a hand around the dressing room. "I was left to my own devices. Because of the botched operation, my knee didn't recover in the projected time period, and I was let go by Rushton City."

There was an intake of breath around the dressing room from everyone. Including Sloane. What a nightmare for Ella. Did she still feel robbed of her career? Sloane knew she might.

"But I wasn't giving up. I worked on my fitness, got a job in a call centre to pay the rent, and signed for East Hampton. I had high hopes. I'd been an England prospect before my injury. I was determined to get back there.

"However, my knee had other ideas. It never felt right. I worked my way back into the reserves, played a few games for the senior team, but always as a sub. Plus, I knew I was playing with nerves. Not with the same bravery and gusto I once had.

"Halfway through the season, my knee gave way, and I had to stop playing. When I went back to the hospital, they told me I'd damaged my tendons and ligaments around the ACL again, and the knee would always be weak and injury-prone. They recommended I not play professional sport again. My next injury – and there would be one – would be worse, and the one after that even more so. I could still kick a ball and train, but professional-level sport was not in my future anymore."

Sloane couldn't quite believe what she was hearing. Ella had everyone's attention for what came next.

"I'm telling you this not to gain your sympathy. Injuries happen. Medical fuck-ups happen. I've got a great alternative career now, plus I understand what it takes to be a footballer. The sacrifices you make. The work you put in. But it can be taken away in a second. Yes, you have better facilities these days, full-time coaches for the physical and the mental aspects of your game, but bodies haven't changed. Especially female bodies when it comes to ACL injuries.

"My point? Live every moment like it's your last. Chase every ball. Close down every player. Run the extra metre, bust a gut to get that cross in. Because tomorrow, you might not play again. This holds especially true when you play in a local derby. Go out there and play this game as if you're never going to play again. Leave it all out there on the pitch. Win this fucking game for the fans, but most of all, for yourselves. Are you ready?"

Ella didn't wait for an answer.

"Then let's fucking go and win!"

A roar from the whole group and everyone clapped their hands and stamped their feet. Ella's words were perfect and had provided the necessary motivation.

"Let's do it for Ella!" Sloane shouted, and the whole team clapped again.

Ella, cheeks flushed from her speech, caught her gaze and gave Sloane the softest of smiles. One she'd never given her before. The effect worked its way from the tips of Sloane's fingers to the studs of her boots. She hoped she hadn't blushed fire-truck-red, too.

"Thank you," Ella mouthed.

"Thank *you*," Sloane mouthed back.

* * *

Sloane could feel the energy crackling off the surface of the field, as well as from the crowd. After winning the Euros in the summer, the initial excitement around women's soccer had endured. Plus, with Salchester Rovers contesting the top spot in the league, their attendances were promising. Both stands either side of the field were stacked with strong numbers of red home shirts as well as Rovers' blue, and the biggest noise came from the stalwart fans behind the goal, roaring their teams on as they ran out. They'd sold over 20,000 tickets for this local derby, which was impressive. Even more reason to win this for the fans.

Their rivals stood, hands on hips, breathing frosty fumes into the sharp November air. Sloane barely registered the temperature. On game days, she was impervious. She glanced over to the sidelines, where Ella gave Welshy a thumbs-up. Sloane wanted to win this for the fans, for herself, but most of all for Ella, and for all the Ellas before and after her.

The whistle sounded and they were off.

The first ten minutes flew by in a wave of hard-fought tackles, the ball mainly sticking in the centre of the field. Sloane only had a few touches, with the opposition nailing their game plan, not willing to let her and Nat have any space in their final third.

Right now, the ball was out on the right wing, and Sloane stood close to her marker, a tall woman named Katy Dempsey who she'd never met before, but who didn't seem at all intimidated by her. Sloane was impressed. Dempsey couldn't have been more than 21. If the shoe was on the other foot, Sloane wasn't sure she'd be the same.

All of a sudden, Welshy had the ball and broke from her marker with a burst of speed. She had that in her game. Sloane jinked one way, then the other, then back again to get Dempsey in the mood. She did it once, twice, three times. Then just when Dempsey thought she was going to do it again, she went the other way and turned on the after-burners, imagining she was Roadrunner in the cartoon. *Beep Beep!* As she ran, she glanced over her right shoulder, hoping Welshy had spotted her run. She had.

In seconds, the ball sailed over Sloane's right shoulder, and bounced into her path with the perfect weight. Welshy could thread a ball as good as the best. Sloane heard her marker's boots thunder on the grass somewhere near her, but she took the ball in her stride, trapped it, then looked up to assess her options. Just outside the penalty area. Nat to her right. Goalkeeper closing down her angles. She had a split second to decide what to do.

As the goalkeeper advanced, Sloane hit the ball with the outside of her right boot into Nat's path, then darted left just in case there was anything to mop up. She saw the whites of the keeper's eyes and heard the expletive that left her lips as she lunged left to grab the ball from Nat's feet, but it was too late. Nat drew back her right foot, and the sweet sound of her boot connecting with the ball filled Sloane's ears. When she looked ahead, the net billowed, and she threw both hands in the air as the stands all around erupted in cheers. Sloane was the first player Nat reached, and she jumped into her arms.

"Fucking yes!" Nat screamed in Sloane's ears, which made her grin. There were many ways to describe the elation of scoring a goal, especially when it was your boot that was the last to touch it before it hit the net. To this day, even after nearly a decade of playing professionally, Sloane was yet to find anything that described it better than 'fucking yes!'

Within seconds, the whole team swamped them, fists

pumped. Moments later, Sloane regained her breath and retook her position at the centre circle to kick off. When she glanced to the dugout, Ella was watching.

She gave her a thumbs-up.

Warmth glittered through Sloane.

Ella was on her side.

The whistle went. They were off again.

The rest of the first half ebbed and flowed, with United hitting a post and Nat skying another good chance. Just when Sloane started to listen for the whistle – she really needed the bathroom – the fourth official put up her board. Three minutes of stoppage time. She could cope with that.

The ball zipped up the touchline towards her, but Dempsey was right on her shoulder, just like the whole of the first half. Kudos to the kid, she stuck to her job. Sloane collected the ball, and looked up. Welshy was beyond her marker. She could dart right and slide it to her. She went to pass the ball with the outside of her boot, but Dempsey put a foot in just when she was mid-motion. The ball left Sloane's foot, but Dempsey's boot crunched into her ankle. Sloane's foot went one way, her ankle went the other.

A lightning rod of pain flashed up her leg as she crumpled to the grass, landing with a thud on her hip. She rolled onto her side, and everything went silent for a few seconds, her mind white. Within moments, reality seeped back in and her ankle throbbed like it never had before.

Or rather, exactly as it had before.

Her bad ankle.

Doom slithered down her.

"You okay, Sloane?"

She cracked open her eyes to see Nat's and Welshy's concerned faces above her.

Judging from the pain that started in her ankle and was now creeping into her eyeballs, she could confidently say she was not.

* * *

Sloane lay on the physio table in United's injury bay. The physio trotted out platitudes to make her feel better as she packed ice around her ankle. None of them were working. Maybe if she was Dempsey's age, they might have.

Injury-wise, Sloane had been lucky. Way more than Ella. However, her ankle was her downfall. After her big injury, her old coach used to say it was made of glass and had to be treated as such. Unfortunately, glass ankles and soccer didn't mix. Not that Sloane blamed Dempsey. Tackling was part of the game and Dempsey was playing it.

Someone knocking at the door made her look up.

Ella.

Just the sight of her made Sloane unclench her fist. "You're missing the game." Right on cue, the crowd outside groaned. Was that a home team miss or an away team goal? She listened further but no cheering ensued. She suspected the former.

"I thought it was worth it to come and check on you." She walked in and pointed at Sloane's ankle. "How's it feeling?"

"Cold."

Ella laughed. "I imagine." She paused, then looked back to Sloane. "I know you have a history of ankle issues, but they wouldn't have signed you if it was chronic. What I'm saying is, don't go jumping to conclusions."

"Easy for you to say."

"Well aware, but my point still counts."

Sloane chewed the inside of her cheek. "Tell me something to take my mind off the fact that my foot feels like it might break off at the ankle any minute. Anything at all."

Ella screwed up her face. "Anything under the sun?"

Sloane clicked her fingers. "Tell me about the best goal you ever scored in your career. Where was it. Who was it against. And did you win?"

A dreamy look crossed Ella's face as she tried to collate her answer. It took a few moments. Time enough for Sloane to take in her pink cheeks, the cute way her thick hair stuck out of the sides of her club bobble hat. Plus, even though she couldn't see it, she knew Ella's training pants would be cupping her butt perfectly. Sloane let her eyelids flutter shut for a moment. Her thoughts were getting worse.

"The Women's FA Cup Final, 15 years ago. It was three months before my injury. I was 19, playing for Rushton City, and I was hot property. I took the ball down from over my shoulder – a little like you did today, good assist by the way." Sloane bowed her head in acknowledgement. "Then I did a Ricky Villa-slalom in the penalty area, feinted one way, wrong-footed the keeper and slotted coolly into the bottom right corner. The crowd, about ten thousand in a small arena just outside Doncaster, went mad, and it was the best moment of my life. I've won the FA Cup, and not many people can say that."

For the second time that day, Sloane was left speechless by Ella. "Why have you never told me that before? Or about your career?"

"You never asked." Ella smiled. "Plus, my job isn't to talk about me. But today, Lucy asked me to. So I did."

"I'm glad." Sloane's ankle throbbed so much, it was like her whole body was on fire.

"Is it helping with the pain?"

"Absolutely."

"Liar."

Sloane grinned. Ella understood. She loved that.

"But you know something? I'd love to kick a ball in a big stadium like you have. We always played in small grounds. Even when I won the FA Cup, we didn't sell out a capacity ground of 15,000. I'd love to score a goal on the big stage. Not in a game, because my knee might have other ideas. Just for fun. And I want to celebrate like I just won the FA Cup again."

"Can't you do that at Rovers?"

Ella rolled her shoulders and shook her head. "Not really. I'm the performance coach. I can kick a ball, but I can't join in training. It's not my job."

Sloane stored that fact away.

"But I meant what I said – it might not be so bad. I doubt it's broken." Ella pointed at Sloane's ankle. "Plus, while you're in rehab, you have me as your coach and your neighbour. I can bring coffee if you're on crutches. I'll make sure you never run out of chocolate digestives."

"They're like crack cocaine." Ella had taken her mind off her problems, even if just for a moment.

Outside, there was a massive cheer from the crowd. Had United equalised? "You should go back out there. You're needed on the sidelines for encouragement."

"I might need to start shouting if they've just equalised."

Ella turned, then looked back at Sloane. "You played well today, by the way. Like a hotshot."

"Apparently I am a hotshot, so someone wise once told me." Sloane held onto Ella's gaze like her life depended on it. Which in that moment, it felt like it did.

Ella went to say something, stopped, then leaned in and placed three fingertips on Sloane's bare arm. The air rushed out of Sloane's system at Ella's touch.

Their gazes were still locked.

Sloane's heart thumped in her chest. The pain in her ankle was temporarily forgotten.

"You're going to be okay."

Sloane desperately wanted to believe her.

Another roar from outside.

The moment snapped in two.

Ella dropped her gaze and took a step back. She stared at her fingertips, back at Sloane, then signalled with her thumb over her shoulder. "I better go."

Sloane nodded. "Don't go!" was what she wanted to say, but she didn't. "Message me the score," was what came out.

More appropriate for work.

Not at all the truth.

What the hell had just happened?

Chapter Fourteen

Ella hadn't been shopping since her first weekend in town, and she hadn't expected it to be so full-on festive.

"It's five weeks to Christmas. What did you expect?" Marina gave her a crazed look as she pushed open the door to Selfridges, battling with a man holding five bags, hence he was the width of a small truck. She lost.

"Five weeks until the big day," she continued as she pushed on the heavy chrome and glass door. Her lipstick was still perfect as she turned to Ella and beckoned her in. Marina was a stickler for freshly applied lipstick at all times. "Five weeks until both you and I spend another Christmas without a significant other, hence another year with no gigantic, statement present. Honestly, our bits might shrivel up and die."

"Speak for yourself. I keep mine active and up to date with a healthy regimen of self-love."

Her cousin stuck out a hand. "TMI."

Ella grinned, but her mind had already skipped to Sloane and what it might feel like to be *her* significant other. She could just imagine the lavish gifts Sloane would give to her girlfriend. She was hardly short of cash. Then again, she might not even have to *buy* the gifts in the first place. She could just pick them out of all the free stuff she was sent.

Ella followed Marina into the department store, thinking about her fingers on Sloane's arm at her last game. Her blood warmed in her veins. Sloane was still vexed about being sidelined. Ella hoped she could take her mind off it, because she of all people knew the injury fear of never coming back. She'd go over this weekend to see how she was doing. Maybe even take advantage of the offer of free clothes.

Moments later, her own mind elsewhere, she proceeded to walk straight into a Nordmann Fir, then rebounded off the festive tree. Ella spat some pines from her mouth, then put a hand to her face to wipe any debris.

"Have I got a pine needle stuck in my cheek?" She moved her hand and stuck her face in Marina's eyeline. She had to keep her mind on the here and now. There were too many obstacles in this department store that could take her down, and she had a hectic festive schedule to fulfil.

Her cousin grabbed a handful of her coat and pulled her towards a spare patch of wall, out of the firing line of the thick and not-so-jolly crowds. "You're pine-needle free," she confirmed, her face up in Ella's grill. "But why did you walk into the tree? It was hardly inconspicuous."

Ella puffed out her cheeks. She wasn't going to tell Marina it was because she was worried about Sloane. Her cousin didn't need any encouragement. "I thought it was a reflection." Ella pointed around the marbled, glitzy interior of the department store. It was weak, but Marina bought it.

She breathed in the scent of cinnamon and spice. Up above, giant baubles and Christmas puddings spun on enormous metal chains. The type that if they snapped, would kill you in an instant. "You're going to have to protect me from other trees and those killer baubles." She pointed upwards. "I've got a lot to do over the next few weeks. Big games. I can't afford to be knocked out by Christmas."

Marina rolled her wide hazel eyes, so similar to Ella's own. "I promise I will do my best. For Rovers, and also because you need to be fighting fit to get a date on Honey Pot."

Marina had messaged her last night to say she'd posted Ella's profile. Ella's response had been to log on, wince, and then ignore the app all day. Ella wondered if it was worth the hassle. Especially as there might be a better option closer to home. Albeit, a complicated and injured option. Maybe she needed to go on a Honey Pot date to get her Sloane obsession out of her system.

"But whether you have a wicked Christmas run-in with the team or not, and whether you get a girlfriend or not, you still need gifts." Marina raised an eyebrow. "We're going to chat about whether you're coming home for the big day, but I know your issue with present shopping, so think of me as Santa's little helper. Got it?"

Her cousin threaded an arm through Ella's and dragged her towards the escalator. A woman dressed as an elf stood at the bottom, half-heartedly offering a squirt of a new fragrance in a bottle shaped like a Christmas tree. Ella had already been attacked by Christmas, so she put Marina in the woman's path, and they made it to the escalator unscathed. The pair rode up towards the women's wear department, where Marina marched to the scarves and pointed at one in the hues of a rich sunset – just like the Californian ones Sloane had described.

"Mum really wants this." Marina held up the scarf. "But it's cashmere, so she thinks she can't have it. You know all about her money issues as your mum had them, too. But I think, with your hotshot new job, you can probably make her dreams come true."

The word 'hotshot' brought an image of Sloane into Ella's mind, and she smiled. How was she doing? She'd been ordered to literally, 'put her feet up'. Was she sitting at home discovering the joys of *This Morning* in her first week off? If Ella was any judge of character, that would last possibly for around an hour. Then Sloane would be itching to get back in the gym. Their building had one, as well as a pool. Marina snapping her fingers in front of her eyes shifted her focus.

"Sorry, miles away." She grabbed the scarf. "Yes, this is perfect, thank you." She paused. "What are you getting her?"

"A subscription to her favourite food magazine, and I've already bought her a necklace. She told me about this last week."

"I am forever in your debt."

"Remember that." Marina bumped her hip as they fell into step. "What you getting me with your big pay packet?"

Ella smiled. Her family appeared to think that now she worked at Salchester Rovers, she was rolling in it. They clearly didn't know how women's football worked. She picked up the nearest thing to hand. A pack of two jade-green tights, size medium. "How about these? I think they'd really suit you."

Marina gave Ella the same look she'd given her when Ella had broken her Polly Pocket, aged six.

"Let's scour the shop and I'll buy you whatever you want, within reason. And then a cocktail in the rooftop bar. Deal?"

Her cousin's face softened. "Deal." She paused as they made their way through the kitchenware department. "I don't want a frying pan by the way." They carried on walking toward an array of shiny coffee machines. "One of these, on the other hand..." Marina fluttered her eyelids as she stopped in front of one Ella recognised.

"This one's pretty good. Sloane has it in her apartment."

"You've been in her apartment? You haven't told me this before." Marina's eyes widened. "You've had a coffee from her machine?" Her voice went up an octave and down in volume.

"We're friends. We live in the same block. So yes, I have."

Marina appeared to vibrate a little on the spot as she took in that fact. "And how was the apartment? Being there? The coffee?" She almost bit back her own words. "You know what, fuck the coffee, I don't care about the coffee." She paused to get her breath back. "How was being in her apartment?" She punched Ella's arm.

It hurt. Ella rubbed it.

Marina paid no heed.

"You never told me you were having coffee with Sloane!"

"I told you I was helping her out. You saw us together!"

"Professionally! Helping her to drive!" Marina shrieked, one hand on the now-forgotten coffee machine. "You didn't say you were hanging out. Having *coffee*."

Ella shrugged like it was nothing. Which it was. Sloane was just a normal person.

But then again, she wasn't at all. She was a Rolls Royce. A Ferrari. She gleamed.

"How's she coping being single?" Marina's gaze seemed to drill into Ella's brain. She only took a few seconds to jump to the conclusion Ella knew she would. "There's nothing you're not telling me, is there? Because you two were very pally when I saw you the other week. I believe I said words to that effect, and you shot me down, telling me it was professional only. But now there's coffee…"

Ella pictured her hand on Sloane's arm. The electricity in the room. The heat between her legs, both now and then.

She needed to nip this in the bud, for herself and for Marina.

"There's nothing going on. I'm her colleague and neighbour." No need to tell Marina about finding Sloane's family. That would only fuel her fire. "We live in the same building, we get on, we work together. I'm helping out a little more now she's injured, that's all." Ella's words were coming out sure and true. She tapped her hand on the top of Marina's, resting on the coffee machine. "But I can vouch for this machine."

Marina put a hand on her hip, and assessed Ella.

She was working out whether she should push this any further.

Ella gave her a sharp look.

Marina raised a single eyebrow. "Okay," she replied, still trapping Ella with her gaze. "How is her injury, anyway? Better or worse than the papers are saying?"

"About the same. Still early days. It might mean two months out, maybe less. Or if it doesn't heal how the doctors want, who knows?"

"Is she going to need an operation?"

"They don't think so. Just recovery time, which is the hardest for any athlete to accept."

"Are you really not coming to Christmas? Is she anything to do with that decision?"

"Of course not!" Ella replied, perhaps a little too forcefully. "I've just got a lot on and I need some downtime. I'm an introvert. It's how we work." It wouldn't be the first time she hadn't gone to see her family. Christmas used to be with her Mum, aunt, uncle and cousins, or just Ella and her mum towards the end. Sometimes, Ella just preferred a quiet Christmas.

"A Christmas away from Brad's kids?" Brad was Marina's brother and had three children under six.

"I never said that." But she gave her a confirmatory smile all the same. "I'll see your parents before, if not on the day, so don't fret." She patted the coffee machine. "Now, are we buying you this baby, or not?" Anything to get Marina's attention away from Sloane. It seemed to work.

"You must be on a wedge of cash if you're buying me this." Marina kissed Ella's cheek. "Just remember, I knew you when you were crap."

Now it was Ella's turn to laugh hard. Her cousin had a way with words.

* * *

Ella got back from her Saturday shopping a little buzzed from her two cocktails, and on a high from life. That's what spending time with her cousin did for her. She only lived two hours away on the coast. Marina had been right about one thing: Ella did need to make more time for her family whether it was Christmas or not.

She glanced at the top of her building as the cab dropped her off: Sloane's lights were on. Should she see how she was? The team had a big game tomorrow, and this was the second one Sloane was going to miss. Once in her flat, Ella messaged Sloane to see if she needed anything. The text came back instantly: *Cream for my coffee!*

Ella walked to her fridge. She had a carton of cream she'd been intending to use in a recipe. Sloane was in luck.

Five minutes later, she stood on Sloane's doorstep, assessing Sloane's sad, gorgeous face. This was the side not many people got to see. The face of the defeated athlete. Luckily, Ella was a pro at dealing with it.

"You smell good." Sloane pushed the door shut and followed Ella through to her lounge, the tap of her crutches and her orthopaedic boot echoing on the laminate floor.

She marched into her lounge, ignoring the way her body lit up at Sloane's words. Focusing on them would only bring complications.

"It's the scent of successful Christmas shopping and two pink gin cocktails. Marina says hello, by the way."

"Sweet freedom. Tell her I say hello back." Sloane lowered herself carefully down to her chaise sofa, then put her injured leg on some cushions. "Whereas I've been sitting here thinking about my wreck of a life. Injured. Single. Wondering if this fresh start is over before it's even begun. If my ankle's trashed, I won't make the international camp in April, then that's my World Cup fucked."

Sloane's words bounced and echoed around the room, which was still devoid of personal touches and soft edges.

Ella raised an eyebrow and put a hand on her hip. "Well, aren't you a ray of sunshine?" She paused. "Shall I make coffee so we can use the cream and put a smile on your face?"

It worked. "Yes, please. On the plus side, I've just demolished two packets of pickled onion flavour Monster Munch and have been wondering where they've been all my life."

Ella could see the damage on the floor next to Sloane.

"How did you get pickled onion Monster Munch when you can barely walk?"

"Nat and Welshy came to see me and brought gifts."

"Gifts of high nutritional value," Ella smirked.

"That's why it pays to have young friends."

Ella filled the coffee machine the way she'd seen Sloane do it a few times since she arrived, and leaned against the island. Her eye was immediately drawn to the cold, crisp evening outside, and the view of Salchester from the roof terrace, lit up like a thousand Christmas trees. It never failed to impress. "You can't mope when you have a view like this." Ella nodded towards it.

"I can if my career's over. I'm only going to be here for a year. I can't spend it on the sidelines."

Ella flinched at the admission. Her stomach clenched, and the room temperature plummeted. Sloane was only going to be here for a year. Ella was already attached. Perhaps it was a good thing nothing had happened between them. "Did you speak to anybody today? It's no good just sitting here, moping. No wonder you're down." She flicked on the coffee machine and it whirred into life, spitting black coffee into Sloane's white mug.

"I spoke to Nat and Welshy."

"About how you're feeling?"

"We talked about soccer, and how good Monster Munch is. And the new garlic hummus they have at Marks & Spencer, which is apparently da bomb. Does that count?"

Ella laughed, grabbed the coffee, added the cream, and brought it over to Sloane.

"Glad to hear you went deep. It must have been difficult to open up."

"You have no idea." A genuine smile grazed Sloane's face.

Sloane held her gaze and the moment shimmered between them. Then she blinked, brought the coffee to her lips, and let out a small groan. "Oh my god, thank you thank you thank you! That is what I've been missing. Why do you people not have Half-and-Half, or the UK equivalent?"

"I'll put in a request for Sainsbury's to stock it. If we say it's for you, the Salchester branch might oblige."

"Unless the manager is a United fan."

They grinned at each other. Being with Sloane was a breeze. Even if she was going to leave next year, Ella could just enjoy the now.

"Things are looking up already. You have cream for your coffee, and you've mastered driving on the correct side of the road."

"Wrong side."

"We'll agree to differ."

"And now I might not be able to drive for ages." She gestured to her ankle. "I won't be able to see my cousin either. I was going to her house next week."

Ella switched into professional mode. "It's a setback. You've had setbacks before. Call your cousin and get her to come here. Problem solved. You've lost games, been injured. You'll come back stronger. Where's your fighting spirit?"

"On vacation."

Whenever Sloane said an American word, Ella was struck by how American she sounded. Now was one of those times.

"It's a temporary blip, so view it as that."

Sloane narrowed her eyes. "You know what would cheer me up?"

Ella shook her head. "Tell me."

"You trying on clothes. I've been asking you to come and raid my wardrobe for ages, but you never do. It's the wish of a dying woman."

"You're dying now?"

"We're all dying, every second of every single day." She sipped her coffee and shot Ella a ridiculous, pleading face. "Please? For me? I'm hardly asking you to do something terrible."

She had to admit that was true. Plus, what could it hurt? Ella blew out her cheeks. "Okay. You're on." She jumped up. "You need a hand?"

But Sloane shook her head as Ella knew she would.

"Where are we going?"

"To my bedroom."

Ella's heart slammed in her chest. She could totally do this. Just wait until she told Marina. But even as the thought formed, she knew she never would. She hadn't shared much about her friendship with Sloane with anyone. She waited for Sloane to position her crutches, and followed her into her bedroom.

She wasn't sure what she expected, but it was similar to the lounge. Devoid of personal touches. As if Sloane didn't believe she was going to stay here. Maybe that was true. Maybe she had a premonition that things weren't going to work out. Ella swept that thought from her mind as her toes sank into the plush beige carpet underfoot. While everywhere else had laminate flooring, the bedroom was kinder to her feet and its acoustics.

Sloane took a seat on a wide, Barbie-doll-pink armchair and dropped her crutches on the carpet. They didn't make a sound. "I'm going to have to guide you here. Normally I'd get the clothes, but I'd be pretty useless." She pointed at the bank of built-in storage ahead. "The sliding door on the left is all the stuff I've been sent that's still in its packaging. Anything you want, take."

Ella slid open the wardrobe door and let out an audible splutter. The rail bent under the weight of the clothes hanging from it. "There's more on this rail than at a Next Boxing Day sale, and that's saying something."

Sloane laughed. "I've no idea if that's good or bad. There's more in another wardrobe, but let's start here. Grab as much as you can and put it on the bed. Then you can sort through, see what you like, discard what you don't, and then try on your selections."

Ella ferried armfuls of clothes and threw them on the bed. "I thought you'd get sports clothes, not fashion."

"Not just fashion, but high-end fashion." Sloane raised an eyebrow and flicked up some imaginary lapels on her plain white T-shirt. "I'm known for my style and flair. Designers and big brands want me wearing them when I go out."

"They might not be so keen on me in their threads."

Sloane shrugged. "They send me the clothes, but I can do what I want with them."

"Seriously, I'm not sure I can take these. Some of this is worth so much money." Ella thought of her mum and her Aunt Ursula, scrimping and saving all their lives to buy things. Then people like Sloane got sent so much stuff? It was obscene.

"You can and you will. Otherwise, it'll just sit in my wardrobe, and that's more of a waste, right?"

That was true. "I guess it would stop me buying more stuff I don't need."

"And save the planet into the bargain, it's the perfect arrangement. Plus, it'd be nice to give you something for a change. You've been a key part of me settling here, professionally and personally. And you brought me cream for my coffee, which means I have a huge debt to pay off."

Ella stared. Sometimes, she had to pinch herself that this was her life.

"Right back at ya. It's been nice living in the same block and getting to know you. Even if it won't be for much longer."

Sloane tilted her head. "What do you mean?"

"The club only paid for my flat for six months. After that, I need to find my own place. Which is up in January, so two months' time."

"You couldn't continue renting it?"

She shook her head. "It's already rented out again."

"Well, shit. I didn't know that." Sloane frowned.

"Why would you? I'm sure the club are paying for this flat for you as long as you want it." She gestured to the clothes. "You don't live in the real world." Ella winced. Had she gone too far?

"I guess I don't," Sloane replied, her voice flat, her face clouded over. Ella couldn't tell if she'd offended her.

"That came out harsher than I intended. It wasn't a dig, it was just facts."

Sloane nodded. "I get it. But if you need some help apartment hunting, maybe I can come with you and take a peek into this real world." She held Ella's gaze. "For now, you can step into mine. Let's get this fashion show started."

Ella flicked through and chose the clothes she liked. The atmosphere was a little frosty after her words, but as Ella held items up and posed in the mirror with Sloane in her ear, she relaxed and so did her host.

"Are you going to try any of this on?"

Ella shook her head. The thought of getting her kit off with Sloane watching made her far too hot under her non-existent collar. "I'll just take them back to mine. Whatever doesn't fit, I'll bring it back."

"Try a couple of pieces. Especially those dark green pants and that red and cream top. For me?" Sloane pulled out her pout.

Ella crumpled. "How can I say no to that face?"

"Works every time," Sloane grinned. "My bathroom is just there if you want some privacy."

She absolutely did.

Ella shut the door with some relief, and put the clothes on. Even with a thick wooden door between them, shedding her clothes in Sloane's bathroom still felt intimate. Like they were stepping over a line she couldn't come back from, which was ridiculous. She glanced in the mirror. She needed a haircut. But when didn't she? She smoothed out the top, so soft it caressed her skin. Everything fit perfectly. Now she just needed a mirror. She opened the door and stepped into the bedroom.

When Sloane looked up from her phone, her mouth dropped open slightly and her eyes widened. Her gaze ran down and then back up Ella's body, stopping at her mouth. At least that's what it felt like.

"What is it?" Ella looked down. "Does this look good or bad?"

Sloane's head shake was quick. "Very much good. You look absolutely stunning. That colour really suits you." She pointed at the wardrobes. "Slide the door beside it. There are a bunch of white sneakers in boxes. What size are you?"

"Seven."

"Seven UK? I have no idea what size that is in the US, but we look about the same." She gestured towards the boxes again. "Try them on. White sneakers would look lit with that."

Ella did as she was told, getting some box-fresh street trainers from an Adidas box. She slid them on and stood in front of the mirror. Sloane was right. Even she had to admit, she looked incredible. "I love it."

"So do I." Sloane's voice cracked when she spoke.

Something in the air had changed. Ella's hand shook as she ran it through her hair.

"Try on something else. That blue suit would look good with the ruffled lemon shirt." Sloane pointed. "Those sneakers would still work." Her face flushed red, and she rolled her neck and looked away.

Ella nodded, got the items, and went into the bathroom. She noticed things she hadn't the first time around. Sloane's Colgate blue gel toothpaste, the same one she used. Her Charlotte Tilbury fixing powder. Her Hugo Boss perfume. She took off the first lot of clothes, folded them and put them on the closed toilet seat. Then she put on the silk shirt, then the suit and trainers. She already felt like a million dollars. She didn't need to look in a mirror. She knew how these clothes made her feel. Like herself. It had been out there all along, she just hadn't known where to look. But with Sloane's help, things were changing. Who knew her new job would lead to this moment?

She stepped out of the bathroom. This time, Sloane was ready and waiting.

"Hot damn, Ms Carmichael. You wear that suit well." Sloane's gaze lasered her body.

Ella steadied her breathing as she stood in front of the mirror. Even she had to admit, she'd never looked like this before. "I look like a fucking movie star."

"And a rock star all rolled into one."

She spun, not caring how she came across. Who knew clothes could make you feel so light? Not Ella. She paused, got her breath back, and glanced at Sloane.

"I'm sorry I had a go at you earlier. But thanks for a peek into this world. I could get used to it."

"If I wasn't on crutches, I'd be up and dancing with you." Sloane held her gaze. "I'm really glad we met, you know. That first day. Off the clock. It's made us… something we might not have been otherwise." Sloane pushed herself upwards, grabbed her crutches and hobbled over to Ella. "I mean it." She was so close Ella could feel her breath on her face. "Even though getting injured sucks big time, I'm glad I moved and found this new team. But most of all, I'm glad I met you."

Delight looped and curled inside Ella. Closely followed by desire.

She grasped Sloane's hand in hers and looked into her blue eyes. "I'm glad we met, too."

Sloane licked her lips.

Ella tried desperately not to follow her tongue, and failed. She didn't care. Her heart punched her chest, and she had no idea where this was going. The one thing she knew for sure? She did not want to pull away. Not one little bit.

"Can I ask one favour before you go?"

"Anything." Staring at Sloane's perfect face, heat swirling

around them, she meant that, too. Whatever Sloane asked for, Ella would do it in a heartbeat.

"Can I get a hug? Being injured and away from home is lonely."

Ella's heart broke into tiny pieces. If she were injured, her cousin would be there, as would her aunt. But Sloane didn't have any family to rely on. Salchester was her family. Perhaps Ella was one of the closest friends she had over here.

"Of course."

Then Ella did what felt completely right. She moved closer so their bodies were touching, and then she wrapped her arms around Sloane in a way she hoped told her she was protected. That what she was doing would work in the long run. That she was loved. She shuffled her body forward a little more and inhaled Sloane's scent of shampoo and Monster Munch.

Sloane settled her head on Ella's shoulder and let out a satisfied sigh as Ella tightened her grip on her waist.

Sloane did the same.

They stood there, Ella's eyes closed, for what felt like forever, simply revelling in being this close, finally. At least, Ella did. But she knew from the contented sounds dropping from Sloane's lips she was providing the comfort she sought too, which pleased Ella. Moving and starting afresh was lonely. Sloane had put up a good front until now. However, slowly, but surely, her defences were melting.

Chapter Fifteen

It was a long three weeks following her injury, and Sloane had spent them focused on getting back to full fitness with long hours on the bike, strength training and a regular icing routine. Eventually, the days nudged into December, Ella delivered a small, decorated tree to Sloane's flat, and she could finally see things might have turned a corner. A recurrence of her ankle injury wasn't how she'd wanted to greet her first Christmas away from home.

However, now the prognosis was that she could be back as early as January if she did exactly what she was told, her mood had shifted to moderately upbeat. If she discounted the fact that Salchester had lost their latest Champions' League group game. If they lost again next week, they were out of the competition. There was nothing Sloane could do about it, but she felt responsible.

When she'd told Ella, she'd received a raised eyebrow in return. As Ella pointed out, they might have lost even if Sloane had been on the field. It wasn't a given. "Plus, you know the drill: stop worrying about things you can't control."

Sloane knew the drill well. It was just easier said than done.

There was no doubt, though, that Ella was a constant plus point in her life. She popped in for coffee and pep talks regularly now, and in the two weeks since that hug, they'd both been skating around it and what it meant. But sometimes, late at night when Sloane was on the couch alone, she closed her eyes and could still remember every intimate detail. The warmth of Ella's thigh against her own. The way Ella had held her just right. The softness of her.

Sloane had held on too long, and yet, it hadn't seemed long enough. When they'd eventually let go, Sloane had stared into Ella's hazel eyes with so much to say, but nothing had come out. Instead, Ella had hastily packed up the clothes she was taking with never-ending thanks, and scurried out the door.

Nothing since. Coffees had been drunk, Christmas trees had been delivered, but there'd been no more hugs. There were a couple of occasions where Sloane thought Ella might be edging towards one, but she'd pulled out at the last minute. It was probably for the best. Sloane was hardly an attractive proposition, was she? Newly single, damaged goods. Ella knew her whole story. Her broken background, her failed relationships. She probably wanted to keep things as they were. Friends.

However, whenever Sloane thought that, she cast her mind back to after her injury. How Ella had looked at her and touched her. To the night she tried on her clothes. That hug. There was something there. But would either of them be brave enough to find out what it was?

Sloane couldn't think about that now. Today, she was meeting her cousin, Cathy, for the first time. Just the thought made Sloane's skin blaze with excitement, but she didn't want to get carried away. Her cousin's son, Ryan, had seemed lovely. However, people could deceive, and her fame might be an issue. All of which meant Sloane was taking the meeting step by step.

If it went well, great. If not, she'd chalk it up to experience. That it was never meant to be. However, before all of that, she had a call with her agent.

Sloane walked over to the kitchen island, and opened her laptop in preparation. She'd avoided speaking to Adrianne since her injury. In fact, she'd avoided speaking to most people, which was what she did. But there was only so long she could put her agent off. Adrianne had Sloane's best interests at heart, but she also wanted to check in on her asset, to see if she was about to lose her 15 per cent. Her agent hadn't been happy with Sloane taking off overseas, but it wasn't her decision. It was the first time Sloane had gone against her advice and it had made their relationship frosty.

Her screen lit up with an incoming call. Sloane grabbed her bottle of water and settled on a stool in her kitchen. She clicked the green button, and Adrianne's face popped up.

"There's my star client!" Adrianne's tired tone didn't match her words. She rubbed her right eye as she spoke, direct from the kitchen table of her Tribeca apartment, not her usual office. In the background, her kitchen counter was stacked with dishes, and Sloane spied a half-empty bottle of red wine. Adrianne always told her she lived in organised chaos, and she wasn't lying.

"I could do with a little more enthusiasm."

"It's 8am, and I haven't had my first cup of coffee yet. That's the best I've got," she replied with a throaty rasp. Sloane always joked that if you imagined a caricature of a New Yorker, Adrianne was it. A feisty, loud-mouth, 40-something broad who *always* got her own way. This morning, her short, red-tinged hair stuck up at all angles, and she had a tell-tale sleep mark down her right cheek. Adrianne carried the aromas of coffee and Marlboro lights with her everywhere she went. If she leaned forward, Sloane was pretty sure she could sniff them through the screen.

"How's the ankle?"

"Getting there. Physio reckons I could be back by mid-January if I don't push it. So, six weeks give or take for a full recovery. It could have been worse."

"No kicking any balls until you're fixed. You're my prize asset, remember."

"I bet you say that to all your clients."

"Damn straight." Adrianne gave her a wide grin. "But you're following doctor's orders? I know you have an issue doing that normally."

Sloane smiled. "I really am. I'm going out of my mind training solo, spending hours on my bike, doing weights, in the hydro pool. But I know it works. I've done it before. It doesn't stop it from sucking big time."

"Just keep doing what you're doing, and things will get back to normal." Adrianne paused. "Talking of which, how's life otherwise? What have you been up to after you finished moping, which I'm sure you gave your all to. I remember your first big injury: you thought it was the end of the world. I'm not there to hold your hand this time, and you wouldn't even take my calls." She balled her fist, pouted, and pressed her fist into her chest. "I've got feelings too, you know. But tell me: who talked you out of your black hole this time? Because I know it was someone. You can't do this on your own. It's a weakness on your part."

Sloane laughed at the accuracy. That was the trouble with

an agent you'd known for over a decade. She didn't take any bullshit, and she knew her inside out.

"I've had a few people. My physio. My manager. And my performance coach, Ella, has been great. I couldn't have done this without her. She's been cheerleading me from the start, and she lives in my building too, so she keeps me topped up with coffee. And cream to go in it, more importantly."

Sloane smiled when she said 'cheerleading'. Such an American term, but also, Ella's term. She realised too late that a smile had taken up residence on her face. Adrianne would notice that. Sloane tried to rearrange her features to a semblance of normal, but feared she was too late. "Did you know this country doesn't drink their coffee with cream? It's an absolute scandal." She was blathering to cover up.

Adrianne didn't respond right away, simply stared into the camera. All of which made Sloane think she'd definitely said too much. Her agent adjusted her position before she spoke. "Is that a Christmas tree behind you?"

Sloane turned, then nodded. "Ella bought it for me. She thought it might cheer me up."

A knowing nod. "Seems like she's really there for your every need." Another pause. "Is she there for *every* need?"

"Everything her job dictates," Sloane replied, sweeping her agent's unspoken questions under the metaphorical carpet. It was time for a gear change. "Did you see the email about me doing schools outreach while I can't train? I did my first this week and it went really well. I was worried the kids might not know who I was, but they all did."

"That's because you're a superstar, sweetheart." Adrianne got up and went out of shot. "I hope you smiled for the selfies and didn't kick a single ball!" Seconds later, she came back with what Sloane guessed was a fresh coffee.

"Of course. I'm always smiling. You know me."

"Unless you speak about Jess. What's going on there? I saw she's all over her socials with Brit now. She didn't even take a breath."

"You know Jess. She can't stand to be alone or out of the spotlight. She can do whatever the hell she wants as far as I'm concerned." Sloane was surprised to realise she meant it, too. "All I know for sure is, I'm glad to be out of it."

"On this issue, I'm in total agreement. Jess could never decide what she wanted. She'll get rid of Brit soon enough, too." Her agent sipped her coffee and lasered Sloane with her gaze. She was just as good at doing it remotely as she was in real life. "I take it with getting injured and moping, you haven't met anybody else yet?"

Ella in those green pants and red-and-white top sailed through Sloane's mind. She pushed the image away and shook her head. "I'm focused on my recovery, nothing else."

"I'd believe that if you were a robot, but I have it on good authority you're not." Adrianne wagged a finger at Sloane. "Tell me when you're ready. I know there's something you're not saying."

Damn her.

"But in the meantime, keep doing the promo and keep healing." Adrianne wrapped her knuckle on her kitchen table. "One more thing: are you coming back for the holidays? I know you weren't initially, but now you're not playing a game every few days, is it a possibility? If it is, I'll start letting the press know you're available."

Sloane hadn't given it any consideration. However, the thought of spending Christmas with her parents and being grilled by the press about her love life didn't fill her with seasonal cheer. Even though people cared about what she did off the field here, it wasn't nearly as much as it was in her homeland. She didn't want to go back to intense scrutiny.

"I don't think so. I'm still a part of the team and I'm still going to all the home games." She hadn't truly allowed herself to think about the holidays too much. If she did, she might feel terribly lonely.

They talked for another half an hour about Sloane's commitments and contracts, as well as how Adrianne's son, Todd, was getting on at college. No, Sloane didn't want to link up with a well-known dog food brand. Yes, she would consider a new, ethical skincare company. Yes to interviews with Vogue and All Out Goals, but only once she'd recovered. "I'm not being photographed on crutches." Todd, apparently, had his first ever boyfriend. Having known him since he was ten, Sloane glowed like a proud auntie. Whereas Adrianne declared the young man, "not Jewish, but cute. It could be worse."

Sloane glanced up at her oven to check the time. She had to go. "I have a meeting in 15 minutes that I have to prepare for."

"Isn't it Saturday over there? What meeting do you have that I don't know about? I'm still your agent, right?"

"Yes, you are, but I need to keep some mystery." Sloane gave Adrianne a wink she knew would infuriate her.

"Something's going on with you, Sloane. I could tell that as soon as I saw you in that button-down shirt. You never wear those on the weekend. Mark my words. I'm getting it out of you next time."

"Bye, Adrianne!"

Adrianne raised a hand. "Before you dash off to meet your mystery woman, I have something else for you. A car, to be precise. You don't have one yet, do you?"

Sloane blinked. "No."

"That's so unlike you. You loved your Subaru, which is still sitting in my driveway. Todd's keeping it going, by the way. He says thanks!" Sloane had given her car on indefinite loan to Todd until she got back to the US.

"I was a bit wary of driving on the wrong side of the road. But Ella's taken me out a few times and gotten me over my nerves."

A smile crept onto Adrianne's face. "Now I know something's going on. You let someone else tell you what to do willingly, and admitted your fears?"

"I'm a professional sportsperson, Adrianne. I take instruction and criticism every day and do it well."

"Uh huh." Her face creased hard with her smile. "Back to the point. Would you like a car? Because I have a sponsor who'd like to give you one."

"Yes please. Although obviously I can't drive right now. But soon. Is it a cool car, and do I get to choose the colour?"

"Already done for you. A silver Jeep. Do I have your blessing."

"You do, and I love you." Sloane could just imagine what Ella would have to say about this gift. Another example of Sloane not living in the real world. A tiny sliver of guilt lodged in her stomach.

"Yeah, yeah. I'll mail you the details. You know the rules. Social media presence showing you in it, I'll send through the contract."

"You're the best, Adrianne!"

Sloane blew her a kiss before she shut down.

* * *

Adrianne was right: Sloane had dressed up to meet Cathy. She was also hella nervous. Her stomach churned so much, her coffee – with cream – was in danger of reappearing. She certainly hadn't been this on edge for her debut with Rovers. Soccer – or football – she knew back to front. Meetings with family members she hadn't known existed until very recently, less so.

When the buzzer went, Sloane pressed it and waited for the elevator to arrive. She still couldn't call it a lift. Moments later, the door opened. The woman who stood there looked remarkably familiar. It wasn't that she looked that much like any of Sloane's family. Rather, she had a familiarity Sloane couldn't quite put her finger on. Her cousin wore a padded pea-green winter coat that could be mistaken for a duvet, her cheeks rosy from the December chill.

"Cathy?"

Cathy beamed, clutching a bunch of colourful flowers. "Sloane." She glanced at her boot. "You weren't joking when you said you were in the wars." Her accent was so thick, you could use it for insulation.

"It'll be off in a few weeks hopefully. But thank you so much for coming to see me instead." Sloane could have gotten Ella to drive her or even the club car, but the thought of hobbling around a stranger's house hadn't appealed. In her own flat, there was far less to knock over.

"These are for you." She gave Sloane the flowers.

"Thank you so much." Sloane didn't have a vase – she'd have to ask Ella. For now, she filled the sink and rested the flowers there. Then she got Cathy settled on her couch, despite her protestations that she could make the drinks. Sloane allowed her to collect her coffee once she'd made it, and then they sat in touching distance. But they still hadn't touched.

They might be family, but right now, they were relative strangers.

"This is a bit weird, isn't it?" Cathy sipped her coffee and gave Sloane a smile.

She'd removed her hat and ruffled her hair, the colour of Sloane's favourite Madagascan vanilla ice cream. Now, one side stuck up at an angle. Sloane smiled internally.

"When Ryan came home and told me about meeting you, I thought that knock on the head he took at that game had affected him more than he realised. However, Matt confirmed you were real, and then I got your text." She shook her head. "Sorry it's taken so long to meet, what with my work and your injury. Plus, I'm still getting to grips with exactly how it all fits together. I mean, you're a world football star and very American!"

Sloane smiled. "Guilty as charged."

"What I know is that your grandad was my mum's brother? I think that probably makes us cousins of some sort?"

She sounded as confused as Sloane. "I think so, but if I ponder it too long my head starts to hurt. Let's go with cousins." She stared at Cathy. "You look familiar, so maybe we share a mouth or a nose?"

"Sounds painful."

That broke the slight awkwardness that had hovered since

Cathy came in. She had a sense of humour. This wouldn't be the longest coffee of Sloane's life.

"Can I say also, I'm glad I came here and not the other way around. This flat is far posher than my house." Cathy got up and stared out the window. "You can see the Arndale from here, can't you?"

"So I've been told."

"I guess this is what happens when you're a superstar for a living. You get to live in flash pads."

Sloane couldn't deny it. She also didn't want to make Cathy uncomfortable. This wasn't a them and us situation. More than anything else, Sloane wanted Cathy to feel at home. "I'm lucky this is where the club housed me." Plus, she got to stay, unlike Ella. She couldn't imagine living here without her. An arrow of sadness pierced Sloane. Who was she going to get a vase from when Ella was gone? She wouldn't think about that now.

"Clearly you earned it," Cathy replied. "I must admit, I wasn't so up on women's football. I tend to go and watch my two sons more. But I heard about your transfer in the news, and I can't believe I'm related to a World Cup winner." She shook her head and sat back on the couch. "It's incredible that you play too, though. There must be a football gene in our blood, because our family history is littered with players, some of them pretty good. You're probably the best, though. Nobody ever had a transfer fee on their head before."

"I'd love to know more about that if you know things. Ryan and Matt at the club told me to ask Barry about the club history? But I got the impression there was a story to tell. Something Matt said about my great-grandmother."

Cathy gave her a puzzled look. "You sound *so* American, it's a wonder we're related. But we are. And yes, there is a story to tell about your great-grandmother. Also, my grandmother."

That comment made Sloane sit back and shake her head. "How mad is that? We share the same grandparents." Her chest went tight and heat travelled through her. This was a real-life living relative. Someone she shared history and bloodline with. Tears bubbled up. She hadn't expected that.

However, when she looked at Cathy, her eyes glistened, too.

Sloane smiled. "This is emotional, isn't it?" She pointed towards the kitchen island. "There are some tissues over there? Would you mind getting them? It's probably quicker if you do."

Cathy obliged and they both took one and blew their noses. Then they laughed.

"This is like an episode of *Long Lost Family*. I was thinking that as I drove over today. I always cry at those too, but they haven't involved me before."

"We have that show in the US, too. I cry a river."

"At least we're on the same page." Cathy blew her nose again. "The big family news is that you're not the first female football star among us. That's what I mean; we have a football gene."

Sloane's ears pricked up at that news. "Tell me more. Did you play?"

Sadness flickered on Cathy's face as she nodded. "I did. But like most kids back when I was growing up, I had to stop. Girls weren't allowed to play football. With so much against you playing, you eventually give up trying. Which is why I'm so thrilled you are where you are. At the top of your game."

"I'm proud to keep the family flag flying. But please tell me the story."

Cathy nodded. "Your great-grandfather, Robert, played for the local team, Kilminster United, as you know. He was a nifty winger by all accounts. But that's not the story. The story is that your great-grandmother played for the team, too."

Sloane narrowed her eyes. "For Kilminster United?"

Cathy nodded. "Yep. Eliza Power was a star striker for a season and a half, until she was rumbled."

"Rumbled?" Even though the British spoke the same language, sometimes they didn't. "I don't get it."

"Your great-grandmother pretended she was a man so she could play football. The FA had banned women from playing on their grounds by then, but she loved the game through her teens. She used to play with her two brothers. They all hatched a plan to get her on the team because she was that good.

"I don't know the proper facts because they weren't recorded, but I know she cut her hair short so she'd pass as a man. Maybe she strapped down her breasts too, who knows? As far as I know, her team all knew, but they all kept it a secret for a good while. But I just love the thought of her wanting to play so much, she was prepared to pretend to be a man."

Sloane didn't know what to say. Pride pressed against her sternum. Amazement nestled alongside. "That is not the story I was expecting." She almost laughed at her understatement. "Was she queer, too? Was the marriage a cover?"

Cathy shook her head. "I wondered the same, but I don't think so. They had a very loving marriage as far as I'm aware. You don't know what goes on behind closed doors, and maybe they had an agreement. We'll never know. But they had three children together, however it happened. Your great-gran met your great-granddad when she was on the team. They were quite the duo: him the dynamite winger, she the star striker."

Fierce admiration and shock burned through Sloane as she pointed her finger to her chest. "Like me." She reminded herself to breathe.

"Exactly like you," Cathy agreed.

More tears welled up, but this time, Sloane didn't try to stuff them down. She allowed them to happen. This was monumental. She was the great-granddaughter of a female soccer star. A trailblazing, pioneering star at that. This was the best news possible.

"I can't believe I come from a long line of kick-ass soccer stars."

"Football," Cathy countered.

"Whatever," Sloane said. She leaned forward and wiped her eye again. "I love that she was so bold, prepared to do whatever it took to play. And she held her own in a men's team."

"She did. More than held her own. Until she was found out by other teams, and made to leave. But she'd left her mark by then, and met her husband."

Sloane held up both her arms above her head and let out a yelp. "I've been feeling a bit sorry for myself since my injury. But you coming here and telling me this has inspired me. I'm going to come back stronger from this injury and score more goals in honour of my great-grandmother. Because I get to do this for a living, something she could never have even dreamt of. I owe it to her legacy to make this season my best ever."

Cathy pointed at Sloane's boot. "You need to get that off first."

"I will. A few weeks' time, every ball I kick is going to be for Eliza."

"She would approve," Cathy said. "I just hope the club can survive in the future, too. The past holds great stories and memories. But the club is fighting for its life. If you have any connections who might think about sponsoring the team, that would be so appreciated. We want future generations to have stories like these, too."

Sloane nodded. "I'll ask around."

When her cousin left, Sloane had too much energy racing around her body. The story of her great-gran was a story for the ages. She wanted to run around her flat, to scream it from the rooftops. It was such an incredible story, it had to be shared. Who to share it with, though? The first name to pop into her head? Ella. Sloane grabbed her phone and messaged her.

I just had the most incredible meeting with my cousin. She brought me flowers. Do you have a vase I can put them in? I have so much to tell if you're free later.

She pressed send and then pulled open the glass doors and walked onto her terrace. Sloane clutched the top of her balcony wall and breathed in the city. The same air her family had been breathing for centuries. She belonged here. Today was the first day she'd truly felt that. If the rest of the season went well, hopefully she could get to know her cousins, too. Optimism flowed through her. This was the new chapter she'd craved after all. She had a new team, new family, new friends.

Her phone beeped. A message from Ella. Sloane clicked on it, smiling. Maybe she could come up and they might even have dinner – or tea – while she told her all about it. Perhaps they might hug again. Even the thought sent waves of hope crashing through her.

I can't tonight, but I'll leave a vase outside your door. I can't stop – I'm off on a date. Marina finally made me swipe right and I got a match.

Sloane's optimism took an uppercut to the face.

A date? Ella had mentioned dating in passing. Sloane had even encouraged her. Why the hell had she done that? But apparently, it was happening tonight.

She had no hold over Ella, but then again, wasn't there something budding between them? Or did Ella only think of her as a friend? But she didn't believe that for a second. They'd shared too many moments. Too many looks. However, they hadn't done anything about it. That was the problem.

Now it might be too late.

Chapter Sixteen

Ella didn't know what the hell she was doing here. She'd dropped the vase outside Sloane's door, then scurried away. It had felt weird to send that message to her, and it would feel just as strange to chat to Sloane when she was about to go on a date. Even though they were just friends. Who occasionally hugged and shared intense, breath-taking stares.

Ella was friends with a gorgeous superstar. If Sloane had wanted anything more, she would have acted on it by now.

Hence, she'd caved and arranged a date. If she couldn't go out with Sloane, she should at least see if she could go out with someone else.

When Ella arrived at the cafe where she'd arranged to meet Minnie for coffee and cake before seeing a movie at a nearby arthouse cinema, her worries only magnified. She'd prefer to be here with Sloane, hearing about her meet-up with her cousin. It sounded like there was a lot to tell. However, Sloane was likely to be gone next year. Which meant that Ella had to live in the real world and see if she could meet someone local. Perhaps someone like Minnie.

When she walked in – it was one of those cafes with local art on the wall and the faint smell of incense in the background – Ella spotted her date right away. It was only as she drew up at the table she noticed her greying hair, the defined lines on her face. How old was that profile photo? Ella would put this woman at closer to 50 than her stated 38. But she was going to give this a chance. She was not ageist.

"Minnie?"

The woman stood and held out a hand. "Ella. Lovely to meet you. Good hair energy!"

Ella frowned. Weird thing to say.

Minnie ran her gaze up and down Ella. "Nice top, too." If Ella was for sale, Minnie may well have bought her.

Ella hung her coat on a nearby rack, then sat opposite Minnie, guilt weighing on her shoulders. She'd worn one of the new tops Sloane had gifted her, but now that decision felt all wrong. Like she was using Sloane's generosity against her. She pushed that thought to the back of her mind.

"Can I get you a coffee? Some cake? I waited until you were here to order."

Ella nodded. "A flat white and whatever cake looks best. Surprise me."

Minnie nodded, smoothed down her black jumper and walked to the counter.

Ella's phone pinged, and she got out her phone. A breaking story about women's football stared back at her. When she clicked, her heart stalled. It was a photo of Sloane and Jess, followed by a photo of Jess and a blonde woman. Ella's mouth went dry. Was this a story about Sloane being back with Jess and returning to the States? Because if so, it wasn't the version of her life Sloane had told Ella for the past few weeks.

However, the story was the opposite. The blonde was Jess's new girlfriend, Britney Navas. The one she'd cheated on Sloane with for months. Their relationship was made official in an Instagram post, which meant it was time for wild speculation and regurgitated photos of Sloane and Jess in happier times. Ella hoped Sloane didn't have the same alerts set up on her phone. What a strange world she lived in. One where her private life was pored over and commented on by strangers.

A few weeks ago, just before her injury, Sloane was snapped getting into a cab after training, and again having a coffee with Layla. It wasn't a world that Ella lived in. This cafe was more Ella's world. Perhaps she should give Minnie a chance. Coffee and cake were more her speed than scandal and paparazzi. Although having spent time with Sloane, she couldn't only associate her with that. Sloane was kind, thoughtful and generous. Also smokin' hot. She'd never clicked with someone so well. But it could go nowhere.

"Here we go. I got carrot and walnut cake, and your coffee." Minnie put the plate on the table. "You're not allergic to nuts, are you?"

Ella shook her head. "I'm not." She put her phone away and focused on her date. It was the least she owed Minnie.

"Lovely to finally meet you. You're my third date this week."

Ella stiffened. She wasn't sure about date etiquette, but she was pretty sure that wasn't in the rules. "Not all in this cafe, I hope."

Minnie shook her head. "I took number one bowling. Number two got a chippy tea. Number three gets cake and cinema."

Reduced to a number within five minutes of meeting. Ella felt like she was on offer at the Asda delicatessen. Perhaps in the discount section.

"What is it you do? I know you said some sort of sports development role?"

Ella nodded, and explained her job.

Minnie nodded, looking vaguely impressed. "I love that you work with all sports, and not just football. I feel like football gets too much of the spotlight, you know? Take the England women's cricket, hockey, or rugby teams. They all won gold or a major trophy long before the football team. Yet it's the football team who gets all the plaudits." She shook her head. "I'm not a huge fan."

Ella's stomach lurched. Minnie hated football? That could be a problem. "I still think what the women achieved this summer was fantastic and against the odds, don't you? They won in spite of the obstacles in their way."

Minnie shrugged. "I prefer rugby. Yes, I agree it was a great achievement, but it's football. Me and football don't gel. Take that woman who just signed for Rovers this summer. The American. Sloane somebody?"

Ella's buttocks clenched. "Sloane Patterson."

Minnie curled her lips in distaste. "Yes, her. I'm sure she's good at what she does, but she got so much hype and press about her move. But she's American. Why are we importing stars when we have great ones here already? It leaves a bad taste in my mouth."

Minnie did not mince her words.

"You don't think it's market forces? That it's good for our players to mix with World Cup winners? Because I do. Plus, Sloane has done a lot of outreach work, too. Pushed for equal pay in the US. She's not just a football star, she's a women's rights activist and campaigner."

Minnie held Ella's stare. "She's probably a very nice person. But I don't like what she stands for. Plus, she's a bit too good looking for her own good."

Finally, something they could agree on.

"What is it you do?"

"I'm an estate agent."

Maybe Ella could get something from this meeting. "Sales or rental? Only, I'll be looking for a rental in a few weeks."

Minnie's eyes lit up. "Maybe this was meant to be. We become a couple, and I find your dream home."

At least one of those might come true. Ella's mind wandered back to when she'd watched the game at Kilminster with Sloane. What she'd said about Jess never wanting to watch a men's game. Ella loved the game in all its forms, just like Sloane. She was happiest watching a game she cared about. She cared about Sloane, which meant she'd cared about watching the club her family played for.

That thought sounded an alarm in her head. Whether Sloane was available or not, Ella didn't want to be here with Minnie. But she couldn't cut and run before she'd even finished the cake. When she looked up, Minnie held out her card. "We're one of the best agents in the city. Take a look at our website and see if anything tickles your fancy."

Ella already knew it wouldn't be Minnie.

* * *

When Ella got home later that night, she already had a message from Minnie saying she'd had a great time and would love to see her again. Ella had gone to see the film in the end, but she hadn't really taken any of it in. She'd skilfully avoided any physical contact with Minnie so she didn't give her the wrong impression, departing with non-committal goodbyes and a kiss on both cheeks, as if they were in Venice and not Salchester on a chilly December evening. Attached to Minnie's message were two rental flats for her to consider. Perhaps this app was Minnie's way of drumming up business.

Ella glanced up to the top floor before she walked into her building. Sloane's light was still on. She'd love to go and see her, find out about her cousin. But it was nearly 11pm, so it was a little late. Yes, they were friends, but they also had boundaries.

However, when she pulled out her phone, Sloane had sent a photo of her flowers in Ella's vase, with two words attached.

Thank you x.

Those two words meant more to Ella than anything Minnie had said to her all night long.

Chapter Seventeen

It was the first time Sloane had been back in the main training gym since her injury and it was bittersweet. She wanted to do all the things everyone around her was doing: jump squats, sprint drills, leg presses. She even missed the sled push, and she hated the sled push normally. However, for now, those were out of bounds.

The good thing? Chatting with her teammates. Yes, they'd visited her, but this was different. Being back among the banter was the best thing for her. She'd had long chats with the other injured players – male and female – when they were with the physios and in the rehab gym, but this was different energy. It was positive. Vibrant.

"How are you, Patts?" Layla skulled a bottle of water, beads of sweat visible on her forehead. It's what Sloane missed the most. Getting sweaty, making her muscles burn, putting everything she had into the session.

"Hanging in there." Sloane added a smile to soften her words. "But the good news is I should be out of the boot by next week, and then I can spend Christmas and New Year really getting fit. The doctor said I could be playing again by the first week of January, but I think maybe a week or two more. But things are heading in the right direction, fingers crossed."

She pointed a finger in Layla's direction. "Now you just have to keep winning our bread-and-butter WSL games so we can keep pace with United. Because they're not giving this up for anybody, are they?"

Layla shook her head. "They're not. But we're not either." She put her hands on her hips. "Going out of the Champions League was shit, but now we can focus on the league and the FA Cup. If we can keep in touching distance and then bring back our star striker, who knows what might happen?"

"Who knows indeed."

Salchester Rovers had only lost once in the league since Sloane got injured, which she was thrilled about. But December was always clogged with games, and this year was no exception. Exiting the Champions League had hurt. Could she have changed the outcome if she'd played? Whatever, they had to learn, look at the positives and go again. That way, she could hopefully step up and make a difference in the second half of the season. That was her goal, at least.

Nat walked over and gave her a hug. "Missing you out there. Especially when it comes to penalties."

They'd got one in the Champions League game against Lyon when it was 0-0. In Sloane's absence, Nat had stepped up, and missed. Sloane hadn't attended the game as the weather had been crazy icy, and Lucy had told her to stay home. She'd watched it on TV though, and had felt Nat's pain.

Sloane stood and gave Nat a hug. The younger striker melted into her.

"You did great. Remember it takes courage to take a penalty. They're all about glory or failure. There's no in between. But you were prepared to step up and take the risk. High stakes.

Sometimes you win, sometimes you lose, just like I told you in my SMS after the game."

"You hardly ever lose." Nat pulled back and puffed out her cheeks.

"Er, hello? I missed a penalty in the World Cup final." It was what drove Sloane to practice as much as she did now. If she closed her eyes and conjured the stadium, she could still feel the itch of failure burned into her core.

Nat gave her a grin. "Even you're not perfect."

"Nobody is. You did great. And you'll learn from it." Sloane gave her a playful punch on the arm. "Because you're Nat Tyler."

On hearing her name, Nat visibly rose in stature. "I am, aren't I?"

Sloane marvelled again at how young and impressionable she was. She remembered when she was the young hotshot coming in and sharing the limelight, ready to soak everything up and learn. Now she was the old-timer. The one getting injured more easily. But she could still help Nat from the sidelines.

"You're doing great out there, leading the line." Sloane paused. "Just remember your movement in the box. Come off the shoulders of defenders, surprise them. You've got youth on your side. Especially when you're playing Leverton this weekend. Their backline is creaky. Jump around. Make them sweat. Sweep them off their feet in the best way possible."

Nat gave her a firm nod. "I will. Are you coming to the game?"

"I hope so. I'm getting my boot off around that time, which will make things easier. But even if I'm not there, I'll be watching on TV. Watching us win." She paused. "Have you decided if you're going home for Christmas yet?" Nat and her parents were on speaking terms, but they still hadn't properly talked.

She gave a slow, wincing nod.

Sloane understood the energy precisely, having lived it in technicolour.

"I want to see my sisters. Plus, if we don't talk, things are never going to move forward."

Sloane gave her another hug. "You always have to be the brave one. It sucks, but you do." She'd always been the brave one, and she'd always ended up disappointed. "I know I haven't been around as much to chat to, but you're always welcome at my apartment if things get rough. My door's always open."

"Thanks. Ella told me the same." Nat gave her a shy smile and wandered off.

Sloane glanced at Layla. "How's things with you? How's Sara and little Darius doing?"

Layla gave her the widest grin in the world. "They're good. We went out this week and bought the absolute cutest outfit for him – jeans, a white T-shirt and a fake leather jacket. He looks like a little dude and yes, I am living the childhood I never got to have through him, and I am here for it."

Sloane laughed. "I can totally get behind that. There are worse reasons to have kids than wanting to dress them up in cute clothes."

"Exactly. My parents are arriving next week, too, so we're not buying him many presents. He's going to be inundated via his Norwegian family. Mum's warned me she's bringing an extra suitcase."

A stab of pain hit Sloane. No matter how many times she thought she was over her parents' lack of love and support, when she heard about Layla's family, who were the complete opposite, it still stung. She loved Layla's family, and she envied her. Layla had invited her for Christmas, but she'd declined. She didn't want to get in the way of their family reunion.

She'd been hoping that maybe she and Ella might spend it together. But now, maybe Ella was about to spend it with her new girlfriend.

Even the thought winded her.

Layla sat on the bench beside Sloane. "How you feeling about Jess and Brit being so in your face?"

They weren't as in her face now she lived here, which she was grateful for. "Life moves on. I have. It's been over for a while. It's only the fans who are shocked."

"It'll blow over."

"I hope so." The smell of Ella's floral perfume floated through her brain. She smiled at Layla. "I'm ready for the rest of my life to start now."

* * *

Sloane hobbled through to the player canteen, and chef Julian kindly brought lunch to her table. Not having two hands to hold stuff was a real bummer, and she'd be happy when she got that ability back. A tray landing on her table made her look up.

Ella.

"Mind if I join you? You look like you could use some cheering up. I'm guessing first day back in the gym means you're questioning your progress all over again?"

It wasn't only in the gym, but Sloane wasn't going to admit that.

"Am I that obvious?"

Ella tapped the side of her nose. "Only to those in the know." She paused while she took off her bag and stowed it on the seat next to her. "Although I don't know why you are. Not only are you a hotshot – which everybody knows – you're also in the top 20 of the Pink Power list as of this morning. Did you see that?"

"My agent sent me something, but I didn't click the link. I'm not feeling very powerful right now, if that makes a difference." Sloane was sure the crease at the top of her forehead got a workout. Her mum sat on her shoulder, telling her to smooth out her brow. Sloane flicked the tiny devil away.

"Not one iota. Although you need to get a whole lot more powerful to overtake the 16 people ahead of you."

"Who are they and have I ever heard of them? I don't think I've made the Pink Power list before. It's a British thing, right?"

Ella nodded. "You're being pipped by someone who came third in *Great British Bake Off*, a reality TV singer turned Instagram star, and a YouTuber, to name but three. But you are the first American footballer to break the top 20, so stand proud."

Sloane made herself sit up straight, then she flexed her arm. "How's that for powerful?" She studied her biceps. "I'm sure they're shrinking."

Ella snorted. "Every time I see you you've just finished a workout, so I doubt that." She paused, glancing at Sloane's lunch. "I see you went for salad. Healthy choice. I, on the other hand, have gone for classic British comfort food: eggs and beans on toast. Would it fly in America?"

"One hundred per cent no." Sloane laughed. It was the first time she'd done so today. Ella had that uncanny knack to make it happen. "How's your morning?"

"Better than yours?" Ella shrugged. "Admin, paperwork, a meeting with the boss. The usual. Last day in this week and I've got the afternoon free after your session," she checked her watch, "in half an hour."

She was in a very chipper mood. Sloane didn't want to know why.

But then again, she did.

"Thanks for the vase the other day. How did your date go?" She scolded herself internally for bringing it up so quickly, but it was out of her mouth before she could do anything about it. Sloane braced for more smiles and tales of dinner by candlelight. She had no hold over Ella. Her role as a friend was to be happy for her. She prepared her happy face.

However, it wasn't needed. Instead, Ella wrinkled her face, sat back and blew a raspberry.

It was the best sound ever.

"Not going anywhere." She stared at Sloane. "She wasn't really what I was looking for. Plus, she didn't like football."

"Ouch." Sloane wanted to punch the air.

"I know. However, she is an estate agent, so she might be useful to me. She's already sent me a couple of properties that are decent." She raised her gaze to Sloane's face. "But back to work. You ready for your session with me?"

Sloane scrunched her face. "Yes. No. I don't know. I wanted to come in here today, but this is showing me what I'm missing."

Ella chewed her mouthful before answering. "There's nothing in the rules to say we have to do it here. We could do it wherever. I have a flat viewing right after. We could go for coffee and chat, and you could come see the flat with me."

Not being at the training ground was exactly what Sloane wanted. "Is your date going to be the one showing us around?"

Ella shook her head. "I think she's keen not to see me either."

Lightness swept through her. "Okay, you're on. Let's go apartment hunting." Sloane grinned. "For the record, if I had this boot off my foot, I might have even driven. Did you see the Jeep my agent got me?"

"I saw it on your Instagram stories." Ella blushed.

Sloane folded her arms over her chest. "Have you been stalking me?"

Ella wouldn't hold her gaze. "No, it just knows I like female footballers, so I got served your car." She finally met Sloane's gaze. "I saw it in the car park at the flats, too, and thought, flashy."

"That's me. Flashy. Hotshot, right?" She gave Ella a perfect grin. "But you might have turned me into a UK driver, which is great. The last couple of times we went out, I didn't try to drive into oncoming traffic. I might be starting to feel at ease on British roads. Now, if they could just make them wider, that would be the ultimate."

"One step at a time." She pointed at Sloane's food. "Eat up, then. We've got flats to view."

* * *

The condo was in a cute three-storey block in a suburban street otherwise full of terraced houses. However, it had space and light, if not Sloane's terrace and views. Sloane knew she was lucky. She could stay where she was for as long as she wanted. She wanted to be supportive of Ella, who was navigating life on her own. Sloane had never really done that. She'd always had soccer to prop her up, even when her family or her relationship let her down.

The agent who let them in was a woman in her fifties with yet another strong northern accent, which meant Sloane caught every eighth word, if she was lucky. The woman said a very long sentence punctuated with what seemed like a lot of tutting, but Sloane couldn't be sure. She caught the words "sofa" and "clearance," but that was it. Thankfully, Ella appeared to understand the lot. That's what came of being a local.

"I need the lot. I literally have nothing, so that would be brilliant."

The agent nodded, then got a phone call. She stared at the screen, then back at Ella. "I have to take this; will you excuse me?"

"Of course."

When she was out of earshot, Sloane leaned into Ella. She smelled delicious. Of apples and honey. Which was new.

"What did she say?"

Ella laughed. "It comes fully furnished. Which is great, because I'm a sad case who doesn't have hardly a stick of furniture." She paused. "I added the last bit."

Sloane peered into the kitchen, big enough for a table, which made Ella produce a small "squee!". When they walked through to the living room, Ella settled on a battered brown couch.

"This chesterfield is not the sofa of my dreams, but it'll do for now." She pointed with her hands. "I see an L-shaped blue velvet one in here eventually. I've already picked it out. I'll have to save to buy it, but I feel like I might finally put down roots. I've got my dream job, maybe it's time to buy my dream sofa."

Sloane hobbled over and sat beside Ella. "I never buy anything big either, because what's the point when I might be moving next season?" She longed for the day she could buy a couch that would stay in one place for a length of time. "Although maybe if you go for this flat, you should. Make a statement. Sometimes you have to make the big decisions, and work out the details afterwards." Sloane wasn't talking about the couch anymore, was she? She ploughed on. "Can you see yourself sitting here? Enjoying a glass of wine on this couch and watching Netflix?"

Ella considered the question, then gave a firm nod. "Definitely." She turned her head. "Can you see yourself sitting next to me?" Her cheeks blushed red as she spoke. "Not that you'd be doing that often. Just on occasion."

The hairs on Sloane's head prickled. Her eyes dropped to Ella's lips and stayed there, as if magnetised. Could she see herself on this couch with Ella, kissing her lips? One hundred per cent, yes. The more time she spent with her, the more she wanted to do just that. But was it something Ella wanted, too? She couldn't be totally sure. If she wanted to keep the most important friendship she'd had since she arrived in the country, she had to tread carefully. She'd rather keep Ella in her life than lose her altogether. But what if she leaned in and kissed her, and Ella kissed her right back? It was a moot point. The agent would be back soon. Now was not the time to make a move.

The problem was, it never seemed to be the right time.

Ella's gaze landed on Sloane's lips, then her eyes, then she stood. "Shall we check out the bedroom?" She put her head down and blushed a little more.

Sloane nodded, and followed her through.

It was spacious, with wardrobes, a white chest of drawers from Ikea, and a large bed.

"Looks king-size, which is perfect." Ella walked around the bed to stand by the main window. "The street looks peaceful, too. I get a good feeling." She turned, then got onto the bed and lay down, getting comfy. Then she patted the space beside her. "Come test it with me?"

What the actual fuck? Sloane's brain melted, then she shook her head. "What if the agent comes back?" This was how photos got out into the world and rumours got started.

Ella tilted her head. "I'm not asking you to have sex with me. Just to lie on the bed. I thought your foot might like the break."

She was thoughtful, too. Sloane did as Ella wanted, and lay next to her. Her heart started to race. When she turned her head left, Ella was *right* there. With all of her charm, her beauty, her hair. There was still an awful lot of hair.

"What do you think? Strong, flexible and able to withstand pressure, like the best football defence?"

Sloane snorted. "Does everything come down to soccer with you?"

"You can equate most things in life to it. In life, you need a strong team around you to succeed. Friends, family, colleagues. You can try to do it on your own, but you won't achieve as much. Just like football. Team sports are always more fun."

She paused. "And that's not just because of the naked showers afterwards."

"They're a nice bonus, though." Sloane immediately pictured Ella naked in the shower. Heat travelled down her body and settled between her legs.

She had to think of something to take her mind off her thoughts. What had Ella talked about before the naked shower part? She eventually landed on it.

"Do you have the team you want in your life?"

Ella took a breath and turned to face Sloane. "I have some good friends and family, but I don't see them as much as I'd like. Luckily, my colleagues are lovely and make up for them." She licked her lips. "There's one in particular who has a funny accent, and just keeps following me around wherever I go."

"She sounds like a nightmare."

"Totally." Ella held her gaze. "But seriously, I like having you in my life. I feel supported. Like you're my new cheerleader. Coming to see a flat on your own is daunting. It's good to get a second opinion."

"I'm glad to be here, even if I do talk funny. But you have to admit, not as funny as that agent."

Ella laughed. "What about you? Do you have the right support team in your life?"

Sloane clicked through her life snapshots. "Same as you: everyone who counts is a little distant right now. But new people have come into my life, and that's brilliant." Her fingers touched Ella's by accident. Sloane flinched then glanced down but didn't move them.

Neither did Ella.

Slowly, tentatively, she moved her fingers closer, then

wrapped the tips around Ella's, as small sparks of heat raced up her arm. Her mouth went dry, and her heart clashed like a kid with a cymbal.

All the things she'd thought about this not being the right time when they were in the living room? They'd flown out of her head now they were horizontal on a bed. It would be so easy to roll over and lay a kiss on Ella's lips right now. Actually, not that easy when she was wearing an orthopaedic boot and literally couldn't get her leg over. She couldn't help but smirk at that.

"But you know what would be great to complete my team? A significant other. Someone I could share things with. Someone to stand at my side. Someone I could count on." Ella exhaled. "I've been doing this life thing solo for quite some time and it's tiring."

Sloane's heart turned its volume up as loud as it dared. "It's also tiring when you have the wrong significant other." She stroked Ella's hand a little more. Epicentres of pleasure popped all over her body, but she kept her breathing steady.

"Maybe we should both work on finding the right person to be on our team." Ella locked gazes with Sloane. She went to say something, but the words got stuck in her throat.

Sloane just nodded. "Maybe we should." Should she lean across? It would be the easiest thing in the world. Was what Ella just said a code to let her in?

Fuck it, she was going to do it. On this rented bed in a Salchester suburb. It wasn't the fanciest of locations, but it was right. Sloane pushed herself upwards on her elbow and turned to Ella. She brushed her cheek with her fingertips. A surge of glitter streaked through her.

She was just about to press her lips to Ella's, when the front door slammed.

"Sorry! That was another client and it was very urgent. But I do apologise!" Northern vowels and consonants spanked the air.

Sloane jumped backwards and would have fallen off the bed had Ella not jumped too, and grabbed her waist.

When the agent appeared at the door, it probably looked like they'd just been making out. If only they had. Sloane closed her eyes and shook her head.

"I see you kept yourself busy, mind!"

She wasn't going to be able to look at this agent for the rest of this viewing, was she?

Chapter Eighteen

"I'm not sure fish and chips – we call this a chippy tea – is the stuff elite athletes should be eating." Ella walked into Sloane's flat, still trying to pretend what happened, hadn't. They were both doing a stellar job. "But it is very northern, so well done on trying to fit in."

Sloane slammed the door with her crutch in a practised move, and hobbled to the kitchen. "If you don't tell, I won't either. Besides, I'll eat minimal chips and hardly any batter. I'll almost be inhaling the taste, rather than actually eating it."

Ella tipped the food onto plates, slid the condiments across the island and joined Sloane on the adjacent stool. Their knees touched under the island ledge. Ella sucked in a breath. She wasn't sure how long she could stay friends with Sloane without saying *something*. What happened in the flat when they'd lain on the bed? That was something. They'd nearly kissed. She'd been frozen with an equal amount of delight that it might happen, and horror because she *really* didn't want it to happen there.

Plus, kissing Sloane would lead to sleeping with Sloane, and that came with complications. They were on different paths, and they lived in different worlds. Sloane got photographed when she went for coffee. She was on the Pink Power list, for goodness sake. Ella just hoped the agent hadn't recognised Sloane, or that could lead to some salacious gossip around town. She didn't get the impression she had.

Instead, Ella focused on the food in front of her. Beside her, Sloane eyed Ella's mushy peas with American-infused horror. "You like that grey-green sludge?"

"Have you even tried it?"

Sloane shook her head. "I don't let anything that colour near my mouth. I'm very choosy."

Did Ella match up to Sloane's pickiness? Did she make the grade?

Over the fish and chips, Sloane related what she'd learned about her great-grandmother being Kilminster's star striker. Ella was suitably in awe.

"Do you think you'll go for the apartment?" Sloane forked a chip and ate it slowly. She was mid-chew when she reached out and grabbed the ketchup and salt to add more.

"I think so. My gut reaction says yes. I could see myself living there, and it's just about in my price range. Plus, it would mean I didn't have to spend my evenings and weekends trudging around more flats, so there's that." Ella paused. "I'm sure you can afford something bigger and better, but this is my reality."

Sloane shook her head and put down the salt. "I'm lucky to stay here with the club paying for it. I know that. But if I were looking, that apartment was perfect." She glanced Ella's way. "We're not as different as you think when it comes to money. I get paid well, and yes probably more than you, but it's not on the men's level."

Could Sloane read her mind? Ella gave her a tight smile.

"You definitely earn more than me, but you deserve to be paid more for your commitment and your skill. You deserve to be paid on a more equal footing to the men, too. You only have a limited window to play and truly earn. I don't begrudge you it."

Sloane cast her gaze to her food, then back up to Ella.

Ella wanted to trail her fingertips down Sloane's cheek. Kiss away the crease on her forehead. But she didn't.

"You know, I can loan you the money for the couch, too, if you want it earlier."

Ella ground her teeth together. Money had always been a pressure point for her. She'd grown up with nothing. She'd built her business from scratch. Self-sufficiency was very important to her. She didn't want to be in debt to anyone, especially Sloane.

She shook her head. "No thanks. I like to do things myself, my way. Money was an issue in my last long-term relationship, and it's come between family, too. I get things when I need them and can afford them." Had that come out too harshly? "But thank you."

Sloane held her gaze. "I get that and admire it." She paused. "And I agree about equal pay. It would be nice. But I know we need the crowds first. We're on our way, though."

Damn, the way Sloane was staring at her right now? Like she wanted to ask her a thousand questions, then listen to every answer as if it was gold? Ella wanted to stop the clock.

Although a kiss from her perfect, full lips would be nice, too.

She sighed internally. Her thoughts were way too confusing.

"But you know, if I had a choice between being paid more or being out and proud, I'd choose the latter. The more money involved, the more pressure on who you are off the field. The women's game is full of queer players, and nobody blinks. I wouldn't want to be a gay man playing soccer. That I can be me is worth more."

"Even though it means you're the subject of tabloid scrutiny just like everyone else."

Sloane smiled. "It's better than the alternative. I am my authentic self every day. If people want to take a shot of me drinking coffee, they're welcome to it."

They finished their tea and moved to Sloane's luxuriously large sofa. Ella carried both glasses of water and put them on Sloane's glass coffee table.

"Although I'm glad that real estate agent didn't have a phone out to take a shot of us." Sloane widened her eyes. "Fuck knows what she thought when she walked in on us."

Fuck knows, indeed.

"Two friends discussing a possible move? Gal pals?"

"Gal pals for sure." Sloane leaned her head back on the couch, then swung her gaze to Ella. "Although, lately I've started to think about you as more than that."

A tingle swept up Ella's spine. She held her breath. Then held it some more.

"Let me start again. It all started with my cousin turning up." Sloane shifted on the sofa, then ran a hand through her hair. "When I learned about my great-grandmother pretending to be a man. But she took a chance, went after what she wanted, which was playing soccer. In the process, she found love.

"I'm living my story, but over the past couple of years, I forgot that. I've been coasting. But moving here has woken me up. I've found a new lease of life playing for Salchester, and I hope to get back to that soon. I wasn't looking for anything else but a new start professionally, but when you went on your date the other day, it brought up some uncomfortable truths. I didn't like it. My ankle started to hurt more. I seized up. I had to ask myself why. You know what I came up with?"

Ella's skin flared hot, as if she was a radiator that had just been turned on after a very long summer. She shook her head. She didn't trust herself to speak.

"It's because I like you, Ella."

The words floated into her ears. Ella turned and sat forward. When their knees touched, she had to stop herself from shaking. However, she wanted to be very clear what was happening here. That nothing was lost in translation. Yes, Sloane spoke English, but American English.

"You like me? As a friend?" She raised her gaze to Sloane's sapphire-blue gaze. "Or you *like like* me?" Had she really said that? You *like like* me? What was she, ten years old?

She didn't have to wait long for Sloane's answer. "I like you as a friend."

Ella's heart sank to the bottom of her life.

At least she hadn't made a fool of herself by trying to snog Sloane.

"But I also *like like* you, as you so quaintly put it. More than you could imagine. In a way that a friend really shouldn't."

Ella's heart rallied the troops and started its advance. Sloane liked her. In the same way that she liked Sloane. In the way that she wanted to devour her mouth right this second. The lights had been red for so long, but now, suddenly, they were green. Ella should act before they went back to red. Or even amber. She'd been in the friend zone for long enough.

When their gazes met, everything inside her clashed, vivid and sharp.

Before she could talk herself out of it, Ella leaned towards Sloane. "In case there's any confusion, I like you, too."

Sloane's mouth quirked up at her words.

Then before hesitation could stamp itself onto the moment, Ella covered Sloane's mouth with her own.

Euphoria streaked through her. Bolts of sensation zigzagged to her chest. Her heart roared, her palms tingled, her brain melted.

She'd imagined kissing Sloane ever since they met in the car park on their first day. Actually, she'd imagined kissing her way before she met her, but it had never been a possibility. Now it was. The reality did not disappoint. Sloane's warm lips moulded around her own with ease. Her kisses were slow and light at first, as if testing whether Ella was completely sure this was what she wanted.

She didn't need to worry: Ella was totally sure. Cast-iron sure. Six-foot deep sure.

Moments waltzed by. Sloane rained down a procession of teasing, slow, sensual kisses. They pirouetted and slow-danced on Ella's lips, making her fight for breath.

If Ella wasn't sitting, she might have keeled over, like a tree felled at the root.

Never moving her lips, Sloane slid a hand around Ella's waist and pulled her closer. Had she been thinking about this, too? Ella would love to ask, but there was no way she was breaking this moment. But she wanted to contribute, too. Not just sit here, filling up with slow, glittery joy.

She lifted the fingertips of her right hand and slid them

over Sloane's delicate cheekbones just as she'd done earlier. Both their lips slipped left, then right, before locking in place.

Warmth rolled through Ella like the best kind of summer day. It was December, but with Sloane's lips on her, Ella had hot sand between her toes, infinite blue skies ahead, the crackle of possibility in her heart. Sloane Patterson's lips made her travel to places she'd never been before.

That was before wet heat slid along her bottom lip. Sloane's tongue. She was about to slide it into Ella's mouth.

Do not faint.

Do not faint.

Do not faint.

Sloane's tongue darted in, then out, like the best secret agent.

Ella tried and failed not to gasp.

Sloane did it again, then once more, until Ella's muscles went weak and her body shook. Then, just when Ella sucked in a huge breath, Sloane slipped her tongue in fully and sealed the moment with a woozy stampede of a kiss.

The lights flickered in Ella's soul. From a slow start, Sloane had suddenly sped up, and Ella was willingly dragged along for the ride.

All Ella's senses flooded with sensation. Butterflies swirled in her stomach and surged through her veins. Her heart stamped an insistent beat. Her legs rattled. Her arms tightened around Sloane's slim waist and never wanted to let go.

Still Sloane kissed her, in a hazy, dreamy, drugged-up state. If the police broke in now, they'd arrest Ella for being under the influence. And she was. Under the influence of one star striker. Sloane Patterson. Hotshot extraordinaire.

She smiled at her own thoughts, then pressed her lips further onto Sloane's.

She let out a small groan, right into Ella's mouth. It travelled all the way down her body and ended up throbbing right between her legs. Ella could already feel how wet she was. How it wouldn't take much to open her legs and welcome Sloane in.

Her eyes sprang open.

Sloane's eyes were on her.

When their gazes locked, Sloane eased her kissing, and then broke their connection.

Ella wilted like a sunflower in winter. She wanted Sloane back. She'd never had that feeling before in her life. Now she'd had it, she never wanted to let it go.

Sloane's eyes searched Ella's before she spoke. "Was that okay?" She sounded fearful of the answer. It made Ella want to laugh uncontrollably.

"That was so much more than okay." She leaned forward and kissed Sloane once again.

An arrow of lust shot through her. Yep, way more than okay.

"That was wholly delicious in the best possible way."

Sloane grinned, slid a hand into Ella's hair, then dropped another light kiss on Ella's lips.

Ella's head spun once more.

"Well, okay."

Ella's chest rose and fell in quick succession as her heart rate thundered on. She wasn't sure it would ever slow with Sloane this close. She suspected this might now be her new normal. She glanced at the skin just below Sloane's neck. Could she lean forward and lick it with the tip of her tongue like she wanted to? Not unless they wanted this to progress tonight.

She *really* wanted this to progress tonight. Every single pulse point in her body told her so.

However, she had a train to catch tomorrow morning very early. A client to see and prepare for. She couldn't stay up all night kissing Sloane. She definitely couldn't let this progress to fucking Sloane. Her clit pulsed at the thought, and she squeezed her thighs together. She was going to have to park this.

"But this is as far as this goes." Ella closed her eyes at her words. Was she mad? Maybe.

Sloane cleared her throat.

Ella opened her eyes. Sloane's gaze shone back at her. Her perfect blue eyes were so bright, it was as if they were Sloane's personal floodlights.

"You're killing me." Sloane swept a hand down Ella's side, and her thumb grazed Ella's breast.

A loud whirring noise started in Ella's brain. Was it her mind and body, sobbing with regret? If they weren't already, they would be soon.

"If this is something we're going to do, I want to do it properly." She glanced at Sloane's injured foot. "I don't want to risk furthering your injury." Ella paused. "Plus, I have a very early train to catch tomorrow. If we don't stop, I don't think I'd get much sleep tonight." She knew that for a fact.

The grin that crept over Sloane's face only confirmed it. "I know you're right." She shook her head as she spoke. "But damn, I didn't realise this boot repelled women."

Ella leaned in and kissed Sloane again. Their kisses were

perfection. She already knew she was going to slap herself when she was in bed alone later. But it was the right decision.

"I'm not repelled, just to be clear." Ella shifted a few inches away from Sloane. "I hope my kisses showed you that."

Sloane nodded. "They did."

"But just to add to the torment, I'm not here all weekend, either. I'm off to see my aunt and cousin before the festivities. I'm away for a full five days."

Sloane covered her face with her palms and groaned.

"Think of this as impetus for you to set a record to get your boot off. More flexibility in your ankle will be required, believe me." Who the hell had she turned into, speaking like this?

The look on Sloane's face told her she was just as confused, too. Hopefully, also turned on. Ella knew she was.

"When is it due to be removed?"

"This week, I hope. I have another X-ray tomorrow."

"Make sure it goes well, then."

"Believe me, I will." Sloane shifted her foot and sat back. "I've been wanting to kiss you for so long." She stared at Ella with a dreamy grin.

"That makes two of us." Ella paused. "But you know this is complicated, right?"

Sloane nodded. "I do. But I never have liked easy."

"I hope you're not trouble, Sloane Patterson."

"I guess you're going to find out."

Chapter Nineteen

The scan results came back, and the news was good: the boot could come off. Now came the next phase of rehab, but Sloane had done it before, and she could do it again. However, this time was doubly important for a few reasons. First, because she wanted to finish what she'd started at Salchester. Second, because of Ella.

Their kiss still burned fresh in her memory. Bright lights illuminated the scene behind her eyes every time she blinked. Kissing Ella had been like a dream sequence in a movie. Scorchingly slow, achingly fast. Ella was everything Sloane wanted in a woman. Ella had taken her time to unlock Sloane, and there was still more to come. They both knew that. The exciting thing was, Sloane got to unlock Ella, too. She wanted to be the person to do that in every possible way.

She made her way along the corridor of the club's training centre, and walked into the empty lounge area. Sloane grabbed a bottle of water from the fridge, and sat on one of the couches. She wriggled her toes with caution, but was pleased nothing crackled when she did. It felt weird not to have the boot on. Her foot was finally free, which meant she was a step closer to total freedom, too.

She glanced at the lounge walls, covered in posters of

soccer formations and tactics. Lucy sometimes gave her match briefings in here to smaller groups, and she'd clearly done one recently for the defenders, highlighting the low block. There was also the obligatory tinsel around doors, and a fake Christmas tree in the corner to provide some festive cheer.

Sloane pulled her phone from the pocket of her tracksuit pants, then frowned. She had 142 notifications, and she'd last looked only 45 minutes ago. What the hell was going on? She clicked, winced, then massaged the bridge of her nose with her thumb and index finger. Sloane flipped left, then left again, and again.

Someone had tailed her and Ella. So much for being left alone here. Perhaps the honeymoon period was over. Seriously, did people not have better things to do? Apparently not. There were photos of them at the service station on the way back from training getting coffee. Photos of them outside Ella's potential new flat. Photos of them laughing and looking very cosy when they left the flat, standing beside Ella's car. The story with it went along the lines of "Salchester's US forward sensation is still recovering from her injury setback, but maybe she's getting a little extra help in the form of the mystery brunette seen here."

Ordinarily, she would have ignored the photos. However, after last night, Sloane looked at them in a different light. Now she'd kissed Ella, to her, these showed there *was* something between them. Something that jumped out of her phone.

Photos like this weren't unusual for Sloane. But they were for Ella, and she was worried about her reaction. She tapped out a quick message to her, asking if she'd seen them. Ella was with her client in London today, so she wouldn't be checking her phone. Sloane hoped she was okay with it. Getting involved with a public figure, however minor, was something Ella had to consider.

The door of the lounge opened, and Lucy walked in. "I saw you pass my door, and I thought you might be here." She waved a hand when she saw Sloane get up. "Stay put. Even though it's clearly good news about your ankle. Let's talk in here – I could do with a change of scene."

Sloane nodded and sat back down.

"Your ankle's doing well?" Lucy pointed to Sloane's finally bootless foot.

"Yep, the physios are satisfied. I just need to work on it over Christmas and New Year, and they're hoping I can return as soon as mid-January."

"That's great. Progress is clearly going well, but what are your plans over the holidays? Are you going back to the US? You're not playing, so if you wanted to, you could. As long as you stick to the fitness program."

"I wasn't planning on it." Sloane never liked going home for Christmas when she was in the same country, so being here was an enormous bonus. She'd have to call her mom and deal with her disappointment, but she was used to that. "I'm going to stay here and get fit. I want to do the best thing for my recovery."

Lucy eyed her with a nod. "If you're sure."

"Positive."

"How are you feeling otherwise? Ella says you're doing well, but I wanted to check on you myself."

Blood rushed to Sloane's cheeks. She couldn't help it. Her boss was asking her about the woman she'd kissed into oblivion last night, and she had to pretend nothing had happened. She would tell her, of course, in due time. But right now, there was nothing to tell. One kiss wasn't enough to proclaim it to the world.

"I'm doing great. The physio team have been by my side through the whole process, as has Ella. I can't complain." An image of Ella's lips coming towards her landed in her brain. She blinked it away.

Lucy stared at her for a few seconds before she gave her a firm nod. "Okay then. Everything sounds like we're on course to have our star striker back in the New Year, which is the news I wanted to hear. But if anything changes, let me know. Anything at all. Physical, mental, I want to be kept up to date."

"You got it, boss."

* * *

Sloane sat at the table by the window in Shot Of The Day. Outside, the sky was the colour of rocks and looked like it was ready to explode. She hoped it didn't happen before she got home, because she was still wearing sliders. She'd told Layla she was happy to go to the counter, but Layla insisted, telling her she had to rest her foot.

"I'm not a princess, I won't dissolve if I get up for drinks."

Layla snorted. "You might. Then Lucy will bench me forever. I'm not taking the chance."

Sloane was still smiling as her friend made her way back to the table. She stopped when a couple of Salchester fans noticed her and came and asked for selfies. Sloane posed with Layla, and the fans thanked them and left. Layla put Sloane's flat white in front of her, along with her own latte.

"Thank you, ma'am," Sloane said, dialling up her American accent just for kicks.

"Have you just come to Salchester direct from the deep south?"

"Seems so."

Layla took a sip of her coffee, then stuck her tongue out. "Too hot." She pulled her phone from her training pants. "But while we wait for it to cool, I wanted to ask you about these photos that appeared today."

Sloane was suddenly terribly interested in her coffee. The pattern on the top was a work of art. Barista Suzy was proud of her skills. She was almost as good at coffee art as her wife had been at keeping goals out for Rovers.

"Is there anything going on you want to tell me as your trusted friend? Or are you avoiding my gaze for another reason?"

Damn Layla. She'd known Sloane for too long. Plus, she knew attraction when she saw it. However, until Sloane confirmed her suspicions, they were just that. Suspicions.

Sloane took a breath, then looked Layla in the eye. "The photos showed two friends going out to view an apartment together. Ella wanted someone else's opinion, and I was at a loose end. Nothing else to it." She chewed on the inside of her cheek to stop herself twitching. She always twitched when she was lying. Even a white lie like this one. Jess had always called her out on it.

Layla narrowed her eyes. "Are you sure? Because I'm really good on body language." She held up her phone, showing the photo of them getting in the car. Just after the agent had caught them on the bed. They'd both been embarrassed and laughing about it. "This looks intimate to me."

Sloane jerked her head towards the cafe windows, covered with festive scenes. "At least we won't be snapped again. They can't see through the fake snow." She was buying a little time, and Layla knew it. Sloane raised both palms in Layla's direction. "We're just friends, honestly. I won't lie, I do like her, and if there's something else to tell you, you'll be the first to know." But it wasn't going to be before Sloane's foot was healed. Or Ella was back in Salchester. Logistics played a part. "Plus, my heart's still in recovery after being trampled by Jess."

Layla leaned back and gave her a full-beam smile. "Now I know you're lying. Just be careful. If anything is going on, make sure you're in it for the right reasons. If it goes wrong, it might cause friction in the team. This is a big season for you, and for us. Make sure nothing derails it unnecessarily. A little advice, one player to another."

Sloane took a sip of her coffee and held Layla's gaze. She had a point. This wasn't something Sloane took lightly.

"I promise. I won't do anything that might affect the team, okay?"

* * *

Layla dropped Sloane back at her apartment after coffee. After she waved her off, she walked past her silver Jeep, still sat in the parking lot, waiting for its new owner to take it for a spin. Hopefully, that would happen in the New Year, so long as her injury healed and she remembered the road confidence Ella had given her.

Sloane smiled. It wasn't just road confidence Ella had given her. She'd made her feel like she had something to give again in her life, too. On the field, Sloane knew what to do. Off it, she'd been a mess for a while. Ella was slowly helping to fix that. The ending with Jess had taken its toll, but now Sloane finally felt like she could get on with her life, wherever that took her. She hoped it might involve going somewhere in her new car, with Ella in the passenger seat. Time would tell.

Sloane pushed open the door to her lobby, said hi to Gareth the concierge, and pressed her key into the elevator panel to take her to the penthouse. By the time she stepped into her apartment, it had started to rain. As well as ushering in sunlight, her roof terrace had the opposite affect when the heavens opened. Fat raindrops bounced off the concrete tiles and slapped her sliding doors with glee. It made Sloane smile. Salchester rain knew this was where it belonged, and it wanted to let everyone know. She dropped onto her couch and looked at her phone.

Over a hundred new notifications, and four messages. What was it with everyone today? It must be a slow news week if photos of her and Ella getting into a car were receiving this much attention. However, when Sloane clicked, a familiar face leapt out at her and made her sit up straight. The expression on her face also made Sloane's stomach curdle.

Jess. Of course it was Jess. Even on a day when the news was about Sloane and even though Jess was on the other side of the world, Jess had made the news and Sloane was still being connected to her. In times gone by, the connection was clear, so she'd accepted it. This time, though, Sloane minded. Because this time, Ella was being dragged into the equation.

Jess Calder shows an ugly face as she and new love Britney Navas row in the Ikea parking lot in their home town in North Carolina. Below that photo – Jess hated Ikea, and Sloane had experienced that post-Ikea mood too many times – was the photo of her and Ella. *Meanwhile, her ex, Sloane Patterson, seems to be getting cosy with a new mystery brunette. Is Jess taking out her jealousy on her new lover?*

Annoyance prickled Sloane's skin. She wanted to make the break from Jess, but would she ever be allowed to? The next message was from Ella. Sloane braced, but it wasn't necessary.

Hey, hope your scan went well and the foot is healing nicely. Can't stop thinking about last night. I haven't seen any photos as too busy today. I'm sure it's fine, don't worry. We hardly snogged in the street, did we? That was later. See you when I'm back. And put your foot up.

Sloane grinned, then did as she was told. The swelling on her foot had gone down, but elevating it was a key part of her recovery. Even when she wasn't here, Ella was still keeping a close eye on her.

The third message was from her mom, asking how she was, but in a tone that told Sloane she didn't really want to know if it involved telling her anything about Sloane's personal life. When Sloane did that, her mom went very silent indeed. However, dutiful daughter that she was, she owed her mom a call.

The fourth was from her cousin, Cathy.

I was thinking after our lovely visit. You want to see some photos. I'd love for you to meet the rest of the family. You said you weren't going home for Christmas. Would you like to come here? Have a think. Someone can pick you up and drop you home if you still can't drive. We'd love to have you.

Sloane blinked and put her phone on the couch. Festive warmth spread through her. Christmas with family sounded great, if a little daunting. But she'd met Ryan and Cathy, and they were both super-welcoming. If it was too much, she could go home early, using her injury as an excuse.

Christmas with Ella flashed through her mind. But was Ella going to her aunt's house? Or was that why she was going this weekend? She typed a message to her cousin thanking her for the invite, but also saying she'd talk to her boss as she wasn't sure about work commitments. It bought her a little time.

Then Sloane grabbed her laptop and pressed to connect to her mom. Duty called.

"Hello stranger, how are you?" Sloane could only see the bottom half of her face: her mom had never quite mastered the use of webcams. This was the way they always communicated. If you could call it communication.

"I'm good, Mom. How are you?"

"Fine. My back's still giving me trouble, but I'm used to that."

She was. "How's Dad?"

"The same."

Sloane tried to elevate her voice to raise her mom's spirits. "And how's your work going?"

"The same."

Moving countries hadn't made her mom any more talkative. But she was sure one topic would get her talking.

"Still trouble with your back, then?"

"Terrible. Some days I can hardly get out of bed. We made it out on Sunday to go to church, but we haven't been out otherwise." Her mom's back had been an issue for as long as

Sloane could recall. She said it had never been the same since childbirth. Sloane had always found it comforting that she blamed her children. It fitted with her persona.

"Sorry to hear that." Sloane took a deep breath. "I just wanted to let you know, I won't be back for Christmas."

"Right." Her mom's chin moved left and right. "I wasn't really expecting you to. You haven't done that for a few years when you lived here. I just hope you'll be going to a church to celebrate the birth of our Lord Jesus Christ on Christmas Day. Goodness knows you need the forgiveness."

That didn't take long to slip the first jibe in. However, Sloane knew better than to reply to that. She didn't want to get into a debate. She knew how it ended.

"Better than that – I'm going to your cousin's house. Cathy, daughter of Sheila? She's invited me over, and I'm considering it." As soon as she said the words, though, Sloane knew she'd go. She didn't have anywhere else to spend the day, and this was a once-in-a-lifetime opportunity. Maybe she'd have more in common with her family this side of the ocean. Cathy was a teaspoon of sugar in her bitter, cold cup of parental coffee.

"Spending Christmas with total strangers and not coming home to see your own family?" Her mom tutted. Sloane was glad she couldn't see her whole face. She knew that tut came with an eye roll. Two for the price of one.

"I think it's going to be great, finding out where I'm from, meeting my distant relatives."

"Be sure to tell them all about us. I hope they're god-fearing people."

Sloane hoped with all her heart that they weren't. In her experience, they were never the nicest.

Chapter Twenty

"Morning Ella!" Head physio Dan gave her a smile as she walked through the main doors. "We missed you at the weekend. You missed a cracker from Nat."

"I caught the goal on the Women's Football Show. It looked like a great game. Shame we didn't get the win, but a draw away from home isn't to be sneezed at."

"We should have won." Dan shrugged. "But no injuries is good for me." He paused. "You seeing some players today?"

Ella nodded. First up, she had two young defenders who'd been drafted up from the reserves to the first-team squad. Ella had been working with them a little in the past couple of weeks, but today was their first full hour with her. Every time she spoke to them, they looked like rabbits in headlights.

For this session, she was taking them onto the practice pitches and was going to chat with them while kicking a ball around. She'd asked Lucy if it was okay, and the boss was all for it. Ella was looking forward to it. After that, she had a session with Sloane. Her whole body fizzed at the thought. However, they were at work, so they had to keep it professional. But they also hadn't seen each other since that night. Since that kiss.

"I'm seeing Cleo and Wren."

A grin broke out on Dan's face. "I love those two! Good luck getting them to talk, though."

Ella grinned right back. "Thanks. I have a cunning plan."

* * *

Ella had her feet up on a chair opposite and was scanning her notes when the door to the cinema room opened.

She turned her head.

Sloane.

Her heart skittered like a lone pinball in her chest. She took a deep breath and got to her feet. She was determined to keep it professional. Even though her breath was already caught in her throat.

"Howdy, neighbour."

Sloane's American drawl was louder today. Or perhaps that was just how Ella was receiving it. It whipped around the room like a lasso, pulling her closer. Ella stood, and gestured for Sloane to sit in the front row. The lighting was just how she liked it for these sessions: dimmed. But now she was thinking about it, was it almost romantic? She shook her head and banished that thought. It was how she did all her sessions. This was nothing unusual. But what about if someone came in?

This was normal.

Ella took a deep breath and gave Sloane a smile that told her she was in control. She pointed to her foot. "No boot. Progress."

Sloane sat in the seat nearest Ella's chair. "I told you in my message, right? Dan reckons another couple of weeks and I can kick a ball again. I can already wear a shoe now, after a few days in sliders. Things are looking up." She held Ella's gaze and gave her a lop-sided smile.

Ella cleared her throat and shuffled her notes. "That's great. Are you back with the team now, too?"

"How was your weekend back home?"

The lights in the room dimmed a little more. Or perhaps that was just in Ella's head. "You've got a habit of turning things around, haven't you? We're not here to talk about me. This is about you."

"Gotcha." A knowing smile played on Sloane's lips. "I saw you out on the training field with Cleo and Wren. You've got a good right foot on you."

She'd seen that? Blood rushed to Ella's cheeks. Somehow, those sessions were meant to be private. Plus, she never wanted her playing to be the focus of attention. However, she couldn't deny she was pleased with the praise from Sloane.

"Thanks. It was just to change it up, get them relaxed and talking. It worked, too."

"And you got to kick a ball."

"I did. Nice to flex the calves again. And my knee held up." Ella tapped her pen on her notes. "But back to you. I know the foot's healing, which is great. How's everything else? No more paparazzi stalking you on coffee runs?"

Sloane sat up. "I'm sorry about you getting dragged into that."

Ella shook her head. "Marina showed me, but you could hardly see my face. Plus, I've never been called mysterious before. I could get used to that."

"I think they finally got bored. They're still linking me to Jess having tantrums in the Ikea parking lot, which is annoying. But other than that, I've been the model of rehabilitation while you've been away. I had one glass of wine with dinner on Saturday."

"Did you go somewhere nice?"

Had Sloane gone somewhere nice with anyone else? Irritation crept up her spine and Ella checked herself. She had no claim on Sloane. Yet. But if she had gone out with someone else, she might be tempted to stamp on her foot.

But Sloane shook her head. "Deliveroo and the Strictly final, even though I haven't watched any of the show previous to this. The bottle's still open if you fancy a glass later."

Relief flowed through Ella. "Probably not the best move."

"I thought we were going to see where this was going?" Sloane accompanied her words with a questioning frown.

"I don't want to do anything that might impact your recovery. You need to have your full focus on getting well over the holidays. Nothing else."

"What if I can do both? I'm an excellent multi-tasker."

"Sloane." Ella's voice held a warning. She hoped Sloane picked it up.

"Ella."

"You know what I'm saying."

Sloane exhaled. "I know exactly what you're saying. But you've helped me immeasurably with this injury. Kept me positive, focused, distracted. Now, I want to turn a little part of my focus to you. To us. To possibilities. All I'm saying is, I don't want to stop spending time with you because of what happened. I want balance in my life. I want you in my life." She paused, then leaned forward. "Not just in this room, either. In real life, out of this complex."

Ella bit her lip. She could see a million complications with this plan, but she also knew what she felt when she was around Sloane. Elated. Lit up. Like she could take on the world. "I want you in my life, too."

"If you don't want to entertain anything until I've recovered fully from injury, then fine. Layla asked me if anything was going on the other day, after she saw those photos."

Ella closed her eyes. This was exactly the situation she was trying to avoid. "You see my point. If we start something, it takes the focus off your game. I don't want to be the cause of you fucking up your limited time here."

"Ella, listen to me."

"Isn't that what I should be telling you?"

"These aren't normal circumstances."

Ella knew that only too well.

"My point is, I can recover and kiss you, too." She locked gazes with Ella.

Ella felt it everywhere.

"Don't you want to kiss me again? Haven't you been thinking about it ever since it happened? Please say yes, otherwise I might start to doubt my memories and my ability."

A slow smile spread across Ella's face. "Of course I have." She paused. "And yes, I do."

"Yes, I do?" Sloane grinned. "My favourite three words in the English language." She relaxed a little in her seat. "How was your weekend?"

Ella swayed as she stared. She was in a Sloane daze, and now all she wanted to do was kiss her. But apparently, Ella had to chat, too. "It was good. Great to see my family." She could multi-task, just like Sloane.

"Will you see them at Christmas?"

She shook her head.

"In that case, I have a proposition for you."

"Isn't that how we got into this mess in the first place?"

"I happen to like this mess. I love chaos. I thrive in it." Sloane paused. "Would you like to come to my family with me for Christmas?" She held up a hand. "Before you say no, or that it sounds like something a couple would do, I could really use the support. My cousin's invited me, but if you came, it would feel much safer for me. Plus, you could drive, which would mean I could leave when I want to."

The logical part of her brain screamed no. The romantic side of her brain swooned that Sloane was asking her out on Christmas Day. Sloane Patterson reduced Ella to a teenager whenever she was around her.

"Say yes? I'm not a great fan of New Year. But if you're here at Christmas, we could spend it together."

It made sense.

"I'll think about it."

"Great. You're coming to the game later?"

Salchester had an FA Cup tie tonight.

"Of course."

"Great."

"And Sloane?"

"Yes?"

"I kinda like that it's something a couple might do."

The sides of Sloane's mouth quirked upwards. "Me, too."

* * *

Playing football on cold, wet December nights was completely doable in Ella's books. Yes, the first time the ball smacked you in the leg it stung like hell, but you soon warmed up.

Not so when you were in the dugout. There, on too-small plastic chairs with no shield from the biting wind, Ella's feet were numb by the time they got to half-time. She was also numb to the performance so far, which she rated as one of the worst of the season. No pressing, no urgency, and a distinct lack of fight from every player on the pitch. Rovers' league form was riding high. Their cup form was about to go out the window. Ella knew Lucy truly wanted to challenge for the FA Cup this year. But at 3-1 down to a team six places below them in the league, they only had 45 minutes to turn it around.

The players were silent as they sat on the thin wooden benches that lined the cold, white brick walls of the away dressing room. The smell of damp earth and disappointment permeated Ella's airways. She pressed her back to the wall, arms folded across her chest, one ankle over the other. Lucy and Sloane were the last to walk in, deep in conversation. In an unexpected move, Lucy sat, and Sloane clapped her hands. Something prickled up Ella's spine.

"Okay, listen up." Her voice was a three-line whip, and Ella leaned in just like everyone else.

"You're two goals behind. 3-1 down. It's not been a great half. But you can't change that." Sloane eyed the group slowly, one by one. She didn't speak again until she was sure she had everyone's attention. "The thing is, you're better than them, but you're not playing with bravery. You're not first to the ball. You're not making challenges, winning second balls, being quick on the transitions. It's killing me I can't run on and help, but that would be bad for me and for the team for the rest of the season."

Her small joke lightened the mood. But Sloane wasn't done.

"But you shouldn't need me. I'm only one person. I'm a team player. The team can function well without me, as you've shown over the past month. Don't let me down now. When I come back in a few weeks, I want to play in the FA Cup. We're already out of the Champions League, and I want to lift a trophy with you this season. I want to play at Wembley. The only way that happens? You all wake up, stop dreaming of Santa Claus or whatever the fuck you were thinking about in that first half, because it definitely wasn't football, and put a foot in. Play as a team. Win the midfield battles. Look forward, play with passion.

"Remember what I told you in my personal session? Nothing is easy. You have to fight hard for what you want. This is the FA Cup. This is history. This is the last game before Christmas. Do it for yourselves, do it for me, do it for your teammates, but most of all, do it for the fans. Because you know what? It's blisteringly cold on the sidelines. They could be at home watching one of those cute Hallmark Christmas movies instead of freezing their butts off out there." She banged her hands together. "You with me?"

The whole team cheered back "Yes!"

"I can't hear you. Stand up!" Sloane waited until it happened. "Everyone in the circle, including support staff. Even you, Lucy!"

Ella put one arm around Dan, the other around Layla.

"I said, are you with me?"

This time, the roar was deafening. The swell was so huge,

it made Ella want to pull on *her* boots, go out there and make the difference.

"Then get out there, score some goals, don't let any more in and let's win this fucking game!"

More cheers, and then the players downed some water, went for a wee, and click-clacked their way back out to the pitch. Sloane high-fived every one of them at the door as they passed. Ella was the last one out.

Sloane held up her hand. "You don't get away with it. High five!"

Ella did as she was told. "Good speech. You could give me a run for my money."

"You better watch out for your job," Sloane replied.

Ella reached up and gave her a short, snappy, sizzling kiss. "You better watch out for yours." Then she squeezed her arse and walked out on the biggest high.

When she looked over her shoulder, Sloane gaped after her.

The look on her face was priceless.

* * *

The team carried Sloane's instructions out to the letter, and by the end of the game, they ran out 4-3 winners. Layla scored the equaliser, much to the delight of her parents who were in the stands. When Nat struck the winner, the first people she came to hug were Sloane, Lucy and Ella, stood in a row, jubilant on the touchline.

"I couldn't have done it without any of you!" she gushed, holding on tight to Lucy at the end. "You're all boss!" Nat was a true scouser.

When the final whistle blew, Ella couldn't believe it. Was

it Sloane's words that had done it, or something else? She couldn't be sure. But this team didn't know when they were beaten. They were just like her. When Sloane caught Ella's eye, their gazes locked, and Ella rocked back on her heels. What was this connection they had? It was so inopportune, and yet, it was there. And she wasn't sure how long she could fight it. Or how long she really wanted to.

Every time she looked at Sloane, she wanted to know her more.

She also wanted to devour her whole.

Minutes later, Sloane finished chatting to Layla's parents and gave them both a hug, before walking towards Ella, arms outstretched. Hugging was something they'd ordinarily do without thinking. So, Ella did it. But this hug had so much more in it. For now, only the two of them knew that.

When Sloane pulled back, she kept their faces close. "What a second half."

"What an inspirational half-time talk."

"It was nothing."

"It was everything." Just like this vibe swirling around them. Ella couldn't avoid it. She knew that Sloane couldn't either. She stepped back, knowing this wasn't the time to discuss it. She tried to steady her breathing, but it wasn't easy. "By the way, the answer's yes. For Christmas Day. My aunt's fine with it, so long as I go and see her before New Year."

Sloane's grin almost broke her face. With her club bobble hat on, she looked about 12, and like she'd just got the perfect gift. "You're coming to my cousin's with me?"

"I can't leave you waiting for a cab on Christmas Day, can I?"

"You won't regret it. And thank you."

Ella held her gaze. "You're welcome." She paused. "One condition, though. No big gifts. I don't have time to shop. If you're getting me something, just something small. Promise?"

Sloane nodded. "Pinkie swear."

Chapter Twenty-One

Sloane changed her bedding to her very favourite 400-count Egyptian cotton sheets, along with her fresh, jade-green duvet set. Even if Ella didn't come back tonight, at least she'd have clean sheets as a Christmas present to herself. But if she did, Sloane wanted to impress.

She'd also spent half an hour changing her outfit already, and when she glanced at her phone, she had to get to Ella's in 15 minutes. She needed to make a decision. Black suit with a crisp, white button-down for a classic look, or high-waisted beige pants with a casual shirt and blazer? Perhaps a suit was too smart. She didn't want to turn up at her new family's house overdressed. Smart-casual was the way to go.

Once dressed, she nodded at herself in the mirror. She hoped her outfit said, 'friendly and approachable'. Making a good impression today was paramount. Sloane touched up her makeup, added a little more product to her hair, and then grabbed the flowers, wine, and bag of presents she'd carefully wrapped. She'd give Ella her gift when they got back.

She rode the elevator down, flexing her ankle in her white sneakers. It was feeling almost back to normal now. Not good enough for kicking a ball just yet, but she'd get there. Just thinking about that made Sloane conjure the smell of freshly cut grass and damp soil, disrupted as she connected with the ball. She couldn't wait to get back out there. Damn, she'd missed it.

Thinking about soccer made her think of Nat. She hoped things were going well with her family. Nat had spoken to Sloane and Ella about it a few times in the past couple of months, and she hoped they'd built her confidence to deal with whatever happened. Life could be unkind.

She arrived at Ella's door, took a deep breath, and knocked. Her heart thumped against her chest as she elongated her neck and concentrated on looking as cool and festive as possible. If she was back home now, there would be pressure to go to church. There was none of that here. Another tick in the box for the UK.

Another key reason appeared now, as Ella opened her front door.

Sloane sucked in a huge breath.

"You look…" She reached for the next word, but all her attention was swallowed up processing Ella's beauty. Life was definitely not being unkind to Sloane. "You look gorgeous," Sloane eventually clarified. It was the truth, and she wasn't sorry she uttered it. Ella's fitted plum pants and simple white shirt were perfect, as was her grey jacket to top it off. The buttons on her shirt were just tight enough to make you look. Sloane wanted to reach out, pop a couple open and lick Ella's cleavage.

She blinked.

Those thoughts were not safe. Not yet, anyway.

However, Ella's clothes were just the outer shell. Her face glowed with something Sloane couldn't quite pin down. Her earrings caught the light, as if Ella was some sort of heaven-sent angel. Her eyes shone, beautiful and bronzed.

They took Sloane's breath away.

Ella ran her gaze up and down Sloane's body. "You don't look so bad yourself."

This was the first time since their kiss they'd been in close proximity, not at work, just the two of them. Whatever it was that had drawn them together was very much still there. That ping of magnetism. Sloane had to hold herself in place not to wrap her arms around Ella and proclaim her off limits to everyone else.

Ella held up a bag of presents. "I brought wine and chocolates, I figured they were safe Christmas gifts?"

"I think they're exactly what Santa gives when he's not quite sure what to leave," Sloane replied. "Although sadly, he forgot to visit my apartment this morning." She gave Ella a sad pout.

"We'll have to rectify that later." Ella's cheeks turned a colour that might be described by a paint chart as Raspberry Bellini. She shook her head. "I mean, I have a gift for you, but I'm not bringing it. You can have it later." Her cheeks went up a paint colour. Perhaps Volcanic Red. "The present, I mean!" She shook her head. "I'm going to stop talking now. Shall we get in the lift and get to Christmas with your family?"

* * *

Sloane wasn't sure what to expect from spending Christmas with a bunch of relative strangers, but it turned out better than anything she dared to dream. Back in her actual family home in Detroit, there were too many rules, too much snow, and far too much religious dogma weighing them down. Sloane had never fitted in, no matter how hard she tried. She wasn't the daughter her parents ordered. Then again, she wasn't sure who would be. Sloane had always relied more on found family than actual flesh and blood. Now she'd met this side of her family, perhaps she'd need a rethink.

Ten minutes inside Cathy's homey semi and she was part of the family, as was Ella. It was extraordinary, and so freeing. Here, she could be completely herself: soccer player, lesbian, coffee-lover, Monster Munch convert. And whatever the hell else she wanted. What's more, she was even celebrated for it. This family were welcoming, and excited to see her. It wasn't anything Sloane had ever experienced before. Would it have been the same with her great-grandparents, Eliza and Robert? She liked to think so. A woman who pretended to be a man to play soccer knew all about the struggles of being an outsider. Every time she thought about Eliza, her heart swelled.

Cathy fussed around in a sparkly top and slippers with reindeers on them, insisting Sloane and Ella sit right in the middle of the massive cream corner couch. To her right stood a six-foot Christmas tree stacked with decorations, guarding a pile of presents underneath. The air was hung with the smells of roast meats and all the trimmings, and jolly gold tinsel spilled from the red-brick fireplace.

"You already know my son Ryan, and this is his girlfriend, Hayley."

Sloane and Ella gave them both a warm smile.

"Huge fan of yours!" Hayley's blonde ponytail jiggled as she spoke, her grin so wide it almost fell off her face. "I cannot believe I'm spending Christmas with Sloane Patterson!" She leaned over Ryan, sat next to Sloane. "Don't worry, though. Cathy told me I'm not allowed to take any photos without your permission." She grinned a little wider. "By the way, that goal you scored to win the championship at LA last season? I've watched it tons of times. Ryan's sick of trying to compete to get my attention because of it, aren't you?"

To her side, Ryan gave Sloane a shy smile. He seemed a little more starstruck now he really knew who she was. "It was a great goal. I've watched it a few times since we met." He fist-bumped Sloane.

Cathy's husband, Rich, walked in carrying a glass of water for them both. "Are you sure you don't want anything to drink? Or is that bad for professional athletes? Ryan tells me he's a professional athlete, but his recovery from injury normally involves beer."

"Dad!" Ryan's cheeks flushed pink.

"I hardly drink during the season, which is why I look forward to summer vacation," Sloane replied. "I've been known to have a glass at Christmas, but with this injury, I'll stick to water, thank you." She turned her attention to Ryan. "How's the rest of the season going? I hope you got some more game time after your concussion. I really am going to try to make it to another game once everything settles down and my schedule allows."

"Knocked some sense into him, didn't it?" Cathy said, taking a seat on the end of the couch. "He was off for a few weeks, but now he's back. Scored a great goal the other week."

Ryan puffed out his chest. "Apparently the Patterson name lives on through me, too. Although I'll probably never score as many goals as my great-aunt Eliza, or you."

Sloane took a sip of her water, still unable to take this in. Somehow, she already felt like she'd been a part of this family for years. She couldn't explain it, but the warm press of home hummed through her body. Sloane stiffened, and tried to swallow down her emotions. Damn it, she couldn't cry. She was happy, but that isn't what tears would say.

Moments later, Ella's hand grazed her knee, giving it a small squeeze. Just to show she was there for her. It gave Sloane the boost she needed. She took a deep breath and gave her new family a broad smile.

"She's who I think about with every step of recovery I make. Eliza Power and her amazing scoring record. I want to get back to full fitness again for her."

"Talking of your great-grandmother." Cathy jumped up, and grabbed a square present from under the tree, topped with a bow. "This is for you." Her warm smile was fixed on her face as she handed it to Sloane.

"I've got you presents, too." Sloane put her water on the wooden coffee table and went to get up.

But Cathy shook her head and tapped her arm. "Open yours first."

The instruction made Sloane's pulse quicken. She remembered the presents from her childhood family Christmases all too well. There were only so many times she could unwrap a Bible and try not to look too disappointed. But if Cathy had bought her a Bible, she would dredge some enthusiasm up from somewhere. She glanced at Ella, who gave her an encouraging nod.

With the whole room watching, Sloane ripped the paper, to reveal a plain white book. But when she flipped the solid cover, she saw it was a photobook. Put together by her new family. As Sloane turned the pages, she gulped, then *really* had to hold back tears. She put a hand to her chest, then looked up at Rich, Ryan and Hayley, then finally Cathy.

"I don't know what to say." Sloane flipped another page and gazed at the sepia-tinged images of her great-grandparents playing soccer for Kilminster United. A short history of where she'd come from and where she got her soccer talent. It was incredible.

"I thought you'd like it, seeing as you came to the ground looking for answers. I've got some personal ones, but I did some digging around the club archives and cobbled together over 20 photos of your great-grandparents, with Barry's help. It's rare to have that many photos of anybody back then, but you can thank the club photographer who was clearly very diligent. Lucky for you."

Sloane shook her head. "This really is the best present ever." She looked up and caught Cathy's gaze. "Thank you."

Her cousin beamed. "You're very welcome. You're carrying on her legacy, and we couldn't be prouder." She pointed at the book. "Turn to page five, though. That's the best photo of your great-gran. She really did look like a man – you can see why she got away with it. But to hold her own in such a man's world." Cathy shook her head. "What a woman."

"If I have half her gumption, I'll be happy," Sloane replied.

A beeping noise from the kitchen made Cathy jump up. "That's my cue to baste. Back in a moment."

* * *

"I might have to lie flat and promise never to eat again after that meal. My body does not know what's hit it." Ella caressed her stomach as she clicked her seat belt into place. "You were far more controlled than me."

"I've got a career and a recovery to think about. You can afford another mince pie."

Ella eased the car onto the road and started the drive back to their apartment complex.

"It wasn't too bad for you sharing the day with me?" Sloane turned her head to Ella. "I really do appreciate it. It would have been fine on my own, but it was far better with you."

"It was better than fine. You've got a lovely family." Ella paused. "How was it, sharing it with them? I know it was probably a million miles away from what you're used to back home."

Sloane shook her head, still processing the past few surprising, golden hours. "It was like the perfect Christmas, you know? The ones I used to dream about when I was a kid. I always used to go to sleep on Christmas Eve, squeeze my eyes tight shut and hope that when I woke up, I'd have the ideal presents under the tree. That we'd all get on, play games, and make Christmas cookies. This was as close as I've ever got. Family, you, the perfect gift. We even played Monopoly." It was more than a little overwhelming.

They arrived back at Sloane's flat, and Ella gave her family a call. Then, at Ella's insistence, Sloane put her feet up while she made them a coffee. She got the cream from the fridge and the look of gratitude on Sloane's face was a sight to behold. Ella laughed when she sat next to her on the couch. "You're very easily pleased, you know that?"

"Tell my mom, please." Sloane's face crumpled. "Sorry. Every time I slate my mom, I'm really aware that yours isn't here." She shook her head. "It's true what they say, the good ones do go first."

But Ella shook her head. "Don't worry. I know she's been with us all day long. She wouldn't miss out on a Christmas dinner. And for what it's worth, you deserve to have all the Christmases you've ever wanted, and more. If your parents don't appreciate you for who you are, it's their loss."

Sloane's gaze lingered on Ella's collarbone, the dip at the bottom of her neck. Now it was just the two of them, these details came into sharp focus again.

"I know that, believe me. I've got the therapy to prove it. Years of it. But it'll never stop me wishing it was different, even if I accept life as it is. My parents don't think women should play soccer; that being queer is a mental illness. My new family think I've got the perfect job, know that I'm gay and didn't blink. The distance between them is hard to take in."

Sloane sat forward on the couch. "But I don't want to bring the mood down. I never expected to fall instantly in love with my new family, which is weird." She laughed, then held up her coffee cup. "I've got so much to be grateful for, and isn't that what Christmas is about? I'd rather focus on the positives. Cathy, Rich, Ryan and Hayley." She turned her gaze on Ella. "But most of all, you. For spending Christmas with me. For driving me around for the past few weeks when I've been useless. For being the best friend and neighbour this lonely American could ever wish for. For giving up your Christmas with your family who you do actually get on with to spend it with me."

"It wasn't a hard decision. I couldn't let you be sad and lonely, could I?"

"Some people might have."

"They're not the ones who've spent the past few months getting to know what a special person you are."

"I'm not sure I'm all that special."

Ella fixed Sloane with her searing gaze. She licked her bottom lip.

Sloane couldn't tear her eyes away. She didn't want to, either.

Ella leaned over and took Sloane's cup of coffee out of her hands. She put it on the floor, then moved closer to her. "You don't see what I see, that's why."

Sloane's heartbeat began to climb as if she was running up a hill. But it didn't feel like effort. This was a hill she was more than happy to climb. A hill called Ella.

Ella's fingers traced a journey up Sloane's left arm, across her shoulder and glided up her neck.

She closed her eyes. Was this going to be the moment she'd been thinking about constantly ever since they shared that dynamite kiss a lifetime ago? She hardly dared to believe it, but her belief was raised when Ella's lips landed on her neck and kissed her gently.

Sloane tingled all over.

"I got you a gift. I could go and get it." Ella's words were warm vibrations on her skin.

Sloane wanted to shout "No!", but no sound left her lips.

"Or else I could give you an alternative festive gift. One I've been saving up just for today."

Blood roared in her veins. This was it, what she'd been

waiting for. Yet even though she'd willed this moment to happen for a while, Sloane found herself unprepared. As if Ella had stripped her bare, yet she still had every stitch of clothing on. But vulnerability looked good on her. Ella had said so. Sloane had practised it enough in her career, just not so much in her personal life. But with Ella, she already felt safe – being vulnerable wouldn't be difficult. That was a big thing. Particularly now that Ella's lips were on her skin, and her words still hung in the air. She wanted to give Sloane a Christmas gift she'd never forget. Sloane was going to open herself up and get ready to receive.

Ella pulled back, her eyes dark with want. She was a portrait of beauty, her lashes thick, her neck the only place Sloane wanted to put her lips. She'd thought about flicking open Ella's buttons earlier, but now she could. Life was a series of moments, of split-second choices. It had that in common with soccer. She decided to take a chance. She always played soccer on the front foot. She was going to do the same now. However, when she moved her hand, Ella caught it, and clamped her fingers around Sloane's wrist.

Ooof.

Sloane really shouldn't be as turned on as she was, but she couldn't help it. She liked a woman who took charge. Her senses tingled with anticipation.

"We haven't specifically discussed this, but you need to trust me if this is going to happen." Ella raised an eyebrow in Sloane's direction, her voice a low, tantalising rumble, her lips a red-hot invitation. To back up her words, she placed a hand over Sloane's right breast and gave it a gentle squeeze.

Desire sluiced down Sloane's body. Ella very much had her attention.

"I'm not normally a dominatrix, but this time around, I'm taking charge. You do what I say, because I don't want any worsening injuries. Understand?"

Right at this moment, Sloane would agree to anything Ella wanted. "Whatever you say."

Ella reached across, stopping just before their lips connected. "Promise?" Her warm breath tickled Sloane's face.

Sloane gave a gentle groan. Enough teasing. "Kiss me, Ella."

A knowing smile worked its way onto Ella's face as she closed the gap between them and pressed her lips to Sloane's waiting mouth.

Sloane's body hummed with the thrill of it. This was still new enough to have a seismic effect. Ella tasted of sugar and spice, sweet and intoxicating. Sloane gave a low growl as she kissed her right back, the perfect pressure creating the perfect storm.

Ella's fingers played with Sloane's nipple through her top.

Sloane's clit hardened on contact. Then a hand slipped around her waist and pulled her closer, and Ella's tongue slid effortlessly into her mouth, out again, then back.

Sloane's mind blanked.

Merry Christmas to her.

In moments, Ella flicked open the buttons on Sloane's shirt, pushed back the cotton and her bra, then gave Sloane a sultry look that made her suck in the biggest breath of her life. Ella ran her tongue over her top lip, then her bottom, before lowering her head and sucking Sloane's exposed nipple into her mouth.

Sloane's brain short-circuited. Breasts and nipples were her downfall. Hers were far too sensitive. She arched into Ella with a groan. Ella took the encouragement and slipped a hand between Sloane's legs, and pressed just where she knew Sloane wanted it.

Sloane's body bucked.

Ella glanced up with a sly grin, but never moved her mouth.

Heat pooled in Sloane's stomach as Ella's tongue worked its magic. She could happily watch this for hours. Although there was a danger she might expire midway. Ella's tongue slid left and right, and Sloane groaned again.

Ella eased herself back. "Bedroom?"

Sloane nodded wordlessly.

"Move slowly," Ella commanded, her voice soft steel. They walked carefully to the bedroom, Ella with a welcome hand on Sloane's back.

Once inside, Ella carefully rid Sloane of most of her clothes. With every item that hit the floor, she applied her lips to the newly exposed part of Sloane's skin. Her light touch made Sloane sparkle all over. Outside her large bedroom windows, the evening drew in and the city shivered. Inside her apartment, it was the complete opposite. Sloane might be naked save for her panties, but Ella's kisses were providing a tropical heat.

When Ella pushed her gently onto the bed, her naked skin connected with the fresh bedding. Sloane was glad she'd made the effort. Ella grabbed a couple of cushions from a nearby armchair and propped Sloane's ankle on them. Sloane went woozy at the gesture.

Moments later, when Ella's gaze raked her body, desire pounded in Sloane's chest.

"You're so beautiful. I can't believe your body." Ella's eyes looked hungry. "Such a hotshot."

Those kinds of words would normally make Sloane blush, but this time, they didn't. She simply smiled at Ella, and stretched her whole frame a little more. "It would be even more perfect with you naked on top."

A blush worked its way onto Ella's cheeks. "I'm not a world-class athlete though, am I?"

"Doesn't mean you're not perfect. I'm sure you are." She didn't want Ella to feel inadequate. She was anything but.

Ella stood at the foot of the bed, took a deep breath, fixed her focus on Sloane, then popped her shirt buttons.

Ever so fucking slowly.

One by one.

All the while moving her hips left, then right.

Was she about to do a strip tease? Sloane didn't have to touch herself to know how wet she was. Ella was bathed by the low glow of Sloane's chrome-and-glass chandelier, and with her flawless skin, it was as if she was lit by the gods themselves.

Ella unclipped her bra and let it fall to the floor, never taking her intense gaze from Sloane. She brushed her palms over her ample-sized breasts, and Sloane thought she might pass out any moment.

Then Ella's cheeks blushed tomato-red and she dropped Sloane's gaze.

Sloane furrowed her brow. "Are you okay?"

Ella wrinkled her eyes, then nodded. "I was going to strip for you, like I'm in a burlesque club. So that it was me who had to move, and you could stay still." She cupped the back of her neck with her hand.

The one that had just been rubbing her breast.

The breasts that Sloane was currently mesmerised with.

"Only, I've come over all shy." She shook her head, lifted her shoulders and crumpled to the edge of the bed, looking like she wanted to be swallowed whole.

Sloane gently lifted her leg off the cushions, then shifted her butt towards Ella. She kissed her shoulder as the cushions fell to the floor. "Come here." It was an instruction, and Sloane wasn't sure Ella would comply. But when their eyes locked and Sloane dipped her head and repeated her words, Ella moved closer. Sloane held her eyes. "I don't need a performance, Ella. I just need you."

Those final four words were the catalyst for Ella shedding whatever embarrassment she had. Something behind her eyes blazed as she leaned over and covered Sloane's mouth with her own. The pressure told Sloane she wanted her, too. More than anything. Ella's kisses didn't just make Sloane's mind spin. It sent it into a luxurious meltdown, but one Sloane slid into willingly. Ella was the first person in a very long time to make her feel this way.

Turned on. Open. Safe.

A few moments later, Ella wriggled out of her pants and panties, and Sloane's mind went rigid. It wasn't the only part of her to do so. That part ached deliciously. She could be patient. Kinda. She stretched out on the bed, and Ella followed. She laid beside Sloane, their bodies almost touching.

Almost.

Sloane reached out to make it happen, but Ella slapped her hand away.

"I'm still in charge." Ella kissed her again, this time with more pressure, more urgency. As she did so, she slid a naked arm around Sloane's waist, and a thigh between her legs.

Sloane ground into Ella in response.

The way Ella groaned into her mouth, she was sure she'd felt how wet she was, even through her underwear. Sloane knew it, too.

Sloane kissed Ella right back with everything she had. She wanted to feel all of her, lose herself in the kiss. Their first had come with an end date, a full stop. This one came with a promise of more.

After an endless stream of five-star kisses, Ella pulled back. She ran her hand up the outside of Sloane's leg, paused at her hip, and reached behind her to squeeze her rear.

Shockwaves coursed through her body.

"You like your bum being squeezed?" Ella pushed her onto her back and straddled Sloane, her naked thighs sinking into her skin, making coherent thought tricky.

"Apparently I do." Sloane's brain rattled and hummed, as Ella reached around, cupped her between her legs, and pressed down.

Sloane's eyelids fluttered shut.

Ella did it again, before taking her index finger and trailing it from Sloane's butt to her clit. She paused when she got there, and circled Sloane's clit through the material.

She was definitely trying to kill her. But she was doing it in such a slow, sweet, sexy way, Sloane couldn't resist. Instead, she pressed her hips to Ella's hand, and let her mind go blank. She didn't need it for anything other than directing her blood to her very core. Ella saw to that.

Eventually, Ella leaned down and kissed Sloane until she had no idea which way was up and which was down. Scrap that, even which century she was in. Ella's fingertips roamed her body as she ground into Sloane, and sucked her nipples one after the other. A strangled sound came out of Sloane's mouth, but she didn't object. Quite the opposite. Her insides reached molten levels, and she sank into the moment.

When Ella laid her body carefully on top of her, providing the pressure and closeness she craved, her mind reclined further. Now wasn't the time to think. Now was the time to feel. A woman was grinding into her and that hadn't happened in a long while. Not just any woman, either. This was Ella. Architect of her dreams. Kisser of her reality. About to make all her fanciful thoughts come true. And there wasn't a photographer anywhere nearby to snap it.

Minutes later, Ella was on her knees, nibbling her way down Sloane's stomach. "Damn, I love athletes' bodies." Ella raised her head. "Yours particularly, of course. Flat stomach. Hard muscle." She cocked an eyebrow. "It's enough to drive us mere mortals completely insane."

"It's the only reason I keep it this way," Sloane managed to croak out.

Ella teased her fingertips up Sloane's inner thighs, dragged her underwear off with her teeth – was there anything more erotic? – then pressed her fingertips back to where Sloane needed them most.

"You're killing me," Sloane growled.

She crawled up Sloane like a wildcat, eyes alight, then shifted her mouth to Sloane's ear. "That's the idea," she replied, as her tongue flicked out and caressed Sloane's lobe. Seconds later, she slipped two fingers inside and pressed them home with her thigh.

Sloane gasped, as flashes of desire arrowed through her.

Her body coiled tighter as Ella worked up a slow, deliberate, teasing rhythm. She glanced up and caught naked need behind Ella's eyes, as well as tenderness. With her injury, Ella was being courteous. Not going too fast, making sure she didn't jolt her ankle. She was jolting every part of Sloane, so that was a lost cause.

But tenderness mixed with lust was an intense combination. Sloane's insides swayed. Her mind reeled. She raised her hips to greet Ella's delicious motion, and when Ella found her G-spot, Sloane's head pressed deeper into her pillow, the moment swallowing her whole.

Desire rolled through her like an express train. She was so close. But Ella wasn't going to make it that easy. She introduced her other hand and circled Sloane's clit, all the while keeping up the rhythm with her fingers.

Sloane tried to slow down her response, but it was hopeless. She'd lost control, and she didn't care. When she pried open her eyes to look at Ella, her sure chestnut-brown gaze was on her. Gauging her needs. Sloane couldn't speak, didn't want to. She just wanted Ella to carry on what she was doing, and do more of it. She loved every part of Ella solo, and every part of them together. In moments, Ella's lips pressed to her own. She teased her tongue beyond Sloane's lips, and curled her fingers inside to make Sloane go wild. It worked like a charm.

Sloane came apart with a low, rumbling groan as luminous pleasure shredded her. Her butt raised off the bed as she ground into Ella as deep as she could, and she didn't care. Plus, she was doing so with some aplomb, her good side taking all her weight. It wasn't just flat stomachs that were a perk of dating athletes. Core strength came into it, too. But her core shook as Ella slid in and out slowly, taking her down, before bringing her back up.

Sloane's butt sank back to the mattress and her gaze locked with Ella's again.

Sloane's breathing hitched. She didn't look away.

Neither did Ella. "You feel so good," Ella whispered, then brought her lips to Sloane. "So right."

Sloane's heart pulsed, quickly followed by every fibre of her being as Ella held her gaze, then circled her once more with her fingertips. Round and round Sloane's hardened clit, and then up and over, back and forth until Sloane fell apart under her hooded gaze.

She was in heaven. Ella was heaven. Christmas Day was heaven.

She already knew she'd never have another that lived up to this.

Chapter Twenty-Two

Ella woke the following morning to the sound of rain battering the window. Her eyelids released and she took in where she was. There had been occasions in her younger years where she'd woken up and wondered where she was. That was in a period just after her mum died, where she went on a bit of a shagging marathon, sleeping with any woman who'd have her for a few weeks, and then dating Reba. It hadn't lasted, just like her relationship. Since that split, she'd lived almost like a monk. Which was why Marina had signed her up for Honey Pot. She smiled to herself. Maybe, now, that wasn't needed.

And then, she'd seduced Sloane yesterday. Because make no mistake, that's precisely what had happened. Ella had planned to hold off. But Sloane's foot was healing fast. So long as she kept any weight off it, it could heal while Ella made love to her. And so, she had. She'd quenched her long dry spell in spectacular fashion.

She glanced Sloane's way. She was in bed with the international footballer of the year. The footballer of the year had mussed hair and looked pretty fucking adorable. Also, highly fuckable.

Would this be problematic? Maybe, but it was also something Ella couldn't even pretend to control. There'd been a pull between them ever since they'd met. This was just the culmination of a whole lot of time spent together.

However, she couldn't pretend there weren't issues. They worked together, but thankfully Ella wasn't on the football side of coaching (out of bounds for relationships), and she had no say in picking the team. That made a difference. Relationships between physios and sports stars happened all the time. She didn't imagine it would be any different for her role. They'd have to be up front, but she didn't anticipate any issues from Lucy, so long as they kept everything professional. Which they would at work.

The bigger issue was that Sloane might not be here long. Plus, she was a star, whereas Ella was very much a private person. The first person she slept with in forever had to be famous, didn't she? She couldn't just meet someone out of the public eye? But Sloane's drive and passion were what made her who she was. If they got together and started dating – she was getting way ahead of herself – how would that work? How would she handle it?

She shook herself. One night together, and she was already anticipating issues. She needed to chill. Relax. Live in the moment, and let whatever was going to happen, happen. You couldn't control other people or the universe. Ella told her clients that every day. You could only control your reaction to it.

It didn't make it any easier to deal with. What she needed to remember was that she'd had an incredible night in Sloane's bed. Which might also lead to more incredible nights to come. Plus, she'd made Sloane's ideal Christmas list. She needed to focus on that.

Sloane stirred and Ella looked left. Sloane's hair stuck up at all angles. But it didn't dent her appeal. She was still bewitching, glossy. A slow, steady drip of desire pooled in Ella's stomach. The multiple orgasms she'd had last night at Sloane's fingers and tongue weren't enough. Not nearly.

"Morning." Sloane's voice scratched the air. "Why are you looking at me like you want to pat me, jump me, or both?"

"Because you look like an adorable puppy. Also, you're pretty hot."

Sloane raised both eyebrows with a smile. "Want me to lick your face?"

Ella wrinkled her nose. "I'll pass."

"Anywhere else?"

The desire drip sped up, as laughter bubbled out of Ella. She bent to kiss Sloane.

Sloane kissed her back, and the already familiar Sloane-shaped euphoria skittered through her veins.

A few moments later, Sloane's hands tangled in her hair, she gave her a final bruising kiss, then got out of bed. "Gorgeous as you are, there's something I didn't give you yesterday."

"I think you gave me quite a lot." Ella threw her arms above her head as she smirked at Sloane.

She looked so beautiful and sexy, she could hardly believe she was in her bed. "That is true," Sloane replied, rifling in her chest of drawers, "but I got so distracted, I didn't give you your present. Bad Santa."

From the back, Ella took in Sloane's perfectly sculpted physique. Ella kept herself in shape, of course, but she wasn't a professional athlete. She was going to drink Sloane in as long as she could.

Sloane slunk back to the bed with a gift-wrapped white box, and sat on top of the covers. Ella had to focus on the gift and not Sloane's gorgeous naked form. It wasn't easy. "I hope this is nothing big. We agreed, right?" But even as she said it, Ella rolled her eyes internally. She sounded like her mum. She had to be more gracious in receiving gifts.

"It's not big," Sloane said. "It only measures three inches in diameter."

Ella lifted the lid on the cardboard box. There, sat on a bed of white satin, was a beautiful round silver necklace with the face of a compass engraved on it. At the four points – north, south, east, west – sat four shiny stones. Were they diamonds? If they were, she was going to kill Sloane. Tears stung Ella's eyes. Sloane had remembered. The necklace was very similar to the one Ella had lost. The one her mum had worn around her neck every single day of her life.

This was, without doubt, the most thoughtful present anyone had ever bought her. It was also the antithesis of 'not buying something big'. But maybe this wasn't big to Sloane? Maybe she bought diamonds for every woman she slept with. It was definitely big to Ella, in every sense possible.

"Do you like it?"

Ella raised her gaze to Sloane. "I…" she started. "I don't really know what to say. It's beautiful, and it's perfect." She touched the pendant with her fingertip. "But I didn't get you anything near this." Her stomach tied itself in knots at the thought of her gift. Her *small* gift.

Sloane moved closer and kissed her shoulder. "I know what we said, but when I saw it in the jeweller's window, I couldn't resist. It screamed at me to buy it." She leaned in and laid a soft kiss on Ella's lips. "Please don't be angry. It was done with the best intentions."

She knew that. Plus, Ella couldn't be angry at Sloane for too long. Not when her lips were so soft and delivered such joy. She shook her head with a wry smile. "Thank you. Really. I love it."

Finally, Sloane grinned. She took the necklace out of the box and held it up. "Can I put it on you?"

Ella nodded. She twisted around, feeling like a Disney Princess. Sloane clicked the necklace on, and then Ella turned.

"Ridiculously beautiful, just like you."

It was too much for Ella. "Stop looking at me like that."

"Like you're the best way to start a morning?" Sloane cupped her chin and kissed her lips. "I can't help it if you are. But I'll put coffee on while you stop blushing in the most adorable fashion. Follow me when you're ready."

Sloane shrugged on her white dressing gown, emblazoned with her initials in gold. She pulled the cord tight, then dropped another gown on the edge of the bed. "For you."

Ella waited until Sloane had disappeared, then slunk into the bathroom and stared in the mirror. She didn't look a fright, but she was hardly love's young dream, either. Still, Sloane had just kissed her with feeling, so maybe that's what she went for. She'd also just given her the most spectacular gift possible.

Ella had intended to buy a replacement for the one she'd lost, but she'd been flat out these past few months. Sloane had stepped in. This was for Ella *and* her mum. She eyed the necklace in the mirror, loving the way it sparkled as the stones caught the light.

"Happy Christmas, Mum," she said to her reflection, then clutched the pendant tight. A few deep breaths, a nod in the mirror, and she was ready. She still had to give Sloane her gift, such as it was. She shrugged on the dressing gown and made her way to the kitchen, where Sloane was waiting. Ella grabbed her present bag from near the front door, then brought it over.

Sloane stood at the counter, coffee cannister in hand.

"Here's my gift to you." Ella held up a far larger present bag. "It's bigger in size, but definitely not cost."

"I'm sure it's perfect." Sloane gave her a pointed look.

"Just take a look and let's get this over with." If she was going to die of embarrassment, she'd like it to happen sooner rather than later.

Sloane put the bag on her island, then peered inside. When she saw what was there, she started to laugh. She reached in and pulled out a box of 60 single portions of Lakeland long-life Half Cream, the nearest thing to Half-and-Half that Salchester could provide. She held it aloft, as if it was the FA Cup.

The look of sheer pleasure on her face made Ella grin.

"I can't even begin to tell you—"

Ella pointed to the gift bag. "There's more."

Sloane put the box down and pulled out the other gift. "Christmas Cookie Baking Set." She glanced up at Ella, put a hand to her chest, and shook her head. "How did you know?"

"You mentioned a couple of times that you'd never made Christmas cookies." She shrugged. "I thought, you've got time over Christmas. Maybe we could do it together."

Sloane took a deep breath, and her eyes went shiny. Then she took a moment, gathered herself, before coming closer to Ella.

Then she leaned forward and kissed her with such passion, it left Ella dizzy.

When Sloane pulled back, she shook her head. "I might have bought you your perfect gift, but you bought me mine. Half Cream? I couldn't ask for more." She patted the box with affection. "The baking kit is amazing, too." Then she gathered Ella in her arms. "Thank you. I love it." She kissed her again. "I cannot wait to have my coffee now."

"You're welcome." Ella reached for her necklace. "I love mine, too. Even though it's too much." Standing this close to Sloane made every hair on her body stand to attention. When Sloane raised her gaze to Ella's, her clit hardened, too. She bit the inside of her cheek as their options for Boxing Day narrowed in front of her eyes. Sloane had mentioned some rehab work today in the gym. But right now, Ella couldn't see past taking Sloane against this counter.

However, she didn't want to overwhelm Sloane. She'd already kept her up half the night. But this feeling she had when she was near her? She wanted to rip off every stitch she wore – admittedly not very much – and ravish her. It was unfamiliar and unnerving. It wasn't who Ella was. Had she been like this in her past? If she had, she couldn't remember it.

This connection.

This *want*.

She couldn't help her gaze lasering in on Sloane's lips. She didn't want to appear pushy, and if Sloane wanted to work instead, she had to be okay with that.

Just being here with Sloane was enough.

"This coffee takes ten minutes to brew. Slow and intense is how it comes out."

But not if Sloane made comments like that.

Heat rushed at Ella's core. "Reminds me of something else." Her tongue skated over her top lip.

"Me, too." Sloane's sapphire eyes flared dark. In a move Ella didn't see coming, Sloane pulled the cord on her robe until it fell open, and stepped into Ella's space. Then she took Ella's hand and placed it on the counter behind her, parted Ella's legs with her thigh, then slipped a hand between them. When they hit their target, Ella groaned, and Sloane did exactly the same.

"You're so wet." Sloane's voice was pure syrup.

"I fell asleep that way. Woke up the same way, too." Ella had no shame, because it was the pure, unvarnished truth.

"Ten minutes, then," Sloane added. "Maybe nine, now." She slid two fingers into Ella and started to fuck her. Fast.

So fast, Ella had no time to think. Or breathe. Or wonder anything, apart from the fact that she never wanted this moment to end. What was it Sloane had said about memories counting? She already knew this snapshot of her life was going to live rent-free in her mind for days.

Ella gripped the counter behind. Sloane added another finger, and Ella thrust forward. When Sloane went deeper, Ella threw her head back and let out a cry. Sloane's fingers filled her deliciously. Ella could hardly remember her name. She threw an arm around Sloane's neck.

"Don't stop," she whispered in a heavy hush. And then, before she could process what was happening, she flushed from the inside out, and started to shake as euphoria rampaged through her. Ella came right there, standing up, Sloane's fingers buried inside her. Hot damn. She was a glorious slut.

Moments later, Sloane bruised Ella's mouth with her lips, then cupped her arse with her free hand. "You're outstanding, you know that?"

Ella couldn't respond. She had no command on anything right now, especially not her speech. Then, Sloane nibbled her way down Ella's neck, gently removed her fingers, and sank to her knees. Ella's eyelids sprang open.

"Your ankle," she said.

"It's fine," Sloane replied, as her fingertips traced their way up Ella's naked thighs.

Ella spread her legs as far as she could, then buried her fingers in Sloane's soft hair. Why had she denied herself this kind of pleasure for so long? Stubbornness, mixed with sheer bloody-mindedness. But now, eyes closed and rainbows dancing on the back of her lids, she sank into it like a boss. When Sloane's tongue pressed into her, the moment sharpened into pristine focus. Ella's grip on Sloane's hair tightened, willing her on. She was about to let go for the second time, and Ella hardly *ever* let go. More surges of desire sparked inside her. She sucked in a deep breath, as a waft of coffee filled the air.

Sloane's tongue swirled around her, sending dizzying bliss to every part of her. Ella loved the way Sloane had cracked her code within 24 hours. Last night, she'd listened to what Ella wanted, and she'd remembered every detail. Every sure circle of her tongue signalled she understood her. When Sloane pressed, Ella roared.

She was glad she'd worn the dressing gown now. Easy access. She'd been anything but over the past few years. But with her easy smile and her generous nature, Sloane had unlocked something inside. Now, Ella just wanted more. For every morning to start like this. Wake up happy, slope to the kitchen, get royally fucked on the counter.

As Sloane's tongue worked its magic, her blood thundered south, to where it was needed most. When Sloane slid her fingers back inside, Ella met every thrust with one of her own, her heart dancing in her chest.

Ella was lost on some distant horizon when a high-pitched beeping shattered the moment.

What the hell was that? Heat swelled inside as her eyelids popped open.

Sloane's tongue stalled. She looked up, and met Ella's gaze. Sloane grinned.

"If you stop now, I'll kill you," Ella wheezed.

A sultry grin invaded Sloane's face. "I'm not that cruel."

And so, to the beat of the coffee machine's beeps, Sloane swept her tongue upwards once more, and hit Ella's jackpot again. Ella's senses rattled, and she hit the heights with a loud groan. Her knees buckled and her brain turned to sludge. Sloane let it play out, then went for more. Ella was so hyped, she came again almost instantly, before reaching down and pushing away Sloane's head.

Sloane placed one more gentle kiss, then stood with great care, reaching over to still the coffee machine's alarm. Back at Ella's height, she kissed her lips once more.

Ella tasted herself on Sloane's lips, which only made her wetter still.

"Well done on coming to the beeping. Some people might be put off by that. But you? You're a professional."

"Some people might call it easy, but I'll go for your assessment."

Sloane laughed.

How Ella loved that sound. Sloane's laugh was light and golden, wrapping itself around Ella, filling her. Her vision was still hazy, but she leaned forward and kissed Sloane's gorgeous, red lips all the same. "You make me easy."

That sounded weird. She screwed up her face. "Ignore everything I say within ten minutes of coming please. Sometimes, it comes out very wrong."

Another kiss to her lips. Then Sloane trailed a finger through Ella's liquid heat.

Ella dissolved on the spot.

"On the contrary, I think it came out just right," she replied.

Chapter Twenty-Three

They were at the counter again the following day, but this time, they waited for the machine to beep without having sex. Sloane wasn't sure whether that was an improvement or not. But she was content with Ella's tongue in her mouth, and Ella's hand on her naked butt cheek.

In the past, Sloane had always considered Christmas as a bit of a disruption to her normal life. An annoyance she had to tolerate. This year, though, she was thrilled she got two whole days off. She'd put them to good use. Meeting her long-lost family, and making sure Ella knew exactly how she felt.

The coffee machine beeped and Sloane reluctantly removed her lips from Ella's. "I could happily kiss you forever." Did that sound corny? She didn't care.

"You'd die of caffeine deficiency. That's very dangerous for a woman like you."

She pressed her lips back to where they most wanted to be. On top of Ella's. Then she slid her fingers inside Ella's panties. Her mind flickered as they connected with Ella's clit.

The door buzzer went.

Ella moved forward, and Sloane's fingers eased into her.

Sloane locked eyes with Ella just as her buzzer went again. She curled her fingers inside.

Ella dropped her head onto Sloane's shoulder. "You're terrible."

"You're irresistible."

The buzzer went again. Sloane paused.

"Shit." She kissed the side of Ella's neck. "I am expecting a package from my friend in the US, so I might have to get that." Sloane winced. "Sorry." She reluctantly pulled her hand from Ella, kissed her lips, then hastily ran some water over her hand and wiped it on the festive tea towel. "Stay right there." Sloane's eyes greedily assessed Ella. "You look perfect. I want to come back to perfection." She glanced at the oversized shirt Ella wore that came down to her mid-thigh, along with her toned, bare legs.

"If you're lucky, I might be here."

Sloane opened the door in her T-shirt and shorts, but it wasn't the expected delivery driver. Rather, it was Nat, dressed in jeans, pristine Nikes, and a hoodie, her short, dark hair flopped in front of her eyes. Sloane had hardly ever seen her out of her tracksuit or kit. She looked even younger, somehow.

Sloane blinked twice before she could get any words out of her mouth. She'd said goodbye to Nat four days earlier, and hadn't expected her back in Salchester until the 29th. This was two days early.

Shit.

Something must have happened with Nat's family.

But this was spectacularly bad timing. Fear sprang up in Sloane's body. She had to stall Nat. She didn't want it getting out to everyone before she and Ella even knew what this was. They hadn't spoken about anything. They'd been lost in their sex bubble.

Nat had well and truly popped it.

"It's you." Bad start. "What are you doing here?" Terrible follow-up.

She was the absolute worst person in the entire world. Ella had told Nat her door was always open, as had Sloane. Here Nat was, taking her up on her offer. Sloane just hadn't laid down specific times when the door might be less open.

Like this morning.

Nat frowned, and Sloane was sure her lip quivered, too.

Yep, Sloane was going to hell on the express train.

"I was just on the way back to my flat, and I stopped to speak to Ella. But she wasn't in. So I thought I'd see if you had time for a coffee. But if this is a bad time?" Her face crumpled, but she tried to hold it together. It lasted at least ten seconds. "I left Liverpool early, it was all just a bit too much." Nat's eyes went shiny. "And I thought..." She shook her head. "I don't know what I thought."

To avoid Nat collapsing on the doorstep and Sloane winning the Biggest Douchebag Friend of the Year award, she put an arm around her shoulder and pulled her in. "What I said was true. Sorry, I just wasn't expecting you."

Evidently, she could lie through her teeth.

But that didn't change the fact that Ella was still in her kitchen, in just panties and a long shirt, in a sexed-up daze.

She had to keep calm. She threaded her arm through Nat's to control her speed, and walked her very slowly down the hallway.

"Coffee's just brewed, so you timed it right, Nat!" Sloane shouted her words, like she was performing in the local pantomime. Apparently, that was a big thing in the UK. She'd seen posters all over town, and it was sold out.

Nat looked at her like she'd gone mad.

But Sloane had to warn Ella. Or perhaps she should have made Nat wait at the front door? Too late, she was here now.

"Did you have a good break?" She was still doing her panto voice.

She wanted to shoot herself in the head.

Nat looked even more confused as Sloane slowed her pace.

"Is everything okay?" Nat frowned. "I just told you I left early after everything was rubbish."

Sloane resisted the urge to bash her own head against the living room door frame. She had to walk through it, but she hoped Ella had heard Nat was here. If she was at the counter, shirt undone, waiting for Sloane, they were both about to die a very slow death.

At that thought, Sloane removed her arm from Nat and bolted into the main living space.

Ella stood in front of the coffee machine. Thankfully, her shirt was completely buttoned up, the festive tea towel in front of her knees. Which only made Sloane melt that little bit more.

"Oh fuck, I didn't realise…" Nat left the words hanging in the air as she looked from Sloane, to Ella, and back. "…that you had company," she finished, eventually. Then she cleared her throat as her cheeks turned the same colour as Ella's. "This is why you didn't answer your door when I tried you first," Nat said to Ella. "Because you're here." She winced. "Fuck, I should go." Then she burst out crying.

Ella dropped the tea towel, walked over and pulled Nat into a hug. "Don't be stupid, you don't have to."

Nat sank into the embrace, and Sloane marvelled at how

much of a confidant Ella had become to the young players. They all trusted her implicitly. It was quite the skill.

After a few moments, Nat sniffed and pulled away from Ella, then wiped her nose on her sleeve.

Ella discreetly stepped back and grabbed her a tissue.

Nat took it with a hasty thank you, then blew her nose properly. "I'm sorry for interrupting, I just wanted to talk to someone. Like I said, I tried your flat first, Ella. I didn't know about you two."

"That's because there was nothing to tell until two days ago."

Nat frowned, and Sloane wasn't sure whether she believed her or not. Right now, it didn't really matter.

"I'm just going to…" Ella nodded towards the bedroom. "Pull on some jeans so I don't feel quite as underdressed. Back in two secs."

Sloane stepped forward and put an arm on Nat's shoulder. "Sounds like you've had an eventful time at home." She nodded towards the couch. "Take a seat, I'll make us some coffee and you can chat to Ella when she comes back."

But Nat pushed her shoulders back and shook her head. "I'll go. Let you two have some space. If it's only been going on for two days, I don't want to be a third wheel."

Sloane shook her head, but Nat was firm. "I do want to chat, but I can go home, unpack, do a work out and come back later. Give you a little time."

That would be better. "If you're sure? I don't want to throw you out."

"You're not." A half-smile twisted onto her face.

"Okay." But there was one thing Sloane wanted to clear up before Nat left.

"Can I ask a favour, though? This is very new, and I don't know where it's going. It could be something, it could be nothing. I'd appreciate it if you kept it to yourself for now."

Nat gave Sloane a firm nod. "Of course. I'll take it to the grave."

"No need for that, just some discretion for now would be good." She didn't want this getting out to the team before she was ready.

Sloane followed Nat down the hallway to the front door. "Go work out and release all that excess energy stored up inside of you. Message me when you're ready and we'll arrange a time. I'm here all day."

Nat nodded as Sloane opened the door. A stab of guilt pierced her. "You sure you're okay? You don't want to stay for coffee?"

"Positive. This has taken my mind off it." She paused. "How's your ankle, by the way?"

"Better. Nearly ready to start firing in your crosses again."

Sloane closed the door, pressed her palm flat against it, and exhaled. Fuck. Maybe she should call Lucy, just to let her know the score. But on December 27th? Maybe not. Plus, she and Ella still had to think about where this was going. What they both wanted. She had no idea.

Footsteps behind her made her turn. There was Ella, looking edible in her plum pants and white shirt. The same clothes that had lounged on Sloane's bedroom armchair since Christmas Day when she took them off. Ever since, Ella had lived in Sloane's clothes, or none at all.

"That was unexpected." Sloane moved towards Ella, but stopped when she got close. The bubble had burst, and

Ella had a barrier up. The energy had changed. A chill sidled through Sloane. "You okay?"

Ella stared, then shook her head. "I didn't much like what you said to Nat."

Sloane's ankle started to throb. "What did I say?" The way Ella's features hardened made it clear Sloane had said something bad. She raked her mind but she was at a loss.

"That we might be nothing."

Sloane chewed on the inside of her cheek. "I didn't mean it like that. It's just, we haven't talked about anything, have we?"

"But I'd have preferred you tell me we might be nothing before you tell Nat." She paused. "Were you planning to fuck me again before you told me, or after?"

Sloane swallowed down a hard lump of reality. "It's not what I meant." She put her hands on Ella's arms. "You don't have to go just yet. Stay. Have some coffee. Let's talk now."

But Ella shook her head. "I need to go and pack for my family visit anyway. I leave tomorrow. I need to get back to my life. I can't just stay here and have sex with you forever more."

That sucked the air out of Sloane's lungs. She pulled Ella towards her. This time, her resistance was slightly less. "Go and pack, and I'll speak to Nat later. But let's see each other after that? Please?"

"I'll let you know." She leaned forward and pressed a kiss to Sloane's lips. Then another. Then one more.

Every part of Sloane broke into applause.

"The trouble with you is, you're very difficult to leave, even when I'm mad at you." A final kiss before Ella stepped back. "But for now, it's time to go back to the real world."

Chapter Twenty-Four

Ella eased her car into the cemetery, then flicked on the heater. The windscreen had suddenly frosted up, and she was almost afraid to get out lest she get lost in the fog that had descended. As she'd driven further north and west, the weather had got decidedly worse. Having grown up here, she was used to it, but it still caught her off-guard. She was a city girl now, living in the centre of Salchester. She easily forgot what it was like living by the bracing northern coast. Despite all of that, driving through the sign that told her she was now in Midcombe always made her smile. No matter where she went in the world, this would always be home. Where her aunt and uncle lived. Where her mum was buried. She steered her car up the cemetery road, and cut the engine near to her destination.

Her mum's grave was well tended, as Ella knew it would be. Her Aunt Ursula brought new flowers every week, and Marina made sure the plot was the most manicured in the cemetery. Ella wouldn't say she was competitive, but if there was a prize for the best-kept grave, Marina was going to win it. She knelt and wiped the marble gravestone, the cold seeping through her thermal gloves. Her mum had loved this weather. There was nothing she liked more than frost and snow. Christmas was her favourite time of year. Ella had vowed to keep up her love of it after her mum died, and not let her death ruin it. She'd mostly succeeded, thanks to her family's help. She placed her bouquet of pink roses at the foot of the grave, then closed her eyes and took a deep breath, just like her mum always told her to do.

"If things get overwhelming, close your eyes, take a deep breath, and count to ten. It will always be clearer when you reopen them."

Ella did as she was told. However, when she reopened them, she wasn't sure it had worked. She'd spent the past two days in bed with the world's best striker, someone she really shouldn't be sleeping with. Yet, it had seemed like it was almost inevitable from the moment they met. When they kissed, she wasn't surprised. But Sloane's response to Nat had been a wake-up call. She wasn't sleeping with just anyone. She was sleeping with someone who was important to her job.

Maybe she could tell Lucy she was just doing this to add extra motivation for Sloane, to keep her happy so she could keep scoring goals for Rovers? She smiled at the thought. Lucy wasn't stupid. She'd been around enough football teams to know relationships were commonplace.

But Ella had never slept with an athlete. Until now.

She blew out a long breath and held her mum's gravestone tight.

"Happy Christmas, Mum." Her breath misted around her. "I'm a little late, but I only drove over this morning. Would you believe I've had no cheese at all this festive season?" In fact, it might be the only one where she'd lost weight, due to eating very little and burning calories in the best possible way. That thought made her smile. But even though her mum was no longer with her, she wasn't going to share that kernel of information. She might be dead, but they were still mother and daughter.

"I'm also in a bit of a quandary. I've met someone. I really like her. She's kind, caring, fantastic at what she does, and I know you'd like her." That was always the kicker in situations like this. That her mum would never get to meet the person who meant something to her.

There was no denying it.

Sloane already meant so much.

"What's the problem then, you might be asking? We're from very different worlds, and I'm not sure how that's going to work. She's loaded, and I know you never trusted people with money." Ella pressed on the front of her coat, and felt the necklace against her bare skin beneath.

"But more than that, she's probably leaving at the end of the season. It might not even be her choice to stay. But I *have* to stay. I've worked all my career for a job like this. I love it so much. But am I making things harder by getting involved with Sloane?"

But even as she said it, she knew it was pointless. She was already involved with Sloane, like it or not. She'd fallen for her long before they slept together. When they'd gone to watch Kilminster United. When Sloane had given her a makeover. When Ella had stopped her crashing into oncoming traffic. When they'd shared sunsets.

It didn't matter what her mum thought, or what Ella thought. She was already in trouble, because she was already up to her waist in feelings for Sloane.

Yes, she might be leaving in six months.

Yes, she didn't know exactly how she felt about her.

But now she'd spoken about it out loud to her mum, Ella knew exactly how she felt about Sloane.

She'd fallen hard for the first time in forever.

That fact just made everything doubly complicated.

Fuck.

Chapter Twenty-Five

"**D**id you like my present?" Layla sat opposite Sloane in the canteen, a grin on her face. "Wasn't it perfect?"

Sloane laughed. "It totally was. A year's subscription to some delicious coffee, delivered monthly. Perfect for me. Does it mean I have to stay here for another year, though?" That was the first thought that ran through Sloane's mind when she opened it. Her contract ran out in June. This coffee contract ran out next December. Did Layla know something she didn't?

They talked about their Christmases, Layla describing hers as "hectic but fabulous." It was her first with children and family staying with them, so Sloane could well imagine.

"How was yours?" Layla scooped up a forkful of chicken noodles.

"The same as yours. Busy, a little crazy." Sloane took a breath. This wasn't as easy as she'd thought. She still had to think about Ella's reaction. How she would feel. But she had to talk to someone. "We met my long-lost family, so we had a family Christmas, too."

"We?"

Sloane licked her lips. It'd slipped out without her even thinking about it. Were they a 'we'? She had no idea. She

Clare Lydon

nodded. "Me and Ella. She offered to drive and came along for moral support."

Layla finished her mouthful of food. "Did she now?" She smiled, put her fork down, then leaned closer to Sloane. "I know that look on your face, Sloane Patterson. I remember when you and Jess got together – the subtle looks, the sly smiles. Ella's not even here and you're doing it. Is there something else you want to tell me?"

Sloane was soothed by the familiarity of their long friendship. Layla knew her.

"Nothing happened before Christmas Day." She paused. "But that changed when we got home, and she didn't leave until Nat walked in on us on the 27th." Sloane winced at the final part.

Layla's eyebrows rose to the ceiling. "Walked in on you? What the fuck does that mean?"

Sloane made a hand gesture that told Layla to keep it down. "Can you not shout it out to everyone here?"

Layla looked around the canteen. It was only half full, with some players and staff given extra time off if they requested it. Nobody in the space had taken any notice.

"It means," Sloane continued in a borderline whisper, "that she walked in and saw Ella was there early on. Without any pants on."

Layla's eyes widened. "My definition of pants, or yours?"

Sloane snorted. "Mine, luckily. Yours would have been a disaster."

"Poor Ella, either way." Layla sat back and shook her head. "You never make it easy, do you? You always fish in the nearest pond."

"It wasn't intentional." It hadn't been. But you couldn't help who you fell for. Had Sloane fallen for Ella? If she hadn't before, she certainly had now.

"You're shagging the performance coach. I guess that means your mental health is tip-top."

"Far from it." Sloane ran her fingers through her hair. It was soft; she'd forgotten to bring her hair wax today. Her mind had clearly been on other things. "I'm all over the place."

"Is she in today?"

Sloane shook her head. "She's gone to see family. It was something she'd intended to do. But it's left more questions than answers. We had two amazing days, but what happens now?"

Layla ate the last of her lunch, then pushed her plate away. "What do you want to happen now?"

"I want us to sail off into the sunset. But I don't know what she wants. We didn't talk much, and then she had to leave." It didn't sound any better when she said it out loud. "We like each other, I know that. We had a great Christmas together." She said the last words with far more confidence, because she knew in her heart they were correct. She didn't know what Ella wanted in the future. She didn't know what she wanted either. But she knew for sure that in the present, when it was just the two of them, they were golden.

Her friend raised an eyebrow. "Makes me happy to be married." She put a hand on Sloane's arm. "But this could be a good thing. Ella is more level-headed than Jess. More than your previous girlfriend, too."

Sloane crinkled one eye. "You know too much about me."

"Far too much," Layla agreed with a grin. "But I could

see you working. Tell Lucy, keep it separate from work, why not?"

"Because what if I fall in love with her, and then I have to leave? This year was meant to be about me putting some distance between me and Jess, and me and my family. It was about finding out who I really am. About showing that I can make it in another country. But I never intended to stay." She already had way too many feelings when it came to the subject of Ella. All of them burnished with flecks of gold and lust. Could they turn into love? She pushed that thought from her mind.

"Life is what happens while you're making other plans." Layla sat back. "My wife told me that when I freaked out after she got pregnant on our first try. I didn't think I was ready. I didn't think I could cope. I did. When something's right, you work to make your life fit around it." She shrugged. "That's what you've got to figure out when it comes to Ella. Does she feel right?"

Liquid glitter flowed through Sloane's veins. She pictured Ella, lying in her bed, gleaming like always.

"More than right."

"Then strap in for the ride."

* * *

Sloane got a cab back from training, then went for a walk along the nearby canal, even though it was bitingly cold. Or "brass monkeys" as the locals liked to say. She was learning more and more UK slang every day, and she had to admit she had a certain fondness for it.

It had snowed for the past couple of days, but the nearby

paths were all cleared and gritted. She was being extra careful as was warranted for someone in rehab. It felt brilliant to be back out on the training ground, doing what she did best. Maybe not scoring goals freely yet, but at least kicking a ball.

She pulled her green woollen hat as low as it would go without cutting off her vision, and shivered as she walked. The ducks on the water looked at her hat with envy.

Her phone vibrated in her pocket and she pulled it out. When she saw who it was from, she frowned. A message from Jess. What the hell did she want?

Just to let you know, me and Brit have split. I wanted to tell you before the media did. I know our affair broke us up, and I still have regrets over that. I'll be back in the UK for England camp. I never should have let you go, and I know I might have burned my bridges. But I'd love to see you, whatever. By the way, I found that ring you loved. The silver one with the black onyx stone? Remember the one you thought you'd lost? I found it in one of my old jacket pockets. I can give it to you when I see you, or I can mail it.

She signed off with three hearts and a single kiss.

Sloane wanted to throw her phone into the water, but that wouldn't benefit anyone. Jess had some gall, coming back to her after everything that had happened. But that was Jess. She got bored easily, but she was always happy to have a second try. It happened when she flip-flopped from learning to play the guitar, to learning the drums, and then back. In this scenario, Sloane was the guitar, and Brit was the drums. She wanted another strum. But Sloane wasn't about to get played, especially not by Jess. Also, the way she'd thrown the ring in casually at the end? She knew Sloane loved that ring. That it would make her reply. It made her want to scream.

Sloane dashed off a quick text to Jess asking her to mail it and reminding her of the address. For a moment, she hesitated, her finger over the send button. Jess probably wouldn't mail it – it would be like her to hold the ring hostage for a meet up. Sloane gritted her teeth, and pressed send.

She was staring at the sent message just as her phone lit up with another message.

This time, it was from someone she wanted to hear from. Ella.

Thinking about you. I'm going to stay here for New Year as my aunt's persuaded me, and also because the snow and fog are driving hazards. I'll see you when I'm back. Do not walk on icy paths. Can't wait to see you.

She signed off with a single kiss.

Now Sloane was very glad she hadn't thrown her phone in the canal. She very much wanted Ella in her life, even if she had to wait to tell her.

Jess was her past.

Ella could be her future.

Chapter Twenty-Six

It was the first week in January, the first time Ella had come back to work since her extended visit to her family. She'd had a good time, but she always felt bad leaving. However, she'd felt just as guilty staying away, too. Leaving Sloane when they'd just started whatever it was.

They hadn't talked about New Year plans, but she'd spent it with her aunt, just as her mum would have. She'd messaged Sloane, but the messages had been cool. As if they were both unsure how they should play this next pass. Ella had no idea. Everything she'd realised over her time away had just confused her more. Given her job, she really should be better at this.

Ella glanced out the window of her office, but could only see the top of two heads walking by. She knew Sloane was in today as she'd messaged her earlier. Ella's day had involved a chat with the whole team (bar Sloane) about getting back on track after taking time off over Christmas, and working their way back to full fitness. They'd told the squad to enjoy a glass of wine with their dinner if they wanted to, but she had no doubt a few had over-indulged. So long as it was only once, they could work with it. But she had to keep on top of the squad's physical as well as mental health, because the two were intrinsically linked. If your diet had gone to pot, it was probably a sign of something far deeper.

Nat was present at the meeting, which was the first time Ella had seen her since she'd met her with no trousers on. She'd blushed when their eyes met, but Nat had barely blinked. Perhaps the whole situation was nothing to her. It shouldn't be an issue. That is, if there was something there to build on. But for that to happen, Ella had to see Sloane again. It was time to seek her out.

She strode out into the corridor and walked past Lucy's office. She was on the phone, a frown pinching her forehead. Ella zipped up her training top, then glanced down at her boots. She still had them on from when she'd been out on the pitch having a performance session with a couple of youth players earlier. They were proving popular for those who found the pressure of face-to-face interaction daunting, and Ella was happy to comply.

Her boots click-clacked on the concrete as she walked from the training centre towards the pitch. The feeling as they sank into the turf was glorious as always. She breathed in the sharp January air mixed with fresh churned soil, then scanned the players in front of her, taking final orders from the coaches. In another life, in another realm, this could have been her. However, in this life, her job was a pretty good second best.

"Alright, good work everyone! If you want extra brownie points, feel free to stay out and train longer. Otherwise, get a shower, and don't forget hydro please!" That was Jonas, Lucy's right-hand man. She'd left today's second training session up to him. At the far end of the pitch was Sloane, doing some solo sprint drills, as well as light ball work with coach Sally. This was the first time Ella had seen Sloane back on the turf, and she could already see her recovery was nearly done. Great news for her and for the team.

"Fancy kicking some pens, coach?" Nat jogged over to where Ella stood.

Ella tried furiously not to blush again. She hoped she could get over this when it came to Nat soon enough.

"No, I'm good."

"Go on. You told us you were quite the player once. I bet you could put one past Becca." Nat nudged her with a grin.

"Nat! You coming?" Goalkeeper Becca jogged towards them, stopping when Nat turned.

"Just trying to convince Ella to join in." She turned back to Ella. "What do you say?"

"I think she wants to say yes."

Just the sound of her voice made Ella's blood heat in her veins.

Sloane.

Silky. Sultry. There.

Ella risked a glance upwards, and saw there was another 'S' to add to her list.

Sweaty.

Two more.

Still sexy.

Their reconnection and the effect on Ella made it feel like this shouldn't be done on a pitch in public, but rather just the two of them. But she couldn't change facts, no matter how much she wanted to reach out, kiss Sloane, drag her inside and strip her kit off. That would have to wait. Funny how Ella had spent the past week agonising over what may or may not happen, but when she laid eyes on Sloane, what should happen seemed like a simple answer.

They should be together. However long it might last.

"Good to see you back on the pitch." Ella's voice came out normal. A good sign. "How's the ankle holding up?"

"Well." Sloane held her gaze as she spoke.

Ella was glad she had bones, otherwise she might have melted onto the pitch there and then.

"I'm ahead of schedule. I had a lot of time to work on it over New Year. I had a final scan yesterday, and got the go ahead to kick a ball again. It's one of the best feelings I've had over recent weeks."

One of them. Ella swallowed down hard as the memory of the other feeling assaulted her senses. Yep, she could still feel Sloane inside her over a week on. Wanted her back there. She took a deep breath. "Great news, I'm thrilled for you."

"Thanks." Sloane turned to Nat. "Seeing as I can't leather a ball yet, and you can, let's do some penalty practice. I'll watch."

At Nat's enthusiastic, "Yeah!", Sloane turned to Ella. "Didn't you say your dream was to score a goal at the main stadium?"

Ella nodded. She had said that. It still stood.

"Then you're coming, too. Get warmed up, because the work up to that starts here."

When it was Sloane doing the talking, Ella didn't need much persuasion. She jogged after Nat and Becca, Sloane falling into step beside her. Every hair on Ella's body stood to attention. She hadn't realised this was how things were going to be when she got back. Sloane was like that Cadbury's Wispa she left in the fridge so she had "something sweet", just in case the urge took her. Yet half the time she opened the fridge, she devoured it in five minutes. She had no control over her feelings for either.

It scared her and excited her all at the same time.

"It's great to see you, even here. I missed you."

Sloane's words slid down her like honey. "I missed you, too."

That was all the chat they got. While Nat fired some shots at Becca, Ella and Sloane knocked the ball back and forth for five minutes to get her warmed up. Sloane even insisted on some sprints and stretches. "You've been sitting on your butt all day."

"Excuse me! I've been strategising and moulding young sporting minds."

"While mainly sitting on your butt." Sloane gave her a wide grin as she walked close to her. "And looking gorgeous as you do it," she whispered as she walked past.

Her words were champagne bubbles in Ella's chest.

"When you two have quite finished." Nat raised an eyebrow. "Do you want a go now?" She offered Ella the ball.

She nodded and took it. She'd hammered a few balls during training, but this was different. This was like she was back in her playing days. She'd taken a few penalties in her time, but not nearly as many as Sloane. Just imagining how she put them in under pressure made her appreciate her skill more. Penalties were 25 per cent practice, 75 per cent mindset.

Ella put the ball on the spot, took five steps back, eyeballed Becca, then side-footed the ball into her arms. She flung her head back and let out a small shout of frustration.

"You need to relax. You're too tight." Sloane walked up behind her. "You're overthinking it. Relax." She picked up the ball Becca had just rolled their way. Sloane locked her gaze with Ella. "Think about where you want to put it. How to strike it, where your body weight needs to be. See it going in. Take a deep breath. Run-up with purpose. Don't lean back."

Ella frowned. "I'm sure penalties never used to be this difficult."

Sloane grinned. "That's because you were used to taking them. You knew instinctively what to do. If you're going to score on the big stage, you've got to start somewhere. Here is as good a place as any." Sloane placed the ball on the spot, then stepped back.

Ella's heartbeat thudded in her ears. She wanted to score this; it was important. She'd told the team she used to play. She didn't want to be seen as a relic, a has-been. More than that though, it was also important to show Sloane she could. She wanted to impress her new lover.

She took another deep breath, focused on the bottom right corner, opened up her body and slammed the ball home. Relief flooded through. Ella wheeled away, arms in the air, and there to meet her was Sloane. Without thinking, she ran into her open arms and crushed her.

"Fucking yes! Still got it!"

Sloane picked her up and spun her around, before depositing her on the ground. "You certainly have." Then she paused, as Nat re-spotted the ball. "Now do it again."

Half an hour later, it was just Ella and Sloane still out on the pitch. Sloane wanted to jog more to get her back in the motion, and Ella joined her. They followed the touchline, not talking, but just the simple act of doing it together was enough.

After 15 minutes, Sloane slowed, Ella did the same, and

they made their way towards the changing rooms. Ella had a million questions slaloming around her head, but she had no idea which one to go with first. Perhaps none of them. She pushed open the door and Sloane brushed past her, pressing into Ella more than was strictly necessary. Ella was all for it. But she had to keep her head here. They both needed a shower. Which meant they both had to get naked.

Which she could totally cope with.

Sloane sat on the wooden bench of the changing rooms and took off her boots. She wiggled her toes and massaged her ankle.

"Still in working order?" Ella asked.

"I hope so." Sloane took off her socks and rolled them into a ball. Then she turned to Ella. "Are we going to talk about the elephant in the room? What you heard me say to Nat. Who, by the way, has been the soul of discretion."

"I know."

Sloane reached out and trailed her fingertips down Ella's thigh.

Ella stilled. Just the slightest touch from Sloane sent her senses into overdrive. It was delicious, but crazy.

"But I only told Nat the truth: that we didn't know what this was yet."

The heat inside Ella cooled for a moment. Where was Sloane going with this?

"I really want to see where this goes, but I know we need to talk about it first. We didn't find much time to do that over Christmas."

Ella swallowed down a huge breath. "We didn't." Her gaze raked Sloane's body. She'd found plenty of time for that.

"Do you feel the same?"

"That I want to touch you right now?" She couldn't hold those words in no matter how hard she tried. "God, yes." Ella moved closer. "I know we need to talk too, but..."

Sloane moved along the bench and pressed her lips to Ella's, igniting her desire like a match flicked onto spilled petrol.

Ella's memories of their kisses weren't a lie. Lying in bed at her aunt's, she'd recalled the way Sloane's lips unlocked something in her, something pure, primal. This time around, it was the same all over again. She'd spent the long, lonely nights imagining what they might do. Her dreams had them coming together at her flat, or at Sloane's. Not at work. But apparently, leaving them alone in a secluded place for a few minutes was the trigger for them to press play after their prolonged pause. When she pulled back moments later, they were both breathless.

Sloane's eyes were dark, mesmerising.

Ella stood and held out a hand. "I only have about 45 minutes before I have to leave for a client. Shall we get clean?"

Sloane's cheeks coloured pink. She stood and stripped off her training top.

Saliva flooded Ella's mouth. She wanted to take Sloane's breasts in her hands and lick them.

They hit the showers together, naked, neither saying a word. Ella lathered her hair with the club's apple-scented shampoo, and Sloane did the same. Then she washed herself, and Sloane echoed the action. Ella's ears were perked in case somebody came in. Her eyes were on Sloane the whole time, and vice versa. This was hands-off foreplay of the highest level. By the time they were done, Ella could hardly breathe.

It was only when they were both clean that Ella turned off her shower, then Sloane's, and stepped into her space, her skin pink and shiny from the hot steam. She pressed her palms to Sloane's breasts.

Sloane closed her eyes and let out a small moan. "Fuck, I missed you."

Ella stepped closer still, until their mouths were centimetres apart.

"I know we only had sex for two days, but it's been longer than that, hasn't it?"

"The months of build-up?" Ella didn't wait for an answer, instead crushing her lips to Sloane's, the hesitation of before now vanished in an instant. She pressed Sloane into the tiles, then took her hand, leaving her lips by her ear. "Come with me," she whispered huskily.

Ella grabbed their towels and led Sloane into the steam room, currently not in operation. They'd have to provide their own steam. She didn't think it would be a problem.

"I'm desperate to feel you." She led her to the edge of the seating and spread a towel. "Put your left leg up on the bench, lean against the wall and hook your arm around my neck."

Sloane raised an eyebrow. "So bossy."

Ella felt those words everywhere. "You complaining, Hotshot?"

Sloane shook her head.

"If you're wondering, having your foot up protects your ankle." Ella paused, pressing her naked body into Sloane, giving the contact they both craved. She put her lips next to Sloane's ear once more. "It also gives me delicious access to your pussy."

Sloane closed her eyes with a glorious moan.

Ella took that as her cue and dipped a finger inside Sloane. She gave an audible gasp at the arousal she found there. "You really did miss me."

"I wasn't lying," Sloane whispered, before taking Ella's bottom lip between her teeth and pulling it, hard. Then Sloane slipped her tongue inside Ella's mouth, and pressed a sultry, sweet shot of a kiss to her lips, one that ticked every box in Ella's body.

"Damn it, you feel so good." Ella pulled back, panting, and slipped in another finger.

Now it was Sloane's turn to groan.

"I wasn't going to fuck you here." Ella teased her fingers out and then back in, a slow drawl of an action she knew would drive Sloane wild. "But I can't keep my hands off you." She repeated her slow thrust, and Sloane's head fell to one side.

"I know the feeling." Sloane reached out a hand, cupped Ella's naked bum cheeks and pulled her closer.

The action drove Ella deeper into her. A rush of lust made Ella stumble forward, the epicentre throbbing between her trembling thighs. She loved fucking this woman. She loved being naked with this woman. If Sloane was in any doubt about that, Ella was going to prove it to her right this minute.

Sloane's kisses deepened as Ella carried on her intense sexual ambush. Her fingers slid to just where Sloane needed them, deep inside and then over her rock-hard clit. When Ella's circles started to gain speed, Sloane spread her legs, her desperate moans vibrating through Ella.

"Can you come standing up?"

Sloane opened her eyes and gave her a languid smile.

"Not before I met you. But it turns out, I have hidden talents."

At that, Ella moved in for the kill, taking in every second as a flare of red spread across Sloane's chest, before her fingertips gripped her, as well as her insides, and she came undone with a guttural moan. Ella made sure she'd given everything before easing out of Sloane, then gripping her with both arms. She kissed her ear lobe, her neck, her cheek, then finally her lips.

Sloane gave her a lazy smile as she grimaced. "Every muscle I own has locked up right now."

Ella grinned. "Put your other arm around my neck."

Sloane lifted an eyebrow.

"I'm stronger than I look. Do it, please."

She did, then Ella lifted her with a firm kiss to her lips. "Let me carry you back to your changing room, madam."

Sloane threw back her head and laughed as Ella did just that. "You are just full of surprises."

Ella started to walk. "You might have to open the door, though."

When they made it back to their abandoned clothes, Ella was relieved to see they were alone. If they'd come back out to an audience, that would have been awkward.

Sloane sat on the bench, then exhaled a deep breath.

Ella got dressed, then put her lips level with Sloane and kissed her. "You're too sexy and adorable, and you're going to make me late for my client who's booked in for 5pm." She checked her watch. One hour's time.

Sloane nodded, then pulled her clean training gear on, stuffing her training kit in her bag. She zipped it up, then stood face to face with Ella.

The electricity in the air was palpable. All it needed was one of them to lean forward again, and the fire would blaze once more.

"We still need to talk," Ella said. "But I did some thinking over my time away. I've no idea where this is going. I've no idea if I'm going to fall for you and get my heart snapped in two. But I'm a big girl. A grown-up. Plus, I can't do anything *but* see where this goes."

Sloane looked deep into her eyes, then took Ella's hand in hers. "I feel the same. We can't walk away from this. We can make this work." She ran her hands over Ella's butt. "I *really* want to fuck you."

Ella closed her eyes and smiled. "You've no idea."

"I do."

For a few moments, the only sound was their breathing. Hot and heavy. Then Sloane planted a bruising kiss on Ella's lips, and grabbed her bag.

Ella grabbed hers, too. "We're agreed? Let's see where this goes? And next time, we really need to talk as well. About who to tell and when. Because this can't be a secret." Ella locked her gaze. "Despite all my protestations that I wasn't going to get involved with anyone at work, it looks like I am. You've pierced my resolve."

"We can print that on our wedding invites." Sloane replied. "One more thing."

Ella raised an eyebrow.

"Have you got time to drop me off?"

"If you're really quick."

* * *

When they walked out of the changing room together, something had shifted. Not just Ella's libido, which was currently grinning from ear to ear. Sloane held the door for her as they turned into the main building hallway, and that's when it hit Ella they were really doing this. Since Christmas, events had been hazy: crisp one minute, blurred the next. Until she spoke to Sloane, stood next to her and breathed her in again, she had no idea how she was going to feel.

She absolutely did now. Luckily it was reciprocated. She and Sloane were each other's people, for as long as they could make it so. They were going to see where this went. As they strode down the corridor, past the main offices, Ella let a smile invade her face. For the first time in forever, she had a kernel of hope in her chest. Which was ridiculous, for a player who was probably going to leave the country in six months. But right here, right now, it was perfect.

Sloane pushed through the main door, and Ella got a flashback to their first day here. When Sloane had also held the door for her, just as she was doing now. They fell into step, walking across the car park to Ella's car. When their fingertips brushed, electricity snaked up Ella's arm. She wrapped her fingers around Sloane's hand, but Sloane shook it off.

That zapped Ella right from her dream.

"I don't want photographers getting photos and outing us, when we've only just worked out what we are. We've still got to talk about who we tell and when."

A stab of hurt hit Ella in the chest, but she nodded. She'd just told Sloane she was a grown-up. Plus, what Sloane said made sense. They'd already been snapped out together. If she was going to be Sloane Patterson's girlfriend, she was going to have to get used to that.

At some point, though, she wanted to be able to hold Sloane's hand whenever she wanted, or this wasn't going to be worth it.

She wanted to live in the moment, treasure every second, just as she always told her clients. Right now, Sloane was making her a hypocrite.

Ella really hoped Sloane was going to be worth it.

That she wasn't going to break her heart.

* * *

Later that evening, Ella's phone lit up with a message from Lucy. The email asked if she'd be interested in working with the men's team for the next month. Many of their backroom staff were off sick, their performance and lifestyle coach had been involved in a skiing accident, and a couple of their mental health team had physical ailments, and so were off for the foreseeable future. It would mean vastly reduced hours with the women's team for the next few weeks while the men's team set up a replacement. It would mean more work, more hours, more opportunity for Ella. She bit her lip as she sat back.

Had Lucy found out about her and Sloane? Was this a way of distancing them, or was this a genuine request? Ella kicked it around in her mind, then deduced it was genuine. Plus, this was what she wanted when she joined the club: the chance to work equally with the men and the women, to experience the different pressures they were under.

However, now she was totally invested in the women's team, and didn't want to step back. But the women's team were in a good place. They sat second in the league and everybody was in a good head space. Ella had contributed to that. The men were currently seventh in the table. Perhaps they needed her more. She messaged Lucy back to say she'd do whatever was needed, but she'd have to see what her schedule looked like with her other clients.

There was, of course, Sloane to think of, too. But Ella couldn't let what may or may not happen with Sloane dictate if she took this job or not. If she and Sloane worked out in the real world, that would be great. But if they didn't, this role gave Ella the experience she wanted.

Ella had to focus on her career goals, just like Sloane.

Hopefully, her heart goals would follow, too.

Chapter Twenty-Seven

"Sloane! Are you good to kick the ball one more time? Can we do that without your boss killing me?"

Sloane laughed. This photoshoot in a Salchester warehouse for *All Out Goals* magazine was taking her mind off the fact that Ella hadn't answered her message from earlier this morning. Scrap that, she hadn't even looked at it yet. But Sloane wasn't going to think about that. She had new job pressures. Sloane didn't want to add any more to her pile.

Instead, she was going to smile with her eyes, focus on activating all her muscles so her legs looked as toned as possible, and look like she'd just played her best ever game, even though her kit was pristine and she had more foundation on her skin than she ever thought possible. She recalled going to the end-of-season awards with Jess two years ago and being caked in makeup. It was nothing compared to this.

"Do you want me to repeat the same set of moves?" Sloane bent down and retrieved the football. She squeezed. It could do with some air.

The photographer, a man named Adam with more tattoos than bare skin from what she could see, gave her a thumbs up. At least he was a cool guy and not a sleazebag. There had been less of them at shoots as the years had gone on. Her first-ever shoot, the photographer had given her his number and asked to meet her for a drink that night. She was 18, he was in his 30s. She'd given him a withering look and requested never to be paired with him again.

"That's it, great, Sloane!"

Sloane stroked the ball into the low goal ahead of her once, twice, three times. Sloane never had an issue scoring, on the field and off. But keeping open lines of communication had always been her downfall. She'd thought Ella and her were on the same page, but it seemed as if Ella wanted Sloane to be both feet in, not tentative steps. Sloane had to work up to that. Plus, the fact that Jess was flying into the UK next month was always in the back of her mind.

Adam stepped out from behind the camera and walked over. "I think we're done for the day. We got some good shots." He gave her a thumbs-up. "When do you think you'll be back playing?"

She lifted her recovering foot. "Depends how it behaves, but I hope a couple of weeks. Things are going well, so fingers crossed. We've got a lot of games to fit in."

"Good luck with it."

Sloane was escorted over to the far end of the warehouse where a makeshift changing room was set up behind a screen. She changed into her jeans, Adidas sneakers, and her black sweatshirt, then was taken to a room at the far end where a journalist was waiting to interview her. Sloane held out a hand and gave Naomi her best smile. They'd spoken on the phone, but this was the first time they'd met in person. She wanted to make a good impression so Naomi wrote good things. She went into full PR mode. A little light flirting never hurt. Even though Ella would roll her eyes.

"Great to meet you finally, Naomi." Sloane gave her a firm handshake. Naomi had an undercut and wore baggy jeans. Sloane would bet the house she was queer.

Naomi blushed, as was Sloane's intention.

"Thank you so much for meeting with me. My friends are all so jealous!"

"No problem at all."

Naomi went straight for Sloane's injury and asked how it was healing, followed by what she thought about Salchester's chances of winning anything this season, along with the club set-up. Sloane gave her truthful answers, flecked with humour and charm. She'd done this dance a thousand times before.

"How are you settling into the UK?"

She exhaled. "I've been here six months. If I wasn't okay by now, you'd know. I didn't even go home for the holidays, that's how much I like it. I have three umbrellas, one for every type of rain. I'm prepared."

Naomi laughed. She was wearing a similar compass necklace to the one Sloane had bought for Ella. She had good taste. Sloane twisted her signet ring on her middle finger. Jess had sent it back, and it had arrived that morning.

"You need them here." She paused, then cleared her throat. "How's your relationship with your manager?"

Sloane fixed Naomi with her intense gaze. "Great. Lucy has been so supportive throughout my injury, as have all the team. I want to pay them back during the remainder of the season by securing the league, the cup, and a Champions League spot for next year."

"Small goals."

"Go big or go home." Sloane licked her lips. Naomi wasn't asking her anything too personal. She had no need to be worried.

Another clearing of the throat. "Talking of the rest of your team and coaching staff. It must be great to be around Layla Hansen after playing together in the US."

Sloane nodded. "It really is."

"She must have helped getting over your ex, Jess Calder?"

Sloane kept her face neutral. She wasn't going to tell Naomi about the messages she'd received from Jess just this morning, declaring love for her again. "Jess and I are still friends and she's having an amazing season. I wish her well."

"What about Ella Carmichael? You've been seen out and about a lot with her. Is there any truth in the rumour that you two are something more than friends?"

Sloane's neck muscles tightened. Almost ambushed, but she was still on alert. She uncrossed her legs, leaned forwards and locked Naomi's gaze once more.

"I'm purely focused on my recovery, nothing else. Ella and all the staff have been terrific. But getting back on the field is my only goal. Plus, friends go out for coffee, and Ella's a good friend. If I was dating everyone I went for coffee with, I'd be in big trouble."

* * *

Ella picked up the third time Sloane called, this time from the fancy executive car her agent had insisted on. It had a tiny TV in the back of the passenger seat, chilled water, and mini packets of Haribo to snack on. She'd already eaten two and was ignoring the others currently staring at her.

"There she is. How's your day been?"

"Long," Ella replied. "You know they say men are simpler creatures than women? They lied. I'm drained."

"Are you home? I'm just on my way back after the magazine interview and shoot."

"I am," Ella replied. "Did it go okay?"

Sloane wasn't about to bring up what Naomi had asked about Ella. That was on a need-to-know basis.

"Went fine. I've still got a face full of makeup. I thought I could come and show it off to you. Are you busy? I've missed you." Ella hadn't been around the women's team for the past two days, instead working with the men. Sloane was also keenly aware it was Ella's last night before her big move to her new apartment. She'd avoided thinking about Ella leaving her building. She'd gotten used to her being around. Her absence was going to be painful. "I could help pack if you've still got stuff to do? I packed all my stuff when I moved cross-country in the US. I'm really good at wrapping glasses."

"No end to your talents." Ella paused. "I do need to finish packing. But I have an early morning tomorrow, so I'm kicking you out before bedtime."

Sloane exhaled. "I promise, no touching, just packing. Plus, I'll order food. Sushi sound good?"

"Sushi sounds superb, thank you."

* * *

"Honestly, it's a whole different ballgame talking to the men." Ella leaned on her kitchen counter and studied the sushi selection. She circled a tuna nigiri in soy sauce and wasabi, then popped it into her mouth. She finished chewing before she continued. "Some of these boys haven't lived at home since they were eight, and they're all over the place. That's one of the perks of the women's game. No investment for years means nobody's left home too early. Everyone's far more grounded."

"Huh, I never thought of it like that. I wouldn't have minded leaving home, but that's just me."

Ella reached out and stroked Sloane's fingers. "I'm so sorry your parents didn't support you."

Sloane tingled all over at her touch. "It's okay. It's mostly in the past." She swirled a gyoza in the vinegar sauce and ate it. "This is delicious. You're going to have to come back and eat it with me even after you move."

"If you play your cards right." Ella snagged a gyoza, then patted her flat stomach. "Although I might be done for today." She was wearing an orange sweatshirt that brought out the colour of her eyes. Her hair was damp like she'd just stepped out of the shower. Which only made Sloane recall soaping Ella's naked body in the shower the other day. She shut down that train of thought. She was here to help pack, and nothing else.

"You ordered too much, you know that, right?"

"Can you ever have too much sushi?" Sloane wrapped a highball glass in newspaper on the opposite kitchen counter, tucking the edges into the top. She recalled doing exactly the same when she left Jess to move to LA. Wrapping glasses always came at pivotal moments. But this time, she hoped the glass owner stuck around in her life.

Ella was really leaving. Sadness slipped through Sloane like sand. "I don't know what I'll do without you living below me."

"You'll have to borrow someone else's vase next time

Cathy brings you flowers." Ella held it up, and handed it to Sloane to wrap.

Sloane licked her finger, selected two sheets of newspaper, and covered the glass. She added another two going the other way. She didn't want to be responsible for breakages. "Exactly. I need to go shopping."

"Or start shagging the new tenant."

Sloane narrowed her eyes. "Salty."

Ella leaned over and kissed her. "Do it and die."

"Only if they've got a really nice vase collection."

"Fair." Ella laughed.

Sloane was going to miss that sound, but she was determined to be supportive. Even though she'd miss everyday intimate moments like this. Moments that warmed her through like sunset on the longest day. Sloane picked up a mug with 'World's Greatest Mum' on it. As soon as she did, Ella whipped it from her hand.

"I'll do that one. It needs bubble wrap. Precious cargo." She stared at the mug, then back at Sloane. "I bought this for Mum when I was eight. She kept it all that time. I'm always amazed the lettering didn't fade, but we never had a dishwasher to batter it. Just me and Mum." Ella stared at the mug a little more.

Sloane closed the gap between them and hugged her tight. She kissed the side of her head, ran her fingers up the back of her neck, trailed them into her hairline and massaged her scalp. Ella let her for a few seconds, then stepped back.

"I'm fine." She wiped her eyes and exhaled. "I just don't want this broken. I know it's only a thing, but it might break me." At that moment, she looked about eight.

Sloane nodded, kissed her lips, and let Ella focus on wrapping the mug. "My mum bought me a mug once. It had a football on it. The only time she bought me something I actually wanted."

Ella swung her head around, her eyes shiny. She grabbed a piece of kitchen roll and blew her nose. "Do you still have it?"

Sloane shook her head. "Our dog, Coco, jumped up on the kitchen counter and smashed it." She'd like to say she'd been devastated, but she hadn't been. She was used to broken in her life. She pointed at Ella's mug. "So please double-wrap that."

"On it." Ella finished, held it up, and they high-fived. Then she paused. Stared into Sloane's eyes. Was Ella's honeyed gaze a little fractured?

"For the record, I'm going to miss living below you, too."

"Yeah?" One word. Big meaning.

A nod. "Yeah." Ella ran her tongue over her top lip. It kept Sloane transfixed. Her eyes were still shiny. Was it just about the mug, or was it something more?

Ella took a deep breath. "I was also thinking." She paused. "Will we be able to hold hands in public soon?"

Sloane rocked on her feet and blinked, hard. They still hadn't talked. It wasn't just her mind it was playing on. "Soon. I just want to get my comeback cemented first. Then there's the April international. I want to get my season back on track and I don't want anything or anyone getting in the way of that. I'm 28. This is likely my last World Cup. I want to be there, playing. My career has to come first. Which means I want to be in control of when we tell people. Not the other way around. Will you trust me on this?"

Ella bit her top lip. "Okay."

Sloane held her gaze and gulped. She could still see Jess's last message on her phone. The one that said she wanted to have a proper catch-up when she was over in April. The other reason Sloane didn't want this out in public was Jess. Sloane wanted to deal with her once and for all, wipe the slate clean. Then she'd go public with Ella. It was just over two months away.

"In the meantime," Sloane said, reaching for the next glass. "This cupboard isn't going to pack itself." She whipped up as much positive energy as she could muster. She didn't want to burden Ella with the Jess stuff. The rest of it was completely true, though. Once she'd taken care of Jess and her season, they could get on with their lives together. "By the way, I can help you move tomorrow after training."

Ella put a hand on her hip and smiled.

The energy changed. Sloane breathed a sigh of relief.

"Actually, I might need your Jeep. I haven't got loads of boxes, but more than I thought." She looked at the pile stacked by the door. "Are you happy to drive?"

"Of course. Anything for you."

Ella turned up her smile. "Thank you." She raised a single eyebrow. "But you might want to tone down the makeup. You look like you're about to go on *RuPaul's Drag Race*."

"I kinda like it." Sloane touched her cheek. "Brings out my feminine side. It's there, just often hidden."

"I know." Ella leaned in and kissed her lips.

The reconnection was exactly what Sloane needed. "Everything's going to work out, you know. I have faith."

"You sound convincing."

"I've lived a million lives."

Ella gave a reluctant sigh, then brought Sloane's right hand to her lips and kissed her knuckle. She stopped at Sloane's silver ring.

Shit.

"Did you get a new ring? I like it. Silver and black. Very butch." Ella grinned. "Goes with your makeup."

A rictus grin worked its way onto Sloane's face. Guilt prickled her skin. But she hadn't done anything wrong. Just reclaimed her property. "It's an old one I found again recently." Found it in the mail when Jess had, after all, returned it.

"It's very you," Ella replied. "But enough chat. Like you said, this packing won't do itself, will it?"

Chapter Twenty-Eight

Ella was glad to be in work today. Her new flat was still a mess of boxes and other people's dust, and she'd had no time to do anything about it. However, the move had gone smoothly, thanks to Sloane, with added help from Nat.

Ella was impressed Nat was playing as well as she was, with her parents still causing issues. However, they had at least started to message her again unprompted, which made Sloane very happy. She was living her alternate reality through her teammate. Ella had everything crossed it worked out second time around.

A knock on her door made her look up. She was about to tell whoever it was to come in, but Sloane already stood in front of her desk, that crease on her perfect forehead, a taut hand pinned in her hair.

"Good, you're alone." She tapped her fingertips on the top of Ella's desk.

Sloane's fingers always got Ella's attention. Something was up.

"What's wrong?"

Sloane held out her phone. "Press play and find out."

Ella did as she was told while Sloane pulled over a chair. A prominent YouTuber had put together a montage of the two of them, set to a Taylor Swift love song, one of Ella's favourites. After watching it, Ella had to admit it was pretty good. If she was a fan, she'd totally believe they were a couple. Which they were. The video and its screenshots were doing the social media rounds. Ella knew there were only so many times they could deny anything was going on.

"What do you think?"

Ella walked around her desk and leaned on the front of it. She breathed in Sloane's familiar bergamot scent, already one of her favourites. She wanted to wipe the frown from her face. "I think we get ahead of any gossip and tell Lucy. Whether she's seen the photos or not, she'll hear about it." She glanced to her right. "She's there right now. Strike while the iron's hot?"

Sloane nodded, then put a hand on Ella's arm. "We're just telling Lucy for now?"

Ella sucked on the inside of her cheek. She didn't like hiding anything, but this was for Sloane more than her. She had to follow Sloane's lead in this. Plus, she didn't want the world knowing their every move, either. She nodded.

When they walked into Lucy's office moments later, questions flashed across her face. "Why do I get the feeling I'm not going to like this?"

Ella dragged a seat across and settled into it. "It's not bad news," she said, allaying Lucy's fears. "We just want to let you know something." She paused, then glanced at Sloane, who looked terrified. Surely she'd handled this sort of thing before? But perhaps it was different with a member of staff rather than a fellow player.

"Have you seen the montage of us on social media?" Ella studied Lucy's face as she reacted.

She shook her head. "I haven't." She frowned. "Should I have?"

Ella risked a smile. "No. But speculation is starting to build about whether or not we're more than friends." She took a deep breath. "It's very early days and we want to keep this on the downlow, but we wanted you to know, as our boss, that we are an item. A new, freshly formed item."

Lucy moved her mouth left, then right. "Okay." She paused. "Since when?"

"Since Christmas," Sloane replied.

"Right." Lucy sucked on the inside of her cheek.

Ella cleared her throat, now incredibly itchy. "We want you to know, just in case you see photos and you're curious. But because we're so new and because Sloane is who she is, we're not going public just yet. But we wanted to keep you informed."

"And let you know that when we're in work, we'll be nothing but professional," Sloane added.

That made Ella blush, thinking about the steam room.

Mostly, professional.

Lucy's gaze landed on them both, before she tapped her pen on her desk and took a deep breath. "First, wow. I have to say, I didn't see it coming, but my wife always says I'm a bit slow on the uptake, so no surprise there. You're both grown adults, and you both know the score.

"Relationships between football coaches and players aren't okay, but we've had physios dating players before. Performance and lifestyle coaches? I don't know, we don't have a precedent. But I'm sure I don't have to tell either of you that as soon as this comes out, there will be more scrutiny on you both, from inside and outside the squad." She pointed at Ella. "If you were a team psychologist, it would be a no."

"I know," Ella replied.

"But you're not, and you're not full-time. Plus, we like what you do, and I trust you both to keep this professional at work." She turned her intense gaze on Ella, then on Sloane. "Can I trust you both?"

Ella nodded. "Of course."

Sloane followed suit.

Lucy blew out a breath. "Don't make me regret being okay with it and giving you the green light, okay? So long as you do your jobs well and don't let any outside pressures into this arena, you have my support." She sat back and folded her arms. "Office romances happen every day. You've got to be on the side of love, right?"

Ella blinked rapidly, and glanced sideways at Sloane. Love? Nobody had mentioned love yet. Sloane's cheeks went the colour of a beetroot. However, she wasn't going to dispute what Lucy had said.

She liked Sloane.

An awful lot.

Everyone had to start somewhere.

* * *

"I think this is the one." Ella stretched out on the blue velvet corner sofa from Heals. It was way beyond her price range, but she figured it was an investment in her future. Sloane's words had made her think she could afford it herself if she paid for it on a credit card and dipped into her savings. That she deserved it. It was going to take six weeks to arrive, and by that time, she already knew she'd be sick of the old one. Her mum had never treated herself, always worrying about the future. That hadn't got her very far. Ella made a promise to herself there and then that she'd live life to the full and get what she wanted and deserved. This sofa was her first big solo purchase.

"It's got your name written all over it." Marina sank into it. "Really comfortable, too. I reckon you could have very intimate times on here with a certain world football star."

"Shhhh!" Ella glanced around the store. "Somebody might hear you." However, there was nobody within earshot.

"Nobody's interested. I still don't get why you can't be out and proud. Are you not expecting it to work? Is that what she thinks?"

Ella would be lying if she said that thought hadn't crossed her mind. But she shook her head anyway. "She doesn't want anything putting pressure on her comeback, which I get. She's just been through the wringer with Jess. She doesn't want new speculation. Plus, she's trying to protect me, I think."

"So chivalrous, or something." Marina raised an eyebrow. "Honestly, your life is like a soap opera."

"Try living it."

Marina lay down and got comfy. "I'm just trying it out for when I stay over. I think this would work to sleep on." She returned to a sitting position and gave Ella a wry grin. "You know what? Even though your start has been a little mysterious, I like that you're with Sloane."

"Are you buttering me up to get free tickets?"

"I assume that's a given." Marina flashed her perfect set of pearly whites, courtesy of a teeth whitening treatment she spent a fortune on last year. She maintained it was worth every penny. "Only, I do need to hang out with her again soon. As your closest family, I feel like I need to properly vet your future wife."

Ella gave her cousin a withering look. "We're not getting married."

"Yet," Marina qualified. "But I like the fire she's lit behind your eyes. You seem different, more alive. I wanted you to find someone, and you have. Now I just have to sort myself out."

"You do," Ella agreed. "But seriously, who knows where this is going. She's gorgeous, talented, and famous, and I can't quite believe she's sleeping with me."

"I can. You're a catch."

"I'm not Sloane Patterson."

"That's good, because I doubt she wants to sleep with herself." Marina waggled a finger in her direction. "She might be queen of the pitch, but you're the queen of her heart."

Ella snorted. "Do shut up, you're making no sense." Then she lay back on the sofa, making sure to keep her feet off the material. She wriggled, then gave a firm nod. "This is comfy. And it's massive. Even a giant could sleep here. You definitely could, seeing as you're a leprechaun."

Marina slapped her in protest.

Ella smiled, and went quiet for a moment. "Do you think it will be okay, though? Me and her? You saw the necklace she bought me for Christmas. It cost a lot, I looked it up." She sat up next to her cousin again, and pursed her lips. "Remember the issues I had around money with Reba? I worry it's going to be the same with Sloane."

But Marina was having none of it. "Your issues with Reba were more than money. You never seemed that happy with her. Whereas you seem smitten with Sloane, even though it's early days. You were never like this with Reba, even after six weeks, when you really *should* be. Yes, Sloane's rich and famous, but in a good way. She earns money doing something she loves. More to the point, something *you* love. From what you've said, she's a good person. And she has good taste in jewellery. Reba earned money as a city financier. Reba loved money for money's sake. There's a huge difference."

Ella hadn't thought about it like that. She and Sloane did have so much more in common. Plus, when Reba had bought Ella expensive jewellery, it had been for show, and not really Ella's style. Whereas Sloane had taken the time to splash her cash on something meaningful.

"Plus, you're older and wiser now, too." She paused. "And if it does all go tits up, at least you can say you shagged a World Cup winner."

Ella burst out laughing, then elbowed her cousin in the ribs. Only someone who'd known her their whole life could say that.

Marina grinned. "Where is she today?"

"Training. She's got her first game back tomorrow. She's really excited, as am I. I've missed seeing her toned, supple legs on the pitch."

"Perve."

"I'm allowed to say that, she's my girlfriend." At least, Ella hoped she was. "We're meeting later at Kilminster. Sloane's meeting her cousins at the local game."

"Can I come?"

Ella shrugged. "So long as you don't say anything embarrassing, sure."

Marina's mouth dropped open and she put a hand to her chest. "Little old me? I'm the soul of discretion."

* * *

Ella scanned the car park as she and Marina got out of their cars, but she couldn't see Sloane's Jeep yet. She led Marina across the gravel to the pitch beyond, carrying a coffee in a portable cup for Sloane, bought from Shot Of The Day.

Marina had called her a sap.

Ella had told her to shut her face.

"Blimey, this looks like the places you used to play in back in the day," her cousin told her as their feet sank into the damp grass. She scrunched her face. "I thought those days were gone." Marina picked up her dainty shoes, not built for muddy fields.

"You were the one who wanted to come." Ella hoped her scowl would shut Marina up. "No moaning."

"I was just saying," Marina replied as they got to the side of pitch.

"Try not to."

"Who rattled your cage?" Marina pulled her grey bobble hat over her ears and raised her chin to the sky, as she did when she was annoyed with Ella.

Maybe she'd been a little harsh on her, but Ella put it down to nerves. Taking Marina anywhere was always like that. She was Marmite. People either loved her, or they hated her. There was no in between.

"Ella, over here!" In the distance, Ella spotted someone in bright green waving in their direction. She squinted, but couldn't quite make out who it was, but assumed it was Cathy. She waved back.

Minutes later, Cathy and Hayley arrived beside them, cheeks rosy, breath swirling around their faces. Ella hadn't seen them since Christmas, but it was as if no time had passed. They hugged her immediately.

"This is my cousin, Marina. These are Sloane's family, Cathy and Hayley."

Marina pulled them in for a hug, and they accepted with grace. "I love this ground. It's so wonderfully retro, with the pitch and the clubhouse." She gave a wistful look. "Just charming."

Ella had forgotten Marina was a grade A actor when she wanted to be, too.

"All my favourite people here at once!"

Ella whipped around to see the one who mattered most walking towards them, a Salchester Rovers winter jacket zipped up over her training gear.

"You made it!" Her heart skipped a beat as Sloane walked beside her and laid a chaste kiss on her cheek, followed by a squeeze of her hand.

"Got to support the family, just like they're supporting me in my first game back tomorrow."

"We can't wait," Cathy confirmed, hugging Sloane. "To see you in action, it's going to be such a treat."

"And when I score, it's for Eliza, remember."

Ella gave Sloane her coffee.

"Is this from where I think it's from?"

"With cream," Ella added. "Suzy's started stocking it just for you."

"I could get used to this service." The smile she gave Ella

warmed her right through. Even her toes. Which up until now had stayed staunchly frozen. That was the power of a Sloane Patterson smile.

"I was just saying to your family what a charming ground this is," Marina told Sloane.

Ella nudged her elbow. Marina didn't have to lay it on so thick.

"If by charm you mean it's falling down, then yes, it definitely is," Cathy said with a laugh. "We're doing a fundraiser again at the end of the season if you want to donate anything, Sloane. No pressure, but it might help."

"I'd be more than happy to contribute something," Sloane replied. "Have you got a new sponsor yet?"

Cathy shook her head. "We had a company interested, but the cost-of-living crisis has affected everyone, so they've pulled out." She nodded at the players. "Hence the shirts are still plain."

Shouts went up from the crowd as Kilminster went close, but their forward leaned back and skyed it at the vital moment.

"Unlucky, Nathan!" Cathy yelled. "Good cross, Ryan!" She tilted her head. "We're going back to our usual places now. You're welcome to join us, or we'll see you in the clubhouse after the game?"

Sloane nodded. "We'll see you in there."

"Hang on, I need the loo," Ella said. "I'll walk with you." As she left, she gave Marina a look which said, 'Do not say anything bad'.

Marina simply gave her a sweet smile in return.

* * *

Clare Lydon

Sloane grinned at Marina, then cupped her hands around her coffee to warm them up. The last weekend of January and the weather was brutal, but she kinda liked it. Plus, she also liked knowing it had an end. She'd missed having seasons in LA. Plus, weather like this reminded her of growing up in Detroit, where you always needed gloves in winter.

"You'll have to come and meet my parents, too, now I've met your family. I know they'd love to get to know you." Marina paused, then pulled back her shoulders. "Now that you and Ella are a thing."

Sloane registered the vibe shift. "Absolutely. I would love to. It probably won't be until after international break now, though." So long as she was selected, which wasn't a given. "Unless they come visit. Then they can meet my family, too."

Her family. She'd never introduced her family to anyone who mattered since she was old enough to have a say. It was nice that Cathy had changed this.

"I know they'd appreciate you going there. It would show you're serious about Ella."

Okay. Sloane had not imagined she was going to get *the speech* standing on the sidelines of a non-league game from Ella's cousin, but that appeared to be what this was. Unless she was misreading the room. That Marina was tiny counted for nothing. She had clearly turned up here with an agenda. Sloane turned to face her.

"I assure you, I am serious about Ella. She's an amazing woman." Sloane assessed Marina as she spoke.

Marina's red lipstick glared in full force, her eyes fixed on Sloane, searching for holes in her words. Ella's cousin had on her poker face. Did she do this to everyone Ella dated?

"She is." Marina took a step forward. "She doesn't open herself up to relationships very often, and when she does, she's all in. You know what I mean?"

"Uh-huh." A prickle of uncertainty crawled up her spine. She really hoped Marina wasn't about to thump her in the stomach.

"I read that magazine article you did recently. Where you said there was nothing going on with you and Ella. I know why you said it, but it left a sour taste in my mouth. It did with Ella, too, no matter what she tells you. I just hope you're not stringing her along for whatever reason. That you're genuine. Because I wouldn't want her to get hurt. You might be famous, but that won't stop me keying your Jeep if anything happens."

"You're going to key my Jeep?" Sloane fought the urge to laugh. She had to hand it to Marina. If Sloane ever wanted someone to go to bat for her, she'd choose her.

Sloane held up her hands, as if Marina was about to shoot her. "I promise, as I've told Ella, I want to protect us and my recovery by taking the spotlight off our relationship. But as soon as the internationals are done, we'll post subtle photos." She tried a smile. "I get you're protective, and it's sweet, but you don't need to be." She put a hand to her chest. "I'm not going to break her heart."

Marina narrowed her eyes, then cracked a smile. "Okay, I believe you."

The crowd roared behind them.

Sloane turned around to see Ryan wheeling away, arms in the air, pursued by his teammates. "Dammit, I missed my cousin scoring."

Marina laid a glove on her arm. "But you got the seal of approval from me."

Chapter Twenty-Nine

"I love this new couch, by the way. Have I told you that?" Sloane stretched out her long legs and eased herself back, groaning as she did.

"You sound about 50, not 28."

"I'm 29 next week. The day I go to camp. Can you believe it?"

"Ancient. I'm going out with an old woman." Ella leaned over and kissed her. "Just know, I'm coming to yours the night before, like it or not." She raised an eyebrow. "I have to give you your early birthday gift, right?"

A thrill worked its way through Sloane's body. Ella had the power to do that whenever she wanted. Plus, she looked so damn sexy in her pink shorts. Her apartment was way hotter than it was outside. "So long as my gift is more Half Cream from Lakeland, I'm down with it."

Ella laughed. "And you should know, with your help, I'm getting far better at spending money on myself, buying treats. I bought this sofa for one, which was a big shift."

"It was."

"For all you know, I might have bought you four boxes of Half Cream for your birthday. Really splashed out."

"A girl can dream." Sloane kissed Ella's full, soft lips again. "I've missed you and your sharp wit."

"What about my awesome bum?"

"That, too." She wasn't joking. Over the past three months, she'd memorised every inch of Ella's skin. Her arse was a particular highlight.

She tapped Ella's exposed knee. "I know I've said it before, but I still can't get over the size of the scars on your knee."

"Medical advancements make a big difference. Plus, fucked up operations don't help. At least I don't walk with a limp and can still kick a ball."

Sloane tilted her head. "Is it just me, or does that top scar have shades of Dan the physio when Lucy's had a go at him?"

They hadn't spent the night with each other because of away games and schedules for over a week, but tonight was going to change that. Sloane had turned up earlier with Thai food, and now they were settled on the couch to watch a key midweek game in the Premier League between Rovers and Blackthorn Stars. The end of March was a crunch time in the men's and women's seasons.

Her comeback so far had proved successful, with her and Nat picking up where they left off. She put that down to hard work, she and Ella being in a good place, and the team working well. They were still in the FA Cup, and still on track to contest the league. Everything to play for.

On screen, a youngster for Rovers broke down the wing and delivered a delicious cross. Sloane let out a low whistle. "That guy can really play football."

Ella whipped her head around. "Oh my god!"

"What?" Sloane's heart leapt. What just happened?

"You said football, not soccer!" Ella raised her arms in triumph. "My work here is done."

Sloane rolled her eyes. "It was a slip of the tongue."

"Busted." Ella nudged her in the ribs.

Sloane opted for a quick subject change. "Are you seeing your family this weekend?"

"Nice segue." Ella grinned. "I am. Driving over on Saturday. I'll be back for the game on Sunday. It's a shame you can't come too – they're desperate to meet you. 'The woman you're seeing but not seeing' as my aunt puts it."

Sloane winced. "After international break – providing I'm selected – I'm coming to Midcombe. Promise."

"I know." Ella elongated the final word with an eye roll. "And you'll get picked, don't be stupid." She paused. "I also have fantastically massive Easter Eggs for them – Marina inhales chocolate – so they're going to be thrilled."

Sloane wriggled, shifted Ella off her, and jumped off the couch. Her ankle didn't even flinch. She spoke to it every morning to confirm it was still her favourite ankle. It was holding up well, but she liked to cover all bases. "Talking of Easter Eggs, I got you one. Just to show you my gifts aren't always flashy."

Ella stroked her necklace. "Don't get me wrong, I like flashy as much as the next woman."

Sloane laughed as she went to the kitchen to get her bag. She marvelled again at how Ella had made this flat so much homier since they came to view it. A retro chrome clock on the kitchen wall. Funky yellow kettle and matching toaster. Fresh flowers on the white kitchen table. Then, it had lacked soul. Now, it pulsed with it.

When she got back to the living room, Ella was lying on the couch like a modern-day goddess, her hair fanned out on both sides. She was so concentrated on the game, she didn't even notice Sloane and what she was holding. Not until she cleared her throat.

When she did, Ella's face lit up. "A Wispa Easter Egg!" She got up, took the chocolate egg from Sloane and danced around the room with it pressed against her chest. She glanced up at Sloane when she stepped closer to her. "This is a fantastic gift. You're good at this." Ella put the egg down, grabbed Sloane and put her arms around her neck, swapping dance partners with ease. "An unexpected gift from my unexpected gift."

When Ella smiled up at Sloane, she took her breath away. The soft rouge on her cheeks, her mess of shiny hair, her rich, caramel gaze.

"You're quite the gift, too." Sloane kneaded her fingers on the base of Ella's spine. Every time they got like this, and she looked into Ella's eyes, she saw a possible clock ticking. But she didn't want this to end, and she was going to do everything in her power to make sure it didn't. Even if Salchester didn't renew, she'd press Adrianne to work something out.

Ella frowned. "What's going on with you? I was just about to kiss you, and you drifted away."

Sloane shook her head. "Not me. I'm right here." She leaned in and pressed her lips to Ella. "Kissing my beautiful girlfriend." She pushed her tongue into Ella's mouth, desperate to feel her hot breath. This was what she needed. No thinking required. This was uncomplicated, it was magical, and Sloane was here for it.

They didn't turn the game off before they stumbled to the bedroom.

***

When Sloane woke the next morning, Ella wasn't there, but she could hear the water running. Her muscles ached from yesterday's training, but the sweet hum of last night still glittered inside. They hadn't declared love for each other yet, but Sloane might be ready soon. It had taken her over nine months with Jess, and that was quick. She wasn't usually someone to fall hard and fast. She feared Ella might have broken all her rules.

She grabbed her phone from the bedside table. Her onyx ring sat beside it. When she saw a string of messages, her heart sank. More from Jess. In the middle of her night. No doubt a little wasted.

She'd started up again over the past week, and this was the third night running Sloane had woken up to them. Jess was worried she wouldn't be selected for the England team, because her form had dipped since she and Brit imploded. She kept reminiscing about the time she and Sloane were together, when they both played fabulously for their respective countries. Last night, she'd written, *Maybe we should get back together when I'm over for the game. We might both score.* It wasn't funny, even said in jest. Sloane had hoped Jess's loss of form would mean she didn't get picked. Then she wouldn't come to England. However, the final message this morning told her otherwise.

Just to let you know, I got into the England camp. Shit knows how. Hopefully we can see each other before, too. I miss you, Sloane. See you in a couple of weeks.

Sloane dropped her phone and closed her eyes, picturing

Ella in the shower. Her round butt, her perfect breasts, her fiery eyes. She didn't deserve Jess walking back into their lives, and Sloane wouldn't let it happen. Maybe she could arrange coffee with her beforehand to sort things out. Would that be wise? She ground her teeth together. She had no idea. She wanted to keep her new life and her old life far away from each other. On the field was one thing. Off it, she could control.

She sent a message back to Jess, telling her she'd see her for coffee at some point to catch up.

Providing Sloane was selected. She wiped her brow. If she wasn't, it would be devastating. But at least it meant she wouldn't have to see Jess.

Silver linings.

Only, this camp was crucial. The final one before the World Cup. If she wasn't selected for this, her chances of making the tournament were slim. Would her five goals since her return be enough to get her noticed? She hoped so. People often thought it was obvious she'd be selected, but not Sloane. She'd experienced the crush of non-selection before, and it had stung. However, she'd done as much as she could to make her case. It was up to the coach.

The bedroom door opened, and Ella came in, a blue towel wrapped around her, her hair a damp bird's nest on top. She looked edible. She grinned at Sloane. "Morning, Hotshot!" She walked over, kissed Sloane, then pulled back. "After last night, maybe you need a new nickname. Something sexy." She put a finger to her lips. "Leave it with me."

Guilt slithered through Sloane. Should she tell Ella about Jess? But she didn't want to knock that smile off her face. Not one bit.

Ella frowned. "Everything okay? You've got your crease back." She pointed to her forehead.

Sloane wiped her face, then plastered on a smile. "Perfect. Just had a funny dream, that's all."

Ella nodded. "Did you see the England team has been announced?" She paused. "Jess is in it." Her eyes clouded, and her energy dipped.

"Is she?" Sloane hoped she sounded convincing.

"She is, so this is your chance to trip her up and show her who won in the end." Ella winked, a dismissal of that subject. "But more importantly, Nat and Becca made the cut. Isn't it amazing? I feel like a proud aunt. Two of our babies being called up."

"Fucking awesome."

Ella towelled her hair, then sat, naked, next to Sloane.

"Do you remember when we viewed this flat? When that agent caught us nearly kissing? She should have seen us last night." She smiled, clearly thinking back. Sloane knew, because she was, too. "You hear about the US team today, right?"

Sloane grimaced. She'd tried not to think about it, but it was big news. "Two o'clock. The coach calls at 9am Eastern."

"You'll be in." She cupped Sloane's chin in her hand. "Who can resist this face?"

Chapter Thirty

"Do you remember where we used to play?" Lucy kicked the ball to her.

Ella trapped, controlled, did a couple of keepy-uppy's just to impress herself, then struck it back to her boss. Nat and Becca had said goodbye to the team today to report for England duty. Along with Sloane, they had six other players out for their country friendlies over the next two weeks, including Layla for Norway. Lucy had asked if Ella fancied a coffee, but as they were both still kitted up from training earlier, she'd suggested a kickabout. Lucy had been all for it.

"Not on pitches like this."

"Not in kit like this," Lucy confirmed. "These kids today, they don't know they're born." She smiled at her own words as she stilled the ball. "When exactly did I turn into an old woman?"

Ella laughed. "You're not old. There's not one grey hair on your head."

"My wife is really annoyed with me about that, too." Lucy picked up the ball and walked Ella's way.

It was early April, the sun was still out, and spring was in the air. It'd been a chilly March, but Ella hoped today was a sign the temperature was about to shift upwards. No matter what the weather, though, she still loved the feel of the grass beneath her feet. The smell of earth in her nostrils. It would always feel like home.

"Shall we call it a day?"

"Yes please. Half an hour is plenty."

Lucy gave her a grin. "Don't tell the players."

They fell into an easy stride together, Ella shielding her eyes from the still-high April sun. In the distance, cars rumbled by on the dual carriageway, but on this pitch, she was in another world altogether.

"How's Sloane feeling about the camp? Big game in the World Cup lead-up."

"I've been trying to get her to focus on other things. I know she was tense waiting for the call-up after her injury. Once that was through, she was fine. Now it's just a case of showing what she can do. I'm not worried."

"England should be, maybe."

"There is that." Ella thought back to the other morning when Sloane had seemed preoccupied, and had jumped when she'd asked what she was looking at on her phone. Maybe she was more worried than she'd let on. The injury had made her doubt herself, but she was back on form now. Her off-pitch life was solid, and that always translated to game-time.

"You two seem good?" It was more a comment than a question, but Ella couldn't help smile.

They were better than good.

They were flying.

"We are, although it'll be nice when we can be truly public." She shook her head. "But I wake up happy, so I can't complain."

"I think you're the ideal couple," Lucy confirmed. "Plus, whatever you're doing for each other, keep it up. I've got a very happy top-notch striker, and a radiant performance coach, both at the top of their game. We missed you for those six weeks you were with the men. It's good to have you back. The men didn't want to lose you. You're in demand."

They reached the dugout at the side of the pitch, and Lucy grabbed bottles of water from the bucket and gave one to Ella. She waited until Ella had loosened the cap and taken a swig before she spoke.

"I wanted to ask as well about your plans. You and Sloane. Have you chatted about next season?"

Ella gulped, then shook her head. "Not really. She wanted to wait until after international break."

Lucy nodded. "Makes sense." She paused. "But if there was a way I could make the budget work, would you be interested in a full-time post? Maybe part-time performance coach, part-time youth football coach? If that's something that interests you, you could take some coaching badges." She held up a hand. "I haven't worked it out quite yet, but I think it could work. You being out on the pitch doing personal sessions with the youngsters while working with the ball got me thinking. Plus, that would take you further out of Sloane's orbit, if she stays. If you went full-time performance coach, we'd have to clear things with those higher up. I don't want to lose you because of your relationship, Ella."

Pure, hot joy sparked inside Ella. "Yes, I absolutely would be interested." Spur of the moment, she pulled Lucy into a hug.

When she let go, her boss stepped back with a grin.

"Sorry, I just… That would be my dream full-time job. A mix of off-field and on-field."

"Slow down, I haven't worked it out yet. But if we're serious about the women's team development, then why not? Especially if things pan out this season, then the top brass have to back me."

"I totally agree."

"Good, I'm glad." Lucy drained her water bottle, and started to walk into the main building. She held the door open for Ella. They both went straight to the changing room and swapped their boots for trainers. "When's Sloane joining up with the team?"

"Tomorrow morning. She's home getting ready now. I'm going around after this for an early birthday tea. She's looking forward to seeing all her friends again. It's been a while." Ella was just glad Jess wasn't American. She'd be teaming up with Nat and Becca. They would give her all the gossip on Jess when they got back.

"Wish her happy birthday from me. She'll have a great time at camp. Apart from losing the game." Lucy grinned, then snapped her fingers together. "Talking of which, come to my office. I got the VIP passes for us. England vs USA at Wembley, and for once, we're only slight underdogs. We're sitting in the good seats. Now, you just have to decide who you're cheering for on the night."

Chapter Thirty-One

Sloane locked her car and strolled towards her apartment block. She was nearly at the door when she realised she'd left her bag in the back seat. She cursed, then turned back to the car. She scanned the parking lot, checking for photographers or fans. Since the US team announcement, she'd had a few more hanging around. She couldn't see any this evening, thankfully. She got her bag, slammed the door again, but when she turned again, a familiar figure stood in front of her.

Jess. She looked thinner, which told Sloane all she needed to know. Jess didn't eat well when she was unhappy. Old muscle memory made Sloane want to put an arm around her, then feed her a bowl of chicken and pasta. But that wasn't on the cards today. Sloane had a birthday meal to eat, and a camp to get to. Ella was due soon. She had to get rid of Jess, and fast.

Slow spokes of anxiety turned in her chest.

"What are you doing here?"

"Hello to you, too." Jess tried a cocky smile, but it didn't quite reach her eyes. "Look at you, driving a posh car like you live here." Her English accent was American-flecked, her lips chapped.

Sloane frowned. "I *do* live here."

"You know what I mean."

Not really. "My first question still stands." Sloane glanced around again. If Ella arrived when Jess was here, that would not be a good look. Sloane needed to get rid of her ex as soon as humanly possible. "I thought you were flying in with the US girls tomorrow?" That's what Jess had told her on one of her many messages.

Jess shook her head. "I was, but then I got an earlier flight so I could see my family for a couple of days."

Sloane raised an eyebrow. "And they've moved into my apartment complex?"

Jess rolled her eyes. "No silly." She reached out a hand and gripped Sloane's arm. "You're my family, you know that." She sighed. "I missed you, Sloane, it's so good to see you. You're looking good. You got all my messages, right? Your replies have been short and sweet, or non-existent. But you said we should meet up for coffee." Jess let go of Sloane and spread her arms wide. "Here I am, ready for coffee, and to wish you happy birthday for tomorrow. I thought if I turned up in person, you'd have to speak to me."

Jess had a point. It did make her almost impossible to ignore.

"Also, I saw that YouTube montage of you with that other woman. Ella, is it?" She leaned in. "Very impressive, these YouTubers. They go to so much effort."

Jess held her gaze. Sloane had to hand it to her. After everything that'd happened, she was brazen. Or a sociopath. She couldn't decide.

"It felt like now was the right time. To come and see you. Have coffee, look into your eyes, show you and tell you I'm not over you."

Really? After everything? Jess had said that back in December post-Brit fallout, but Sloane thought she'd be over it by now. Sloane hadn't encouraged her. But then, Jess was never good at reading between the lines. Sloane had tried to be kind. She knew what it was like to be far from home and alone after a break-up. Maybe that had been her downfall.

Perhaps now was the time to be blunt.

Sloane's ears flared hot, and her stomach churned. She was just about to spit out her killer opening line when Ella's car sailed around the corner.

Breath backed out of Sloane's body, as alarm skidded in.

She wanted to disappear, but she couldn't. There was no way she could get rid of Jess before Ella spotted her now. She knew very well what this looked like, because every time Jess was mentioned in the press – particularly concerning this game – Sloane's name never seemed to be far behind. It didn't matter they'd been officially split for months. As far as the world was concerned, they came as a pair.

Sloane had to try some damage control before Ella got here.

Maybe she could appeal to Jess's better nature – although she wasn't altogether sure she had one. "You've come to tell me you still want me? Are you fucking high right now?"

Jess blinked, then looked confused. "Brit was just an interlude, Sloane. I never stopped thinking about you. Never stopped loving you. I said that in the messages I sent."

"Yes, but you had an affair with someone else!" Sloane tried to keep her voice level, but she was pretty sure she shouted the last bit. She couldn't help it. How could Jess be so dense? Sloane glanced behind. Ella was approaching, her face scrunched tight.

Sloane knew the feeling. But here it was. The meeting she hoped would never happen. Her former life and her current life colliding.

"Hi, Ella." Sloane leaned in and gave Ella the lightest kiss on the cheek. Did Ella turn away at the last minute? Damage control was very much the mode she had to assume now. "I just got back and look who was waiting to see me." She hoped her heavy tone told Ella she wasn't pleased to see Jess.

"I can see. Nice to meet you, Jess. I'm Ella, Sloane's girlfriend."

Pride surged up Sloane's spine. She had to hand it to Ella. She was taking control of this situation. Something Sloane should have done months ago.

Jess's confusion notched up a level. "Girlfriend? I knew you were seeing her, but I didn't know it was *official*."

"It's official," Sloane said, before there could be any other conclusion drawn.

"And you're here now because?" Ella asked Jess, her words like granite.

Oh fuck, what was going to come out of Jess's mouth? The sinking feeling was back.

"Because I came over early for camp so I could see my family. But I arranged to see Sloane, too. Because we're family. As well as unfinished business."

"You are?" Ella eyes widened as she turned to Sloane.

Sloane stepped forward. No, no, no. This couldn't be happening. The night before the biggest game of her life, and her personal life was blowing up in her parking lot. She had to stop this and make it right. This wasn't how tonight was supposed to go. She had a special meal planned. Marks &

Spencer food to eat. This was not how this night was going to end. She reached out and caught Ella's arm, now folded across her chest.

"This is as much news to me as it is to you."

"I did tell you I was coming in my messages," Jess replied. "After I sent your silver and onyx ring back."

"She sent your ring?" Ella's controlled mask slipped. Bafflement streaked across her face, closely followed by hurt.

This was worse than anything Sloane could ever have imagined. Desperation looped and coiled inside her. She never wanted to be the cause of hurt for Ella. "I promise, I won't break her heart." That's what she'd told Marina. But she had to tell the truth. "Jess found the ring in her jacket."

Jess folded her arms and leaned against the Jeep. "And we agreed to meet for coffee."

"But not today!" Sloane responded. Before realising her mistake.

Ella stepped back, eyeing the pair of them. "You've been messaging?"

Double fuck.

Triple fuck.

"Of course we have. We were engaged," Jess said, as if it was obvious. "We split up. I didn't die."

Sloane grimaced, glancing from Jess to Ella. Nothing she said here was going to be right. But she had to make this right for Ella. To show her this was not what it looked like. But the more she looked, the more she saw that it was exactly what it looked like.

"Sloane? Is that true? Have you been speaking?"

Gritty, black fear lodged in the back of Sloane's throat.

If she denied it, Jess would only dispute it. She might even get her phone out to show Ella.

Sloane had to fix this. Even though Ella had already stepped backwards. One foot out of Sloane's life.

"Technically, yes. But it's more that Jess sends me messages, and I respond." That sounded cleverer in her head.

Ella glanced from one to the other, and then she flinched.

Sloane followed her line of sight. Ella was staring at Jess's left hand.

"Are you still wearing your engagement ring? The one that Sloane gave to you?"

Even Jess seemed slightly embarrassed by that as she nodded.

Say something, Sloane! Anything to break this moment!

But Ella was quicker to react. "Let me get this straight. You told me your ring turned up – but conveniently forgot to mention Jess found it. You've been messaging your ex-fiancée, who all the papers and fans want you to get back together with, and you'd arranged to meet. Meanwhile, you told me we had to keep our relationship a secret until after the international break, so that you could focus on your comeback and get Jess out of your life for good?"

Ella's cheeks flared red. "Pardon me for calling bullshit. Maybe the real reason you didn't want to go public with our relationship was because you were keeping your options open? Waiting for Jess to come back to the UK. See which one of us you liked the most?" She glared at her with a ferocity Sloane didn't even know existed.

"It's not like that!" Despair lapped the shores of Sloane's heart. She could see how this looked. But Ella had to know this wasn't the reality. However, judging by the look on her face, maybe not today. Or even next week. She had to listen at some point though, right?

A hollow opened in Sloane's chest. She could really lose her.

"You know what? Fuck you, Sloane. Fuck you and your superstar, player ways." Ella's eyes shone as she spoke. "I can't quite believe you were stringing me along this whole time, when really, you were just filling time, waiting to get back to the USA and back to being the golden couple." Ella put her fingers to her compass necklace. When they connected, her face soured, and she ripped the chain from her neck. She yanked open the fingers of Sloane's right hand, and pressed it into her palm.

"You can have this back, too. You lied to me." Ella took a shaky breath. "You've been in contact with your ex for months and not said a word."

Ella's words were like machine-gun fire. Every one lodged in Sloane's heart. Her mind flailed for ways to turn this around, but her scrambling senses came up with none. Tonight, she already knew this was a lost cause.

Ella turned to Jess. "You're welcome to her. You're clearly as bad as each other."

With that, Ella shot Sloane a murderous look, turned on her heel and stalked back to her car. The tyres squealed as she accelerated out of the parking lot.

When she'd gone, Sloane turned back to Jess, then bowed her head. "I cannot quite believe that just happened."

"I'm sorry," Jess said.

"Bit late for that, don't you think?" Sloane pocketed the necklace, then leaned her palms on her thighs and bent over, winded. What the hell was she going to do now? She glanced up at Jess. "Do you cause this much havoc everywhere you go?" She held up a hand. "You know what, don't answer that. In Ella's words, fuck you, Jess."

Jess winced. "I didn't know you were a proper item. I thought we still stood a chance."

Sloane shook her head, disbelieving. "Whether Ella and I are together or not has no bearing on us. We stand no chance of getting back together. Am I clear?"

"But I thought—"

"You thought what?" Sloane squared up to her, hands on hips. This, she had to know.

"That we were destined."

Sloane wasn't sure, but by the look on Jess's face, the penny might just have dropped.

"We were destined when I asked you to marry me, and you said yes. But then you fucked someone else, so destiny did a sharp U-turn." Sloane shook her head. "You are such a hot mess, you know that? Go to camp, Jess. Play football. You're good at that. But before you try to get together with anybody else, maybe try a little introspection and growing up, too."

Jess held her gaze, went to say something, then obviously thought better of it.

Did Jess understand what Sloane was saying? She had no idea.

"You really pick your moments to proclaim undying love. You never did that when we were together."

"I didn't realise what I had then. I do now." Jess paused, then caught Sloane's gaze. "We're really done?" Her shoulders slumped in preparation for the answer.

Sloane nodded. "We really are."

"And you like this girl a lot?"

"Yes." She could hardly get the word out.

Jess stood straight and folded her arms. "In that case, it sounds like you've been dicking around unnecessarily. It's about time you showed her, isn't it?"

Chapter Thirty-Two

Ella couldn't recall a time in her life when she'd felt like this. She'd swallowed all of Sloane's lies as if they were gospel. Yes, keeping their relationship close to her chest had taken a toll, but the light at the end of the tunnel, which she thought was so close, had turned out to be a mirage.

She felt ridiculously stupid, like one of those women in a magazine article who knew nothing about their partner's secret life. Jess's words kept coming back to her. "We split up. I didn't die." Was everything between them a lie? Had Sloane just been filling time? She couldn't quite believe it after everything they'd shared, but all the evidence was staring her in the face. Even though things didn't add up. She was living in a topsy-turvy world. Her mum had been cheated on by men enough times in her life, and Ella remembered them all. Maybe it was a genetic disorder she and her mum shared when it came to relationships.

That night, Sloane had sent messages and tried to call, but Ella had ignored them all. She'd been in no mood to talk. One thing Ella was sure of: she wasn't going to the England vs USA game now. She'd had enough humiliation for one week.

The first person she spoke to about what had happened was Marina. Her cousin told her she'd drive over as soon as possible, which told Ella how upset she must have sounded.

Marina wasn't the drop-everything-for-no-reason type, but she'd always been there for Ella throughout her life. She was the sister she never had. Plus, as Marina said, "I need to be there with you to watch that England versus USA friendly, otherwise you're going to drive yourself mad."

Ella had started to refute she was going to watch the game, but then she'd stopped. There was no point. Her cousin was right. Ella was going to watch the whole game and clutch the sofa when Sloane and Jess got anywhere near each other.

On game day, to add insult to injury, somebody had leaked a story about her argument with Sloane in front of the apartment block, saying they'd had a lover's tiff involving Jess. It wasn't gaining huge traction, but it was out there. Ella was too tired to look at too many responses to it, but she'd watched one YouTuber who said she was thrilled with the thought of Sloane and Jess getting back together. Did these people not know there were real people with real feelings involved?

Marina turned up at 7pm with two bottles of merlot and the Deliveroo app open on her phone. She squeezed Ella extra tight and kissed her cheek. "You'll get through this, you're a strong woman. Whatever the outcome." She touched her cheeks. "You look pale. You need wine."

Ella knew she was right on both counts. Who wouldn't be pale, when they were about to watch their (ex?) lover play football on TV with her former fiancée? Ella couldn't quite believe this was her life, but it was 100 per cent real.

They settled down with their curry: chicken bhuna for Ella, beef madras for Marina. Ella pulled the coffee table closer so they had somewhere to rest their plates, then she cracked open the wine and put on the football.

Marina immediately grabbed the control and turned it off.

Ella frowned. "I thought we were watching it? I really need to watch it. It's not just because of Sloane, who I will try my best to ignore. Our goalie's playing, along with our other striker, Nat. It's her first call-up, and she might get some minutes. She's so excited." That, at least, put a smile on Ella's face. Nat had truly earned her call-up through hard work and huge talent.

"We will watch it. But before you put yourself through that torture of watching your girlfriend—"

"Not my girlfriend." Ella slumped on her brand-new sofa. The one she and Sloane had lain on only last week, talking about their future. Now in the bin.

"We'll discuss that later. Before you do that, tell me what happened again."

"I already told you."

"You were in a state. Tell me again in a more rational way."

Ella did.

Marina frowned. "When you turned up, Jess was there, but Sloane said she wasn't expecting her?"

"No, but they'd been messaging. Jess sent her a ring, and they'd arranged to go for coffee. Jess also said she wanted her back." Ella gave an exaggerated shrug. "I mean, short of taking out an advert in the paper, Jess was very clear in her intentions, and Sloane didn't deny any of it."

"What did Sloane say, exactly?"

"She admitted they'd been messaging. And that Jess sent back a ring Sloane had lost. I told her where to go, and left."

"Hmmm."

"Hmmm? I don't know why you're on her side. Just because she's famous doesn't mean she's beyond reproach. Famous people can be arseholes, too. Or maybe it's like before with Reba. That I'm not on her level fame-wise or with money. If she wants Jess back, maybe that plays into it. I don't have the fame or the caché she needs."

But Marina was already shaking her head, and waving a forkful of curry about.

Ella grabbed her hand and put it down. "Not around my new sofa, please. Curry and blue velvet do not mix."

Marina put it down and turned to Ella. "I'm here to tell you, money and fame are not what Sloane wants. Most famous people don't want someone who steals their limelight. Fact. Which means you're ideal. But Sloane likes you for you: famous or not. She's one of the good ones. I only met her a couple of times, but I could tell. Plus, I told her not to break your heart, and she agreed not to."

"You did what?"

Marina shrugged. "It was nothing, thank me later. But my point is, I think you need to hear her side of the story before you go off the deep end. Although, yes, I know you've already technically dived."

"Tom Daley levels of expertise."

"Agreed. 9.7s across the board."

They both smirked. The light relief was needed. They ate some food and processed for a few moments.

"But she's tried to contact you?" Marina asked eventually.

"Yes, ever since. She's sent me messages every day. She's persistent."

"Why do you think that might be?"

"Because she can't bear to be the one who's dumped?"

"Sloane Patterson is one of the most level-headed footballers I've ever met. She also likes you. A lot. I would lay bets this has all been a misunderstanding."

"Why are you defending her?"

"Because I like her, and I love you. I think she might be a little in love with you already, and vice versa. Put that all together, and that's why I'm defending Sloane. If she's a schmuck and I turn out to be wrong, I'll have to revise my entire view of human nature. Don't write her off just yet."

Ella picked up her phone. "I'll message her now, shall I?" Sarcasm dripped from her words. What did Marina know about relationships? She was still single, after all.

Marina rolled her eyes, plucked the phone from Ella's fingers and put it on her wooden coffee table, face down. "You don't have to do it now. She's a little busy."

"Playing with her ex."

"Playing *against* her ex. There's a significant difference."

Ella huffed. It was hard being mad at Sloane, even when she was in the wrong. Because feelings didn't just turn off overnight, did they? "Okay. I'll think about it." She glanced up. "Can we watch women play football now?"

"You're not going to throw anything at the TV?"

"No promises."

They switched it on. It had just started. The USA were already on the attack, and their other striker, Lena Jackson, rifled a shot at Rovers' keeper, Becca. She got her full weight behind it and fell on the ball.

Ella clapped her hands. "Go, Becca!" She was definitely cheering for England tonight. On the right side of the screen,

Sloane jogged away from goal. Ella's mouth went dry. She still looked good in her kit. That hadn't changed.

Becca bounced the ball, then put it down for a goal kick. Ella leaned into Marina. "I scored a goal against her in training. Did I mention that?"

"Once or twice," Marina replied.

* * *

Ella woke the following morning with a small kernel of hope that maybe she and Sloane could get things back on track. That maybe Marina was right, and there was a logical explanation for Sloane and Jess. They shared a lot of history. Plenty of lesbians were friends with their exes. Did plenty of exes' land on top of each other and roll around on a grass pitch in front of millions of viewers worldwide, as Sloane and Jess had done last night? Ella was glad Marina had watched it with her and kept repeating that it was their job to get stuck into their tackles. Otherwise, Ella might have paid too much attention to the commentators who kept mentioning that they used to be engaged.

"How strange to be tangling on a field in front of millions with someone you were engaged to only six months ago. What do you think, Alex?" one had asked the other.

Ella wanted to punch the screen.

This morning, she grabbed her phone from the bedside table and called up the latest message from Sloane. She'd sent it after the game last night, which had ended in a 2-2 draw. England had led 2-1, but then Sloane had won a penalty, after being hacked down in the box. She'd stepped up, and in a show of ice-cold precision, slotted it past Becca.

Ella hadn't known how to feel. Sad for England? Happy for Sloane that she was back scoring on the big stage?

But also, fuck Sloane. For being so good. And looking so hot in a football kit.

Sloane's message told Ella she had her voice in her ear when she took the penalty, telling her it was just her, nobody else, just her and the ball. One goalkeeper, one goal, just like they'd practised. Ella shook her head. She was pretty sure Sloane had mastered penalties way before they met, but she was touched she'd tried to include her as part of her achievement.

Should she reply? She took a deep breath and thought about what she might write.

Great game last night. Fab penalty. Really loved the way you rolled around with your ex, too. Or is she your ex? Yeah, maybe she wasn't ready quite yet.

Marina popped her head inside Ella's bedroom door. "You're holding your phone. Have you seen the photos from last night yet?" Her voice was tentative.

The blood drained from Ella's face. "What photos?" Her voice sounded as tired as she felt.

Marina walked over and sat on Ella's bed. "I'm sure there's nothing to them. But have a look anyway." She handed Ella her phone.

What Ella saw made her drop her phone on her bed covers, and close her eyes. Photos of Sloane and Jess hugging on the pitch after the game, and then afterwards, chatting and hugging in the English team's changing room. At least they were wearing tracksuits, and they weren't naked. She had to be thankful for what she could get.

"I know you said not to jump to conclusions, but even

you might say this was a bit much. We've been seeing each other for nearly four months. She's never wanted to hug me in public. But she sees Jess for five minutes and they're all over each other?"

Marina nodded. "I get it. I'd be pissed. But it was a friendly game. She hugged others on the English team as well." Her kind eyes rested on Ella. "Speak to her. Sloane is genuine. I'm sure of it."

But Ella wasn't in the mood to speak right now.

She wasn't sure when she ever would be.

Chapter Thirty-Three

Three weeks later, Sloane walked into Salchester's training ground, giving receptionist Beth a wave as she passed. Her feet knew the way to the locker room, but they curled in her sneakers as she walked, knowing they had to pass Ella's office on the way. When Sloane did, she held her breath. Just as she had the previous three days, too.

Ella's Bodum coffee mug was on her desk. Her jacket was on the back of her chair. But she wasn't there.

Sloane picked up speed as she walked by, just in case Ella was in the bathroom and about to exit. She wanted to get to her peg, change, get out on the field and run off all her worries. As soon as she crossed those white lines, the rest of her life faded into the background. Some people meditated. Some did Tai chi. Sloane's happy place, the one that kept her balanced, was the soccer field.

Or at least, it had been, until Jess showed up and shredded her life.

The international camp had gone okay, although her coach had noted how subdued she was. Sloane hadn't told her why. However, Sloane had got assurances that if she kept progressing from her injury, she'd make the World Cup squad. Good news, at last. Now she knew what she had to do, she was up for the challenge. A bigger challenge, however, was getting Ella back on side.

She'd sent her a number of messages, but Ella had told her to give her some space. Sloane knew when to back away, she was good at that. She'd had practice with Jess. So she complied. But she'd been back from camp for a few days now. She'd given Ella weeks of space. Those hours and minutes had dripped all over each other. Surely space had an end date?

Sloane kicked herself for the photos of her and Jess saying goodbye after the friendly match, but that was all it was. Nat had dragged her into the English team's locker room to meet a couple of the England girls, and Jess had been there. Somebody had snapped them hugging, saying a final goodbye. Jess had even wished her luck sorting things out with Ella. She'd told Sloane she might take some time out of relationships for a while.

How could she make Ella see there was nothing going on? Soccer was a small world, and Sloane couldn't avoid Jess forever. The World Cup was this year, and she had no doubt they'd see each other. She had to convince Ella it would mean nothing. Ella was intertwined with Sloane's life now. When Sloane woke up, she was the first thing she thought of. How she missed waking up with Ella's wild hair on the pillow next to her. She stared at the ring on her finger, the catalyst for their current standoff. She had to let Ella know she meant everything to her. That her relationship with Jess had taken place in another life. Now, she was just somebody that she used to know.

But even as she thought that, Sloane knew it wasn't true. The reason she'd been so reluctant to let go of Jess was because, in the absence of blood family, Jess *was* her family. She'd provided the first stable relationship in Sloane's life. The first where she felt loved for who she was. That was hard to let go of. And perhaps, in some twisted way, when Jess treated her badly, she expected it. After all, it's what family did.

Sloane sat on the locker room bench. She put her head in her hands. Her relationships with family and with Jess were fucked up. Her relationship with Ella hadn't fared much better. She had to change that, and fast.

"You okay, Patts?"

Sloane looked up. Layla. She blew out a breath and jumped up. "Yeah, good. Just a bad night's sleep."

Layla stared at her. "That all?"

Sloane nodded. "Just want to get out there again." She'd played one game for Salchester since she got back from international camp. She'd been slow to the ball, sluggish. The only way to remedy that was back out on the training field.

"Ready to slay like the queen you are?"

Sloane stood and nudged Layla with her elbow. "Don't overdo it," she replied with a smile.

"You look like you need cheering up."

Sloane stripped off her trackpants and climbed into her shorts. "Let's go kick some balls."

Show time.

* * *

Sloane was glad when the training session finished. She'd been off her game again. To make amends, she grabbed Becca, then placed the ball on the spot. She imagined a game situation as she always did. The roar of the crowd. The itch of anticipation on her skin. Then she went through her practice routine, one ball at a time. It was always that way, just like life. Live in the moment. Take each second as it came. Only, these kicks weren't going in quite as planned. Twenty-seven out of fifty. She even missed the target eight times. Layla practised beside her, and she scored more than Sloane. Unprecedented.

"You feeling okay today? Or are you just saving yourself for when it matters?" Becca asked as they walked from the field.

Sloane shook her head. "Just one of those days." Or one of those weeks. Perhaps the whole month.

When Sloane got into the training centre, she checked the time. If this was affecting her penalty taking as well, she had to sort it out. To catch Ella before her next session. She took off her boots, slipped on her white sliders, and wandered down the corridors to the offices. Lucy clocked her as she walked past, and frowned. Sloane glanced into Ella's office. She was at her desk.

Sloane rapped on the door frame with her knuckles.

Ella looked up, and stopped whatever she was writing. Her face was as blank as a winter sea. She wasn't going to make this easy.

"Can I come in?"

It took a few moments, but eventually, Ella gave her the slightest nod.

Sloane sat in the chair in front of her desk, suddenly wishing she was showered and fresh. Coming direct from the training ground put her at a disadvantage. But she was here now. She should say her piece and get out.

"I wanted to catch you before you left."

Silence.

Okay, she wasn't going to make this easy.

"I was papped on the way to work the day after those photos of you and Jess came out." Ella sat up in her chair. "Someone was waiting for me to leave my flat." She put a finger to her chest. "Me. I'm not a famous footballer. I'm not you, I'm not Jess."

"But you're Ella. You're definitely someone."

Ella's wince made Sloane's stomach clench. Unease kicked her in the gut.

"Not someone who should be photographed at will, though. I'm behind the scenes, not in front of the camera. Maybe you knew that when you didn't fully commit to us for the past few months."

"I already told you I'm sorry about all of that. Jess turned up unannounced. She wanted to talk, and I thought I could chat over coffee. Get it done without worrying you. I know now I should have told you she'd been in touch, but I thought I could handle it. Turns out, I couldn't."

"My point still stands. Maybe you'd be better off with someone like her, though. Someone who likes the limelight. I don't."

Sloane was getting that vibe. "I don't think so. For the record, I don't like it either."

"Your game's suffering."

Sloane had missed a sitter in her first game back, and the team were now third in the league. Next up was the FA Cup semi-final.

"That's because I'm not happy. You know everything has to be right off the field, for it to work on it. I just notched 27 out of 50 penalties today. A new low. I need to sort this out with you."

A knock on the door frame made them both look up.

Lucy. She walked in and closed the door behind her. She stood to the side of Ella's desk, arms folded across her chest. "I'm glad I got the two of you together. I've been wanting to since we lost the other night." She sighed. "Remember when I said I was all for this, so long as it didn't impact the team?" She glanced from Ella, to Sloane, then back. "Tell me this isn't impacting the team." She pointed at Sloane. "You're not training well, and from what I saw just now, your penalties are suffering too, am I right?"

Sloane nodded. She cast her gaze to Ella, then to the floor. This was like being told off by the principal. It wasn't what she was used to.

"And you," Lucy said, staring at Ella. "Pre-international break, things were going so well. Now, you're working from home every chance you get. Hiding in the toilet when you think Sloane might walk past your door."

Ella's mouth dropped open. "How did you—"

"—it's my job to know these things."

Now it was Ella's turn to blush and look at the floor.

"Put simply, I need my two best performers back on form. This is the crunch point of the season. I can't have Ella avoiding the team, and Sloane misfiring. It doesn't work." She blew out her cheeks. "Here's what I need you to do. You're grown adults. You know what's at stake. Please sort this out, so that Sloane's form isn't affected, and Ella's sad face doesn't haunt the rest of the team. I need happy staff and fired-up players, not people at each other's throats. Can I rely on you to do that?"

Sloane glanced at Ella, and they both nodded.

"Absolutely," they said in union.

"Good," Lucy said. "Now I'm going to get out of here before this tension suffocates me. Remember what you like about each other. Please. At least until the end of the season. And remind me never to be a soft touch about staff-player relationships again."

Sloane waited until Lucy shut the door before she turned to Ella. She wasn't leaving until Ella knew how she felt.

"I guess we really fucked this up."

"I guess we did." Sloane sighed. "But I can cope with disappointing Lucy. I can't cope with disappointing you. I really missed you while I was away at camp. I missed talking to you, as well as everything else. You're part of my life, Ella. A massive, non-negotiable part. I don't want to lose you."

Ella blew out her cheeks too, mimicking Lucy. "I don't want to lose you either. But this isn't cut and dried, Sloane. You've been in contact with your ex. You might be leaving in a few months. Look at it from my perspective. Should I put my heart on the line, only for you to walk away? Maybe now's the time to step back. We can still do well until the end of the season if we agree to be civil."

Fear streaked through Sloane. She'd been at this junction before in games, where she'd thought everything was lost. She'd turned it around numerous times in her life. She wasn't giving up on Ella that easily. This was not how they ended.

"What happened with Jess was my fault. I've told you that. But I need you to know, I want to hold your hand in public now. The reasons for not doing it backfired spectacularly on international break. I was stupid. I want to be not stupid from now on. I'm not going anywhere, Ella."

But Ella shook her head. "For now. What happens when you leave at the end of the season? You never want to think long-term, Sloane. I have to. Maybe that's why we should cut our losses."

* * *

The look on Lucy's face told Sloane all she needed to know. They had five league games left, and Sloane hadn't scored in the last two. More than that, she still wasn't on her game. Only seven points split the top three, with everything still to play for. The problem? They weren't gaining ground.

Things still weren't resolved with Ella, and they weren't going well with her game.

Sloane was not fulfilling her end of the bargain.

Tonight's FA Cup semi-final was crucial to their season, and after extra-time, it was 1-1. Sloane had missed an easy strike that would have won the match.

Nat's parents had told her they'd come, but they hadn't turned up. She'd scuffed a shot, and hit the corner flag with her next effort. It was only Layla getting a tap-in that had kept them in the tie, along with Becca having the game of her life.

The team gathered on the sidelines, the crowd humming with anticipation and frustration. They'd been the better team. They should have won in 90 minutes. When Sloane glanced right, she could see the supporters still in scarves, even though it was April. She was boiling, but that's because she'd played 120 minutes of soccer and somehow failed to score. She was going to put it right on penalties. She was up first.

Lucy made sure she got eye contact with her and all the penalty takers before she spoke. "This is still all to play for. This is season-defining. Go out there and score for us all. Make sure that all the effort we've put into getting this far in the campaign was worth it. We want to get to the final at Wembley, don't we?"

The huddle broke. The referee had the ball. Layla, the team captain, lost the toss, which meant Rovers had to shoot first. Sloane strode across the grass with purpose. She was shooting into the away end, something she'd done a thousand times before. Behind the goal, supporters waved their arms to try to put her off. But Sloane had practised. She knew what she was doing. Low and hard into the bottom right corner. She eyed the keeper. Took a deep breath, then five steps backwards.

Then, all of sudden, a movie of her recent practise misses started to play in her mind.

Over the bar.

Wide of the right post.

Straight at the keeper.

What the actual fuck?

She closed her eyes, then refocused. She could do this. She did it every day. Even though yesterday, she'd missed eight times. Eight times, two days in a row.

Did Ella still want her?

Focus!

She gulped, exhaled, ran up, hit the ball.

She knew as soon as it left her foot it was over the bar. She had a sixth sense where the goal was. Today, it wasn't where she'd put the ball.

The wind whipped around her face.

The crowd behind the goal went wild.

Her stomach sank without a trace. Right through the ground. To the galaxy below. She wanted to stop the world, and jump off. She wanted to be anywhere but here. Sloane was a big-game player. This was not what she did.

She ground her teeth together, then trudged slowly back to her teammates. She couldn't look at the bench. Didn't want to see the disappointment on their faces. Or those of Cathy, Rich, Ryan and Hayley, who were somewhere in the stands.

All here to see her fail.

Sloane didn't fail. But she was failing in every area of her life right now.

Maybe it was a blessing that her family never came to games.

When she arrived at her teammates, Nat was the first to hug her.

"Don't worry, we'll score the rest."

Sloane took her place in the line of players, arms around shoulders.

Layla squeezed her shoulder.

The opposition scored their next, as did Salchester. But then their opponents scored again. Each side had taken two spot-kicks. Salchester were down.

1-2.

The next two penalties were expertly put into the bottom corners by both sides. Welshy hit hers low and true.

2-3.

Crunch time. Sloane wasn't sure she could watch as Nat stepped up. Her family had to be playing on her mind. She took five steps back, just like they practised. However, instead of placement, as they'd also practised, Nat went for power and put her laces through it. Right down the middle as the goalie sailed left.

The net billowed.

3-3!

The Salchester line yelled and punched the air as one.

They were level. As Nat sprinted back to the line, everyone hugged her. Sloane placed a kiss on her forehead; in return, Nat gave her a grin.

"What did I tell you?"

Sloane wasn't going to speak and jinx it. This was far from over.

Next up, the opposition's number 10 walked slowly to the spot and placed the ball. She'd scored the goal in normal time. She was experienced, and this shouldn't ruffle her. But Sloane would have said the same about herself.

Sloane closed her eyes. She couldn't watch. She willed her rival to miss, or Becca to pull off a save. She'd given her enough practice every day. Surely it had to pay off? If their striker scored, it meant Layla had to score their final kick to keep them in it. If they lost, it would be down to Sloane.

She squeezed her eyes tight shut and tried to steady her breath. Adrenaline hurtled through her. Beside her, Nat gripped her shoulder.

The next noise Sloane heard was her teammates screaming all around her, bodies leaping nearby.

Sloane opened her eyes, and saw Becca yelling, while waving her clenched fist in the air.

"Did she save it?"

Nat shook her head, eyes wide. "She blazed it over the bar."

Wow. It really was never over until it was over.

Out of the corner of her eye, Sloane saw the opposition forward trudged back, head in hands. Sloane knew how she felt. But she was too elated to feel sympathy. Relief swamped her as she looked to the sky. Then to the bench. Lucy and Ella stood side by side, stoney-faced.

The score was still 3-3. Both teams had missed one penalty. Now they each had a kick to avoid sudden death.

The final penalty was down to Layla, because they'd elected to put their strongest kicker, Sloane, first. They'd practised together for the past week, but would it work out? Sloane gave her a fist bump and a "You got this!" before she walked to the spot and placed the ball.

Sloane made herself watch this one. She owed it to Layla. Every muscle she owned tightened as she willed her friend to score.

Layla's shoulders went up, then down. She took three steps back, then with a trademark burst, she arrowed the ball into the top right-hand corner. Bang! Nobody was going to save that.

For the first time since the shootout started, they were ahead. Sloane allowed herself to believe. She clenched her fist by her side, let out a yelp, but it wasn't over. The whole team knew that. It was down to the next kick. If the opposition scored, the game went to sudden death. If they missed, Salchester were through to the final.

Layla returned to a flurry of hugs, then took her place back in the team line. All ten outfield players had their arms around each other on the halfway line, all facing the goal.

Now it was the turn of the opposition number five, a stalwart defender who'd marked Sloane with authority throughout the game. Her walk was slow. This was the ultimate pressure penalty. Way more than Sloane's, because from her miss, there was still a way back, as her team had shown. But for this defender, miss and they were out.

On the back of her red jersey was her name in bright white. Stoneson. She placed the ball on the spot. Walked backwards, then stopped, hands on hips. The referee blew her whistle. Stoneson looked left, then ahead, then ran up.

Miss it. For the love of god, miss the fucking penalty.

The thud as her boot hit the ball was loud. The shot was good, headed for the top left of the goal. It was a solid penalty. Sloane narrowed her gaze as Becca flung herself towards the ball, and stretched her arms as far as she could.

Was she going to save it? Sloane sucked in a breath.

Becca got fingertips to the ball, tipped it onto left post and away from goal. She landed in a heap on the floor, and the penalty-taker dropped to her knees.

The Salchester team let out a collective gasp, untangled themselves and started to run towards their hero, arms raised. The Salchester Rovers half of the stadium erupted. The home fans behind the goal sank.

Becca had saved it! They were through! They were going to Wembley! Sloane wanted to laugh, cry, and scream all at the same time. She let out a primal yelp, sent up a thank you to a god she didn't believe in, then stirred her feet to join the rest in smothering Becca. When the commotion died down, Sloane looked to the sidelines.

Ella beamed her way.

She had to find a way to make this okay.

For herself, for the team, and for Ella.

Chapter Thirty-Four

It was the second week of May, the end of another work day, and Ella had the EasyJet site open on her screen. The season finished soon, and then she got a few weeks off. She needed to get away. A holiday somewhere in the sun sounded good. Palm trees, blue skies, gorgeous sunsets. But that only made her think of Sloane. Every day without her was an assault course of emotions.

Ella focused on the screen. On the photos of people laying on sunbeds, with a cocktail and a book. That sounded perfect. Maybe Marina would like to go? Only, when she pictured it, it wasn't Marina who came to mind. It was Sloane. Always Sloane. She tried to block the images of Sloane in a swimsuit, looking outrageously sexy, but they lived rent-free in her head.

After the semi-final win, Ella joined in the celebrations as best she could on the pitch and in the changing room, before sneaking away, hoping she wouldn't be missed. The elation of the night and the emotions tied up with Sloane were overwhelming. They were going to Wembley. Ella could hardly believe it.

After Sloane missed that first penalty, she'd thought they were done. But this team constantly surprised her. When the staff had joined the team on the pitch, they'd hugged each player in turn, with particular attention paid to Becca and all five penalty takers. Whether you scored or not, it took huge courage to take one in the first place. Ella remembered it from her playing days.

When it came for her turn to hug Sloane, they'd both hesitated. She didn't want to avoid her and make it seem like something was wrong. There again, if she hugged her, she might not let go. In the end, they'd settled on an awkward hug and a couple of backslaps, then stepped away from each other at speed. When Ella had clocked Lucy staring, she'd felt as if they'd been caught red-handed. The fact that every sinew of her body leaned towards Sloane like a plant seeking sunlight? She'd ignored that. Right now, Ella didn't trust her thoughts or feelings.

All she knew was, Salchester's season was reaching its ultimate climax. In the game yesterday, Sloane had scored a brace. However, with one league game to go, they couldn't catch United for the title. They'd come achingly close. However, the FA Cup was still very much in their grasp. The game was at the forefront of everyone's mind.

The Wembley final was coming up this Saturday, May 12th.

Sloane had tried to talk to Ella. To corner her. To message. But Ella had held firm. Restarting anything was pointless because Sloane was leaving.

Ella was just getting her bag ready to leave, when Lucy stopped by her office.

"Have you got a minute?" She tilted her head towards her office.

Ella shut down her screen and walked next door, her stomach rolling as she did. Last time she and Lucy had spoken in a formal fashion, it hadn't been pleasant. Was that going to happen again? She sat in the chair opposite and waited for her dressing down.

"There's no need to look so scared. Last time out, Sloane hadn't just scored a brace." Lucy gave a tentative smile. "Have you two made up?"

Ella drew her lips into a pencil-thin line. "No, but we've called a truce of sorts."

"If it helps, I want to keep her here next year. It depends if she wants to stay, and if her agent likes the deal. She drives a hard bargain, but Sloane's worth it. Despite her injury and her brief dry spell, she's still second top scorer in the league. She might even win the Golden Boot. You can't argue with those figures."

Would Sloane stay? She hadn't told Ella that. Surely if she was thinking about it, she would have? Then again, Ella hadn't really given her the chance. A flicker of hope burned in her chest. Quickly followed by defeat. Maybe she'd use the offer to get another one in the US or elsewhere in Europe? Somewhere warmer than Salchester?

Lucy cleared her throat and looked Ella dead in the eye. "But it's not Sloane I want to talk about. It's you. Sloane isn't the only one I want to stay. I've talked to Paulo, as I said I would, and we've hashed out a deal where, if you agree, the club can offer you a full-time contract as Salchester's part-time performance coach, and part-time youth football coach, along with a good pay rise." Lucy sat forward. "You'd be working mainly with the women, but there's a possibility to work with the men, too, when needed." She shrugged. "It was my concession to getting it pushed through." She paused. "What do you think?"

For once in her life, Ella was gobsmacked. She'd only been at the club for a season, and she already loved it more than she ever thought possible. But getting to work on the actual football side, too? It was beyond her wildest dreams.

"You're okay with me keeping a couple of my clients on the side? I feel it's not fair to leave them in the lurch. But it won't affect my dedication."

Lucy nodded. "Of course. We understand that. So long as you can give us full-time hours and be at the games, we want you. What do you say? Does it sound appealing?"

"What do I say? A huge, unreserved, 100 per cent fucking yes!" She slapped a hand over her mouth. "Shit! I've never sworn when accepting a job offer before." She blushed. "I swore again, didn't I?"

Elation fizzed around Ella's system. She wanted to tell her mum, like always. Marina. Aunt Ursula. And then, someone else popped into her mind. Ella pushed her out. "You don't know what this means. I won't let you down. I could kiss you, but that's how rumours start."

Lucy barked out a laugh. "You've earned it. For what it's worth, the men's team wanted to hire you permanently, too, as their performance and lifestyle coach is leaving. But I staked my claim."

She stood and walked around the desk. She shook Ella's hand, pulled her in for a hug, then held her at arm's length. "You've got so much to offer, Ella. You've been fantastic this season, and I've no doubt you'll only build on that next season." She gave her a tight smile. "I know it's not been plain sailing with you and Sloane, but I hope you can work things out and come back refreshed next season."

She walked out of the training complex, her skin still flushed, lit with adrenaline. She was going to be a proper football coach. She clenched her fist as she approached her car. Parked next to it was Sloane's silver Jeep. She was here late. Probably still in the gym. There was a reason Sloane was as good as she was. She worked hard, every single day.

Ella desperately wanted to tell Sloane her news. She also desperately wanted a congratulatory kiss. It had been weeks since it happened. Far too long. Her resolve wavered.

This was an about turn, but maybe her news had shown her who was important. As had her possible holiday booking. She didn't want to do life without Sloane. Should she wait for her? Ella shook her head. Instead, she threw her bag into her back seat, then tried her aunt. No answer. Then she tried Marina. Same deal. Godammit, where were her family when she needed them?

She got into the driver's seat, phone still in hand. She scrolled to Sloane's number, and her finger hovered over her name. All the reasons she should press strolled through her mind. Quickly followed by all the reasons she shouldn't. Why was all this so bloody hard?

All she wanted to do was tell her that she'd been offered a new job, and she was taking it. She was staying at Salchester for the foreseeable future, and if Sloane felt anything for her – anything at all – then she should stay too. But Ella wanted Sloane to stay because she wanted to. Not for her. But she couldn't bring herself to call. To spit out the words. To make the first move. Because what if it was too late? What if Sloane had already decided she was going elsewhere? What if she'd decided Ella wasn't worth the hassle after all?

"She's already a bit in love with you, and vice versa." That was what Marina had said. Was she right?

A knock on her window made her look up.

Sloane stared down, sunglasses on.

Ella's heart made a noise like wind chimes. Her ear lobes glowed hot as she lowered her window.

"I hoped I might see you today." Sloane's words were unsteady, as if she'd just learned them.

"I was just wondering whether to call you."

Oh fuck, she'd said that out loud.

But it was the truth. At least Ella didn't have to wonder any more. Fate had lent a hand. Sloane was here in person.

"You were?" Sloane paused. "In that case, what are you doing right now? Would you like to come back to mine so we can talk?"

Ella sucked in a huge breath. The wind chimes turned to drums. Yes? No? Maybe? All of the above?

But then Sloane leaned in, and took off her sunglasses. She tilted her head and gazed at Ella with an intensity that made her melt. "I should tell you, I'm not too proud to beg." She licked her lips. "Please?"

All Ella wanted to do was rise up, take Sloane's face in her hands, and kiss her. Perhaps Ella should listen to what her body was telling her.

Sloane had made the move, taken a chance. She'd repeatedly told Ella she wanted to make this work, and Ella had rebuffed her. Today was different. Now she took time to truly assess, the answer was simple.

Yes.

* * *

Sloane's flat felt different. More welcoming. She spied plants. Pictures on the wall. A new rug. Sloane had been busy in her absence. On the far side of the lounge, sunlight streamed in through the patio doors and windows. This flat was already a work of art – now it seemed almost homely as well. Ella had missed it.

Ella snagged her gaze. "I like the new look."

Sloane threw her a tentative smile. "I thought you might. You always told me I needed to soften the place." Sloane swept her arm across the space. "I had some spare time after camp. I hope I made good use of it."

"You did."

They'd both suffered. But maybe they'd needed to, so they could arrive at this point.

"The next thing I need to soften is you. Can I get you anything to drink?" She stopped mid-turn. "But also, why were you going to call me?"

Ella sat on one of the kitchen stools, then exhaled. "Because I just got news. Lucy offered me a full-time contract. I'll be the club's part-time performance coach, working with both teams, but I'll also be the part-time youth football coach." She gave an exaggerated shrug, coupled with a full-scale grin. She couldn't keep this joy inside much longer. "Honestly, it's a dream come true. And the first person I wanted to tell?" She held Sloane's gaze. "You."

Sloane sat on the stool next to her. She raised her hand as if she were about to touch Ella to congratulate her, then took it back. They weren't quite there yet.

But dammit, Ella wanted to be. She desperately wanted

Sloane to touch her, hold her. It turned out, the thing she'd been denying herself was what she'd wanted all along: Sloane by her side. But she hadn't known it for sure until now. She'd been too busy expecting the worst. Now, she hoped, however things turned out, the fog might be clearing.

"That's such fantastic news, and nothing less than you deserve." Sloane locked eyes with Ella.

How she'd missed looking into Sloane's exquisite gaze. She wanted to stop time, and stay here for days.

"Can I hug you? Is it allowed?"

A wave of warmth washed through Ella. "You better hug me, or I might expire."

Sloane did as she was told, and just like that, the world got brighter. In Sloane's arms, Ella felt supported, safe. In response, she wrapped her arms around Sloane too, and breathed in her smell. Apple shampoo and Sloane's bergamot perfume.

Sloane nuzzled her nose into Ella's neck. Somehow, this felt different. To the months they'd done this, with one eye open, always looking over their shoulder. This time, Sloane's body was relaxed, in the moment. Just like Ella always told her to be. She could do it on the training ground. Now she had to do it in real life.

Slowly, Ella pulled back, and locked eyes with Sloane. A roar of attraction revved inside her. She'd never wanted anybody like this. In moments, their lips reconnected, and a shimmer of joy cascaded through Ella. When she was around Sloane, all she wanted was her. Their attraction was magnetic. Now, she could finally have what she wanted.

When they finally untangled their lips, Sloane tipped her head back and blew out a long breath.

Ella frowned. "Was my kiss that bad?"

Sloane smiled. "Far from it. Kissing you is easy. Talking to you is where it gets scary. But I want to be honest with you, because dishonesty hasn't gotten us very far, has it?"

Every muscle Ella had tightened. Was this about Jess? Had they slept together after all?

"And before you go thinking the worst, this has nothing to do with Jess."

Damn, she was easy to read. "What is it, then?"

"Let's take this to the balcony. It's sunny, I don't want to waste it." Sloane got up and offered Ella her hand.

Ella took it, her heart rolling out the red carpet. She'd wondered if this was going to be awkward. She had her answer. Sloane pulled back the glass door, and they stepped out. She pulled out one of the white chairs, and Ella sat next to her. The afternoon was summer-holiday warm. If anyone had clothes on the line, they'd come in smelling of sunshine.

Sloane waited until Ella was settled before she spoke. Below them, someone tooted a car horn and tyres screeched. Above, the sky was combed with cirrus.

"First, I have to say I'm sorry. A million times, sorry. In fact, sorry isn't nearly enough. About it all. For keeping you a secret. Not telling you about Jess being in touch. For being dishonest. I did it for the right reasons, but the outcome was all sorts of wrong. From now on, that stops. One hundred per cent honesty."

Ella liked where it was going, but she knew there was more. Her reply was short. "Apology accepted. Go on."

"I got a call from Adrianne this morning. My agent. She's had an offer from a big US team. New York wants me to come back and play for them, make me a statement signing. Playing for Salchester was only ever meant to be a short-term project, that's what I told Adrianne when I moved. The upshot is, she wants to know if I'm interested."

The upbeat mood was immediately extinguished, as if Sloane had snuffed a candle by pinching the flame with wet forefinger and thumb.

Ella closed her eyes. Disappointment slammed into her at speed. After all of this, she'd been right. It was depressing to realise. She would have liked to snog Sloane a little longer before their bubble burst. But that was not to be.

However, Ella was a grown-up. She always knew this might happen. But she was still more than gutted that her worst expectations were playing out in front of her.

She took a deep breath before she spoke. "I get it. You have a limited career, and you have to take whatever comes your way. A big pay out especially." Ella shrugged. Tears bubbled up behind her eyes, but she was determined to keep them in. They'd had a fling. It was always going to be nothing more. She had to accept that and move on. "Congratulations. It sounds like something you can't possibly turn down."

Okay, maybe those words had come out a little harsh.

A slight smile graced Sloane's features.

She thought this was funny? Ella folded her arms across her chest in defence.

"You're very cute when you're flustered. And you're a terrible liar, just so we're clear."

Ella sat up, hackles rising. She wasn't having that. "You just told me you're moving back to the US. Excuse me if I'm a bit upset about that." She pressed her index finger to her chest. "I'm trying to be the bigger person."

"And failing gloriously." Sloane paused, then took Ella's fingers in hers.

Small fireworks exploded in Ella's chest.

Damn Sloane. Damn every last little thing about her.

"You said I couldn't possibly turn it down. Nine months ago, that would have been true. But now, I've met you. I always thought if I met someone here, I'd keep them at arm's length. Not go all in." Sloane held up her hand. "To some extent, that was true. But even if my body was cautious, my heart never was. You could never have been a fling, Ella. I've fallen for you. But like you say, I have to think about what's best for the handful of years I've got left in my career. I have to choose wisely, and it can't just be for you. But" – Sloane held up a finger – "Lucy wants to talk to me after the FA Cup Final. They're still thrashing out the deal, but Salchester have an offer on the table as well. Adrianne needs to do her thing to get it the best it can be. I don't know how it matches what New York have offered yet. Not until I speak to Adrianne and Lucy. But everything's on hold until after the final."

Ella sat, transfixed by Sloane's gorgeous red lips. Her fluttery eyelashes. Her hair, ruffled from the ever-present breeze on the rooftop. Sloane had uttered many words, but the only phrase that stood out was 'I've fallen for you'. It was lit up in her mind like a glow stick. She hoped it was enough.

"But I want to stay. I want to be where you are. If you say yes, then I will, too." Sloane turned the full power of her gaze on Ella.

Ella wallowed in its heat, its passion.

"I want to wake up with you. I want to fall asleep with you. I want to watch more sunsets with you. I want to spend every holiday with you, not just Christmas." Sloane leaned over and squeezed Ella's hand. "If Salchester give me a decent offer, should I say yes? Can we start again?"

Those words made Ella shake her head. "Are you insane? I'm not starting again. The moaning about the lack of cream? About driving on the wrong side of the road? Your inability to call football the right name? That's not going to work." Ella stood, and pulled Sloane with her. As she did so, her heart lifted higher still. There was hope. Big hope. In the end, hope was what she needed.

If Salchester came in for her, Sloane was staying. Lucy had told Ella they were serious about wanting Sloane. And Sloane wanted to try again. She was sorry. There would be ground rules. But Ella knew in her heart the answer she wanted to give. It was yes. It was always yes. She'd fallen for Sloane, too. Now they just had to learn how to catch each other better.

"No, we can't start again. But we can pick up where we left off. Just me and you. I've fallen for you, too, Sloane."

The sides of Sloane's mouth turned upwards. "Thank fuck for that." Then she leaned forward and covered Ella's mouth with her own.

It felt like home.

Chapter Thirty-Five

"Okay everyone, huddle!"

Sloane had been in the same locker room only last month to play the game against England. What a difference a few weeks made. Back then, she'd been surrounded by American accents, which had been strange. She was used to British voices, now. Whoever would have thought that?

That last time, she and Ella were also on shifting sands. Today was a different story. Yes, her contract discussions were still on hold. However, this morning she'd woken up with Ella, just as she wished for. Everyone in the team knew they were an item. Sloane walked to the centre of the group.

"Welcome to the FA Cup Final, you beautiful humans!" She looked around the group. Nervous energy radiated off them. But that was a good thing. They could use that. "I asked Lucy if I could do this talk, and also team captain, Layla. They both kindly said yes. This is the biggest day in our club's short history. The women's team is less than ten years old. We've come a long way. *You've* helped this club come a long way. I've only been here a year, but I'm hoping to carry on building in future years. Unfortunately, we can't win the league, although we gave it our best shot."

Sloane was still pissed, but that was football.

Soccer.

Damn it.

"But you know what we can win? The FA Cup. At Wembley. Isn't that what childhood dreams are made of? But we're not only doing it for us and for the fans. We're doing it for all those who came before us. All those who wanted to play football but were told they couldn't because they were women.

"Some of you might have heard me talk about my great-grandmother, Eliza Power, later Patterson. She wanted to play football, but she wasn't allowed. So she cut her hair, strapped down her breasts and pretended to be a man. And she scored and scored and scored. Until she was found out and kicked off the team.

"When you're out there playing today, think of her, and all the other Elizas all around the world. We're allowed to play. It's a privilege, and one we should never take for granted. Go out there, express yourself, and make this a day for every Salchester Rovers fan to remember. Don't be daunted by the crowds: they're here for you, so let them lift you. In the words of the wonderful Shania Twain: let's go, girls!"

Sloane finished off by going round the team, high-fiving her crew. When she reached Lucy, the manager clasped her hand tight and pulled her in for a hug.

"I couldn't have said it better myself."

Then she came face to face with Ella. Her new love. She gave her a high five, followed by a hug. When her mouth was level with Ella's ear, she whispered. "I'm going to beat them for you, too. Because they treated you so badly when you needed them all those years ago." They were playing against

Rushton City, the team that had let Ella go. Sloane kissed her ear, then pulled back.

"It's not about me," Ella told her. "But go and beat those bastards."

Sloane grinned, then followed her teammates into the tunnel.

* * *

They came out for the second half after Lucy had put a rocket up their arse for their lacklustre performance so far. They deserved it. Only two shots on target in the first 45, and the one that had come from Sloane had been an easy save. She, and the whole team, had to do better.

Sloane wasn't sure what was going wrong, perhaps nerves? Passes were going astray, and the slick Wembley turf seemed enormous. But she'd experienced this before and come back stronger. She could do it again. Luckily, their opponents, Rushton City, were playing their own jittery brand of soccer too, even though their dynamite striker had scored a scrappy goal. They all counted. Luckily, they still had the second half to redeem themselves.

"You can do it, Hotshot!" Ella shouted as Sloane ran past her and onto the field. All around, flags fluttered, and the crowd roared. Sloane breathed in the smell of game day, then gave Ella a thumbs-up and a grin. Ella was right. If Sloane wanted to live up to her nickname, she had to score a goal and change the game.

Nat walked up to her and they slapped hands at waist height.

"You ready to win this?"

"Never readier."

"You can do it, Natalie!" shouted Nat's mum, three rows behind the dugout.

Nat blushed, and waved at her family. Her dad hadn't turned up, but her mum and sisters had. Sloane was thrilled for her. It was a start.

Sloane flicked her head back to the May sunshine. A sudden calm descended. She could absolutely do this. All she had to do was channel who she really was. Who she wanted to be. The very best version of herself. The one that Ella saw. The one that Ella made her.

The referee blew her whistle, and they were off.

The first 15 minutes were end to end, with Rushton going close, but Salchester going closer. Becca pulled off a close-range save from their striker, and Nat went so agonisingly close, she reeled away with her head in her hands. She knew she should have done better.

Ten minutes later, and Salchester couldn't get out of their own half. The opposition's speedy winger dinked one way, then the other, cut into the box and let loose a shot that Sloane stretched her right leg to block. She just about did it, too, but in sliding, she felt something in her thigh tweak. She was pretty sure she could run it off, but she stayed down to give her team a breather.

Dan ran on with his medical bag and knelt next to her.

"You okay? Where's it hurting?"

"My ego?" Sloane whispered. "Nothing a bit of spray and a magic sponge won't cure."

Dan bit down a smirk, and administered the necessary lotions and potions. Her teammates milled around, grabbing a drink as the sun beat down. After a couple of minutes, Sloane got up, stretched the muscle out and ran back to the centre.

Becca took the goal kick and punted it long. Sloane watched the ball all the way, but was outjumped by Rushton's six-foot-plus number seven. She headed it on, their attacking midfielder slotted it out wide, and all of a sudden, the opposition had a quick overload.

Fuck.

Salchester couldn't go two down, that would be a mountain to climb. Sloane galloped towards the box again to defend the cross, as did Welshy. As it came in, Welshy inexplicably raised a hand towards the ball and it connected.

Her arm was not in a natural position. That was a definite penalty.

Sloane winced as her teammate fell to the ground, the shouts of handball all around from the players and the crowd. She didn't need to look at the referee to find out what she'd given. Sloane heard the whistle and held her breath, as the referee had no hesitation in pointing to the spot. The crowd roared. Welshy got up, tipped her head to the sky and cradled the back of her neck in her palm.

Fuck.

This was beyond bad. There wasn't long to go, and the stadium was a cauldron of whistles and cheers. They had to hope Becca could save it. Or that they could score three. Nothing was impossible. Sloane put an arm around Welshy's shoulder and led her out of the box.

"Don't worry, we've got this."

She squeezed Welshy tight, and glanced at the clock. Seventeen minutes to go, and they might go 2-0 down. She wasn't sure if she believed her own words, but she couldn't say anything else. It was never over until it was over. That much, she did know.

City's tall, red-headed striker placed the ball and steadied herself. Sloane focused on Becca. As the striker started her run up, Sloane clenched her fists by her side. She hit it straight down the centre, and as Becca went to go right, she stuck out a boot and saved with her foot. The striker followed it up with another shot, but Becca smothered, and fell to the ground with the ball cradled to her chest.

Cue delirium from her teammates and the crowd. Sloane hugged Welshy tight – she looked like she wanted to cry – then ran up, and as Becca stood, she cupped her face and pressed a kiss to her forehead. "I owe you my first-born," she told her.

Becca grinned amid the bedlam of noise, which had just cranked up a notch. "All that penalty practice finally paid off for me, too. Just score a fucking goal or two now, will you?"

Sloane had extra impetus. She raced back up the field, and Becca launched it long again. This time, Sloane won the header, played it to Welshy in midfield, and Salchester calmed play, keeping the ball, moving it smoothly. Until Layla saw a run Sloane had made and slotted an inch-perfect pass that sliced their defence. Sloane took the ball down the channel, looked up, and crossed for Nat. She anticipated, rose majestically and steered a thunderous header into the net.

One all!

Suddenly, Salchester were back in the game.

The relief was palpable, from the players and the crowd. Sloane sprinted across and jumped on the huddle by the corner flag, with Nat at the bottom.

Nat hugged them all, then punched the air as she saluted the crowd. "One more for the win!" she screamed. The atmosphere was electric, and Sloane's skin prickled all over.

As they jogged back to restart, the momentum had shifted. Now they had to capitalise. Next goal to win it. Do or die.

Sloane glanced at the clock as their opponents restarted.

Ten minutes to go.

Game on.

Rushton swarmed forward from the restart and won a corner. Salchester took their places, only Sloane and Nat not in the box to defend. Their corner-taker fizzed the ball in, but Becca got a good punch on it, and Layla brought it out of the area. She passed to Welshy, who found Nat. At that moment, Sloane knew Nat would have only one thought. Surge forward.

Sloane was on her wavelength and ran ahead, turning on her afterburners. Her lungs burned as she powered up the field, knowing Nat was behind her. Sloane knew what would happen next, and when Nat released the ball, it sailed over Sloane's head. It bounced once, she controlled it, then got it on the deck.

Now it was just her, an oncoming defender, and the keeper.

Sloane cut into the area, swerved around the defender, who slipped over. One down. She eyeballed the keeper as the world slowed and the crowd noise faded out. Sloane leaned one way, then the other, and was just about to go around her when the keeper reached out an arm. She connected with Sloane's ankle. Sloane went down almost in slow-motion with a yelp.

The referee wasted no time awarding a penalty, but this time, it was at their end. In front of their blue and white fans, who at this moment, were going ear-piercingly crazy.

Sloane got up, wiped herself down, and walked over to the referee, who held the ball. She took it and placed it on the spot. Were her parents watching? She had no idea. But Ella was. Her new family was. They were all the inspiration she needed.

She breathed in, then out.

Focus.

Five steps back.

Six minutes on the clock.

One kick for glory.

She closed her eyes, and conjured a vision of Eliza. *This one's for you, Great-Gran.* Sloane eyeballed the keeper, ran up, struck it sweet, and the ball flew into the top right-hand corner.

Elation burst out of her. The roar of the crowd didn't dent the roar that came out of her mouth as she wheeled away, arms aloft, running towards the fans. Sloane reached the barriers, her grin threatening to engulf Wembley, just as her teammates landed on her. She crumpled to the ground. One of these days, she was going to get really hurt when they did that. But not today.

Today, she was Teflon.

Today, they were 2-1 up in the FA Cup Final.

Today, they were going to win.

* * *

When the whistle finally blew, Sloane sank to her knees and rested her head on the hallowed turf. Soon, she was swallowed up in hugs from her teammates.

"We fucking did it!" Layla screamed, arms tight around Sloane's neck.

Yes, they had.

Sloane got up, was twirled around in a bear hug by Lucy, and then engulfed in her favourite floral perfume on the centre circle when Ella reached her. Her hug was epic. It should be placed in the Hug Hall of Fame. When Sloane pulled back, Ella shook her head.

"I know you practice, but that penalty." She shook her head some more. "Where you get the strength, I'll never know." She paused. "I'm in awe of you, Sloane Patterson." She hugged her tight. Then whispered in her ear. "But I'm going to stop hugging you now, as we're on national TV."

Sloane snorted. "Probably wise." She was lucky that her ankle had healed in time to play in such a historic game, at the home of football. She'd won the World Cup, along with every honour in the US. But the FA Cup was special. Her great-grandparents played in early rounds. Now, she'd carried on the family name and finished what they started.

"I'll be right back. There's something I have to do before I can properly celebrate."

Sloane squeezed Ella's hand, then ran to the sidelines, searching behind the dugout where she knew her family were. When she heard her name called, she looked up and connected with Cathy's huge grin.

"You did it! You're a bloody superstar!" Cathy screamed, her arms aloft.

Sloane didn't care what she looked like. She vaulted the barrier, took the steps up to the tenth row, and amid much back-slapping and congratulations, reached her family and hugged them all in turn. Hayley looked in shock. Ryan couldn't stop smiling. Rich kept patting her back. And Cathy just grinned.

"You were just brilliant," she said, clutching Sloane's chin. "Nerves of steel to take that penalty. I could hardly watch."

Ryan nudged his mum in the ribs. "You didn't watch! You had your hands over your face."

"I was watching through my fingers." Cathy blushed bright pink. "I'm so proud of you. Your whole family is. But I know especially that my grandparents, your great-grandparents, are both looking down on you and saying, 'Go on, girl'!" She punched the air as she said the last bit. "You're a chip off the Patterson block."

Sloane nodded. "That one was for Eliza."

Cathy wiped away a tear. "I know it was, love." She put her hand over her heart. "I felt it here."

Sloane couldn't help but smile.

She'd come to the UK to find herself.

What she'd actually found was a new family, a new love, and a new home.

Chapter Thirty-Six

Sloane was waiting when Ella got down to the street outside her flat. She kissed her, with a wide grin. She wore ripped jeans and a black parka, because the weather had turned from blue skies to Baltic, even though it was nearly June. Salchester's season was done, and Sloane had called saying she had news.

"Well?" Ella put a hand on her hip. She hoped it was the news she'd been waiting for ever since their last game of the season. They'd missed out on the league by three points, but it was still their best-ever finish. Lucy had thanked the whole team and staff, and told them to go and enjoy their time off. Ella wouldn't be able to do that until Sloane's future was settled. Sloane kept telling her to relax. Easier said than done.

"Get in the car, you sexy thing. We're going to Shot Of The Day."

She gave Sloane a look. Nobody looked sexy in a rain jacket.

"The news is we're having a coffee?"

"And a Danish if you play your cards right."

Ella checked her watch. "You know damn well they'll be sold out by now."

Sloane gunned the engine and plugged in her phone. Taylor Swift filled the car, singing about being 22.

"I've wondered, ever since our pre-season. Would this have been the one you'd have chosen to sing? When you ducked out of karaoke, as I recall?"

"That would be telling. I can't give away all my secrets." Ella grinned as Sloane pulled onto the road with ease. She drove regularly now with no hiccups. Ella liked being driven around. It had never happened in her life before. It felt like being taken care of. It felt nice.

"I'll just have to make sure you sing a song at this year's pre-season then, won't I?"

Ella let the words sink in for a few seconds. Then she sat up. "Hang on, does that mean?" She turned in her seat.

Sloane pulled up at a red light, turned, then nodded. "It does." Her grin said it all. "Just got the call from Adrianne. She managed to get what she wanted. She's happy. I'm happy. And I hope you are, too."

A wave of love washed over Ella. Right at this second, she didn't think she'd ever been happier. She put an arm around Sloane's neck, pulled her in and gave her a bruising kiss. A reel of their past few months whizzed by in her mind. Sloane was staying. Life was good. It was only about to get better.

"I should drive around telling you life-changing news more often."

Sloane's gaze warmed Ella right through. The lights went green, and Sloane pulled away.

"But why are we going for coffee at Shot Of The Day?"

"Why not? It's a glorious day, the sun's shining, and they serve the best coffee. Apart from the stuff in my apartment. But I've run out of those tiny, delicious Half Creams."

Ella snorted. "Now we're getting to the crux of it."

"Also, double good news. I've been selected for the USA World Cup team. I leave for camp at the weekend. Let's enjoy the time we've got."

Ella threw her hands in the air. "You're telling me all this while you're driving and I can't snog you? Unfair!" She laughed. "But congratulations, Hotshot. Of course you got in. Duh."

Ten minutes later, the sky the colour of nightmares, Sloane jumped out of the car and ran around to Ella's side. When she opened the door, she held out her hand. Ella took it. Sloane kissed her hand, slammed the passenger door, and didn't let go. Instead, she pulled her towards the coffee shop, but stopped in front of the floor-to-ceiling windows. Inside, customers stared out at them. A couple, seeing who it was, raised their camera phones. Sloane still held Ella's hand.

She glanced down at their entwined fingers, then back up to meet Sloane's focused gaze. "You're still holding my hand." That was still unusual.

A broad grin. "I know. I hope that's okay. Because I want to hold it now, and for the foreseeable future, if you'll let me." Sloane paused. "Ella, I want this to be our local coffee shop. And if holding your hand means we might be photographed, there's nobody I'd rather be photographed with." She squeezed Ella's fingers tight. "I've been offered a two-year contract at Salchester, and I've said yes. For two reasons. First, because I've fallen in love with the club and the area." A fat raindrop fell on Ella's nose. Followed by another. They both laughed.

Sloane kissed it away.

Ella swooned.

"But most of all, because I've fallen in love with you. I should have told you earlier. I've been stupid. I think I mentioned that.

348

But I'm telling you now. I love you, Ella. And wherever you are, it's where I want to be. I know your mum's not around to be your main cheerleader anymore. But if the job's still open, I'd like to apply."

Ella's eyes grew hot and wet, as her mind, on high alert, got to its feet and gave a standing ovation. All the weeks of hurt and the days of heartbreak. But now, Sloane stood in front of her, offering her heart, with added pompoms. She couldn't be more perfect. Ella was ready to accept with everything she had.

"I love you too, Sloane Patterson, and I'll have you as my chief cheerleader any day." Her heart boomed. Sloane wasn't moving back to the USA. She was staying here, and she was in love with Ella. This was turning out to be one heck of a day. "Although I can't believe I'm telling you this while stood outside Shot Of The Day."

"I can't think of anywhere better." Sloane's eyes sparkled as she spoke. "I'm even in love with the constant rain."

"Let's not go overboard." Ella was done holding Sloane's hands. She needed to get closer. She threw her arms around Sloane's neck and kissed the woman who was in love with her. She'd never tire of hearing that. "But I can't believe you've gone from no PDAs to snogging in front of a whole cafe," Ella mumbled into her lips. "You think we can go inside now before we get soaked?"

When they got there, Suzy and Michelle gave a slow clap. "Quite the show, ladies."

Also, sat at the counter were Nat and Layla. They'd had an audience the whole time.

Ella blushed like mad. Maybe she needed to get used to public affection, too.

"Thank goodness you're out in the open and I don't have to watch what I say anymore," Nat said, hugging them both. "But does this mean you're staying, too?"

Sloane's grin covered her face as she nodded. "Two more years. Next year, we're going to win the league."

"Yeah we fucking are! I'll get coffee to celebrate." Layla shooed them away. "Go grab some seats. We'll bring them over."

Sloane and Ella sat on the sofas by the window. Ella hadn't been here half as much as Sloane, but she could see its charm. The main charm today being Sloane.

She took Ella's hand in hers and kissed it. "One more thing. You're coming to the World Cup, yes?" This year, it was in France.

Ella grinned. "I just thought. Am I a WAG now?"

"The very best one," Sloane replied. "Once we've won, I've got two weeks off. I've booked an all-inclusive stay in a resort in Mexico. I was hoping you might come with me?"

"Once you've won?" Ella shook her head, but she loved the bravado, the arrogance. It was why Sloane was who she was. A winner. "Also, are you trying to buy me with an exotic holiday, Sloane Patterson?"

"I'm offering my body, too, whenever and however you want it."

Ella's grin was wide. "You drive a hard bargain, but you've got yourself a deal."

Epilogue

"I cannot believe you've managed to organise this in a month," Ella told her. "Or that you got the club to agree to it in the first place."

Sloane swung her Jeep into a free space in the club parking lot, then cut the engine. The silence was golden for a few seconds, as she sat, composing herself. "You should know, once I decide I want something, I normally get it." She leaned across and placed a light kiss on Ella's lips. She still couldn't believe she got to do that every day, with no worries. Ella's new role had been rubber-stamped, with management having no objections to their relationship continuing. Sloane was free to kiss her girlfriend whenever and wherever she wanted. "You were on the list of things I wanted, just in case you were wondering."

"I figured." Ella smiled as she unclicked her seatbelt. "How many tickets have you sold?"

"In the region of 25,000, which is outstanding for a game with nothing at stake."

"Your star power behind it."

"I have superpowers I never even knew." The sun's rays tickled her face as she got out of her car, and put on her new shades. She waited at the hood for Ella, and they walked to the stadium hand in hand.

Ella squeezed it before she spoke. "Everyone's coming today. My family. Your family. Everyone together for a meal. Are you nervous?"

Sloane shook her head. She'd be nervous if it were her parents. But Cathy and co? She couldn't see a day where anything they said or did ever dimmed her love and admiration for them. Ever since they'd come into Sloane's life, they'd brought nothing but positivity. She wasn't sure she'd ever be able to repay them for showing her how family could be.

"It'll be grand. We've got the Big Shootout, we're getting Kilminster off to a flier, and the new women's team is getting some much-needed publicity and funds. What's not to love?"

Ella pushed through the stadium doors, before turning to her. "You're not just a pretty face, Sloane Patterson."

"I know. Apparently, I'm a hotshot, too."

* * *

They were in the tunnel, tension carved into the faces of all the penalty-takers. Including Ella. Sloane was used to pressure penalties, but sometimes, she forgot the simple act of running onto the field could cause anxiety. She'd been doing it her whole life, it was second nature to her. She clapped her hands and got everyone's attention in seconds.

"First, welcome to the Salchester Rovers' tunnel. I hope you're drinking it in. This is where so many greats have stood, pre-game. Now, you're in the same club."

Nervous chuckles filled the air. This would be so different in her homeland. There, every person would be high-fiving and vocal. But here, they'd all shrunk into their shells, contemplating what was ahead. The cultural differences were never more stark. It was Sloane's job to relax these people, make them believe.

"Second, thank you so much for supporting grass roots football, and for paying £500 to take a penalty against Salchester's men's and women's keepers in the Big Shootout. There are 100 of you, 50 men and 50 women, which means you've raised £50,000 for Kilminster United with your generosity. That's before they take their share of the gate for the match afterwards. Your money is helping save Kilminster men's side, and helping to create a Kilminster women's team, too."

Pride prickled all over her skin. "My great-grandparents played for the team, my family still do to this day, and I'm proudly donning their new kit this afternoon in the friendly game between Salchester and Kilminster." She paused, and stared around these faces she was so very grateful to. "From the bottom of my heart, thank you." Sloane took a breath. "But now is the moment you've all been waiting for: you get to shoot your goal. Do you want the advice of someone who's done this a million times?"

"Yes please!" shouted the woman next to her. She was kitted out in the new Kilminster shirt, sponsored by Sloane in honour of her great-grandmother. The words 'Let Women Play' were emblazoned on the front, with 'In honour of Eliza Power' far smaller on the back. Sloane had spent ages trying to come up with something clever, but in the end, the answer was the most obvious. Those were the words Eliza would have wanted, because it was what she'd wanted way back when. With Sloane's new sponsorship deal, and this fundraiser's total, she hoped Kilminster would be set for a good couple of seasons ahead.

"Here's my advice, which is solid if you've never taken

a penalty before, or if you've taken dozens. Enjoy it. Relax. Decide where you're going to put it, and stick with that plan. Also, remember that doing this takes guts. Yes, even in a non-game situation. You're still stepping up and putting yourself out there, beyond your comfort zone. Life is all about experiences, and you're about to experience something that most people never will. Have fun, and let's try to score 100 great penalties out there, shall we?" She paused. "Ready?"

One hundred pairs of wide eyes stared back at her.

To her right, Ella mouthed the word "No!" in her direction.

Sloane bit down a grin. "I said, are you ready?"

This time, she got the response she wanted.

"Then let's go!"

* * *

Ella took deep breaths, and tamped down her nerves. Her heart thumped in her chest as she gazed out into the rapidly filling up stands. The match was due to start in half an hour, but plenty of supporters had got in early to cheer the penalties. Every run up had brought a cheer from the crowd, and every one that hit the back of the net had been celebrated as if it were a cup-winning goal.

Running onto the pitch in full kit had stirred up all sorts of emotions which Ella thought were well behind her. Apparently not. But now, here she was, the 50th female penalty taker in this charity shootout. At the other end, the men's keeper Fraser Holt still had five of his 50 to go. Women got on with things with far less fuss.

"Ready for your shot at the big time, Carmichael?" Sloane placed the ball on the spot and held her whistle in her hand, just as she had for the previous 49 penalties. Sloane's officious side turned Ella on far more than was necessary, but she pushed that thought from her mind. She wasn't going to glance at her girlfriend's muscular, firm thighs that she'd licked earlier this morning. Not even for a second.

"Remember what I said?"

Ella narrowed her eyes. She didn't need a Sloane penalty masterclass right now. "Shut up now, please."

Sloane mimed zipping up her lips and throwing away the key, then stepped back.

This was Ella's turn to shine. Her chance to score in a big stadium. Her dream could finally be realised.

She took a deep breath, then took seven steps back. The crowd behind the goal started their low run-up roar. Ella's previous career flashed before her eyes. It could have been so different, but weirdly, she wouldn't change a thing. She was where she was, at the time that she was, for a reason. Next season, she was going to be training young stars on the pitch, sharing her knowledge, watching them realise their dreams. That was more than enough for her.

The roar got louder as she started her run-up. With every step, Ella sank more into the moment. When she reached the ball, she sent up a silent prayer to her mum, then she struck it low and true towards the bottom left-hand corner.

The ball arrowed away, and Ella held her breath.

Becca guessed the right way.

Ella winced as she waited for the keeper to reach it.

She did, but the power behind Ella's shot was too strong. The ball hit the back of the net and the crowd behind the goal threw their hands in the air and roared their approval.

Ella stood, arms in the air, turned to Sloane, and flung her head back.

"Yes!" she cried, just as Sloane reached her, picked her up, and swung her around.

"You fucking did it!" Sloane shouted, still wheeling her around. "How does it feel to be the hotshot yourself?"

Ella grinned as her feet hit the ground. Mentally, she was still soaring.

"Not gonna lie, it feels fucking ace."

* * *

The friendly finished 6-3 to Salchester, which wasn't a terrible score considering there were six leagues and hundreds of teams between the two sides. Nat scored a brace for the mixed professional team, showing her breakthrough year was no fluke. Sloane couldn't wait for the upcoming season to start.

Sloane had played for Kilminster in honour of her great-gran, and even scored a goal. She got a photo of the moment, and stills with the whole squad that were set to be hung on the clubhouse wall at Kilminster's ground in the near future. Sloane would always be welcome there; manager Matt had made that very clear when she'd phoned to tell him about her proposed sponsorship.

As they walked off the field, Nat caught up with Sloane and gave her a tight hug. Her undercut was freshly buzzed, and she glowed with pride at her performance.

"Well played, not-so-rookie," Sloane told her.

"Cheers, Hotshot."

Sloane's title was being challenged, and she couldn't be more thrilled. When she glanced up to the family section behind the goal, it wasn't just her family there. Nat's mum and sisters were three rows back, along with a dark-haired man. Sloane turned to Nat, and tilted her head.

"Is that who I think it is next to your mum?"

Nat's grin nearly split her face as she nodded. "His first game, after my mum told him she'd divorce him if he didn't come."

"Well played, Mum."

Nat waved to them, and her dad gave her a nervous smile and waved back.

Sloane nudged her. "Looks like he might need to loosen up. Go give him a hug."

The pair vaulted the barriers to reach their loved ones. Sloane embraced Cathy, Rich, Hayley and Ryan, as well as Ursula, her husband Gary, Marina, her brother Brad, along with his wife Sarah and their three kids. More family than she'd ever had in her life.

"I loved the game, Sloane," Ursula told her. With her enormous chestnut hair, she could only be Ella's aunt. "I haven't been to many since Ella used to play. I've missed it." She turned to Ella. "You'll have to get us tickets for this season."

"You should come to Kilminster, too," Cathy told her. "Then come for tea. I can cook you that chicken recipe I was just telling you about."

"And the chocolate dessert. To die for," Rich added, kissing the tips of his fingers.

Sloane smirked. "Did you watch the game?"

Cathy laughed. "All of it. Never missed a minute." She winked. "You played so well, shame you didn't win." Cathy leaned forward and brushed something out of Sloane's hair.

Weirdly, Sloane didn't mind. Her new family's tactile nature was something she'd got used to pretty quickly. She kinda liked it. Beside Marina, Ella sat in her Salchester training gear, still glowing from scoring her penalty. Sloane didn't think she'd loved her more than she did right at that moment.

She looked content.

Sloane knew the exact feeling.

"Today wasn't about the result, it was about saving Kilminster." Sloane glanced around the slowly emptying stands. "I hope we achieved it."

"You absolutely smashed it," Ryan said, offering his palm for a high five.

Sloane slammed her palm into his. "I hope so. It was important. I'm hoping a few of these supporters make it to the Kilminster ground this season."

"Fingers crossed."

Sloane took a deep breath. "I'm going to get changed, but I'll see you all at the pub later for dinner?"

They all nodded.

Before that, she had something to ask Ella. Nerves jangled inside her. She couldn't wait.

***

"You were amazing out there today. Ice running through your veins taking that penalty." Sloane slung her arm over Ella's shoulder.

Ella gave her a broad smile. "I learned from the best."

"Our first meal out with all of our families, too. Feels significant, doesn't it?" They walked up to the pub entrance, and Sloane paused.

Ella stopped and gave her a quizzical look. "Aren't you coming in?"

Sloane nodded. "Of course. I just have something I want to ask you first." She removed her arm and turned to Ella. A prickle of fear ran up her. If asking this was stressful, Sloane hated to think what it was like to propose.

"When I'm starving and about to get hangry?"

That was the Ella she knew and loved. "I would never come between you and your food." Sloane grinned. "We're spending a lot of time at each other's places right now. And my place is far closer to the training ground than yours." She took both Ella's hands in her own. The tips of her ears tingled. "The thing is, what would you think about breaking your lease? The six months is done, and you can do that now, right? You already sleep at mine 75 per cent of the time, anyway."

"I'm not sure that much sleeping gets done," Ella replied, an eyebrow quirked. "Are you asking me to move in with you, Hotshot?"

Sloane frowned, then nodded. "I guess I am."

"Are you ready for us, 24/7?" Ella pursed her lips.

"Born ready. But most of all, I was born to wake up every morning with you."

"You're so adorably corny and American sometimes." But Ella's face lit up with a smile all the same.

"Suck it up. I'm just telling the truth." Sloane pulled her closer, then leaned in. "What do you say, Ella Carmichael?" She stared into her dark hazel eyes. The colour she'd never tire of. "Is that a yes to doubling your wardrobe? A yes to a roof terrace?" She pressed a gentle kiss to Ella's lips as her heart boomed inside.

"When you put it like that, how can I refuse?" Ella kissed her again, then stepped back. "You're the Half Cream to my coffee, Sloane Patterson. I underestimated you when we met. Just so you know, you're way more than just a hotshot." Ella held out her hand. "Shall we go tell our families the good news?"

Sloane nodded. "Let's do it."

THE END

Want more from me? Sign up to join my VIP Readers' Group and get a FREE lesbian romance, **It Had To Be You!** *Claim your free book here: www.clarelydon.co.uk/it-had-to-be-you*

Did You Enjoy This Book?

 If the answer's yes, I wonder if you'd consider leaving me a review wherever you bought it. Just a line or two is fine, and could really make the difference for someone else when they're wondering whether or not to take a chance on me and my writing. If you enjoyed the book and tell them why, it's possible your words will make them click the buy button, too! Just hop on over to wherever you bought this book — Amazon, Apple Books, Kobo, Bella Books, Barnes & Noble or any of the other digital outlets — and say what's in your heart. I always appreciate honest reviews.

Thank you, you're the best.

Love,
Clare x

Also by Clare Lydon

Other Novels
A Taste Of Love
Before You Say I Do
Change Of Heart
Christmas In Mistletoe
It Started With A Kiss
Nothing To Lose: A Lesbian Romance
Once Upon A Princess
One Golden Summer
The Christmas Catch
The Long Weekend
Twice In A Lifetime
You're My Kind

London Romance Series
London Calling (Book One)
This London Love (Book Two)
A Girl Called London (Book Three)
The London Of Us (Book Four)
London, Actually (Book Five)
Made In London (Book Six)
Hot London Nights (Book Seven)
Big London Dreams (Book Eight)

All I Want Series
Two novels and four novellas chart the course
of one relationship over two years.

Boxsets
Available for both the London Romance series and
the All I Want series for ultimate value. Check out
my website for more: www.clarelydon.co.uk

Printed in Great Britain
by Amazon

30375270R00211